I0748527

OVERNIGHT SENSATION

OVERNIGHT SENSATION

SARINA BOWEN

TUXBURY PUBLISHING LLC

This title is published by Tuxbury Publishing LLC.

Cover photograph by Wander Aguiar. Cover design by Hang Le.

Editing by Edie Danford of Edie's Edits.

[1]

I wish you to know that you have been the last dream of my soul.

- *CHARLES DICKENS, A TALE OF TWO CITIES*

JASON

"Gentlemen." I lift my beer bottle high, signaling the start of a speech. "It was the best of scrimmages, it was the worst of scrimmages..."

The moment I utter my version of Dickens's most famous opening line, there are groans as well as laughter.

"Oh, brother," my teammate Bayer complains. "Here we go with another speech."

"It was the afternoon of victory, it was the afternoon of too few shots on goal. It was the epoch of belief, it was the epoch of '*holy shit,* I should run more sprints before training camp!'"

O'Doul, our team captain, snorts as my other teammates shake their heads. They're used to my antics.

"It was the season of lamplighters," I continue. "It was the season of exhaustion, it was the autumn of hope, after the summer of despair. We have eighty-two games before us, we have nothing to stop us, we are all going direct to Heaven, except whichever of you asswipes tripped me during the second period..."

There's more laughter around the long table, so I pause for a swig of beer.

"Does he always quote Dickens after a scrimmage?" asks Heidi, the girl I've been eyeing all night. If I'm honest, this little show I'm putting on is for her benefit. Although I'm not sure if I should be trying to attract her or trying to drive her away.

"He usually quotes Shakespeare," answers Silas, my new roommate. "But I guess it's more of a Dickens kind of night."

"In short," I wind up for a strong finish. "The scrimmage was the same gongshow as last year. And all the noisiest authorities predict—for good or for evil—that every goddamn day of the new season will be a familiar struggle!"

A cheer rises up because I stuck the landing. I lean back against the paneled wall of the tavern and chug the rest of my ale, spilling a few drops of it on my team T-shirt.

"Classy," Silas snorts. He's one of our goalies.

"Yeah?" I slam the bottle down on a table that's already littered with our empties. "Where's your speech, then? I'm listening."

"I meant the mess you're making." He swats at my shirt with a cocktail napkin, and I grab him quickly into a headlock.

"Fuck," the goalie says from my armpit. "Let go."

"You're just lucky I showered," I say, not letting go.

Silas laughs, but it's a fake-out. The second I relax, he wrenches out of my grip and tries to knee me in the balls. I'm saved by my lightning-fast reflexes. I swivel my package out of harm's way.

"Children, cut it out," Bayer says with a sigh. "If you knock over the bottles, Pete won't serve us until we clean 'em up."

Grinning, Silas and I take our hands off each other. We have some excess adrenaline to burn off. Anyone would.

I'd forgotten how the beginning of a season feels. Training camp has me stirred up inside and raring to go. Dickens had it right. It's the best of times, and also the worst of times. Sixty guys fighting for twenty-three slots on the opening-day roster. Any player who says he's relaxed tonight is a goddamn liar.

We've just finished the big scramble where all the new prospects skate with the veterans. It's like Hunger Games on Ice—a flock of youngsters trying to show us up and take away our roster spots. And it's our job to smack 'em back down to the minors where they belong.

I know all about it. It took me three tries to make the Bruisers' roster. Last year was my first full season in the big show. I had a killer year with gaudy stats.

Until it all went wrong at the very end. Regrets? I have a few. The stupidest thing I've ever done—and there's some competition for that award—is to imagine that once I made it to the big leagues, things would feel easier.

They don't. Not ever.

There are a few perks, though. The plush charter jet is a lot more comfortable than riding the bus in the minors. And these days someone else carries my pads into the stadium and hangs 'em up at my locker.

But not one thing in my life is relaxing. Every game is a brutal test of my staying power. Should I fail, there are a hundred other guys lined up to take my place. And after the inglorious way my last season ended, some days I think one of them will.

That was a Dickens kind of day, indeed. They all are.

But tonight we celebrate. I've earned this beer. Next week the roster will be posted, and I'm going to be on it. I'm healthy, I'm fast, and I was exactly the kind of playmaker in today's scrimmage that the team needs.

"I think we should switch to shots," I say, upping the ante. "Silas, you can choose—tequila or vodka."

My roommate groans. "You know we have to get up early, right?"

"I'm aware. Rookie!" I snap my fingers. "What's your name again?"

"Drake," says the kid.

"Right." I stripped the puck from young Drake in our scrimmage today at least twice. But he fought back like a beast, and I give him a fifty-fifty chance at making it onto our roster. Now I hand him my credit card. "Ask Pete for a bottle of good tequila and some shot glasses."

"And limes!" Silas calls out as Drake walks away.

"Okay," the kid says gamely, turning his big shoulders toward the bar.

"*Okay?*" I gasp. "How about *yessir!*"

There are chuckles, but I'm only half kidding. I just spent the summer reading books in a hammock and trying to forget that it was *my* missed shot on goal that sent us into overtime in game seven of the championship. If I'd rotated my stick two more degrees before I shot, we would have hoisted the cup over our heads at the end of the period. There would have been a parade through Brooklyn and all the other bullshit that comes with being top dog.

But the puck hit the pipe and bounced off. And I will never stop seeing that black shape flip against the white ice, or hearing the condemning sound of buzzer announcing the end of the third period.

Less than a half hour later we lost the championship in overtime.

If I'd made that goal, I would have been the leader of that goddamn parade. I would have hoisted the cup first. The video clip of that goal would have played on repeat whenever the Bruisers were mentioned on TV. Forever, probably.

Pass the tequila.

The rookie comes back with a tray and a message. "Pete says he doesn't need this—" The kid flips my credit card onto the table. "—because he's got the number memorized. And he said to tell you to take it easy."

"Right," I snort. "Because that sounds like me for sure."

"Oh, Castro's always easy," Bayer says. "Just ask the ladies."

"You shut up," I scoff, plucking the shot glasses off the tray and lining them up. I count heads around the table. "You in? Who's in?"

That's when my gaze collides with Heidi's. My gaze does that entirely too often.

"Tequila?" I ask her, my tone borderline rude, and I don't even know why.

She smacks the bar with her hand. "Yes *sir*."

And my mind leaps *right* into the gutter. I'd like to get her to say that again later. When we're alone.

"Jesus, don't call him sir," Silas begs. "The power will go right to his head."

Or other places. Fuck me. I pour out shots of tequila. "Ladies first," I say, passing a shot glass to Heidi.

When I've doled one out to all takers, O'Doul lifts his shot. "To old friends and new challenges," he says.

To fewer last-minute disappointments, I privately add as I lift my glass.

The sound of six or eight shot glasses meeting for a toast is the backdrop of my life. It's a good sound. We all toss the tequila back, and I watch Heidi drink hers with wide eyes that turn red as she swallows.

"I think you need this," I say, nudging the bowl of lime wedges in her direction.

"Thanks," she gasps, reaching for a wedge and plunging it between her pink lips.

My body stirs. *Tonight, then.* I'll take her home with me. Finally.

Heidi and I have been circling each other on and off since last spring, when she turned up to help the team out during a personnel crisis. One day at the practice facility I heard a peal of uproarious laughter. And when I turned the corner, there she was—all bouncing curls and curves and a big smile. She's five-foot-nothing but full of personality.

And since that very first moment, I've been yearning to fill her with something else. She's open to this idea as well. I see it every time our gazes collide. And they do that a lot.

It hasn't happened, though, for a couple of reasons. In the first place, I only hook up with randoms. Hockey is my life, and there's no room for emotional entanglements.

Also? She's the office intern. The aftermath could be awkward. She doesn't strike me as needy or crazy. But it's not like I can put a lot of distance between us afterwards. Worst-case scenario is that I avoid the office wing of the team's headquarters for a semester, or however long her internship lasts.

I've done stupider things, though. And tonight I don't think I am going to be able to resist her. Every time those big blue eyes land on me, I'm a little closer to giving in.

That's how distracting she is. I'm not the only one who thinks so, either. My teammates have given her a nickname that suits her personality: Hot Pepper. That's because she's attractive, but also lively.

If I'm honest, she reminds me a little of the girl I fell in love with at sixteen. I have very few regrets in this life. A lost love, and a lost goal. Tonight I've got both of them on my mind, damn it. But I'm going to let Heidi distract me from both things.

Problem solved.

"Shhh!" Silas says suddenly.

We all fall silent without knowing why. There's a look on Silas's face, as if angels are speaking to him from a higher plane.

"Um, what are we listening for?" the rookie asks.

"New song," Silas says. "It was just released yesterday."

A groan rises up from the table. Silas is a devoted fan of the singer Delilah Spark. He plays her stuff from sunup to sundown and seems not to mind all the ribbing we give him about it.

"You just *shushed* me so you could hear this singer again?" Bayer asks. "Don't we get enough of her leaking from your headphones on the jet?"

"Try living with him," I point out. "It's only been a month, and I already know every lyric to every song. I don't even have a choice."

"Have you tried those noise-canceling headphones?" Drake asks. "You could give those a whirl."

Silas doesn't even acknowledge us. He slips past me and heads for the bar, where the video for the new song is playing on one of the TVs.

With a snicker, Bayer moves off to harass him, and O'Doul follows.

Our little group thins out, leaving me basically alone with Heidi. I should probably make an excuse to talk to my team-mates. I should walk away. I don't, though, because I feel about Heidi the way I feel about the last cookie in the cookie jar—I should resist, but I don't really want to.

"Not a big fan of tequila?" I ask her. That's my opening line. It isn't too smooth, but she's already watching me with those big baby-blues.

"I'm not accustomed to shots," she says. "My mama would be appalled."

"Why? You're no worse for wear."

"It's not ladylike to drink fast, eat too much, or wear white shoes after Labor Day."

"God." I laugh. "Why?"

"It's just impolite."

Heidi has a hint of a southern accent, and the word comes out as impo*laht*. The delicate way it rolls off her tongue does something to my groin. Something very impolite. I'm determined to have her in my bed tonight.

"How was your summer?" I ask, because I'm a gentleman. Or at least I can fake it.

"Pretty dull, if you want to know the truth." Her perfect lips tense for a moment before relaxing again. "I spent six weeks trying not to argue with my father. I was hoping he wouldn't lose his mind when I told him I wasn't going back to Bryn Mawr."

"But he did anyway?" I guess.

"Absolutely. Total conniption."

"Oh, man." I know all about parental disappointment. "He yelled?"

"He yelled, and he threatened. My mistake was thinking that we could have a sensible conversation about it. There's no arguing with that man when he gets his hard head set on something he wants. And he does not want me in Brooklyn."

Ouch. "Your father doesn't want you working for the team?"

"No sir, he does not."

Sir. I want her to call me that when she's naked. But we'll get to that a little later. "Maybe your father doesn't like hockey players."

A strange reaction flickers across her face and then disappears immediately. "I think it's me he doesn't like. I spent the first twenty years of my life trying to be Daddy's good little girl. But it's impossible to please that man, and I am done trying."

I would have never guessed that Heidi and I had so much in common. "That's funny because my parents aren't so wild about having me in Brooklyn, either."

"My goodness, why? You're killing it for the team."

Her expression is full of wonder. God bless the girls who have a thing for hockey players. "My family is a bunch of nerds.

They think I'm wasting my life playing a brutal sport when I should be getting a doctorate."

"Oh," Heidi says softly. "That sounds familiar."

It's actually a little more complicated than that. They think my whole lifestyle is self-destructive. And isn't that ridiculous? Me with the eight-percent-body-fat ratio and low-resting heart rate.

"The booze and the women," my dad says when he's lecturing me. *"They're eating away at you."* He says this with a straight face and the paunch of a guy who sits at a desk much of the day.

"But it comes down to this," Heidi declares, patting my hand to get my attention. "Who gets to say who's wasting his life? Why do parents think they have that right?"

"Exactly." I use my thumb to trap her hand against mine. Then I lean forward and look into her blue eyes. There's no mistaking my interest.

"Right?" she squeaks as twin spots of pink appear on her cheekbones. But she doesn't pull her hand away.

"Lucky for me," I say. "My sister is an academic. So at least someone is following the family plan."

Heidi blinks. Her gaze drops to our joined hands before returning to mine. "I have a sister, too," she confesses. "But she does what she wants and they love her anyway. And they treat me like a convict just because I won't finish my liberal arts degree."

"Is your father an academic like mine?" I ask. Wouldn't that be a funny coincidence?

"Um, no," she says slowly. "But my mother went to Bryn Mawr. Now she is a full-time stay-at-home wife, and the world's most eager country-club member." She rolls her gorgeous eyes. "That hacks me off even more. 'Stay in school, Heidi Jo. So you can graduate and never use that degree!' They'd be thrilled if I'd settle down with a nice lawyer and start popping out the grandkids."

"I have so many questions." I chuckle. "Heidi *Jo*?"

"That's what my family calls me. But I call myself Heidi so I don't sound so..."

"*Gone with the Wind?*" I guess.

"Right."

"And your parents really want you to get married? Why?"

She shrugs. "That's the extent of my mother's imagination, I think. Also, she'd have a wedding to plan. Marrying me off to a lawyer in a ballroom somewhere is her dream come true."

"But you're not down with that plan?" I stroke my thumb across her hand, and Heidi shivers almost imperceptibly.

Her gaze returns to our joined hands. "Weddings are a snore. Lawyers are, too. The ones I've met, anyway."

"Your taste runs more to hockey players, I assume?"

Now her cheeks are on fire. "When the mood strikes," she says primly, removing her hand from mine. "More tequila, maybe?"

When the mood strikes. Jesus. She's going to make me work for it. And I'm a hundred percent down with that.

This girl is teasing me in the best possible way. She pushes her shot glass closer to me, then raises that kissable face to look at me. And there's a challenge in her eyes that I plan to answer with a whole lot more than a couple of drinks.

For now, though, I pick up the bottle and pour.

[2]

HEIDI

I'VE ALWAYS KEPT a wish list. When I was a preteen, it lived in one of those journals with the tiny lock and key. But now I keep it on my phone, updating it whenever the mood strikes.

My list is pretty long. Some of the wishes are awfully materialistic, like designer shoes and luxury cosmetics. I could really use a shade of lipstick that's just a little pinker than Sassy Petal, but not too pale.

But some items can't be bought in a store. For example, I need to figure out if I have any marketable skills. That's close to the top of the list. And while I'm at it, I *really* want one of the Katt phones that the Bruisers players all have. Those are super cool. The team owner—Nate Kattenberger—only gives them out to official employees of the team. My internship doesn't count.

But also? I've been wishing *hard* for a hookup with Jason Castro. And tonight it seems possible. Somebody pinch me, and please let it be him.

As I watch him pour tequila into my shot glass, I have to

wonder where my good fortune is coming from. Why tonight? I've angled for this before, but he never responded. And maybe I shouldn't count unhatched chickens. I still need to seal the deal.

"Here you are," Castro says, passing the shot glass back to me.

There's a little drip on the rim. I tidy it up with my fingertip, and then suck the drop of liquor off my finger.

And—dear Lord—Castro's eyes go one shade darker than they already were. His gaze focuses on my lips. Just to be sure I'm not crazy, I draw it out a moment, tonguing the tip of my finger.

He makes a low sound that's impossible to describe, except for the way that it affects me. My body tightens in a host of private places. No man has ever watched me as intently as he is right now.

And it is *intoxicating*. Forget tequila. I feel high on a brand-new drug—*courage*.

"Cheers," I say in a perky voice, and then we clink our glasses together. I toss my second shot back and then reach for the limes. This time I'm ready for the alcohol's burn. I always was a quick study. I could rock that psychology degree if I wanted to.

But I don't. So here I am, watching my favorite athlete pour his tequila shot down his beautiful throat.

Up until this moment, today has been wretched. Daddy blew up my inbox with angry voicemails, until I had to shut off the phone completely. He's *furious* that I'm not going back for my senior year at Bryn Mawr. I don't think he'll ever get over it.

I'm just going to have to learn to be okay with that.

Not that it's easy. I'm used to being a good girl. I never refuse Daddy's calls, and I never drink shots of tequila with the team in the bar.

Tonight, though? It's time for a change. *Take that, Daddy*. And who knew I could slug back tequila like a party girl?

The problem is that I don't know what to do next. I've never had a one-night stand. And every time Jason looks me up and down with those sinful eyes, I feel a little thrill of excitement.

And—fine—nerves. Although the tequila will help with that.

Besides, when you need a job done right, you're supposed to hire an expert. And that's what I want from Jason Castro. He's the most notorious hookup artist on the team. He's hot as blazes, and a real smooth-talker. I like everything about him, from his rich, bronze-toned skin to his hypnotic brown eyes.

He can talk me through it. I'm a quick study.

And I'm not a virgin. There have been boyfriends—four of them. But not one of them ever managed to... There's no polite way to say it. Nice Southern girls aren't supposed to speak in detail about sex. But let's just say I've never been very satisfied by my sexual experiences so far.

That will all change tonight. This is not an opportunity to be squandered. In fact, it's time to up the ante. Just because I don't have a whole lot of experience seducing men doesn't mean I'm clueless about life in general.

Slowly, I ease my body a little closer to his. Two inches, maybe. Then I smile at him.

And—holy heck—the results are instantaneous. His eyes sweep down my body. And it's almost as if he touched me with his hands, too. I feel that gaze burning me up everywhere it lands. Then he looks up again and gives me a hot smile. We're having an entire conversation without words.

This is a revelation. I feel bold and a little wild.

"So what happens next, Hot Pepper?" he asks.

Oh my. That thumping sound is my heart taking off like a jackrabbit running a fifty-yard dash. I thought I had some more time to get used to the idea before we actually made our move.

"Are you gonna stay in Brooklyn and finish your internship, even if it causes family strife?"

"Oh," I say slowly, because, whoops! I'm the one who's gotten ahead. "I'll stick with the internship. Heck, yes. I have no marketable skills." My internship doesn't pay very much. But I can live in Daddy's Manhattan condo and ride the subway to work.

Soon I'll turn twenty-one and inherit some money. Although my father could make my life very difficult if he chooses to. I heard that thinly veiled threat too many times this week already.

"Good for you," Jason says.

"It's an easy decision," I agree. "I need to start living differently, or I'm in danger of spending the rest of my life trying to please other people."

"That's no good," he agrees. We're still standing way too close together, and we're still flirting. But I can tell he's actually listening.

"I was deeply unhappy at school last year. And my parents didn't care. You know what's funny?" I can hear myself talking too much, but his attentiveness encourages me. "When I was a teenager I actually took classes on how to please people. It's called charm school."

His deep laugh vibrates through my belly. "To learn to be charming? I can already tell you got an A-plus."

"That's natural ability," I tease. "But they taught us etiquette —which fork to use first and how to set a table for six courses. How to daintily remove an olive pit from your mouth. How to introduce two people when there's an imbalance of power."

"How do you do that?" he asks, leaning in just a few millimeters closer.

"You're supposed to address the person of higher rank first. 'Mr. Important Person, I would like to introduce Mr. Lesser-person.' And then you offer any further details that are appropriate to the situation." I can smell his aftershave. It's clean and spicy. I have the strangest urge to lean in and kiss his angular jaw.

"Who knew?" He moves imperceptibly closer. "And now I'm wondering how many times I've been put in my place like that without realizing it."

"Oh, please," I tease him. "Try being the office intern for a day. I might as well wear a nametag that says, *Hello My Name Is Lesser Person*."

"What *else* did they teach you at charm school?"

"How to foxtrot. The proper way to phrase a wedding invitation. Penmanship. How to dance with a boy you don't like in order to save his feelings. In other words, how to be a good girl even when you don't want to be." The more I think about it, the more it sounds like brainwashing.

"Hmm," Jason whispers. We're so close together now that the word vibrates against my cheek. And then he leans in and lets his lips coast past my temple. It's so faint that it can't even be called a kiss. But it makes me shiver just the same.

No wonder this man gets any woman he wants. I'm practically quivering for him, and he hasn't even kissed me.

Then his voice drops low, and he asks, "Would you rather be a *bad* girl, Heidi?"

Holy heck in a handbag! It's the cheesiest line ever, but my girl parts shimmy all the same.

And then he puts his mouth right beside my ear. "Are you —" He drops his voice to barely a whisper. "—thinking of wearing white after Labor Day?"

I wasn't expecting a joke, which makes it twice as funny. All the tension in my fluttering chest just sort of erupts. I let out an actual snort, which I haven't done since fourth grade. We don't snort in charm school.

But it's been a long day, so I can't stop. I laugh so hard that tears form in both eyes.

"Well? Are you?" he asks, laying a hand at the curve of my hip.

His touch sobers me, and I lean into it. "Probably not." I wipe my eyes. "And it's a crying shame, because I just bought a nice little pair of white jeans on sale and Labor Day has passed."

Jason tips his head back and smiles. "You're right. You *do* need more tequila." He's already pouring me another shot. "Here's to breaking some rules."

I feel a shiver of excitement as I raise my glass, and we toast. His dark eyes watch me while I tip the little glass back and drink. *So this is how the other half lives.* My ex-boyfriend—Eric—wouldn't even recognize me. Although he never once looked at me the way Jason is right now.

But, ouch. Tequila is strong. With watering eyes, I casually take another wedge of lime from the dish and bite it as daintily as a girl can.

Take that, Daddy. The fact that he'd hate me drinking makes it all the more fun.

Castro pounds his shot in one easy gulp and sets his shot glass down on the table. He doesn't even bother with the limes. "You know, we're built to care what other people think," he says, as if he can read my mind. "That's what civilization means."

"Sure," I agree with a sigh. "It's just not very convenient sometimes. Maybe I need to practice not caring."

"My mother has an embroidered pillow on the sofa in the den. It says—*Do one thing every day that scares you.*"

"Omigod!" I squeak. "My mom has that same pillow! Is it khaki, with red piping?" His hand is still warming the juncture of my hip and my rib cage. I cover it with mine, and his knuckles feel sturdy beneath my palm.

Then he surprises me by flipping his hand and capturing

mine. As his long fingers close around my own, I fight off another shiver.

"I'm not in the habit of taking advice from home furnishings," he says, his voice dropping low. "But I love breaking rules." With his free hand, he turns me to face him. And then he pushes a lock of hair out of my face, tucking it behind my ear.

It's not exactly an erotic maneuver. Still, I'm aware of every nerve ending in my body. And I can't look away. The moment he started touching me, I fell into the tractor beam of his attention.

"In your case…" His palm captures my chin and tilts it upward so we're eye to eye. "I think that pillow has it just a little wrong. Instead of doing one thing each day that scares you, try one thing a day that scares your father. He'll get used to it."

"Like, aversion therapy." My voice comes out all breathless and odd. As if I'd said, *"Ravish me against the wall."*

"Yeah." His smile is swift and hot. "Like that."

"Well. He wouldn't like *this* at all," I confess. And by *this*, I mean Jason touching me.

Although—and this is fascinating—it's dawning on me that Jason doesn't know who my daddy is. And I'm *not* about to tell him. Experience has taught me that hockey players won't seduce the commissioner's daughter. They usually steer a wide path around me.

"This?" he whispers. "Which part of this?"

"All of it. The tequila shots. The…" *Hot caresses.*

"Maybe he has a point," Castro says slowly. "I don't think your daddy would like the thoughts I'm thinking right now."

I smile up at him, because I'm so happy I could squeal like a little girl who's just been given her first pony. Men like Jason Castro don't usually want anything to do with me. And I *crave* this. I want him to take me home and show me how it's done by a man who isn't afraid of my daddy.

"You want a soda or something?" he asks. "Maybe it's time to switch to something non-alcoholic."

"No, one more shot first," I insist. If this is a night for rule-breaking, then I'd better get the full experience.

Also, I'm a little nervous. And the warm buzz of alcohol is settling over me like a cozy blanket. If things go as planned, I'll soon be *naked* with the hottest hockey player I've ever met.

"Fine, a small one. What the lady wants, the lady gets," he says with a grin. Then he reaches for the bottle. I watch his fingers clasp it, and wonder how they'll feel on my body.

Amazing, I'll bet.

Silas comes bouncing back to the table. "Dartboard is free," he says. "Who's in?"

"Oh, I don't know." Castro's eyes flick toward me. "Darts are a lot like my day job."

He's giving me an out, but I won't take it. "I'm feeling extra lucky tonight," I announce. "A dollar a point. Let's go."

"She's on my team," Castro says immediately.

And I sure like the way that sounds.

[3]

JASON

AT THE DARTBOARD, Heidi lives up to her nickname. Hot Pepper is *en fuego*. And I'm not too busy checking out her very cute ass to notice that she's weirdly good at darts.

It's me and her against Silas and Bayer. I expect to lose, because Heidi just doesn't seem like the kind of girl who's spent a lot of time hustling darts. But I swear there's a magnet under the bullseye whenever she steps up to throw. We win and we win some more.

"You should play hockey," I say after she wows the bar with another bullseye.

"Good girls don't," she says with a sigh. "Silas, you're up, sir. Time to take your beating."

We lose only the final game, because Heidi has a couple of unlucky throws at the end.

"Maybe you actually wore out the bullseye," Bayer says. "Never seen anyone hit it so many times."

"Or maybe the problem is that last tequila shot," Silas says under his breath. He reaches out to wrap an arm around Hot

Pepper, and I feel a hot spear of jealousy. "Easy, there," he says. And that's when I realize my roommate is only steadying her. Because she's swaying.

Uh-oh.

"I think we should call it a night," Bayer says with a chuckle. "It's late, anyway."

Heidi looks up at me and gives me a big drunken smile. "Bedtime!" she says.

Oh, *hell*. There goes my hookup. I should have done a better job monitoring her tequila intake. But she was so enthusiastic. "How about I take you home?" I say. "Where do you live?"

"Manhattan," she slurs. "But we can't go there. I can't have sex in Daddy's apartment."

Both Silas and Bayer are barely concealing their amusement. "Need a hand?" Silas asks.

I wave him off. "Don't wait up. There might be a long taxi ride in my future."

Silas sort of parks Heidi's floppy body against mine, the way you'd lean a bicycle up against a tree. "Nighty-night, kids." He and Bayer walk off, chuckling to themselves.

"Now," I say. "You've had a little too much to drink, missy. Where can I take you?"

She lifts her chin, and her lips brush the underside of my jaw. "Wherever *you're* goin'."

"That sounds like a very fun time," I admit with a sigh. "But let's have a little chat." I steer her into a chair and sit down beside her. "Now tell me your Manhattan address."

"Nope!" She punctuates this with a burp. "I thought you were hitting on me. I really did."

"Oh, I was," I say, rubbing a hand in slow circles over her back. I'd like to undress her slowly and worship every inch of her. Some other night, though. "We're gonna have to have a raincheck."

"But I can't go home like this. It won't go over well."

"Why?"

"Daddy." She makes a face. "I might as well wear a sign that says, *I'm the fuckup you accuse me of being*." Then she claps a hand over her mouth. "I don't usually drop f-bombs. That was pretty fun, though." She giggles. "Fuck. Fuckity fuckity fuck fuck..." *Hiccup*.

She's getting drunker by the second. It's alarming. I don't really want her father flipping out at me, either. He sounds like a real piece of work. "Okay—here's what we're going to do. I think you'll fit really nicely on my sofa bed." I stand up and offer her my hand.

"Ooh!" she says. "Netflix and chill! And *then* the dirty sex!"

Pete the bartender gives a snort of laughter from behind the bar. "Got your hands full, there, I see."

"Literally." Heidi is standing again, but barely. I balance her against my chest and unlock my Katt phone. "Can you grab a car for me?"

"Can I touch your phone?" Heidi asks suddenly. "I want to fondle it. They don't give the intern a Katt phone."

"Later," I promise.

Pete laughs as he opens the ride-share app and summons a car for me. "Two minutes." He passes me the phone. "And let me pull your bar tab."

I'm using both hands to keep Heidi stable. "Can you just sign that, too? We'll be outside. Night, man."

"Take care." The older man says something quietly under his breath, and it might have been, "And better luck next time."

At least the car shows up on time. I steer Heidi into the back seat with me. "Last chance to let me take you home to Manhattan."

She shakes her head vehemently.

Right.

"Okay. Water and Bridge Street, then."

"Where's that?" Heidi asks. Her eyes are closed.

"My place."

Heidi lifts her head and does an awkward fist pump. "Wow. Yes!"

That seems like a lot of enthusiasm for sleeping on my couch. But whatever.

On second thought, I wonder if I'm supposed to take the fold-out couch. I *am* a gentlemen. But I'm also six-three, and she's at least a foot shorter. She'd totally fit on my sofa...

These are my thoughts as Heidi stirs beside me. Even with her limited dexterity, she's able to climb into my lap. And then kisses me very sloppily on the corner of my mouth.

"Whoa, Nellie!" I pull my head back. "None of that."

"But I can't *wait*," she says in a breathy voice. "Finally..." She leans in again.

I weave out of the way, like a prizefighter trying not to get punched. "Um, when I said we were going to my place, I just meant—"

"Sex!" Heidi says, her warm body settling more firmly onto mine. "Dirty, filthy sex. Sweaty, clawing, pounding, burn-your-soul-to-the-ground sex!"

I let out a groan of frustration.

But my drunken companion misinterprets it. "You're going to really *fuck* me, right?" she asks, blinking at close range.

Parts of me rise up and cheer. "Maybe. But not tonight."

"Please," she says breathlessly. "Boys are always too polite with me. The ones who'll date me are afraid of Daddy. I'm starting to think that polite sex is worse than no sex at all."

I'm wondering—who the fuck is her daddy? Maybe Heidi is a mob princess. Maybe her father controls all the gambling in Brooklyn or runs guns in Jersey.

"What's polite sex like?" asks the driver. "Just asking. For science."

"It's too gentle," Heidi says, relaxing against my chest. "Too sweet. Maybe I just attract the wrong kind of man. I need to know if headboards banging against the wall is a real thing."

"Oh, they bang," I say with a sigh.

A small hand runs up my chest and then back down. Then fingers dip beneath the hem of my T-shirt. "You're so...hard," she says dreamily.

You have no idea.

"How soon 'til we get there?" she asks, her lips coasting up my cheek. "Someone wrote on the ladies' room wall that you like to tie women up when you have sex. Will you show me?"

"Damn," the driver comments from the front seat. "Can I come, too?"

How much longer can this night get? "Listen, Heidi. When I said we were going to my place, I just meant that you need a place to—"

"Here we are!" the driver announces cheerfully.

"My body is ready," she whispers.

I wonder if they teach that at charm school.

Heidi opens the door and climbs out. And then? She tumbles to the curb.

I curse as the doorman comes running outside, but I get to her first. I scoop Heidi off the pavement and into my arms. She slumps against me.

"Everything all right, Mr. Castro?" asks Miguel.

"It will be. This one had a little too much to drink, and now she's going to sleep it off."

"You smell nice," Heidi says, wrapping her arms around me like an octopus.

Miguel laughs. "You need help?"

"Nope. I got this," I say, beginning to tow her toward the building. He runs to open the door for us.

"Are there stairs?" Heidi mumbles. "I don't think I can do stairs."

No kidding. She can't even do flat pavement. It's only about fifteen feet, but I'm basically carrying her toward the door. I turn around just as we reach it and see the driver grinning at me through the open window of the car.

Laugh it up, buddy.

Somehow we make it through the lobby, and Miguel has already summoned the elevator. When it arrives, he blocks the doors open for me. "Good night, Mr. Castro."

"Night," I grumble. "Thanks for your help."

"Anytime." He tips his hat to me as the shiny doors close.

He didn't press the floor button, though, so now I have to do it myself. "Let's see," I say, parking my elbow against the paneling so I can stabilize myself and Heidi at the same time. Her body is in my way, and the first time I reach out to hit the button for the third floor, I miss.

"Goodness," Heidi gurgles. "You're like my ex-boyfriend trying to find my clitoris." She smacks her hand on the console and presses the button. As well as two others.

That'll do, I guess.

"Your ex-boyfriend?" I ask by way of conversation. "Let me guess. He was a hockey player?"

"Yup," she says, snuggling her face into my neck. The elevator begins to move upward. "You're my type. I love your body. It's so..." She doesn't finish the sentence. But one of her hands wraps around to explore my ass. "Wow." Her hand travels all over my backside, then runs right up the center between my—

I twist away from her. "Getting a little fresh, are we?"

She kisses my neck. And I won't lie—she smells good, too. Like citrusy perfume and bad decisions. I'm not immune to those soft lips on my skin. But she's wasted, so we're not going there. Maybe ever. Screwing a coworker was a bad idea from the outset, right? This is fate's way of slapping my hand.

Ding! says the elevator as it arrives on my floor.

"Come on. Everybody out," I say as the doors part.

"Sleepy." Heidi puts her head on my shoulder. Then her knees buckle again.

But this time I'm ready and catching her is easy. "So it's gonna be like that, huh? Miss Perky passes out?" *Great.* I'm talking to a sleeping person.

With a sigh, I tuck her head against my body and lift her cute butt with the other. I stagger into the hallway and toward my apartment door.

I would bet any amount of money that Miguel is watching this via the security cameras and laughing his ass off right now.

When I get to my door, I have a problem. Both hands are busy, and I still need to unlock. It's a keycard setup, but the card is in my wallet.

"Come on now, Heidi," I coax. "Now would be a good time to do your share." I set her feet gingerly on the floor and nudge her arms to close around me.

She hugs me, thankfully, and I reach for my wallet.

"Is this your place?" she whispers in my ear. "Take me to *bed*."

My lizard brain hears only the word *bed* in that sentence, and for a split second I can picture it in my mind. Peeling off our clothes and getting hot and heavy sounds much more fun than putting a drunk girl to bed and hoping she doesn't puke everywhere.

But we can't always get the things we want.

I fumble the door open, grasp Heidi, and carry her into my apartment. She doesn't say a word, and I have the strange sensation of starring in that movie about the dead guy they haul around—*Weekend at Bernie's*.

My life. So glamorous. A glance at Silas's bedroom door shows me that he's already turned in for the night. Lucky guy.

Heidi is completely limp as I carry her to the sofa and pour her onto it. "Ow," she says, even though I'm careful not to let her hit her head.

"What hurts?"

"My stomach."

Oh, fuck. She sits up quickly, alarm in her eyes. "I think I'm going to—"

She stands up fast and runs for the rear of my apartment.

"On the left," I bark as she sprints. The girl is surprisingly agile for someone who was limp as a ragdoll a minute ago. But every hockey player knows that adrenaline has superpowers.

Not even four seconds elapse before I hear the door slam and the sound of retching.

I sit down on my sofa and put my face in my hands. I allow myself a chuckle. At least I didn't insist on taking her home to Manhattan. She might be puking on me in the back of a car right now.

Things could always be worse.

Heidi appears a few minutes later, looking pale and sheepish. She sits down beside me on the couch and lets out a drunken sigh.

"Are you okay?" I ask.

She clears her throat. "Yeah. I don't usually drink." There's a slight slur to her words.

"Because it's impolite?"

A giggle escapes her. "Don't tease! It's embarrassing enough already. There's no mess, though. I'm a *very* ladylike puker."

That makes us both laugh.

"I borrowed your mouthwash," she confesses. "Sorry."

"You borrowed Silas's, because that's his bathroom. But we can do even better than that. Come on." A glance at my phone tells me it's midnight. In six hours I have to be up and on my way to Long Island, where the next part of training camp is scheduled to happen.

I need to sleep, and that can only happen after I make sure my unexpected guest is comfortable. Heidi follows me into the giant master bedroom, and then the huge en suite bathroom. "Wow. Nice place."

"Thanks." It is a nice place. Silas and I are paying exorbitant rent, although some of our teammates bought their units. We refer to this building—a hundred-year-old factory that was renovated into luxury condos—as the Million Dollar Dorm. It's pricey, but its proximity to the practice facility is irresistible. So a significant percentage of the team lives here.

I haven't tried to buy my unit yet, since I don't want to jinx myself by assuming the Bruisers will keep me. Especially after the way last season ended.

"Here," I say, fishing a new toothbrush out of the medicine cabinet. "And let me find you a T-shirt and a pair of shorts."

Ten minutes later I tuck Heidi into one side of my king-sized bed. And then I climb into bed on the other side. I'm not sleeping on my couch—not if I have to scrimmage tomorrow under the watchful eye of coaches who are still trying to cut players.

Besides, if Heidi is here with me, I can keep an eye on her. And—bonus—the bathroom is nearby.

This will only work if she doesn't get frisky, like she was in the cab. I shut off the lamp, plunging the room into darkness. All is silent for a moment, and she stays on her side of the bed. Then I hear her sigh. "The room is sort of..."

"Turning?" I guess.

"Yessir. How did you know?"

"It's called having the spins." She wasn't kidding that she doesn't drink very often. Who's never had the spins? "Should we find you a bucket for beside the bed?"

"No." She groans. "My stomach isn't sick anymore. Now it's only my head. But I hate it. It's like I'm turning through space."

"You're not, I promise." I reach across the bed and take her hand. "See? I've got you."

She squeezes my hand with her smoother one, and then she wiggles backward. Suddenly my arms are full of warm, curvy girl. Her back is to my chest, and she pulls my arm over her body and hangs on tightly to it, as if I'm the only thing tethering her to Earth. "That's better," she whispers.

Her hair smells like flowers. And she's just as soft and warm as I thought she'd be, damn it.

"We're not having filthy, dirty sex right now," she observes.

"No, we're not," I say firmly.

"Because I puked."

"Because you needed to puke," I correct.

"And that's off-putting. It's not ladylike. Maybe Mama was right all along."

"Nah." I smile into her hair. "That's not the reason."

"No?"

"Nope. The reason is that having filthy, hot sex—"

"Filthy, *dirty* sex."

"—is that having filthy, *dirty* sex with wasted girls isn't gentlemanly. Turns out I do follow a few rules."

"Oh. I thought tonight I would finally be a wild child. I guess I lost my shot."

"Yeah, you did. But I still think you're pretty wild. It isn't often I beat Bayer and Silas at darts, three times in a row."

"I'm handy at skeet-shooting, too."

"No shit?" There is something deeply appealing about the image of Heidi blasting clay plates out of the sky with a shotgun.

"No lie," she says, and the way that "lie" is flattened a little to "lah," makes my body respond. Or maybe it's the fact that she's stroking my hand with her softer one. Then she sighs and wiggles a bit in my arms.

Goddamn it, now I'm hard. Of course I am. I'm lying in my

bed with a beautiful girl who I've been staring at since the day she showed up on the team jet last spring. And her perfect lips keep repeating the words, "filthy, dirty sex."

You'd have to be a dead man not to respond. And I'm very much alive. If I shifted my hips a couple of inches, we could be…

I hold back my impatient groan. So much for a good night's sleep.

"Good night, Jason Castro," Heidi whispers. "Thank you for being such a good guy."

"I'm not," I argue.

"No, you are. You listened to me. Earlier, when I was upset."

"Oh." She really is drunk. "That's nothing." She was damned entertaining.

"It's not nothing. Not at all. You made me laugh and told me to be daring."

"I was only trying to get you naked," I admit.

She sighs against my pillow. "But that's nice, too. Nobody ever does that, either."

I squeeze her hand in mine, wondering how that's possible. She's not the only one who feels a little disoriented, either. I'm not usually a cuddler. I don't usually snuggle up to my hookups, because I don't want to send the wrong impression. But it's unexpectedly pleasant to feel Heidi's smooth skin against mine.

I'll never be anyone's boyfriend again. That's by choice. But I'd forgotten what this was like—holding someone who needs me. Years ago I used to sneak through my high school girlfriend's window so I could hold her all night just like this.

And now I'm both horny and wistful. What a strange night. I feel stirred up inside, but I lie still, unwilling to disturb the sleepy princess beside me. My eyes drift closed, and I find myself wondering what it would be like to have someone in my bed every night like this.

It's not like me to have these thoughts. While my body runs hot, my heart is pretty cold. But something about Heidi warms me all the way to the center. She's willing to tell me her flaws. And she's unafraid to say she doesn't have all the answers.

And I sure as hell don't, either.

On that happy thought, I fall asleep.

[4]

JASON

WHEN MY ALARM goes off the next morning at six, I'm not alone.

Unfortunately, the other person in my room is *not* the hot blonde woman with long, silky legs that tortured me last night. Instead, my roommate Silas is standing at the foot of the bed, nudging me with his knee.

"Aren't you getting up?" he asks, drinking deeply from the Delilah Spark Fanclub mug that my teammates bought him for his birthday. It was meant as a gag gift, but Silas drinks from it every morning.

"Yeah, I'm coming. Jesus." It wasn't a great night's sleep, unfortunately. Too much tossing and turning against Heidi's body. Too many horny dreams.

"The bus leaves in thirty minutes," Silas reminds me.

"You know what?" I squint up at him. "Let's just drive out there. Fuck the bus."

"In your new car?" he asks brightly. "I'm so there!"

"Sure, I'll drive you—so long as there's more of that coffee."

I lift my head and look toward the bathroom. "Did you see Heidi anywhere around here?"

"Jesus, did you actually fuck her?" Silas's eyes pop wide.

"Of *course* not. Didn't you see how sloppy she got?" I should've known she couldn't hold her liquor.

"Good thing." He shakes his head. "Banging the commissioner's daughter is not a great career move."

I play that sentence back in my head, and it still doesn't make sense. "Wait—whose daughter?"

The question catches Silas in the middle of a sip of coffee, and he has to gulp it down to avoid choking. "Seriously? You don't know who Heidi is? And her nickname didn't clue you in?"

"Hot Pepper." The truth hits me like a punch to the gut. "As in... Tobias Pepper?"

Silas laughs. "What rock have you been living under?"

"A big one, I guess." *Jesus.* My mood plunges. What a terrible mistake I almost made. "Did you hear her leave this morning?" It's just after six, and there's no sign of her.

"Nope, and I've been up for a half hour already making coffee."

Hmm. "Pour me some? I'll be your best friend."

"You already are." Silas heads out of the room.

I sit up and shift my feet to the floor. I check in with all of my muscles, half of which are stiff. But that's how it always is during the season.

My phone is on the bedside table so I grab it and scroll through my contacts. I'm pretty sure I have Heidi's number; last spring she was in charge of transportation for one of our road trips. And—bingo. I shoot off a text. ***Morning, sunshine. I hope you're feeling better today.*** It's a nice, friendly little message. And that's the only kind I'm going to send this girl.

I almost fucked the commissioner's daughter. Who knew?

"Are you packed already?" Silas calls from our kitchen. "We could leave in thirty."

"Yeah, already done," I grunt. My garment bag is hanging on the back of the closet door, and my golf clubs are standing in the corner. I even remembered my bathing suit.

In spite of the five-star accommodations, this boondoggle on Long Island isn't my favorite preseason ritual. Who wants to wear a tuxedo and mingle with rich fans after a long day of hockey? Not me. Tomorrow, at least, I get to play a round of golf on one of the best courses in the nation.

But even the golf won't be relaxing. It's a charity event, so I have to make small talk with rich preppies while we play. Last year our foursome included a guy named Maximillian Rothchester Barrington III. That was his real name. But—and this is where it gets weird—preppies have strange nicknames. This guy was called Bink.

That's what I'm up against.

My conscience tugs at me even as I finish that thought. *Oh poor me! The soul-grinding punishment of golf and expensive resort food...* So I'm a whiner when I'm tired. Sue me.

Silas reappears with a giant cup of coffee in a stainless-steel travel mug. "This is for you," he says. "You can drink it in the passenger seat while I drive us to the Hamptons."

"Nice try," I snort, and he laughs.

"Aw, come on! If I had a brand-new car like that, I'd let you drive it."

"Would you really?"

He shrugs, and then gives me the lopsided, innocent grin that shows up on Instagram every other day. Chicks dig his innocent face.

I don't have an innocent face. I just don't. Ask my mother. And it's just as well, since there's nothing very innocent about me. Not anymore.

My new ride is a Tesla Model X in Pearl White Multi-coat, and she is beautiful. Zero to sixty in four-point-nine seconds, and a ride so quiet it's like you're shooting directly through the space-time continuum.

Or at least shooting along the Long Island Expressway, which is where we are right now.

Fact: it's completely impractical for a man who lives in Brooklyn and walks to work to own this car. But that only made me want it more. I'm a single guy who earns almost a million a year. No wife. No responsibilities. This car is the first decadent thing I ever bought myself, unless top-shelf liquor counts.

My family doesn't understand. When I told my dad I was thinking of buying a car, he suggested a Honda CR-V. "You can get a used one coming off a lease for under twenty grand," he'd said.

When I spent a hundred large on the Tesla, he almost burst a vessel. But the point of the car is that it's beautiful, not that it's practical.

"Just listen to that quiet," I say as I pass a Honda CR-V with the noiseless, instant acceleration that only a Tesla can manage.

"Can I listen to the silence with the radio on?" Silas asks.

"No, you *cannot*. Jesus. I get enough of Delilah Spark at home. She and I are on a first-name basis now, because we see so much of each other."

"Are you, now?" Silas says in a low voice.

"Yeah. We're going steady. Are you jealous?"

Silas doesn't take the bait. He's immune to our teasing at this point. Also, my phone is ringing. At least I think it's mine. The billionaire—Nate Kattenberger—who owns the team, provides every player with the same model of phone, and sometimes we get confused.

"That's yours," Silas says. "How come you don't have it linked to the car?"

"Didn't get around to it yet." I'm not that interested in gadgetry that doesn't go ninety miles an hour. You can keep your apps and photos.

Mercifully, the phone stops bleating.

"I'm going to hook you up," Silas announces, reaching for my phone.

"Oh, baby. You're really not my type."

Ignoring me, Silas reaches into my gym bag on the floor behind my seat, and retrieves my phone. Then he spends a few minutes tapping on the Tesla control screen.

"Unlock your phone for me," he says, tagging my hand off the steering wheel so he can press my thumb to the screen.

"If you want to hold hands, all you have to do is ask," I say as the phone beeps in recognition.

"Please," Silas complains. "I don't want your body, but I'd probably sleep with you anyway if it meant I could drive this car."

That cracks us both up. We're still laughing when the phone rings again. "Who keeps calling me at seven a.m.?"

"Uh-oh," Silas says. "It's Tommy."

"The new publicist?"

"That's the guy."

"Don't answer. We'll see him in an hour, anyway. You told the travel team we weren't gonna be on the bus, right?"

"Of course. All they said was 'drive safe.'"

"Ready for some acceleration?" I ask as we gain on a slow-moving tractor trailer.

"Scare me," Silas says. I barely have to touch the pedal and the car shoots forward. It's like flying. The acceleration is so swift that it pushes me back against my seat.

"Jesus," Silas says. "This car is everything. It's better than sex."

Are you sure you remember? The dig is on the tip of my tongue, but I don't say it. I don't even know what's stopping me. With my teammates, pretty much anything is fair game at any time. But I get a lot of action, and it's not nice to brag.

Besides—Silas doesn't hook up. Ever. I don't really know why. And I don't want to make assumptions that might be wrong.

My phone chimes with a text. And then another one immediately follows.

"Uh-oh," Silas says again.

"Tommy again?"

"Yeah. And…shit. There's a picture of you on a sports blog."

"So?"

"It's you and Hot Pepper."

I'm still not seeing the problem. "What, we're playing darts?"

"No. You're sort of…" He sighs. "Dragging her. It doesn't look good. You'll have to look at it to see what I mean."

"Shit! Really?"

"Tommy is not a happy man. He says to call him right away."

I steer my baby off the next exit and stop in a convenience store parking lot. "Show me this picture."

Wearing a grim expression, Silas hands me my phone.

And it's *bad*. Silas is right. The shot was taken just after we got out of the car in front of my apartment building. Right after I'd scooped Heidi up off the pavement where she'd tripped.

That *should* be no problem. The caption I'd have given this moment of my life is: *Dude lifts woman who's trying to nap on the ground*. And images don't lie, right?

Well, this one misleads. I guess it's the violent expression on my face—I've seen it before in photos where I'm lunging for the puck. In this photo, I'm frowning like a grumpy beast while holding Heidi in my arms, and she looks *blotto*. The overall effect is somehow menacing. And the blogger writes, *Bruisers are aggressive on and off the ice.*

A sick feeling rolls through me. "That is so wrong."

"Just call Tommy," Silas suggests. "But do it from the road, or else we'll be late."

Fuck! Showing up late will only add to my difficulties. So I tap the control panel to open both the driver's and the passenger's doors. They lift like wings to let us out. "You drive."

Silas makes a little noise of glee and climbs out of the car. We pass each other in front of the hood. "Hell, I'd have taken that picture myself if I knew it meant I could drive."

"Not. Funny." I glance at the picture one more time, hoping it won't seem as bad the second time I see it. But, fuck. It does. "Christ almighty. *Hulk hauls blond princess back to his lair.* I'm so screwed."

"She does look awfully helpless," Silas concedes.

"She *was* helpless. And I helped her." But we both know that some people will assume that I also helped myself to the goods.

Silas's forehead wrinkles as he fastens his seatbelt. "The picture isn't that bad, dude. It's just a moment's worth of gossip. The tricky part is that the commissioner is probably on the guest list for this shindig tonight. I'll bet that's what Tommy wants to tell you."

"Fuck my *life*!" That hadn't even occurred to me, although the commissioner had been at the event last year. Last fall was my first season as a full-fledged team member. I spent the two prior years getting bounced back and forth between Brooklyn and the minor-league team in Hartford.

Last year I was as happy as can be to play in the golf tournament and be one of the boys. I had a great season. All my dreams were coming true. Until a certain shot didn't find the net during game seven.

And now this bullshit.

I press the button to return Tommy's call. Might as well take my licking now, or else I'll have to endure it in a crowded changing room later.

"Jason," Tommy says when he picks up. "What the hell is that picture?"

So I guess we're skipping the small talk. I don't know this new publicist at all, but already I don't like him. "That photo was taken by a ride-share driver with a death wish. He's getting a one-star review for sure," I tell him. That's the only possible explanation, unless there had been somebody else lurking across the street. "Heidi got toasted and fell down outside the cab. I picked her up."

He's quiet for a second. "The photo has multiple interpretations."

"Yeah, I noticed that, too, because I *have eyes*." I leave off the end of that sentence which is, *you dumbass*. Because I'm nice like that.

"Hey—I'm on your side, here. Are you and Heidi Jo a couple?"

"No. And not that it's anyone's business, but Miss Pepper and I have never had, uh, an intimate encounter. Not last night, and not ever."

I'm making that point awfully loudly. But now I have my hackles up. This is one of those situations where I can't help but wonder if the publicist would ask different questions if it wasn't the team's only brown guy in that shot.

Am I paranoid about this? Maybe.

He sighs. "So that photo is just the office intern getting some assistance from a team member."

"Right."

"She's the office intern, but she's also drunk and underage."

"Under...*what?*" I feel ill.

"She doesn't turn twenty-one until next month."

"Oh." *Phew*. For a second there I thought he was saying she's a minor. That would have stunned me, but I've been stunned before. "A twenty-year-old in a bar is not exactly a national scandal, Tommy. Girl gets drunk a month before her birthday. Film at eleven."

"It doesn't help to be flip," the publicist growls. "Did you buy her the drinks?"

Well, fuck. "I bought a bottle of very good tequila and served it to everyone who was there last night. Don't make my generosity into a plot point."

"You're the only two in the photo."

"You think it would look so much better if there were seven guys hauling her drunk little butt off the pavement?"

Tommy actually laughs, giving me some hope that his sense of humor hasn't been surgically amputated. "So you helped her off the pavement, and then what?"

"Who's asking?"

"I am, you—" He doesn't finish that thought. "Tell me, so I can help you craft your message."

"There is no message. Hot Pepper didn't want to go home to Manhattan and wouldn't tell me her address. I took her up to our place, where she puked in our bathroom. Then I tucked her in and let her sleep it off." I edit out the part where we shared a bed. "When I woke up she was gone. Probably embarrassed. Haven't heard from her since." A little prickle of worry hits me as I say those words. "She's okay, right?"

"She's fine. She's on the bus with the team. It's you I'm worried about. I don't think the commissioner is going to like his baby's picture on the blogs..."

...getting manhandled by a league player. He doesn't even have to finish the sentence. I can hear how it ends.

"So what do I do?" I ask him. "I mean, I didn't do anything wrong. So I can't apologize."

"No," he agrees swiftly. "You can't. It's not that kind of situation. I just have to be ready to answer any questions that media outlets might ask. I've already got one newspaper guy asking me if she's okay, and what does her father have to say about the photo."

Ugh. I'm sorry I ever poured that girl a drink. I don't need this headache. And neither does she. Hers is probably an *actual* headache, too. "Let me know if there's anything I can do," I grunt. "But I think staying the hell away from her is the best course of action."

"Couldn't have said it better myself. No drinking with the ladies this weekend, okay? This party is going to be all nosy socialites and season ticket holders."

"No kidding." His little warning irritates me. "I was there last year." *Unlike you*. "I'll be a good boy."

"Sounds like a plan. See you after practice for the team photos."

I say goodbye and hang up the phone. We're flying down the L.I.E. toward the Hamptons. "You having fun at least?" I grunt at Silas.

"You know it. Was Tommy pissed at you?"

"Not sure. I didn't do a thing wrong."

"I know that." He casts a glance in my direction. "Then there's nothing to worry about. Except for her dad making a scene."

"That's when I leave the party through the kitchen."

"I'll follow you out," Silas says. "We'll go for another joy ride." Then—with obvious glee—he floors it.

[5]

HEIDI

THE BUS RIDE from the team headquarters in Brooklyn to the golf resort is unending. I have a white-knuckle grip on the armrests of the luxury coach as we speed toward East Hampton. It's three hours of torture. My head aches, and my stomach is foamy and hot. Little waves of nausea pass through me every few minutes, worsening each time the bus makes a turn.

I chose a seat near the back of the bus, just in case I needed to sprint toward the coach's little bathroom. But now I realize this was a mistake. I feel claustrophobic back here where I can't see the road. When I was a little girl who got carsick, Daddy always told me to look at the horizon to steady myself.

My stomach gives another angry lurch, and I start praying again. *Dearest Lord above, I'll never drink again if you could just make it stop. No more tequila. No more darts. No more climbing into hockey players' laps in the backs of cars and begging them for sex.*

That mortifying memory brings the taste of bile to my throat. I swallow hard, feeling sweaty. If I could just get off this bus, everything would be fine. I need to stand outside in the sunshine and breathe the fresh air.

I check the map on my phone for the tenth time. We're still twenty minutes away from East Hampton. I've almost survived the trip, but these last miles are crawling by. If I don't find some relief, I'll lose my mind.

There's a text from Castro, checking on me. I should answer the man, but I'm not feeling well enough to think of something pithy to say. How does a girl beg for forgiveness in this situation?

In charm school, I learned to write condolence notes and thank-you notes. But they didn't prepare me for this situation. *Dear Jason, I'm sorry I got senior-prom-drunk and then begged you for nookie.*

Every time I remember the words I used, I want to die all over again. I thought I was living life out loud, and being true to myself. But I was only humiliating myself.

The dot on my phone's map creeps forward too slowly. I need air.

Rising onto unsteady legs, I shoulder my handbag and then lurch toward the front of the coach. The only saving grace is that Jason Castro is not on this bus. Some players opted to drive to the Hamptons instead.

Thank you, Baby Jesus. I couldn't face him right now.

I toddle forward. In the second row, there's an empty seat beside Bayer, who's dozing with his head against the window. I slip into the empty seat and fix my eyes on the road.

And it's a little better up here. There's less motion, and I can see out the giant front windows. I take a deep breath in and then exhale slowly.

"Hungover?" Bayer asks without opening his eyes.

"Seems so," I grunt. It's not the most ladylike response, but I can't afford to be polite right at this moment. I can barely breathe through my misery.

There's a chuckle from the seat beside me. "Have you eaten anything yet today?"

"Lord, no. Didn't seem like a good idea." Not to mention that I was pressed for time. I took a five a.m. subway ride back to Manhattan. I snuck into my father's apartment, quiet as a mouse. After a hasty shower and some frantic packing, I snuck out again while my father was in the shower.

I barely made the team bus, saving myself the embarrassment of missing it. Although, if I barf everywhere before we arrive at our destination, the point will be moot.

Bayer rises in his seat and fishes a hand into the duffel bag at his feet. "Here." He hands me a small bag of pretzels. "These are the perfect hangover remedy. I always have some handy."

"You are a prince among men," I gush, which makes him laugh.

I tear open the bag and put one of the pretzels in my mouth and chew. Even the first bite of salty, bland carbohydrates is restorative.

He reaches into the duffel again, then hands me an unopened bottle of water. "Now have some of this, with two of these." He fishes out a bottle of ibuprofen and takes the cap off.

"That settles it," I say gratefully. "I'll name my firstborn after you."

Bayer laughs. "Learning to cope with a hangover is just part of hockey. I have to keep up with these youngsters around me."

"I hope you're not sacrificing your best weapons for little old me." Later today I will find a bag of pretzels and a bottle of water to replenish his stock.

"I'm good." He chuckles. "I had just one shot last night. No need for the arsenal today."

"If only I'd stopped at one." I could have saved myself a full helping of mortification. I distinctly remember straddling Castro's lap and asking him if he'd tie me up. And it's possible that I said the word "clitoris" out loud at some point.

Even if the bus driver opened the door of the moving bus and tossed me out, I don't think I could be any unhappier than I am right now. Every time I think about last night, I want to die all over again.

There should be a charm-school course on how to hold your liquor. *Gather 'round ladies, tonight we're drinking tequila!* The idea would be funny if I weren't so distraught right now.

I fix my gaze on the highway as the miles roll by. I eat a few more pretzels, sip the water, and count down the minutes until our arrival.

At last the bus leaves the highway. We begin to roll past carefully manicured properties and tidy little shops. You know you're in the Hamptons when everything is decorated with beachy paraphernalia and expensive landscaping.

Beside me, Bayer is poking at his phone. But he's also stealing glances at me.

"What?" I finally ask. "Something the matter?"

He opens his mouth and then shuts it again. "Suppose not."

"Thank you again for your kindness," I say as the bus comes to a stop outside a hotel. "I feel worlds better."

"You're welcome. Anytime."

Before we can exit the bus, the doors open to admit Rebecca Rowley, who will soon become Rebecca Kattenberger, as well as the new team owner. She and Nate Kattenberger announced their engagement right at the end of last season.

And—if I'm lucky—Rebecca will become my permanent boss. She's going to hire someone to replace herself as the office manager. I plan to be first in line for that job.

"Morning, champs!" she says. "We have a full day ahead of us. You have forty-five minutes to check in to your rooms and prepare for practice. This bus will leave at ten for the rink. You'll practice, eat lunch, have a meeting with the coaches. And then you'll scrimmage for the public at three thirty. Veterans against the younger guys and rookies. Then it's back on the bus, and back to the hotel for two hours of rest before the black-tie cocktail party. Everyone attends. Any questions?"

Bayer's hand shoots up beside me. "What do the veterans get if we beat the rookies again this year?"

"My undying respect," Rebecca says with a smile. "And free drinks at a stuffy cocktail party. Now off you go."

I practically launch myself off the bus, I'm so happy to breathe the fresh air. I know I'm not the first stupid girl to ever have a hangover, but I sure do feel like I survived three hours of torture.

"Heidi Jo? A word?" Rebecca waves me over, using the name my father calls me.

But I don't correct her. If I can interview for the office manager job, I don't care what she calls me.

"Yes, ma'am," I say, stepping out of the way of the players who are streaming toward the hotel.

"You ma'amed me?" Becca says with an exaggerated gasp. "Did I age significantly over the summer?"

"Oh, stop. I'm just feeling humble this morning. Enjoy it while it lasts."

Rebecca's smile fades quickly. "Are you okay?"

"Absolutely," I say quickly. Not only do I feel loads better now that we're off the bus, I never want to show weakness to the boss. "What can I do for you first?"

"Well..." She makes a grim face. "I have two items of news for you, and neither of them is good."

Oh, dear Lord. My stomach dives for the hundredth time today, and it's not even nine o'clock. "Did you fill the position already?"

"No," she says quickly. "It will be a couple weeks before I get around to working on that."

I relax a little, but then I notice that she does not.

"Look, I need you to step inside and speak to our publicists for a moment. Would you follow me?"

"Of course," I say, feeling sick all over again. I can't imagine what they want with me, unless they want me to do a publicity rotation as part of my internship.

She ushers me inside the East Hampton Lawn and Golf Club, and as we head for a small conference room open off the lobby, I get a quick glimpse of dark wood paneling and chandeliers. It's a fusty, old-money look. *Our blood is bluer than yours,* it whispers. *We're too genteel for bling.*

The co-heads of publicity are already seated at a table when we enter. There's Tommy, who I don't know very well. And Georgia is a real sweetie, but today she looks grim. "Hi, Heidi Jo," she says. "How are you today?"

"Um, fine?"

"We have to show you a photograph," Becca says, taking a seat. "It popped up on a sports blog in the wee hours. And I need to ask you to tell me what's happened here."

When she holds up her phone, I'm confronted with an image that brings all my nausea back in force. "Oh my God." I actually sway on my feet.

Rebecca reaches up to grab my arm. "Hey, take a breath. And a seat."

"That picture!" I sputter. "My daddy will *shoot* me." I turn my face away from the photo, as if that would make it go away. I look exactly like my parents' worst nightmare. Like a brainless tramp. Daddy will yell, and Mama will cry.

I sit down heavily in a chair. If the floor opened up and swallowed me right now, that would be okay, too.

"I'm sorry," Becca says softly. "But I have to ask—how did things work out for you after this was taken?"

"Oh, *terribly,*" I babble as Becca's eyes widen. "Last night I tried to be a fun party girl. But the night ended with Castro listening to me puke in his toilet. Then he gave me his clothes and tucked me into bed like a second-grader. I woke up at five with a pounding head and snuck out of his apartment."

Everyone around the table visibly relaxes. "Okay, well…" Rebecca clears her throat. "There are worse nights. We all do it."

"Not you," I whisper. "The other girls say that nobody holds their liquor like you do." Honestly, I want to be Rebecca Rowley-soon-to-be-Kattenberger when I grow up. She's fierce and smart *and super fun.* Yet she still manages to have everyone's respect.

"It's a gift, handed down from my Yorkshire ancestors, along with sturdy hips." She winks. "I'm glad to hear that you're all right. But this picture is circulating. We're getting questions."

A fresh wave of horror rolls through me. "Is there anything I can do to shut it down?"

"That's what we're trying to decide," Georgia says quickly. "This photo looks more like a predator and a helpless college girl than two friends out on the town together."

"Oh…" I say slowly. "Is Jason going to get in trouble over this? That's not fair. All he did was pick me up off the sidewalk." I remember the doorman's laughter. And the too-bright lights in the elevator.

Jason had looked grumpy as heck, but who could blame him?

"It will be okay," Becca says quickly.

"In a case where there's no real story, people tend to lose interest pretty quickly," Tommy agrees.

"I hate that you called it a *case,* though," I point out. "There's no case. There's only me making a fool of myself and a player who was in the wrong place at the right time."

"All right," Georgia says kindly. She rises to her feet. "We won't call it a case. We'll call it an unphotogenic moment. It's possible we'll ask you to take a photo with him that looks better. The two of you passing out visors at the golf tournament tomorrow, or something."

"Can I wear a T-shirt that says—*Look, I can stay upright without assistance?*" Everyone laughs, but I'm only half kidding.

"We probably won't need a photo at all," Tommy says, following Georgia out of the room. "Not if the story dies quietly. Hang in there, Heidi Jo."

I wait for the publicists to leave the room. And then I ask Rebecca, "What's the other bad news?" I haven't forgotten that she'd said she had *two* things to tell me. Is there any point in hoping that the photo was the worst of it?

"The other thing might not be so bad," Becca says, leaning back in her chair. "Your father called me this morning."

"Uh-oh. Did he see the photo?"

"I'm not sure," Becca admits. "All I have is a voicemail. He wants to talk to me about renegotiating the terms of your internship."

"Oh," I say slowly. That could be bad. "We had a huge fight yesterday. He's mad that I didn't go back to school. But I don't see how that affects my job with the team."

"Maybe it's no big deal, then," Becca offers.

But I'm not convinced. My father has a very forceful personality, and he loves to go on about meaningful consequences. Yesterday, Daddy ranted about all the horrible jobs I would have in my life if I didn't finish school. He regrets arranging my internship. "*That was my mistake. The job is too cushy for a slacker like you.*"

That one hurt because I am a hard worker. I always have been. Just not at Bryn Mawr.

"You won't fire me, right?" I ask Becca. "I mean—I work for free right now." My father has been paying me a stipend out of his own pocket.

"Best deal ever." She beams at me. "I'm not sure what your father wants, and I thought you might know. But if not, we'll reconvene after I speak to him tonight."

"Well…" I clear my throat. "If he stops funding my time in

Brooklyn, I'll have to find a paying job. I'm still hoping to work for you after you transition into the owner's office."

"Let's just see how it goes," Becca says, pushing her chair back from the table.

"All right," I agree. "I'd better check in so I can make it to the bus on time. What do you need from me this afternoon?"

When I stand, Becca hooks her arm in mine, then leads me toward the check-in desk. "I need you to help Georgia and Tommy with the swag," she says. "They have goody bags for the guests tonight, and something like keychains and game schedules for the people who watch the scrimmage this afternoon."

"Okay. What else?"

"When we all get to the practice space, there will be something to fix or untangle. There always is."

"Sounds like my life." I sigh. "I'll see you in a jif."

"And Heidi Jo?"

I turn back. "Yes?"

"Don't get your picture taken with Castro tonight."

I feel a new flutter of panic run through my body. "Don't worry about that." I don't even want to *see* Jason Castro again. I'm so embarrassed. The things I asked him for...

Becca walks away, and I pull out my phone and finally answer his text. *I'm fine! And I'm SO sorry I made your evening harder than necessary. And sorry about that awful photo, too.*

His response comes almost immediately. *Glad to hear it, kiddo.*

Kiddo?

Once more, my cheeks flush with shame. Only children get stumbling drunk. And there goes my shot at seducing him. I've just been demoted from hot-girl-in-a-bar to drunken idiot.

It's almost more depressing than having my blotto face on a sports blog.

Almost.

[6]

HEIDI

It's a long day of running around at the Hamptons practice rink and trying to look like I don't feel nauseated.

When lunchtime comes, I help the caterer set up a buffet in the hallway at the practice facility. Instead of eating with the players, though, I grab a sandwich and two Diet Cokes and disappear to a bench outside.

The food and the fresh air do me some good, too. But I'm not out here to admire the hydrangeas. I'm hiding in shame. And that's not something that the Pepper family ever does.

It's time for a consult.

I pull out my phone. Ignoring a dozen waiting text messages from people who saw *that photo,* I dial my sister. "I need help," I tell her. She loves it when I ask for help. She's two years older than me and super bossy.

"I'll say you do," she says immediately. "You need to examine your life choices if you're too drunk to focus on that hottie in the picture."

"You saw it, too?" I squeak. That's bad news, because my

sister does not follow hockey. If the photo made it all the way to Jana, things are worse than I thought.

"I hope Mama doesn't see it. She'll have a conniption. Did she call you?"

"Not sure. I've been avoiding my phone. But I made an exception for you, because I need some advice."

"About men?" she asks hopefully. "Did you catch yourself a new hockey player?"

"Negative." But not for lack of trying. "My question is about something simpler than men. Eye makeup."

"Oh, precious one." My sister lets out a dramatic sigh. "There is nothing simpler than men."

That may be true for Jana, who always seems to have men falling at her feet. But Jana and I are not the same kind of girl. She likes nice boys that she can control. And I'm just the opposite.

Just once, I want a bad boy to be interested in me. How will I ever take a walk on the wild side if the wild side is put off by Daddy?

Or put off by *me*.

"So what is this makeup emergency?" she asks.

"My eyes are red. As red as Uncle Wyatt's face after Aunt Dorothy runs up his credit card."

"Ouch."

"I know. And my dress is pink."

"Hmm," my sister muses. "What shade of pink?"

"Shell."

"Oh! That's not so bad. I was afraid you were going to say coral. And there'd be nothing I could do. Almost nothing."

"So? Tell me what to do. I have the Dior palette in cool shades."

"Okay—write this down. Dark navy eyeliner on the upper lids, but not the bottoms," my sister says, her voice ringing with authority. "That will help with brightness. Do you have a white or shimmery liner?"

"Maybe?" I didn't look carefully at my cosmetic bag this morning. I was too busy trying not to puke.

"Use it for the lower lids if you have it. And then try the grayest color on the shadow palette. That purple in the corner. A silver highlight wouldn't go amiss."

"All right. Thank you." I sigh. "Could be a long night. I'm pretty sure *he'll* be there."

"Castro? The hottie in the photo? He's a player, Heidi. I looked him up today."

"Why?"

"Because he's in a photo with my baby sister! *Why*, she asks." Jana sniffs. "How did you get so drunk?"

"Tequila is the short answer. The longer answer is that Daddy was an ass and I wanted an adventure."

"An adventure with Jason Castro?"

"Is that so wrong?"

My sister is quiet a moment. "No, I suppose not. But you're not the one-night-stand type."

"Who knows if I am or not?" I ask. "Daddy sent me to a college for women only because he obviously hates me. And every boy I ever dated was afraid of Daddy."

"So? Every boy you ever dated treated you like gold," my sister argues. "What's so bad about that?"

Plenty. My high school boyfriend never took me to bed. His fear of my father ran that deeply. He was a hockey player, and therefore dazzled by my father's pro and coaching careers. Then, while at Bryn Mawr, I dated a college hockey player from the next town over. He's in awe of Daddy, too. And maybe it's a coincidence, but when we finally did the deed it was…

Very *polite*. One might even say perfunctory.

It's possible that sex isn't all that it's cracked up to be. But I suspect there's more to it. When I watch the Bruisers fight like animals for control of the puck, I can't reconcile all that testosterone with quiet, missionary-style-only-on-Tuesdays lovemaking.

I want to experience that kind of brute power off the ice. My sister doesn't understand the appeal. She never dated a single hockey player, nor watched a single game that Daddy wasn't either playing or coaching.

"You're very wise," I tell my sister just to appease her. But if Jana can't understand what I'm looking for in a man, I don't think I can explain it. A lot of the words I'd need to use aren't part of the Pepper family vocabulary.

"Nobody slipped anything into your drink last night, did they?"

"What? No! Why would you ask that?"

"Because it's not like you to get drunk and stupid. Mama will be worried for your virtue."

We both laugh at that. Because even if Jana and I don't ever *discuss* sex, that doesn't mean we don't partake. Jana lost her virginity to Dwight Hawkins on prom night her junior year of high school. It took me a little longer.

But since we're unmarried, my mother actually assumes we're virgins. It's probably a willful dismissal of the truth rather than sheer stupidity. My mother is smart. She got straight A's at Bryn Mawr in Russian Literature. But then she married my father and never spent another hour of her life on Dostoevsky or Tolstoy.

That's what my parents expect of me, too. A degree in a nice, quiet field. And then suburbs and children.

Is twenty too late to become rebellious?

"I drank tequila, Jana. It was fun so I drank a lot of it. I'm pretty sorry about the whole thing now. But it's nobody's fault but my own."

"Glad to hear that," she says with a sigh. "Get busy with the eyeliner. Skype me if you run into trouble."

"Will do."

Back in my little hotel room after the scrimmage, I spend a lot of time straightening my hair and babying my skin.

"There is no such thing as too much concealer," I tell my reflection. Then I get to work.

Seventeen cosmetic products later, I look pretty darn good. My hair falls in golden layers around my face. I'm wearing a long, lean cocktail dress in a pale shade that shows off my summer tan. And sparkly shoes, because sparkly shoes make everything better.

Mission accomplished. I look different enough from the girl in that awful photograph that I can hold my head up high.

Tucking a tiny sparkly clutch under my arm, I leave the hotel room with my game face on. And I use my phone to summon a taxi to take me to the beach club where the party will be held.

It's beautiful here, with manicured lawns and hedgerows as far as the eye can see. The air has a salty scent, and I can hear the distant crash of ocean waves on the beach.

A lovely breeze plays on my shoulders as I climb out of the cab. I hope the party is outside.

And it is—sort of. I follow the signs to a patio strung with fairy lights. I can't see the beach, because there is a ten-foot hedge surrounding the patio. Hamptonites value their privacy.

"Do you have a ticket, miss?" asks a young man in a waiter's vest.

"Oh, certainly!" I pop open my clutch and hand over the pass that Rebecca gave me earlier.

"Welcome," he says. "Can I offer you a complimentary glass of champagne?"

My stomach raises a small objection, but I smile and take one anyway, just as an accessory. "Thank you."

Dozens of guests are already clustered around the players. I feel a little sorry for our boys. If I'd played hockey all day, I don't think I'd want to put on a tux and shake hands with season ticket holders.

I do a slow circuit of the patio. There are waiters carrying around silver trays of hors d'oeuvres. I see tiny bites of salmon tartare on rice crackers, and boeuf en croûte.

My mother frowns on eating at a party. She says it's difficult to look like a lady when you're shoving food in your mouth. Since my ladylike persona took a serious hit last night, I won't risk it. So I hold my glass of champagne and wait for an opening to ask Rebecca if there's anything she needs.

I really need a chance at that job. Becoming Rebecca's office manager would buy me some time to figure out what I want to do with my life. And I could be a *great* manager. Thanks to my upbringing, I know tons about hockey. And—thanks to charm school—dealing with people is easy for me, too.

I locate Rebecca in the center of the space. Nate Kattenberger stands beside his future wife, looking resplendent in a charcoal tuxedo. His bowtie is Brooklyn aubergine—the team color. There's a line of well-wishers to greet them both.

Stepping back against the hedgerow, I scan the crowd. If I didn't already have a thing for hockey players, I'd probably develop one right now. There's a lot of testosterone on this patio, and it looks twice as good in a bowtie. Leo Trevi is chatting with the team captain, Patrick O'Doul. Whereas Leo has a pretty-boy face, O'Doul is more rugged.

Which is better? Who's to say? It's like ice cream flavors. There are so many good ones that it's hard to choose.

When my gaze finds Castro, though, I experience a cascade of reactions. First up is *OMG how can one man be so hot?* He wears his traditional black tux as impeccably as an Oscar nominee.

The perfect starched collar of his shirt stands out against his shapely, olive-toned jaw.

He's holding a glass in those long fingers—the ones I still haven't experienced on my body. Or at least not in the way that I want to. The man did hold me while I fell asleep last night. While I was too drunk to appreciate it. Or even remember it properly.

In the grand scheme of things, last night doesn't qualify as an actual tragedy. But I feel bereft nonetheless.

He must feel me watching him, because he turns his head and catches me staring. My face reddens, which seems to happen a lot when I'm looking at him. But just as the embarrassment kicks in, something unexpected happens. Castro's eyes heat. And he makes a slow sweep of my dress.

Lordy. It's a good thing I'm wearing a lined bra under this gown because otherwise I'd have to blame the ocean breezes for the way my nipples are suddenly tight and sensitive. That man's gaze could be sold as a weapon of female destruction.

His slow perusal of me ends when we lock eyes. And then he actually scowls before looking away.

"Heidi Jo?"

I look back toward Rebecca so fast it's a good thing I don't snap my neck. "Evening," I say quickly. "How are you both?"

"Just fine!" Becca says with a smile, her diamond ring glinting in the fairy lights. "How are you holding up?"

"I feel terrific," I say quickly. And it's almost true. My headache has finally receded into the background. I take the tiniest sip of champagne, but it doesn't appeal to me right now. "Are you excited for the golf tournament tomorrow?" I ask her.

"I don't know if 'excited' and 'golf' belong in the same sentence," Becca says.

"That's my girl!" Nate toasts her.

"But we're going to raise a lot of money for charity. And I get to drive the cart," she says with a smile.

"Good plan. What can I do to help?" I'm fixing to ask that question seventeen times a day until she realizes the new assistant's job belongs to me.

Becca shrugs. "Just be ready at eight thirty, okay? I'm sure something will come up for us to worry about. Something always does." Becca's gaze focuses on someone entering the party. "Heidi Jo, your father has arrived."

"*Here?*" Even as the word comes out of my mouth, I know I shouldn't be surprised. Money, golf, and hockey are his favorite things. So what if we're a hundred miles from midtown? His driver brought him. Or else he took a helicopter.

I should have known.

A few seconds later, he arrives at my side. I open my mouth to greet him when he removes the champagne glass from my hand. "You won't be needing this, sweetheart," he says, his voice grim. "Good evening, Nate. Rebecca."

"Evening, commissioner," Nate says. "Are you ready to raise some money for adaptive sports?"

"Anytime." My father chuckles.

"I didn't see your check, though," Nate adds.

My father scowls. "Maybe it got lost in the mail."

Nate grins. "Just teasing you. I don't ever see the checks. It's probably on Becca's desk."

I'm not even listening, because my face is on fire. Daddy took that glass out of my hand as though I were a naughty teen. I'm used to him treating me like that, but usually it happens in private.

"Hello, Daddy," I say as he turns to me, taking a deep drink of *my* bubbly. "I didn't know you were coming."

"I'm invited every year," he says, glancing around the crowd. "And since you haven't returned my calls today, I did not have the opportunity to tell you."

Yep. I walked right into that one. My face burns even more brightly.

"But since we're all here," Daddy continues, "let's spend a few moments talking about Heidi Jo's internship."

"She's been a big help so far," Nate Kattenberger puts in. "If you'll excuse me—I have a few hands to shake." He slips off, the way I wish I could, too.

"What did you have in mind?" Rebecca asks. So I guess we're doing this now.

My father removes a piece of paper from his pocket. "There won't be any desk jobs this year. I've made a list of the more utilitarian jobs at the rink—the ones you end up in when you don't finish college. Take a look at this."

"Oh," Rebecca says slowly. "That's an interesting approach."

I want to kick him in the knees with my sparkly shoes. But I won't make a scene. I look up at him with clear eyes, even if I'm dying inside.

Rebecca takes the list from my father's hand and skims it. "These are the jobs you think Heidi Jo could do?"

"No—these are all the jobs she *will* do. All of them. One job a week for ten weeks," he says.

"Hmm." Rebecca flashes me a quick look of sympathy. "Covering the stadium ice is a union job," Rebecca says. "She can't work with those guys."

"Then cross that one off." My father smiles cheerfully. "There's more than ten things on that list. She's going to be paid *exactly* like everyone else who does those jobs—on the payroll—and I'll personally reimburse each business unit. My assistant is ready to tackle the paperwork for those weeks when she's..."

"Selling hotdogs for the stadium vendor?" Becca clarifies, still studying the list. "Cleaning locker rooms with the maintenance crew?"

Oh Lord, deliver me.

"For starters," my father chirps.

"All right," Rebecca says. "We can work with this. For now.

A little later in the season, though, there may be an entry-level job that Heidi Jo can apply for—"

"No," my father says immediately. Because interrupting people is his favorite pastime. "She will complete at least ten of the tasks on that sheet, or there will be financial consequences for her."

My heart sinks again. I don't have to ask what he means, either. My father is the trustee of the trust fund my grandfather left me. He can vest me any time after I turn twenty-one in a few weeks. But he doesn't *have* to vest me. He can wait if he chooses.

And Daddy's been hinting that college dropouts don't deserve Grandpa's legacy.

But *ten* jobs? Ten weeks? The job I want will be long gone by then. Rage bubbles up inside me, and I have to take a deep cleansing breath just to keep it inside.

"In fact we'll start now," my father says, crossing his burly arms. "Heidi Jo will be parking cars for the rest of the evening. Please go outside and report to the bell captain. They're waiting for you."

"Parking cars?" I squeak. "What does that have to do with hockey?"

"Nothing," he barks. "But it has a hell of a lot to do with real life. It pays minimum wage. Do you know how much that is?"

I swallow hard. "No, sir," I say softly. *Please don't make a scene.*

"Eleven seventy-five in the New York suburbs. Thirteen-fifty when you're inside city limits. Now go on. The bell captain's name is Roger. Don't keep him waiting."

There is a horrible awkward pause. I can feel sympathy radiating from Rebecca. Her expression is stunned, with a side dish of appalled. She opens her mouth and then closes it again. My father's antics are putting her in a very awkward position right now.

The last thing I need is for my future boss to be stressed out over something to do with me. And a well-raised Southern girl always knows how to do the graceful thing that puts everyone at ease. There's one clear option open to me, and I take it.

I lift my chin as if I own the whole resort. "Good evening, then," I say to Rebecca. And—without a glance at Daddy—I leave the party to go park some cars in an evening dress and sparkly shoes.

[7]

JASON

THERE HAVE BEEN nights when I've regretted my life choices. But this really isn't one of them. I won't hide from the league commissioner, because I've done nothing wrong.

I stand my ground, shaking hands with fans and nursing a beer that would probably taste better from the bottle than from the stuffy goblet the bartender handed me.

The evening passes slowly. But at least I don't have to avoid Heidi all night, in that killer dress and those fuck-me heels. I have no idea what her father said to her, but she lit out of here no more than two minutes after he arrived, and I haven't seen her since.

Not that I ought to be looking.

Eventually the commissioner makes his way over to our cluster of players. "Good evening, boys," he says, shaking O'Doul's, Bayer's, and then Silas's hand. "I expect more great things from the team this year."

"So do we," O'Doul says easily.

The commissioner is well-respected, even though he's only

held the job for a couple of years so far. He had a hell of a career in Nashville before retiring to become their defensive coach and then general manager. He's known to be a shrewd negotiator who always gets what he wants.

When he turns to me, I offer my hand, and I'm not entirely surprised when he attempts to crack all of my bones at once.

"Easy," I say smoothly. "I'm going to need that hand to score."

"My daughter is off limits," he says immediately.

Out of the corner of my eye, I can see my teammates' stunned faces. They didn't expect him to go right for the jugular. "Not a problem, sir. That photograph does not tell an accurate story."

Speaking of photographs, I can hear the telltale click of someone's camera shutter right now. Some asshole is taking a picture of the commissioner trying to intimidate me.

I hate my life tonight. It's a fact. But I smile anyway, damn it.

So does he. "Glad to hear it," he says, and somehow his smile makes him look like he still wants to snap my neck. "She shouldn't be out drinking with the players."

"We have no reason to shun her, though," O'Doul says, jumping in to rescue me. "We're a friendly bunch. And even if she had a little too much to drink last night, these two made sure she stayed safe." He puts a hand on both my and Silas's shoulders.

"I can see that she's fine," the commissioner says with a chuckle. "And she has nothing but good things to say about you gentlemen." He actually rolls his eyes. "But she's an impressionable young thing who's got her head on a little backwards right now. So any reminders you can give her that adult life is not one extended party would be appreciated. Now you boys take care, and I'll see you on the golf course tomorrow, bright and early."

Having said his piece, he moves on to shake more hands.

"That could have gone worse," Silas says.

"You still have your balls," O'Doul says, and then he laughs.

"Yeah, yeah. Laugh it up." I track the commissioner across the room. "Sucks to be Heidi, though."

"Because she's forbidden to get into your pants?" Silas asks. "Any girl would be inconsolable. I hear there's a waiting list."

"Yeah, poor girl. I meant, though, that she has him for a dad. No wonder she decided to try tequila."

"At least he cares," Silas points out. "Not everybody has that."

"Truth," O'Doul agrees, just as Tommy the publicist steps into our circle.

"Evening, boys. Who's ready to golf tomorrow? I've got O'Doul in a foursome with Silas."

"You know I'm a hack, right?" O'Doul asks. "I don't actually keep score for myself. It's too embarrassing."

"I taught him to score each hole with a smiley face or a frowny face," Bayer adds. "It's better for morale than to write a double-digit number on the sheet."

"Double digits, eh?" Tommy chuckles. "Oh, man."

"Who are you putting me with?" I ask Tommy.

He looks surprised. "I don't have you down to play."

"Seriously?" My hackles are up again already. "You don't think the Latino can golf?"

"We need Castro," Bayer says immediately. "Put him out front. He's the only one on the team with a handicap."

Tommy blinks. "The reason I don't have you down for golf is that your clubs were not on the bus. So I assumed you don't golf."

"Oh, shit," I say, feeling like an ass. "They're in my hotel room. I didn't ride the bus."

Tommy pulls a sheet out of his pocket. "I'll redo the foursomes."

"Feel free to cut me from the roster," O'Doul volunteers.

"I'll take it under advisement." Tommy strides away.

"Anyone want anything from the bar?" O'Doul asks.

"Not from this bar," I say, peering into the dregs of my beer. I'm not fit for company tonight.

"Suit yourself," O'Doul says before he heads for the bartender.

"Time check," I say to Silas.

He glances at his designer watch. "It's nine, big man. You're almost off the clock."

I drain the beer I've been nursing. "I think I'm done here. I took photos with dozens of people. I signed autographs and made small talk. Want to hit the hotel bar instead?" I can't wait to take off this fucking bowtie that's choking me. I love my team, but this is just one of those nights when professional hockey looks more like a dog-and-pony show than a sport.

"Maybe," Silas says. "Leo wanted to go out for pizza, though."

"You go without me." I'm just not in the mood for people. "I'll see you back at the hotel."

I set my beer glass down on a table and glance around the room. Coach Worthington isn't watching me and neither is the PR team. All great hockey players know how to find an opening, and I've just found mine.

Ten seconds later I've ducked from the patio into the lobby, and I'm making a break for the front doors. That buzzy, preseason energy is back, and it needs someplace to go.

Training camp has been great so far. It feels good to be back on the ice. But now I have to spend this ridiculous weekend in the Hamptons. It's not a vacation. We're here to impress fans on that undersized rink and at tomorrow's charity golf tournament.

There's no shortage of rich Long Islanders who will pay two grand each to get stuck in the sand trap with us. The course is supposed to be a real doozy. I hope I can write off the hundred dollars' worth of balls I'm going to lose.

It's a waste of time. I feel twitchy to skate and eager to prove myself.

I walk outside, fishing in my pocket for my wallet. I pull out a couple of singles. "Can I get my car?" I ask a waiting bellman. "It's a..."

"Tesla Model X in Pearl White Multi-coat!" says a female voice. "This one is all mine, boys. Hand over that key."

I blink, but Heidi Jo Pepper is still here. She's curbside in that sleek dress that's cupping her irresistible tits and fuck me-heels that glitter. As if my night weren't long enough already.

And now she's squabbling with the bellman, apparently over who gets to fetch my car.

"You *said* the next one was mine!" she says, holding her hand out for the key. "You promised not three minutes ago!"

"Miss Heidi..." the man says. "It depends on the vehicle."

"Roger!" she gasps. "You're kidding me! Don't tell me you're one of *those*. A man who thinks there's something wrong with the way women drive!"

The little dude looks completely tongue-tied. And I'm betting he's totally one of *those*.

"Hand it over," she snaps. "Have you heard the term 'hostile work environment'?"

This girl. Holy shit. It's a struggle not to laugh.

Looking completely cowed, the guy hands over my key fob. "I parked it over by—"

"Oh, I *saw* where you parked it," she snaps. "When you sent me to go get that 1994 Celica." She tosses her hair. Then she turns to me. "Just a moment, *sir*."

And then I'm watching her walk away into the darkness of the parking lot, her hips swaying defiantly in that sleek pink dress that I want so badly to unzip and peel her out of...

That's when it hits me. She's going to drive my baby. And suddenly I'm the same kind of asshole who's worried about her skills behind the wheel.

So I take off after her. "Hey—Hot Pepper. Wait up!"

She doesn't.

"Yo! You don't have to get the car for me. I'll get it."

She lifts a hand and shows me her...pinky finger.

"What does that mean?" I ask as I finally catch up to her.

"It means I want to give you the finger but I'm too polite."

Po-*laht*. There's that word again. I want to know how polite she'll look when she's naked in my arms, begging me to let her come.

Jesus. My raging attraction to the commissioner's daughter is really inconvenient. "Have you ever driven a Tesla before?"

"It's a car, Jason. How hard could it be?" She stops in front of my baby, which is practically glowing in the moonlight. She opens her fingers to reveal my key fob, which is basically a small, smooth replica of the car itself, without any buttons.

She turns it over in her hand, and I can practically hear her gears grinding as she tries to figure out how to open the door.

This time I can't fight off my grin. "Need some help?"

"Okay, this is weird," she grumbles. "No buttons?"

"Touch the driver's side of the little car in your hand."

She taps it, and my car door opens slowly. "That is seriously cool!" She taps the model twice more, and now my back doors rise, too—bat-wing style—up over the car.

"You've got it now," I say.

But before I can even finish the sentence, she's tapping those sensors like crazy, opening and shutting all four doors. The car looks like a bird that's flapping its wings for takeoff.

Jesus. "You're draining my battery right now."

"Oh, *please*," she says. "Like you never did this?"

Fine. I totally did.

She marches over to the driver's side and gets in. Then all the doors begin to close at once.

"Whoa," I say, ducking under the backdoor, forcing it to

pause in its descent. I drop into the backseat of my car, a place I haven't admired before now. "Hey, it's roomy back here."

"Shall I climb on back, then?" Heidi asks, turning around to face me. Her pretty face sizes me up. There's a challenge in her eyes.

Unngh. This girl is gonna kill me. "Very funny."

"What if I wasn't joking? I want another chance."

"Another chance at…?"

"*You*. Jeez." Her expression is defiant, but a telltale blush hits her cheekbones. "I'm not drunk, and I've sworn off alcohol."

I clear my throat. "Well, I've sworn off you."

"Because of the picture?"

"The picture doesn't help," I admit. "We both know that people will believe what they want to believe."

"Which people?" She narrows her eyes. "Does this have to do with my father?"

"Sure it does," I admit. "Do you know how he greeted me tonight? With, 'My daughter is off limits.' That was his opener."

Heidi whips around to face the front again and thumps herself back against the driver's seat. "FML."

I snort. "You say it that way when you're sober*?*"

"Yes. It sounds cheap when a woman drops f-bombs."

"Depends *when* she's saying it," I point out. "I'm rather fond of hearing it when we're naked and she's begging for it."

"I wouldn't know," she snaps. "I guess there's nothing more to say. Let's deliver you and your hot guy vehicle to the turn-around, shall we?" She reaches forward and…

I wait.

"Castro," she says in a low voice. "I know there's no key. But where's the magic button?"

"I can't help you find your magic button, baby," I tell her.

Heidi growls. "We already went over that. I mean on the *car*."

I laugh. "There's no button. It's always on. You step on the brake to close the doors. Then you put it in gear and hit the pedal."

"That's just weird," she grumbles as the doors close. She moves the lever into reverse.

"No, it's awesome. My baby is always ready to play. She's—"

The car leaps backward so fast that I'm thrown forward.

"Whoops!" Heidi says as we halt just as fast. "I guess those Tesla engineers aren't fooling around."

I'm absolutely terrified now. "Maybe you should let me—"

"Nope," she snaps, guiding the car out of the parking space more carefully now. "I've got it." She touches the control panel, shutting off the air conditioning. Then she touches it again to lower the windows. "I want to hear the silence."

"Okay," I say with a sigh. Everyone does.

She glides gently past the row of parked cars. "That is super cool," she says. "We're in stealth mode."

"Stealth mode is awesome," I admit. Everything about this car turns me on, including watching her drive it. Not that I'd say so.

"Does it really accelerate as fast as they say?" she asks.

"Totally."

"Awesome," she says, passing the entrance to the turnaround.

"Where are you going?" I ask as she puts on her turn signal.

"To try it out! Duh." Heidi makes a right onto the country road.

"Oh. Well. There's a gas station about a half mile from here. You could turn around there."

She says nothing. And when we reach the gas station a minute later, she blows right by it.

"Uh, Heidi?"

"Don't worry. I'm just going to have a little fun. I have to get my kicks somewhere. I mean—I'm totally down with giving you a blowjob instead right now. But I think you said that's already off the table."

My poor brain is instantly filled with images of Heidi unzipping my tuxedo pants and bending over me, her hair sliding around on my body as she takes me inside her mouth...

The car turns onto the highway entrance ramp and accelerates further. "Holy shit. Where are we going?"

"Can't go ninety on the side streets," she says. "That'll be dangerous." She taps a button to close the windows. They slide up as the car shoots forward onto the sparsely populated roadway.

Thank God it's a Wednesday night and not rush hour. Because we are *flying*. I watch my speedometer climb to eighty and then ninety.

"Jesus, slow down!"

"You are wearing your seatbelt, right?" She puts her hands at ten and two on the steering wheel. "How does she handle at high speed?"

"You don't need to know! Let's go back now."

But Heidi ignores me. There's a Taurus in the left lane that isn't moving quite so fast, so Heidi slips into the right lane and passes it.

"Careful. You don't want a ticket," I say a little breathlessly. "Wouldn't that be a bad way to finish the night?"

She slows the car, and I'm immediately grateful. We roll along at a nice quiet fifty for a moment. I'm breathing a little easier, but then she asks, "Have you done a hundred? I bet you have. Hey—time this. Count of three."

"What? Don't—"

"One, two, three—" She floors it.

The only thing I'm timing is how quickly my balls recede into my body as Heidi rips forward down the highway. It's one thing to press down the accelerator yourself. It's quite another to be at the mercy of someone else.

Heidi gives a little shriek of joy as we hurtle down the road at high speed. The speedometer lurches upwards, through seventy and eighty in a heartbeat. Then ninety.

It's dark, for fuck's sake. So many things could go wrong. A deer in the road. A drunk driver coming home from happy hour. My heart is in my throat as I glance at Heidi in the front seat. Her eyes are locked onto the road, her sleek arms gripping the wheel like she's a NASCAR driver in formal wear. She's completely focused.

"A hundred," I gasp as the speedometer shows triple digits. "You did it. Feel free to slow down."

"Yes!" She eases back on the pedal.

And that's when we fly past the police cruiser in the median. "Uh-oh. Shit."

"Cop?" she squeaks. She doesn't freak out, though. "Did he pull out?"

"Well..." I crane my neck to watch the road behind us. "He was facing the other way. Like he'd have to do a K-turn to get you." We're making tracks away from him. But just when I think we're out of the woods, I see cruiser lights flip on. "Uh-oh. He might be coming."

Heidi doesn't say anything. She makes a lane change that's sudden yet smooth and heads off the upcoming exit. "Hey!" I gasp, grabbing the seat in front of me. I'd be impressed if I weren't busy preparing for my sudden death.

It's a short exit ramp, and she has to break hard at the bottom. The tires squeak as she makes a short radius turn, heading away from the highway.

"This is just going to get you into more trouble," I complain.

"Possibly," she grunts as we head down a street dotted with low-slung buildings. "But the universe owes me one."

"It doesn't work that way for me," I point out from the backseat.

Although maybe it does for her. Because Heidi pulls into the entrance of an automated carwash and drives around to the back.

This will never work. Those are my thoughts as her sleek arm reaches out of my lowering window, a credit card on offer. She dips it into the waiting instrument panel and the carwash door begins to lift ahead of her.

Heidi taps on the screen several times at top speed. And then my car glides into the bay as she raises the window again. "Now you won't have those dead bugs on your windshield," she says as the door closes behind us.

"I'll be in jail, but at least I'll have a clean car. There's a window on that door. See? The cop will be sitting out there waiting when it opens."

We both stare at that window as the water begins to spray the car. My heart rate is accelerated, and the buzzy feeling in my chest has returned. I feel more alive right now than I have in a long time.

"What do you think the citation is for evading a police officer?" I ask, because I'm a dick. "Misdemeanor or felony?"

"Gosh. Stop it," she says, reaching back to slap my leg.

But I grab her wrist and hold on tightly. She turns around, fire in her eyes.

I feel lit up and happy. It makes no sense at all. Neither does my next move—reaching out to palm Heidi's jaw with my free hand, and tugging her closer.

Our mouths fuse before I even realize what I'm doing. But it's already too late. She tastes like cherry lip gloss and heat. My first kiss is slow, and she makes a soft sound of surprise. Emboldened, I lick her lower lip. She opens on a hot gasp that goes straight to my crotch.

Damn it all to hell. Why does this girl get under my skin?

As soapy water rains down on my car, I try to figure it out by weaving my fingers into her hair and exploring her sweet mouth with my tongue.

But there aren't any answers here. Only the click of teeth as I get even closer. Her hands grasp tightly to my shoulders. She wants this, and yet she shouldn't. She ought to understand that this is a bad idea.

My kiss turns punishing, my tongue scraping against hers. My grip tightens on her hair. *Run, little girl. Or I'm going to hike up that soft pink silk and do you right here on my premium upholstery.*

She moans.

So it's like that? *I'll give you something to moan about.* With my free hand, I cup her breast. It's heavy in my hand. And as I give her one more impossibly deep kiss, I pinch the nipple through the fabric.

"Yes," she pants against my mouth. "More." She ups the ante by skimming a hand clumsily down my chest. She's twisted around, trying to reach me, basically trying to climb into my mouth from the driver's seat.

Fuck. I'm torturing both of us. I'm the stupidest man alive. With a groan I ease back, breaking our kiss.

That's when the carwash door opens automatically, revealing the police cruiser outside. The cop is standing there, arms crossed, waiting.

"Oh, fuck," I breathe.

"Let me handle this." Heidi hits the dash control to open her door, then hops out.

Still a little stunned, I scramble to open my door, which takes me a second because I've never sat back here before. Then I hop out, too.

The cop is ranting. "—and you thought you'd just take a joy ride in the dark, on a public highway?" He takes in Heidi in her strapless silk dress and heels. And his eyes scan me as well. I hate wearing a tuxedo, but when you have to face down a cop, I guess it's better than a hoodie and ripped jeans.

I open my mouth, but she's already apologizing. "I'm so sorry, officer. My boyfriend just bought this car, and I wanted to teach him a couple things about torque and traction so he'll be extra safe when poor weather arrives. But he complained about the dead bugs on the windshield, so I offered to get a carwash, too."

Wait, what?

The policeman's eyes widen. He clearly doesn't know what to make of her. That makes two of us. "Back up, now. Where are you coming from tonight?"

"The East Hampton Beach Club. We were at a fundraiser," she says sweetly. "I apologize, sir, for going over the speed limit. I wanted to demonstrate the cross effects of acceleration and transient force, and the road was so quiet. Still, I should have waited." She digs into her pocketbook. "Here's my license. Oh —and my racing license."

My jaw is on the asphalt.

He studies both of them carefully. "Let me run your license. One second." He trudges back to his cruiser and gets inside.

"Your racing license?" I sputter when he's out of earshot.

Heidi shrugs those smooth, bare shoulders. "I went to racing school one summer. That's what bored rich girls do when they're sick of tennis camp. Nashville has a speedway." She bites her lip in contrition.

I'm officially speechless, but no less horny. I'll be trying to fall asleep tonight while picturing Heidi zooming around a race-track in a strapless dress.

The cop comes back with her license and a smile. "No outstanding warrants. No tickets. I'm gonna let you off with a warning."

"Oh, thank you officer," she says, giving him a big smile. "I promise to be good, sir."

My dirty mind proposes recreating this scene later. Naked. I'd need some handcuffs…

"You have a nice night, now," she says.

"Drive slow," he adds, tipping his hat to her before he climbs back into his vehicle.

He pulls away, and we just stare at each other for a moment. "I thought you had no marketable skills? Getting out of tickets is nothing to sneeze at."

She rolls her eyes. "I have a lifetime's practice appeasing men. Now you'll take me back to your hotel room, right? I'll let you drive."

I groan. "No can do."

"I was afraid you'd say that." Her face falls.

"We are not going to happen," I say quietly. "I just spent the day telling everyone that you and I are not a thing. Rebecca. Tommy. My agent." Now there was a fun call. "So we can't be a thing. I shouldn't have kissed you."

"But I liked it."

"Oh baby, I know you did." I liked it a lot, too.

"We'd be so good together."

"I'm sorry," I grunt. "We'll have to live with the mystery. Hand over that key fob. I'm driving back."

"You're a cold man, Jason Castro." She pouts.

"You're right. Exactly." It's time she knew. "Now get in the passenger's seat, Miss Pepper. I'm going to enforce your curfew now."

The ride back is silent. But at least nobody's in jail.

[8]

HEIDI

I'VE NEVER TRIED to fit my whole life into a suitcase before, and it isn't pretty. Most of my belongings are going to have to stay here in Daddy's apartment. Do I leave behind my Theory cardigan, or my Burberry trench coat? It's like choosing a favorite child.

My parents have no trouble choosing a favorite child. They'd pick Jana any day of the week. On that happy thought, I zip my giant wheeled suitcase closed.

As I wheel the suitcase out of the room, I realize what a pain it will be to haul this sucker down the subway stairs. I can't afford to Uber to Brooklyn. I can barely afford dinner after laying out my first month's rent.

"Heidi Jo? Where are you going with that bag?"

I freeze at the sound of my father's voice. He's not usually here in the middle of a workday. But when you run the entire pro hockey league, your schedule has some flexibility. So there he is, holding a copy of the *Wall Street Journal* and a mug of coffee.

Crap. I'd planned to make my exit while he was out, even though I hate myself a little for sneaking around. I'm twenty years old, I shouldn't care what he thinks.

"I'm leaving," I say, lifting my chin.

"I can see that. For where?"

"An apartment I've rented in Brooklyn."

"You can't afford an apartment in Brooklyn."

"Not a very nice one," I admit. "But I can't stay here."

"Sure you can. Don't be foolish."

Ah, but there's the problem. "I'd rather not be foolish. But you insist on making me look foolish just to amuse yourself." It's been two weeks since he ruined my internship with the Bruisers. During the first week, I was assigned to the janitorial contractor at the stadium. I cleaned the women's bathrooms during and after a Grateful Dead tribute concert. And last week I sold hotdogs during the hockey team's preseason events.

I survived. It's honest labor. No reason to be ashamed. Yet every time I come home on aching feet, smelling like hotdog water and spilled mustard, Dad is waiting here with a smug expression.

Like the one he's wearing right now. "You can quit anytime, you know," he says. "You can go back to school if you hate it so much."

Trying to humiliate me into going back to school won't work. That's my father's idea of parental love. So I'm outie. "Bye, then." I roll my case a little nearer to the entryway.

"Where are you going?"

"I told you. Brooklyn. A rental."

His face is full of confusion. It has never occurred to Daddy that I'd actually defy him. But that's on me. Twenty years of obedience is a habit that's hard to shake. "Where'd you find this apartment? Are you moving in with friends?"

"Nope. I found it on Craigslist."

His coffee mug stops halfway to his mouth. "That's dangerous, Heidi Jo. It's unregulated."

"I'm careful," I argue. I couldn't afford to use a rental agent, because they charge broker's fees.

"Is this a ploy to get me to vest your trust fund?"

"You wanted me to learn to be independent," I snap. "Here's what that looks like." I roll my suitcase onto the marble tiles in the entranceway and then march out of there.

It will prove to be my last smug moment for a while, though. My newest assignment from Daddy's list of jobs starts today, and it's worse than selling hotdogs. This week I'm working stadium security, and they've stationed me at the employees' entrance.

Here's what I've learned so far about low-paying jobs—they have a million rules and those rules don't have to make sense. My boss for the week—Mr. Dunston, who has salami breath—has instructed me to spend sixty seconds on everyone who comes through the back door. No more. No less.

"Seventy-seven percent of security breaches in tier-one urban facilities come through the backdoor," Dunston lectures as I inspect the tote bag of a bored-looking ticket-taker.

"Yes, sir."

It takes me fifteen seconds to establish that she's got a functioning employee ID, a paperback book, and a salad in Tupperware. No weapons of mass destruction. But I still have thirty seconds to burn. "Please raise your arms?"

She does, with an eye-roll. Not that I blame her. With my face heating, I make a couple of non-invasive, half-hearted pats at the pockets of her cargo pants and then stand up really slowly. "You have a nice shift at work," I tell her by way of an apology.

"Will do," she mumbles before grabbing her tote bag and striding away.

"That was only forty-one seconds," the boss complains.

"Sorry, sir. I'll do better this next time." He must have other people to intimidate, right? If he would just go away, everything would be fine.

The door opens, ushering in my next two victims. And as soon as I see Silas's face, I feel immediately cheered. Unfortunately, it's quickly followed by the one face I've been trying—unsuccessfully—to avoid.

Jason Castro, ladies and gentlemen. The sexiest, most eligible bachelor of hockey is in the building. And he's staring right at me with those grumpy brown eyes.

"Hello, boys," I say, lifting my chin. But embarrassment has already set in. And it's not the navy-blue polyester uniform that's caused it. Two weeks ago I kissed that man like the world was burning down around the carwash.

Then he rejected me. And I am so not over it. His kisses didn't just curl my toes. They curled parts of me that I didn't know were curlable.

But never mind. Another day, another small humiliation.

"Hey there, Heidi," Silas says cheerily. "New post?"

"Yes, sir." I glance at Jason, and his eyes darken immediately. He gets that dark look all the time now when he looks at me. It must be irritation. We keep bumping into each other. Last week when I was wearing a smelly brown polyester uniform, I swear I bumped into him a dozen times.

Every time, I get that same unhappy look from him—like he can't believe he kissed the loser girl whose daddy took away her trust fund until she does ten weeks of manual labor.

And now I get to frisk him.

"Step right up, boys," I say, patting the security table. "Would you kindly lay your bags on the table, please?"

"Sure thing." Silas gives me a big grin, drops his duffel on the table, and unzips it for me. "Careful, though," he says. "Some of these bags will have that hockey stench."

"Trust me, it's the scent of my childhood." Maybe that's why I have a thing for hockey players; I'm immune to the odor of sweaty pads. Silas's bag is almost empty. Just a pair of headphones, a bottle of coconut water, and a tablet computer. No trouble here.

Unfortunately the whole inspection takes about five seconds. And Silas is about to step on past me.

Behind me, the boss clears his throat. "Security first!"

"Would you mind unbuttoning your jacket?" I ask Silas as embarrassment creeps up my neck.

"Not at all," he says as his strong hands take care of the buttons. Players are required to arrive at the stadium in a suit and tie. Silas wears navy gabardine, a white shirt, and a tie in the team color—eggplant.

Just to use up seconds, I come around the table at a geriatric pace. Then I pat each of his suit pockets with all the force of a house fly landing on a windowsill. Because—*come on*—this is the biggest waste of time in the history of sports.

But logic does not prevail. And it's not about post-9/11 fears anymore. The head of stadium security has a staff of fifty people, and he needs to keep them all busy so he can look important. I've worked here for less than two hours, and I've already got his number.

"Have a good game," I tell Silas.

"Will do!" He winks and walks away.

Ignoring Jason has been easy enough so far. But now I turn and expose myself to the blast furnace of his studliness. Jason Castro in a suit is not a sight for the faint of heart. The jacket and pants are charcoal and cut to show off the perfect taper from his chest to his waist. The white shirt cuffs shine against his copper skin, and his green tie sets off the unusual brown of his eyes.

"C-could you please, um..." I briefly lose my train of thought. *Could you please undress me?* That's what I want to ask.

He bails me out. "Here," he grunts, dropping the bag on the table. "Watch out for the sandwich."

"Is it ticking?"

"No." He snorts. "But I don't want to eat a squished sandwich."

"It's peanut butter and strawberry jam," says another player from the doorway. There's a line forming now. "Has to be strawberry. This one is superstitious."

"Good to know," I say, taking a quick look inside the bag. Aside from the sandwich, there's a set of rosary beads, and a paperback book. *A Tale of Two Cities*. Castro has fancy taste in literature.

You could learn a lot about a guy doing this job. What if his bag was full of jock-itch powder? Or GasX?

I close the bag hastily.

"Check the pockets," grunts Dunston.

"You're right, sir," I say grumpily. "Mr. Castro looks like a very dangerous man."

The players lined up behind Jason all give hoots of laughter, but Castro just frowns down at me. I unzip the outer pocket at one end of his bag, and then immediately wish I hadn't, because there are a handful of loose condoms in there. The only small mercy is that I don't pull them out for everyone else to see.

I do, however, look up into Jason's eyes with an expression approximating that of a kicked puppy.

His face is unreadable.

Hastily, I unzip the other pocket. When I plunge my hand inside, I only find a square object. I pull it halfway out to identify it.

It's a silver picture frame the size of my palm. And the photo is of a laughing teenaged girl. A senior portrait, maybe. She has strawberry-blond hair and daring eyes.

Once more I glance involuntarily at Jason, who's scowling up a storm now. "All good!" I say with forced cheer.

"Twenty-seven seconds," Dunston announces.

"Seems like plenty," Jason mumbles.

"Body check," the boss says.

"Oh, fuck me," Jason says on a sigh.

If only.

"Sir, please unbutton your jacket."

But he's raised his arms already. So I unbutton them, just to hurry things along. The tip of my thumb grazes his abs as I work. "Wowzers," I whisper. "Someone keeps up with the core exercises."

His jaw tightens, and he looks away as I spend about one second patting his pockets the way they taught me during my thirty minutes of training.

The last step is to check for an ankle holster. Because whoever directs these procedures watches a lot of TV. So I sink down onto my knees and quickly pat down the muscular lower legs inside Jason's suit pants.

"All set," I say, which I'm sure is a relief to both of us. I raise my eyes from my kneeling position, ready to offer my favorite hockey player an apologetic smile.

But that's not what happens. First, my gaze snags on the bulge in his trouser pants that wasn't there a minute ago. And it is a *bulge*. At close range.

I feel my jaw flop open. And then when I manage to raise my chin, my gaze finds a set of lust-darkened eyes staring down at me over a jaw that's locked tightly.

We regard each other for one more fractional second as I realize the position we're in. And then we both come to our senses at the same moment. I leap to my feet while he takes a quick step backward, buttoning his suit jacket with hasty fingers.

"Good game!" I say in a shrill voice. "Knock 'em dead! Make 'em cry!"

"Will do." He takes one eager step away from me.

But he only gets a few feet toward the hallway when Bayer calls after him from the line. "Wait up, Castro!"

Jason stops, but he's gritting his teeth. As usual, he's eager to get away from me. But I don't mind half as much as usual, because it's dawning on me that Jason Castro is still attracted to me. No matter that I puked when we were supposed to be hooking up, and no matter that my daddy wants to kill him.

That bulge, though. And the lust in his eyes when I looked up at him? It's the only good news I've had today.

Bayer puts his gym bag down on the table and unzips it. I poke inside, mindful of the forty-five seconds I'm supposed to use up. There's a pair of sneakers.

"I wouldn't get too close to those if I were you." He says.

"They could be a security risk, sir," I say. "Stench weaponry?"

Bayer chuckles.

Dunston moves closer to hover like the grumpy barnacle that he is. "Oof," he says as his foot finds something I've hidden underneath the table. "What's this?" He bends over, where he'll be treated to an eyeful of my giant rolling suitcase. "Hold on! Unidentified luggage? That's a security risk."

"It's mine," I say quickly, zipping Bayer's gym bag. "Don't worry about that."

But Dunston has already rolled the bag out of its hiding place. "This can't stay here. It's against security regs."

"Sir, there's no place secure for me to put it. Can I lock it in your office?"

"You may not bring personal effects to work. It has to go."

I swear the whole flipping team is lined up to get in now. And they're all listening to this little humiliation. "I'm on the clock, though. What would you have me do?"

"There's always the incinerator," he says darkly. "That'll learn you the rules."

"What?" I squeak. "My Manolos are in there."

"Oh, for fuck's sake," Jason snarls. "I'll take the bag. Can we just get a move on here?" He leans forward, grabs the handle, and jerks it toward his body. "This will go with me."

"Nice color for ya," Bayer pipes up.

I bend over and pat Bayer's ankles with zero finesse. I do not, however, kneel at his feet with my face near his crotch. That's a lesson they won't have to teach me twice.

"That was twenty-seven seconds," Dunston complains as Bayer departs with a grumpy Jason Castro.

"I'll do better, sir." I hold back my sigh as the next player steps up.

"Security first."

"Yessir."

[9]

JASON

THERE ARE JUST three minutes left in tonight's preseason scrimmage. That's a relief, because I'm dog-tired.

"Cross-body vision," the assistant coach yammers at me as he leans over me on the bench. "Just as soon as you adjust your line of sight, you'll be all set."

"Cross-body vision," I mumble so he thinks I'm paying attention.

"Get ready," he says. "Your line is up."

"Born ready," I say. But it's a total lie. My muscles are screaming, although that happens at the end of every game. My problem tonight is that my brain is fried, too. Last season I was able to relax into the rhythm of the game. But there's been no relaxing since Coach Worthington stunned me by asking me to change positions.

Correction—he didn't ask. The morning after the Hamptons golf tournament he just clapped me on the shoulder and said, "Think you can play right wing?"

I believe my clever response was, "Who, me?" Because I'm a

lefty shooter who plays left wing, and always has.

"You're playing right wing now," Coach had said. "Starting today. Let's get out there."

After two weeks of bumbling practices, I'm still unsettled.

But now is no time to panic. I stand up on command and vault over the wall as Leo Trevi returns to the bench. We used to be on a line together, but now we can't be anymore, because we play the same position.

Coach has me with Bayer and the new kid, Drake. To say that I'm disoriented is putting it mildly. I still launch myself into the game, accepting a pass from our D-man, Beringer, but the pass is coming into the wrong side of my body, of course.

Everything is just wrong wrong wrong.

I find an opening and get the pass off to Bayer before the opposing D-man can squish me. But the transfer feels less smooth than I'm used to.

It's a long three minutes of trying to attack from the wrong side of the room. Driving a car in England on the wrong side of the road would probably be easier than this.

When the buzzer goes off, I'm full of relief. And—damn it—that's not now I want to feel at the end of a game.

I skate past our rivals from across the river with a scowl on my face, shaking hands and good-game-good-game-good-gaming it as fast as I can.

When that's done, I follow Silas off the ice. He yanks off the goalie's helmet and gives me a giant, sweaty smile. "They don't stand a chance in regular-season play."

"Nice job tonight," I grunt. Silas only let in one goal, and we won it 2-1.

No thanks to me.

"You look about as happy as a mushroom cloud."

"I'll come around," I bark. Silas is my buddy, but it's not my habit to let people know when I'm suffering. Ten months ago when I started on my scoring streak, the sports news described me as an "overnight sensation."

Somehow I don't think I'm going to be seeing those words in print for a while.

The locker room is the usual mayhem. Someone is blasting the Beastie Boys' "No Sleep Till Brooklyn"—our win song. The head coach is congratulating Silas on his game. Everybody is pumped up that our up-and-coming goalie is finding his feet. They'll use him more this year.

Ten bucks says Coach won't seek me out for any back pats today, though.

I chuck my helmet onto its shelf and strip off my sweater. I'm shucking off my pads when I hear a voice behind me.

It's Miranda Wager, a journalist I despise. And behind her hovers my favorite publicist, Georgia.

"Evening, Mr. Castro," Miranda chirps. "Can I have a word?"

"Certainly," I say, trying to keep my cool. But she's just about the last person I want to talk to right now.

"Congratulations on your win," she says. It's just a ploy to soften me up.

"Thanks." I brace myself for worse.

"What's with the new suitcase?" She smirks at me. "I like your style."

I glance down and remember Heidi's suitcase. I'm sure as hell not mentioning her name to a reporter. "That's my favorite color. Got a problem with that?"

"Nope," the reporter says, her slick smile still in place.

Behind her, Georgia mouths the word *relax*.

As if.

"How's the preseason feel for you so far?" the reporter asks.

"I love the preseason," I say, because that used to be true. "It's a great way to get some early action without having to travel. And the fans love the cheaper tickets and the relaxed atmosphere."

I'm apparently the only one who's not relaxed.

"But what about *you,*" she presses, and I want to kick something. "How do you feel about Coach Worthington asking you to switch to right wing?"

I toss my chest pad aside and face her bare-chested. I'm a pretty fine specimen, so I suppose there's an outside chance that my strapping, naked torso will distract her from this line of questioning. "I'll do whatever my team needs. That's how we roll in Brooklyn."

"But what's it like to suddenly switch? How long have you been a left wing?"

I chuckle, trying to sound lighthearted. "Since I can remember." The last time I skated on the right side of the ice, I was probably twelve, had a baby face, and still thought Marvel superheroes were the shit. "It's going to take some work. But hard work is what I'm here for. Change is always a little bracing, but I got here by tackling each new challenge head-on."

Georgia beams at me from behind the journalist, so I must be doing okay.

"I noticed you didn't get a goal or an assist during the game," Miranda presses. "Last season you averaged a point a game."

"Yeah, thanks for remembering that," I say with my most plastic smile. "But that's an average. Should we go over how averages work?"

Georgia puts a hand over her mouth. I'm sure she'd rather put it over mine.

"That won't be necessary," Miranda says. "I'll just watch your next game for two points, so you can even things out." She smiles like a cat who's ready to pounce.

"You do that," I say, because I've backed myself into a corner.

"Have a nice night," she says. "Good chat." And then she finally walks away.

Georgia shoots me a look that implies we'll be having a talk later. One that I totally deserve.

Ugh. I need a pizza and a beer immediately. And maybe a massage.

But first a shower.

By the time I've put on my suit and tie again, it's ten thirty. "Who's up for Grimaldi's?" I ask.

"Always," Silas says. "But seriously, what's with the pink suitcase?" He's already wearing his suit, but he's got one foot parked on the bench, where he's stretching his hamstrings like a good little goalie.

"It's Heidi's," I grunt. "Holding it for her." I don't even know why I made the impulsive offer to help. I need to get Heidi out of my brain, not see her after the game to give her luggage back.

"Let's find her," he says. "Then pizza."

"Cool."

"I think she said something about moving into her own place? Maybe today's the day."

When we exit the locker room, she's right outside in the hallway. And I swear to God, this girl is like my personal Kryptonite. Even in a dumpy polyester uniform she makes my blood quicken. She's biting her lip when I spot her, which makes me want to bite it, too.

"Omigod, thank you!" she says as soon as she spots the suitcase behind me. "I didn't know what else to do!"

"No problem," I murmur. "Here you go." I reach down and grasp the handle to move it around my body. But that fucker is heavy. "What do you have in here? Your collection of encyclopedias?"

"It's just everything I can't live without." She sighs. "Well, I'm off to Bleecker Street."

"Hey, nice address," Silas says.

"It's the, uh, Bleecker Street in Bushwick. Wish me luck."

I open my mouth to say goodbye. But there's something very wrong about that statement. "Bushwick? What's a nice girl like you doing there?"

"Moving in. There are some very nice parts of Bushwick."

"Is your new place in one of them?"

Heidi wrinkles up that cute little nose. "Not exactly." She grabs the handle of her suitcase. "See you later. Thanks for the help." She turns and rolls it down the hallway, which isn't easy because there are people in the way and that bag is enormous.

"How do you think she's getting that thing to Bushwick?" Silas asks, echoing the question in my own mind.

"No idea. Yo!" I call out as Silas and I head for the same exit. "Hot Pepper! You call a car?"

"It's handled," she says over her shoulder.

We follow her out, though, because Silas and I are leaving, too. And damn if she doesn't head right for the subway entrance. At the top of the steps she tugs on the handle of her giant suitcase, barely clearing the ground before she yanks it down a stair.

All I can picture is Heidi squashed like a bug under its weight at the bottom of the stairs.

"Wait up!" Silas and I both yell at the same moment and then run for it.

Heidi jerks her chin over her shoulder. That's when her bag topples against her and she grabs wildly for the handrail. I see her start to tip just as my hand closes around her wrist. And Silas grabs the bag at the same moment.

None of us goes flying down the stairs, thankfully.

"That bag is too heavy," I wheeze. All the cells in my body are hungering for nourishment. Or for Heidi. It's hard to tell at close range, where I can smell her perfume.

"I noticed," she says quietly.

"Let's put you in an Uber," Silas suggests, dragging her bag onto the level pavement again.

"Okay, thanks." She lifts her eyes up toward the dark sky as if praying for patience.

Silas unlocks his phone and starts tapping on the screen. "Two minutes," he says.

"Where'd you find this new apartment, anyway?" I ask as we step out of the foot traffic on the sidewalk.

"Craigslist," she says.

"What? That's danger—"

She cuts me off with a glare and by getting into my face, at least as well as someone who's eight inches shorter than me can do. "Thanks, but my daddy already gave me that speech. He just wants to keep me under his thumb."

"Well, this isn't Bryn Mawr, Pennsylvania. I just want you to stay in one piece."

"Why do you care?" she demands from four inches away.

"Because…" *There are too many dead girls in my life already*. But I'm not going there. And I'm a little distracted, anyway. Her pink lips are *right* there.

Silas clears his throat. "The car is here." He rolls the suitcase toward the vehicle at the curb. When the trunk opens, he makes the grunting noise of an Olympic weightlifter and heaves the bag inside. "Jesus." He closes the trunk. "Does your new place have an elevator?"

Slowly, the hottest, most maddening girl I know shakes her head.

"I was afraid you'd say that." Silas opens the rear door and slides into the car. "Come on, guys. Time's a wasting."

And there goes pizza and beer.

[10]

HEIDI

BLEECKER STREET in Bushwick is farther out than I remember. I only came to see this place once, a few days ago. As the car takes us farther and farther into Brooklyn, I try not to panic. The buildings shrink, but the street traffic is still lively at this hour of the night. That's not a bad sign, right?

Maybe I've been too impulsive.

I wanted to smack Jason when he said we weren't in Bryn Mawr anymore. But the truth is that I've never lived in a big city alone. Okay—any city. Last spring doesn't count because I was staying in Daddy's condo. His driver took me to work some mornings.

Holy hell—I'm truly the pampered little shit that everyone thinks I am. Although that's not entirely my fault. It's not like I've ever been allowed to make choices for myself.

These are my depressing thoughts as I sit pressed up against Jason. He's wearing a spicy cologne I can't identify, but it's driving me a little bonkers. I swear he hasn't said three words to me since the night he kissed the stuffing out of me in the carwash.

And now here we are, three across in the back seat. So cozy, and so unsatisfying.

"You got kinda snappish at that reporter," Silas is saying. "Miranda what's-her-name."

"Because she's a bitch," Jason says.

"Miranda Wager?" I gasp. "I love her. She's so sharp."

Jason growls, and Silas laughs. "He didn't used to hate her," Silas says. "Last year she kept calling him an overnight sensation. But last week she wrote that Coach didn't know what to do with him. Which is—let's be honest—hardly the worst thing that's ever been written about an athlete."

Since I'm mad at Jason for being hot and bossy and also unwilling to give me more of those kisses, I'm totally willing to wade into this disagreement. "Think of how hard her job is," I point out. "She's a terrific sports analyst. Yet every time she goes into a locker room, some Neanderthal tries to embarrass her." I totally read a story about this. "And no matter how well she covers hockey, her Twitter DMs are full of unsolicited dick pics."

"Well, I'm not guilty of any of that," Jason points out. "And I still don't have to like her."

"He just gets hangry," Silas explains. "Most game nights he'd be halfway through a large pizza by now."

Well, crud. "I'm sorry you're in a car to Bushwick instead."

"Maybe there's food here," Jason grumps, ducking his head to see out my window. "Hey! That's a Caribbean joint. Sally Root's. Looks open."

My stomach growls. I ate a really meager hotdog during my ridiculously short dinner break five hours ago. I'm afraid to spend much money until I finally get a paycheck. My bank account is down to almost nothing.

"Which corner?" the driver says from the front seat.

"Anywhere," I say, because all the buildings look alike and I can't see which building is 415. "You guys can just make the return trip, okay? I'll be fine."

"No, you don't," Jason says with a sigh. "We're not just dumping a helpless—"

I elbow him for using the world "helpless."

"Ow!"

"Sorry, reflex," I say quickly, hopping out of the car.

Silas cackles. "Didn't you just play the Rangers?"

"I had pads!" Jason complains as he extracts his long legs from the car.

I run back to the trunk, but of course I can't get my suitcase out, and Silas has to rescue me. So much for my independence. It's not going that well. And things go even more poorly when I identify number 415 and march inside.

"At least there's a doorman," Jason mutters.

Although the man in question looks to be about ninety years old. "Help you, señorita?" he asks.

"I'm here for apartment 212. Bobby said he'd hand over the keys tonight."

"Bobby?" The frail doorman adjusts his blue cap. "We don't have a Bobby."

"The superintendent?" I ask, my voice rising in alarm. "Big fellow? Earrings in lots of places?"

"Dios mio." The old man shakes his head. "He have a scar right here?" He traces an invisible line above his eye. "And he advertise on Craigslist?"

"Yes! That's him. Can you ring him?"

The old man shakes his head. "He don't work here no more. Hasn't for years. But he still has the keys. Sometimes he come back and rent out the places that don't need renting out."

"Wait, *what?*"

"He show you a place with somebody else's stuff in it, right?"

My heart drops. "Yes. He said they were moving out the next day."

"Señorita." The geezer's face turns sad. "He always say that. 212 brought home a pizza two hours ago. They up there right now."

"Can she check?" Jason asks. "Just in case there's been some misunderstanding."

He shrugs. "I suppose it can't hurt nothing. Let me guess—you don't have a lease with his signature on it."

"We had a handshake deal," I say in a quavering voice. "He said we'd sign it tonight."

In stereo, both Jason and Silas make noises of dismay. And I have never felt like a bigger idiot.

"You just knock," the elderly man says. "And if 212 answers, you tell 'em they need to have their locks changed. Tomorrow you call the precinct and report your money stolen. But he done this three other times and they haven't found him yet. He bring you in the basement door, right?"

"*Yes*," I croak. My throat is dry and tight and my eyes are burning.

A big hand lands on my shoulder. "Don't panic," Jason says. "Can you cancel the check you wrote him?"

My embarrassment is complete. "He said it had to be—"

"—cash," Jason finishes on a sigh. "Oh, little buddy. Okay—listen. We're going to get some Caribbean food and sort this out."

Twenty minutes later I'm watching Jason and Silas devour braised oxtail and jerk chicken. And still trying not to cry. The food looks great and my stomach is empty. But I didn't order anything.

Neither did Jason and Silas, come to think of it. The

moment we walked in the hostess's eyes lit up. "Good *game*, guys! And you're here with us tonight? This is amazing! Sit sit sit. You need food?"

"So badly," Jason had said.

The hostess—Clara—put a hand to her heart. "Let me just dash into the kitchen to tell them they're not done yet. I'll be right back to take your drink order!"

That was fifteen minutes ago. Since then, Clara and the wait staff have made a dozen trips to our table, bringing all manner of small plates and beverages. "And what will the lady have to drink?" a server asked at one point.

"I'm not drinking," I'd said quickly.

They brought me a homemade soda made with cucumber, lime, and strawberry. I'm sipping on it balefully right now and questioning all my life choices.

"Okay," Castro says, putting down a chicken bone. "That took the edge off. Now I can think."

"This food is really over the top," Silas agrees. "We need to come here again."

"No problem," I grumble. "The next time I'm swindled like a fool we'll just drop by."

Jason clucks his tongue. "You need some of this chicken," he says. "It'll change your mood." He grabs a meaty piece off the platter and puts it on my empty plate. "Don't do that dainty girl thing and pass up this food. And here—some tostones. Fried plantains."

"It's not a dainty girl thing," I argue. "Jeez." I pick up the chicken and take a bite. The skin is crispy and spicy, and the meat is juicy. I let out a little moan.

"None of that," Jason says. "Now tell us what the hell happened back there."

"Just a minute. I'm communing with this chicken." Silas chuckles while I take another bite, and then eat a plantain. I'm stalling, because I really don't know what I'm going to do. "I didn't know how to find a place that I can afford," I say eventually, wiping my fingers with the napkin Jason hands me. "So I took a chance on Craigslist. And now I don't even have my deposit."

I want to cry all over again.

"Weren't you staying with your dad in Manhattan?" Silas asks.

"Yes. But he's made a big point of teaching me a lesson. I can't stay with that man." Although I don't really see any alternatives.

"You can stay with us for bit," Silas says. "Right, Castro?"

Jason's cocktail glass pauses halfway to his mouth. "What?"

"She can have the couch," Silas says, grinning. "We're leaving on a road trip in two nights, anyway."

"*My* couch?" Jason asks. He gives me the side-eye.

"You don't have to do that," I say.

"It's no problem," Silas says cheerfully. "Right, bro?"

"Sure," he grunts.

Oh dear. I don't know what to do. Nice girls don't impose. On the other hand, being a nice girl isn't working so well for me. And I really, really don't want to run home to Daddy.

Still, though. Jason doesn't want me on his sofa.

"Guys, it might be three *weeks* until I can earn back what I lost. I earn almost nothing, and they hold onto my pay forever."

Jason closes his eyes. It's a long beat before he opens them again. "Don't worry, okay? Just eat the chicken and take a breath and then you can stay on the couch."

He doesn't look thrilled about it. But I feel a rush of gratitude, anyway. "Thank you! Thank you so much!" I lean in and hug him. I'd hug Silas, too, but he's on the other side of Jason and I don't have gorilla arms.

The hug doesn't last long, though, because Jason makes a growly sound. I guess he's not in the mood for a hug from a freeloader like me.

"Good deal," Silas says. "Let's get the check, shall we? It's getting late."

"I might need another one of these rum drinks first," Jason grumbles. "Heidi, eat that food."

"Yes, *sir*," I say.

He gives me a dark, unsettling look.

But that's okay. I have excellent food and a couch to sleep on. I won't have to admit defeat just yet.

[11]

JASON

"YOU ARE A PAIN IN MY ASS," I hiss at Silas. "You know that?"

We're in his room, and Heidi is currently singing to herself in my shower. Silas is propped up in bed, cackling to himself while I glower at him from the doorway.

"I should be forgetting my troubles, hooking up with a hockey fan right now," I complain. "Not hosting a sleepover!"

"Were you going to throw the girl out on the street? I bet you couldn't do it."

He's right, of course. I'd never leave Heidi in danger. "Her daddy has a penthouse on the Upper East Side," I point out. "Let's not pretend she was going to end up sleeping in a cardboard box under the bridge."

"My bad," he says with an arrogant grin.

"What is your goal here?" I demand.

"Entertainment." He tucks his hands behind his head. "When she's around, you're not a broody cat. You're more like a slobbering dog."

"I'm not here to entertain you!" Jesus. I used to think of him as a good roommate.

"Someone should," he says with a sigh. "And entertain you, too. We were such grinds last season. And look where it got us."

"It got me twenty-seven goals and you a one-way contract." Last season was epic.

Maddeningly, Silas just shrugs. "Success is nice. But we don't have anyone to share it with except each other. And you're not into dudes, so..." He shrugs again.

"You think you can *set me up* with..." I jerk a thumb toward the other room.

In the silence, we hear the commissioner's daughter singing about hills that are alive with the sound of music.

"She likes show tunes. You're a showboat. I think it's a sign," Silas says with another irritating grin that makes me want to choke him.

Getting nowhere, I stomp off to find the sheets and blankets for the fold-out couch. It takes me fifteen minutes to get that sucker set up. I'm just fluffing the pillow when Heidi emerges from my room wearing a tiny sleeveless T-shirt and shorts that could get a girl jailed in several countries.

I need to stop noticing her. But the outline of her nipples against the soft fabric taunts me. And the smooth skin of her legs goes on for miles...

"Everything okay there?" she asks. "You look a little woozy."

"Fine," I grunt and force myself to look away. "You're all set up here."

Her expression softens. "Thank you. I would have done that."

"S'okay." She turns me into a caveman. One word at a time is all I can manage. As she slips past me, I get a whiff of citrus and honey.

She sits on the edge of the sofa bed and tests the mattress

with her hand. "Wow, nice. I appreciate you letting me stay here."

"No problem." I shut off the lamp. Then I sit down beside her. I tell myself it's because I'm trying to be less grumpy and more friendly. But it's really because I'm drawn to things that are bad for me. "My parents are the only ones who ever use this sofa bed."

"Do they visit often?"

"Couple times a year."

She puts one silky hand on my arm. "I promise to be out of your hair soon."

And that's my cue to leave. Because I like her touch way too much. "Goodnight, you pain in the butt."

She smiles at me in the dim light. "You don't have to go, you know."

"Yeah, I really do."

"Do I get a good night kiss?"

Oh hell. We both know how good that could be. "That's a bad idea." I stand up before I give in. "You sleep well. Tomorrow you can call the police, okay? File a complaint against the asshole who took your money."

"I will," she says with a sigh. "But they won't get it back."

I put a hand on her head, and then I lean down and kiss her hair. I meant it as a friendly gesture, but even the sweet scent of her as my lips brush over silk is too much. "Night," I say in a husky voice.

Then I retreat to my own room and shut the door.

It isn't a great night's sleep. My dreams are charged with coaches yelling at me. And then, towards dawn, I have a sexy dream about a certain girl with blue eyes and soft hands.

When the alarm goes off, I open my eyes warily. I'm turned

on and overtired. It's not a nice combination. I want to roll over and close my eyes again, but morning skate starts in an hour, and later I need to pack for our first road trip.

So I get out of bed and do some stretches to wake myself up. When I'm dressed and ready, I open my bedroom door to a curious smell.

Is that...bacon?

I pad into the kitchen to find Silas seated at our table, looking like a king at a banquet. He's eating a waffle with a fried egg on top. There's also bacon and a wedge of cantaloupe on his plate.

"Whoa," I say as Heidi turns to face me from the counter. "What happened here?"

"Breakfast," she says with a forehead wrinkle. She looks at me like I'm an imbecile. "Don't you eat breakfast?"

"Um, yes?" It's just that it doesn't look like this. "You don't have to cook for us."

Silas makes a noise of dismay and then a slashing motion with his hand. "Will you please shut up? Do you not see all this good food?"

"It's the least I can do," Heidi says. "Here's yours." She offers a plate, and it's just like Silas's. The scent of waffles and bacon fills my nostrils, and I begin to come around to Silas's way of seeing things.

"Thank you," I say, sitting down hastily and grabbing the silverware that she's already put out for me. "We have a waffle iron?"

"You sure do," she says. "But I peeled a sticker off it. I don't think you ever used it before."

"Oh." I wonder what else is in my kitchen? "Where did you get these groceries?"

"I ran out this morning."

"Save the receipt," I say.

"It's already on the fridge." She points at a slip of paper

trapped with a magnet. "I'm happy to run errands, but cash is tight."

I put a piece of waffle and fried egg in my mouth and then moan a little. "Is that cinnamon?"

"Yes," she says, stacking more waffles onto a piece of waxed paper. "The little store didn't have real maple syrup, and fake maple syrup is garbage. These waffles are going in your freezer. If you microwave them for twenty seconds and then toast them in the toaster, they will be very good for leftovers."

"Can I have another one right now?" Silas asks.

"No," she says shortly. "Too carby. But you can have another egg if you need more calories."

Silas and I exchange a curious glance. "Got it," he says as we both try not to laugh.

"While you're away—assuming the police don't magically find my money, and that I don't also find an instantly available apartment I can afford—I can take in your mail and do errands and water your plants."

"There aren't any plants," I point out. "But thank you."

Silas chews a piece of bacon with a thoughtful look on his face. "You know, this is a big issue for some players during the season. They need sporadic help with errands and groceries and stuff. If you're looking to pick up extra cash, you might want to offer your services. You could charge by the hour. Bunch of guys live in this building, so you could take in everyone's mail at once."

Heidi sets a half melon down on the counter and turns around to face Silas. "Really? That's a thing?"

"Sure." He shrugs. "Every year guys are trying to figure out how to get their groceries delivered right as the jet lands in New York. How to get their suits to the drycleaner's. There's services for all that stuff, but it's piecemeal. And they'd trust you with a key. It's like a different level of service."

"Silas," she breathes. "I could kiss you right now. You're a flipping genius."

Something goes wrong in my gut at the idea of Heidi kissing Silas.

And then it gets worse when she lunges over to him and hugs his head, which effectively puts his cheek against her boob. She says some more gushy words about how excellent his idea is.

Silas pokes his head out from under her arm and grins at me.

Annnnd I'm done here. I stand up suddenly and carry my empty plate over to the sink for a rinse.

"Just leave it," she says. "I'll load the dishwasher in a minute. You have practice, but I don't have to show up for my security shift until four."

"What's there to guard when there's no hockey game?" I ask.

"No idea," she says. "But I already know it will be unpleasant."

[12]

HEIDI

THE BRUISERS ARE HEADQUARTERED in a restored warehouse that's part of the Brooklyn Navy Yard complex. After I pull the large brass door handle and step into the lobby, I am treated to the sight of a highlight reel playing on a big screen.

Someone changed the video over the summer, incorporating all of the team's best moments from their winningest season. I pause to take in a clip of O'Doul scoring a goal against the D.C. team during the first round of last year's playoffs. This is followed by a clip of Jason's goal against Tampa. He rushes the net and puts it between the goalie's legs. They call that the five-hole in hockey.

This week I've watched all three of my boys' away games. Sadly, Jason never found the five-hole. Or any other holes. The best he could manage was a single assist on a power play. My favorite forward is still really shaken up over his move to right wing.

He's going to be a grumpy bear when he gets home tonight. Any athlete would be.

I cross the lobby and then follow a glass tunnel down toward the brand-new practice facility. I'm on an errand for Bayer, and he's not paying me to stand around watching tape.

When Silas suggested that I offer to do errands for the team, he was really onto something. That first morning I mentioned it to just two other teammates, and by noon I had incoming texts from another dozen hockey players. In the last five days, I've done errands for the lot of them.

For O'Doul and Ariana—the team masseuse—I checked on the progress the contractors were making on their renovation two blocks away. I made sure their doors were locked in the evening after the workers left.

For Trevi and Georgia, I took in the mail and the drycleaning. And I bought the groceries they wanted on hand for their return. I did the same for Beringer.

Now I'm here to pick up Bayer's medical file from the training department. It's x-rays of his knee, or something. I don't ask questions, I just fetch things. I'm charging twenty bucks an hour, and everyone's getting their first emailed invoices tonight.

My apartment money will be replenished twice as quickly this way.

The folder I need has been left for me on a desk outside the treatment room, as the receptionist had promised. I tuck it into my messenger bag and turn around to leave the facility.

"Hey!" Rebecca says, stopping to greet me. "Long time no see. What brings you here?"

"Errands for the players. It's my second job."

She blinks. "That's very resourceful."

"It was Silas's idea. My next stop is Trader Joe's on Gold Street. I'm delivering food to six different apartments before the team jet lands."

"How are you going to manage it all?"

"I'll take a cab back to Water Street and then split my

carfare cost among my clients. I bill twenty bucks an hour in six-minute increments, plus incidentals."

Becca bursts out laughing. "You're going to run the world someday."

"Maybe." As soon as I get out from under my dad's thumb.

"I hope you're not working around the clock," the new team owner says, her hands on her hips.

"Nope. Last week I was assigned to stadium security, but they could barely give me any hours while the team was on the road. Wednesday I got called in to work some kind of banquet across town, though. I thought that was odd. It didn't have anything to do with the team."

Rebecca's eyes get round. "What? Where was this event?"

"At a social hall on Court Street. I can forward you the email telling me when and where. Do you think the security company is padding your bill, or something?"

"Probably not?" Rebecca says, but she looks thoughtful. "Send me the details, and when we receive our bill at the end of the month, I'll check it over thoroughly."

"That's a great idea," I agree, edging toward the tunnel back to the street. "I'd better get going."

"Let me walk you out," Rebecca says. "You're giving me ideas."

"What kind?"

She's quiet as we pass the doors to the practice rink. "Could I trouble you for a report on every department where you're working? You could bill me your standard rate."

"You want me to spy?" I squeak.

Becca stops walking. "Is that awful?"

"No! I *love* espionage." This is going to be great. "Did you know the hotdog seller uses cheaper buns for the cheap seats? But charges the same price?"

"Get out of town!" Becca gasps. "That's awful."

"I think they're selling off-brand beer and mislabeling it, too.

I wasn't really paying attention but I swear someone hooked up a tap with a beer of a different label."

Becca leans back against the glass bricks of the tunnel and closes her eyes. "I shouldn't be so surprised, right? But I still am. What if everyone is cheating us?"

"Don't panic. I'll take a second rotation through concessions if it helps you. I'll smell like hotdogs twice for you, Bec. So long as you appreciate it."

She lets out a peal of laughter. "You really want that office manager job, don't you?"

"Badly," I whisper.

She taps her chin. "It's not going to be easy to leave that position open for another two or three months. But I'll try."

"I'll be worth it, I swear."

Becca grins. "I don't doubt it. Where are you working this week?"

"Licensed apparel. It's boring but not smelly." I've only done two shifts so far, and I can't complain. "I'll write you a report for everything I've done so far."

"Good work, intern." She slaps me on the back. "I'll read every word."

I have never seen so many groceries.

Shopping takes me a really long time, because everyone's list needs to be kept separate. And, as I shop for six hockey players, certain trends emerge.

One—hockey players eat a lot.

Two—hockey players like avocados. I have never bought so many avocados. If there's an avocado company listed on the New York Stock Exchange, I'm going to direct Daddy to invest part of my trust fund in it. When I finally get my hands on that money—in fifty years, when Daddy has eventually forgiven me—my inheritance will have quadrupled.

"You must be very hungry," the cabbie says as I load fifteen shopping bags into the back of his car. I've already written every player's name on the bags in Sharpie marker.

But this guy doesn't know that. "Actually, I'm eating for four," I say, patting my stomach.

His brow furrows as he closes the trunk. He can't decide if I'm kidding. "Congratulations," he says eventually.

"Thank you. If only I knew who the father was."

The man climbs into the front seat in a big fat hurry, while I give myself a private high-five. Nice girls don't make tasteless jokes. But I'm breaking all the rules these days.

In the back of the cab, I pull out my phone to see if I've forgotten anything. But no. Every single item on my to-do list is checked off. Tonight I can send out my invoices and collect my moonlighting cash.

There's only one thing missing. My little business needs a name. I'm considering Mighty Heidi, because it almost rhymes. But it's not quite right…

A text pops onto the screen. It's from Eric, my ex. My finger hovers over the notification to dismiss it, but then I happen to glimpse a snippet of the message. ***I'm in town for an interview and I'd like to take you to dinner.***

Well, crumbs. If he's in town, can I really refuse to see him? That's breaking about seventeen different rules of etiquette.

I tap on his name and call him. Half of me hopes he won't pick up. But then he does. "Heidi Jo," he says in a soft voice. "To what do I owe the pleasure of hearing your voice? Please tell me you didn't butt dial me."

"No," I say, already wishing I hadn't called. "I saw your message."

"Can I see you?"

"Well, it really depends on the day. My father has me

working some strange jobs lately, and the hours are pretty unpredictable."

He chuckles, as if that's just so adorable, and my temper flares. The men in my life never take me seriously. "Well, I'm only in town for thirty-six hours, but I'd really love to see you. I miss you so much. I'd like to take you out and spoil you."

"That's really nice, Eric," I say gently. "Maybe that could work."

"I hope so." He sighs. "Still don't know why you had to leave school." *And me.* I hear those extra words at the end of that sentence even if he won't say it. "Pennsylvania isn't the same without you."

"I'm pretty sure Pennsylvania will survive." Although I'm so tired right now that Eric's nostalgic tone is wearing me down. Maybe I'll have dinner with him, if my schedule permits. Is it awful that I miss having a guy who calls me every night before bed and whispers *I love you?*

"Look, I'm thinking of graduating early," he says. "This interview is for a job that would start in February. In the analyst-training program."

"Wait, what?" That wakes me from my reverie. "But that's right in the middle of hockey season."

His chuckle is low and warm. "Figures that would be your first concern. But the Villanova Ice Cats will just have to make do. It's my last season to play anyway, Heidi Jo. It's not like the Brooklyn Bruisers are going to come calling."

He's right, I guess. Most college hockey players are done with the sport on senior night. But who could ditch his team right before the playoffs! "It must be a great job opportunity. Is it at a bank?"

"Goldman Sachs. It's top-shelf. If they offer me the spot, I'm taking it."

"Oh," I say slowly. "Well, I'm sure you'll wow them with your smarts."

"I'll wow them, and we'll celebrate with a nice dinner. I'll send you my itinerary. If I'm in town for two nights instead of one, that doubles my chances of seeing you, right?"

"Yes, I guess it does." I'm just not sure how I feel about it.

"You take care, honey. Can't wait to see you."

We sign off just as the cab pulls up in front of my boys' Water Street condo building. I get out on tired feet and begin to pull grocery bags out of the trunk of the cab.

The condo's doors open and Miguel emerges, rolling a brass bellman's cart. That solves the problem of how a girl can deliver groceries to five different apartments. God bless millionaires. They've thought of everything.

"Where to, miss?" Miguel asks. I've confused the heck out of him this week, as I come and go from a half-dozen different apartments.

"It's complicated," I tell him. "Could I borrow your wheels for fifteen minutes while I make my deliveries? I need to get these perishables into the fridge."

"Of course." He steps back. "The drycleaner also dropped off shirts for…"

"…Trevi," I say. His were the last to arrive, because he uses a different shop than the rest. "Load 'em on here. I'll take care of everything at once."

My feet are screaming by the time the freight elevator doors open to accommodate the cart.

If Becca was right, I will run the world someday. I only hope that world domination comes with foot rubs.

[13]

JASON

EVERY ROAD TRIP IS HARD. But usually I'm not feeling quite so discouraged.

We won two and lost two, but my contribution was poor. I'm worried, and I know my teammates are, too. Because they're being so fucking *nice* to me right now. Bayer is holding the door for me as we all trudge into the Million Dollar Dorm. And Silas let me pick the music in the cab on the way back from the airport.

That's how you know it's bad. If these dudes thought everything was okay, they'd be assholes like usual.

"Pizza and beer at our place later?" Silas offers to our teammates. "I need a dose of Grimaldi's, but I'm too tired to go out."

"Sounds good," Bayer and Beringer both agree.

"Maybe," Leo says. "Gotta see if Georgia made any plans."

"Gotta check with the little wife," Bayer prods him. Then he makes the sound of a whip. But Leo just smiles to himself, like he knows a secret. Leo has two goals from our first road trip.

His season is well underway. He doesn't need anyone's approval, and he knows it.

Must be nice.

Silas and I ride the elevator in silence and then trudge toward our door. He unlocks it.

"Every traveler has a home of his own, and he learns to appreciate it the more from his wandering," I say as we drop our luggage on the floor like always.

"Shakespeare?" Silas asks.

"Dickens," I say. "Maybe I jinxed myself quoting Dickens during training camp. Like—now my whole season is going to be like *Oliver Twist*. 'Please, sir. May I have a goal?'"

Silas snorts. Then he lifts his nose and sniffs the air. "Do you smell that? It's like…"

I take a deep breath. "Yeah. Our place smells like lemons instead of feet."

"Wow. Huh. I like it." Silas walks toward the refuge of his bedroom with a happy sigh.

I linger a moment in our living room. I'd been trying not to think about Heidi staying in our apartment, because I have enough distractions right now. But there's her suitcase, tucked against the wall.

There aren't any other signs of her, though. The sofa bed has been put away, and every surface is tidier than it usually is. The stack of *Sports Illustrated* magazines is straight, and there aren't any abandoned water bottles lurking on the coffee table.

Heidi has been here even though there's no sign of her.

I grab my travel bag, hoist it onto my shoulder, and trudge toward my bedroom where a nice hot shower awaits. I'm mentally turning on the faucet when I happen to glance down at the bed.

Holy fuck. Heidi has face-planted onto my mattress. She's lying the wrong way across the foot of the bed, on top of the quilt, asleep. She's even snoring gently.

One glance is all it takes, and I'm already feeling an unwelcome flash of lust. A split second is all I need to admire the golden skin of her arms as they stretch overhead, and the round shape of her perfect ass in those jeans.

White jeans. And it's way past Labor Day. Someone's been naughty. I want to kneel on the bed and peel those off her body…

Fuck. I drop my bag on the floor again and remove my suit jacket, which I drop onto the bag. Then I make a beeline for my bathroom. I lock the door and shed the rest of my clothing and climb under the warm spray.

I will not jack off to the commissioner's daughter.

Just kill me already.

Ten minutes later I emerge, freshly shaved and wearing a towel. Because it's my damn house, and I don't own a bathrobe. Not only have I made tons of noise, but I can hear the chick music blaring from Silas's room already. We're not quiet people.

But wouldn't you know? There's still a sleeping, off-limits princess sprawled on my bed.

This time she hears me, though. Heidi's eyes fly open when I open my underwear drawer. "Oh my goodness!" She sits up fast. The stitching pattern of the quilt my mother made for me is carved into her pink cheek. "Sorry! I just meant to sit down for a minute." She scrambles to her feet and takes a deep breath. "Welcome home."

"Thanks. Glad to be back." I wait for her to leave.

She still has that half-conscious look of the recently awakened. As I watch, her big blue eyes travel slowly as she looks me up and down. I can feel her gaze like a caress as she takes in my bare chest and abs. "Wow," she says, her voice full of appreciation.

"Unless you want to see even more, you might want to step out," I grumble.

She doesn't move. Instead, her eyes go a little soft, and she sighs dreamily.

Holy shit. That's probably how she looks right after she's been well-fu—

Argh! "Out you go," I snap, turning to face my dresser.

"Sorry," she whispers and then sprints on out of my room, closing the door behind her.

But the damage is already done. My body feels tight and ready for sex. And the room smells lightly of citrus and honey. Hell, my bed probably smells like her.

I stomp around the room, getting dressed, hanging up my suit and unpacking. I'm tired, my hockey game is in the shitter, and I need pizza, beer, and sexual release.

But only the pizza and beer are forthcoming, damn it.

When I finally venture into the kitchen, Silas is there with Heidi. He's happily munching his favorite snack—avocado slices topped with fresh salsa. "Heidi shopped for everybody who lives in the Million Dollar Dorm!" he says. "It's really nice to come home to groceries."

"Oh, cool." I'd given her a list, too. "That's great. Thanks for that."

"My pleasure," she says with a smile.

I step up to the cabinet and open it, looking for some chips. Hmm. "Where are you hiding the Doritos?"

"Oh," she says. "You got those instead." She points.

I grab the bag off the shelf. But these chips are *green*. "These are made of…kale?"

"Yes," she says. "They're delicious. And for dip you got this." She opens the fridge and pulls out a tub of organic hummus instead of the onion dip I like.

This is a freaking disaster. "But that's not the same! Are you telling me you changed the orders of six players to whatever you think is best?"

"No way." She tosses that silky hair and purses those kissable lips. "Just yours. Nobody else asked me to buy anything with yellow dye number five in it."

Silas laughs, that fucker. I tear open the bag with a scowl. And then I have a truly horrible thought. "But what about my sandwich? Did you get—"

"Whole-wheat sandwich bread, creamy peanut butter, and strawberry jam?" she asks.

"It *has* to be strawberry," I thunder, sounding like a lunatic. Some things cannot be fucked with. Like fate.

Heidi walks over to another cabinet and opens the door, revealing a loaf of bread, and jar of peanut butter. And a jar of Bonne Maman strawberry jam. "I'm not crazy enough to take on your superstitions," she says.

"Thank you." I exhale in a mighty gust. "Did you save the receipt?" I'll need to pay her back.

"What do you take me for?" she yelps. "Tonight you'll get a fully itemized invoice. And—by the way—I'm only billing you for the groceries. You two don't pay for labor. Don't tell anyone, though. I need to keep my market price on an upward trajectory."

"Got it," Silas says with a smirk. "Thanks."

"No—you can charge me," I argue. I get why she did that—we're letting her stay here for free. But I don't want to owe her anything. And the faster she earns the money, the faster she can stop torturing me with her tiny pajamas and that tight little body that I want to—

Yeah. No.

I'm so frustrated right now. So frustrated that I grab the kale chips and rip open the bag. Then I shove one in my mouth.

It's not awful.

Hmm.

"Let me know when it's time to order pizza," she says. "I'll text your friends for their orders and then put everything in my spreadsheet."

"Don't forget the beer!" Silas says cheerfully.

"I won't!" Heidi walks out of the kitchen, her ass swaying just enough to torture me.

I shove a handful of kale chips in my mouth so I won't say or do anything I'll regret.

[14]

JASON

THE FOLLOWING week is a shit show. Practice is awful. My stats suck. Every coach in the organization has spent serious time trying to help me. I know that's supposed to be a *good* thing. But there's only so much advice a guy can absorb in a day.

It's only October, and this is already the longest hockey season of my life.

To make matters worse, Heidi is still prancing around my apartment and prancing through my dreams. It's torture. I'm full of pent-up frustration, and I can't exorcise it the way I want to—by pushing her down into the sofa cushions and having my filthy way with her.

Friday night it's the same damn thing. We lose our home game to Buffalo, of all teams. And then when the team retreats to the Tavern afterward to lick our wounds, Heidi is there, too, looking luscious in a tight-fitting sweater.

"Hi Pete!" she greets the gray-haired bartender.

"Hello, miss." He gives her a big smile.

"I'd like a shot of tequila with a whiskey chaser," she says.

Pete rolls his eyes. "You're underage. We've been over this. Besides—nobody orders that. We have to work on your smack talk."

"What do I order if I want to make a statement?" she asks, pulling out a barstool and plunking her cute butt onto it.

"A buttery nipple," Pete suggests.

"What if I'm avoiding dairy?"

The bartender laughs so hard he practically has an aneurism. That's the thing about Heidi. Once you've noticed her, it's hard to stop noticing her.

Or maybe that's just me.

"You could try a dirty martini," Pete says after he regains control of his executive function. "Always a classic. Or a glass of bubbly, if you want something lighter."

"Good tip," she says. "Oh, hey, Castro! Come here a sec. I have something to discuss with you."

That's what I get for staring at her so subtly, I guess. I do as I'm told, and take a seat next to Heidi.

"What non-alcoholic drink am I pouring you?" Pete asks.

"Club soda with lime. Thanks. Now, Mr. Castro." She turns to me. "Before I left the apartment tonight, someone left a message on the landline answering machine, and—"

"Oh, that's my—"

Heidi holds up a hand, silencing me. "Do not interrupt a lady's story. I did some excellent sleuthing, okay? She greeted you with a name I didn't catch. But then she said something about how Mom isn't coming to your game next week after all. The caller apologized for the change in plans, but she's convinced your mom to come visit her instead of you and help out with your nephew's birthday party."

"Oh, okay." I can't say I'm too upset that Mom isn't coming next week. I'm in too much of a rut. If things go on like this, I won't be in much of a mood to entertain her.

Fuck. I feel glum just thinking about it. Last year when my parents visited, I had two goals in one game, and we all went out for dim sum the next day.

"Which leads me to my next deduction." Heidi snaps her fingers. "Stay with me, Jason."

"Lay it on me," I say, although it's unclear whether I'm referring to her message or Heidi's body. She's like a beam of sunshine. And my cloudy ass could really use some of that.

Theoretically, anyway.

"It was your sister calling, right? And you have a nephew who's about to turn three?"

"Yeah. My sister Jackie has... Oh, shit!" I forgot about his birthday. I'm the worst uncle ever. "Could you possibly help me—"

"I'm a step ahead of you," she says.

Of course she is.

Out of her very large bag she pulls a Brooklyn Bruisers toy hockey stick. "Every little boy needs a hockey stick."

"Good call, Heidi."

"There's more." She beams at me. "I hope you like it, because I talked them into doing a rush job. Tonight was my last shift in licensed apparel." She pulls out a brown teddy bear wearing a Brooklyn jersey. It's adorable. And when she turns it around, I see the bear has CASTRO and my jersey number on his back.

"Holy crap," I say, laughing. When she hands me the bear, his fur is soft and cuddly. "This is amazing. I think I need one for myself."

"No, you don't." Heidi snatches the bear back from me. "This is going in a FedEx box tomorrow. I just need your sister's address. Oh—and I need to see a photo of your nephew."

"Why?"

"Because toddlers are cute!" She rolls her eyes. "You're in a *mood*."

I really am. I pull my phone out of my pocket and open up some photos. "Here he is." The picture of my sister and her oldest makes me grin.

"Aw!" Heidi coos. "Such an attractive family. I hope he turns out nicer than you."

"What?" I squawk.

Heidi sips her soda. "That's all the business I have for you," she says, waving a hand at me. "You're excused."

"Thank you." I blink. "Did you just dismiss me?"

"Yes, I did." *Yes, ah did.* Her Southern accent is very subtle, but it softens her in a way that really gets to me.

"If I stay here on this barstool, are you going to bill me in six-minute increments for your time?"

She rolls her eyes. "I don't bill you for services rendered and you already know that. But you're cramping my style right now."

"How's that?" This is a hockey bar. *Our* hockey bar. There's not a woman in here that would chase me off. As a matter of fact, there's two of them already giving me the fuck-me eyes.

"Maybe I'm hoping a great guy will come along and chat me up," Heidi says, stirring her soda with a straw. "He sees you sitting here, he'll just move on."

"Which guy?" As a reflex, I look over one shoulder and then the other. The place is full of guys, of course. Half of them are my teammates. They won't pick up Heidi.

Will they?

And here I thought I couldn't get any grumpier.

"Or—here's a plan. You could take me home yourself," she says. "It's not like you don't want to."

She's right, of course. "You have a key to my home," I point out.

"That is *not* what we're talking about, Mr. Castro," she whispers. "I still want my chance."

I swallow hard. "You know that's not going to happen." Although the way we're staring at each other right now, I'm feeling less sure than I should be, damn it. So I force myself to look away.

"Right." Heidi clears her throat. "So get lost, then."

And I'm speechless.

"Hey, Jason?" Pete asks. "Do me a favor and bring this over to your pals in the back corner? I'm short-handed." He sets down a platter of chicken wings.

"Um, sure," I grumble. I grab the wings and a stack of napkins, and carry the whole thing away before I say something to Heidi that will get me in trouble.

Growing up with two sisters taught me a thing or two about keeping my trap shut. Although if she thinks she's going home with some random stranger, she's got another thing coming.

I take the chicken to my pals and help myself to a couple of wings. Swear to God, it only takes about ninety seconds until some college guy wearing a backward baseball cap takes the barstool I've just vacated, and starts chatting up Heidi.

"Your girl is making friends tonight," Bayer says with a chuckle.

"She's not my girl," I grunt.

"Just keep telling yourself that," Silas whispers.

"Hey, Drake?" I say, snapping my fingers at the rookie. "I need a favor."

"Yeah?" The kid wipes buffalo sauce off his mouth. "What is it?"

"Go order us a pitcher of beer. And say hello to Heidi while you're waiting."

The rookie looks over at the bar and then chuckles. "You don't like that guy?"

"I don't *know* that guy," I correct. "And our little friend has a way of getting herself into situations. She's kinda sheltered."

"But they're just *talking,*" Bayer points out. "How much trouble could he be?"

"He's a frat boy," I grumble.

"So were you," Silas says gleefully.

"*Exactly!* I know how they think. Drake—you don't have to chase him off. Just let him know that Heidi has friends in the bar."

The rookie shakes his head. But since he knows he has no choice, he takes our empty pitcher of beer and lumbers toward the bar. He puts one hand on Heidi's shoulder as he reaches over to hand the pitcher to Pete.

Heidi pats his hand, greets him, and then shoos him away.

But I don't miss it when the college boy glances in our direction with widening eyes.

About two minutes after Drake returns with the beer, the frat boy shakes Heidi's hand and then gets the heck out of there. He exits the bar through the front door, leaving Heidi by herself.

She looks down into her soda glass and sighs. Nobody else sits on the vacant bar stool, and my rusty conscience gives a little burp of discomfort. But then, as I watch, Heidi straightens her spine. She shoulders her bag and gets up.

Then she walks straight towards me.

"Uh-oh," O'Doul says under his breath. "Incoming."

"You think that's *funny*?" Heidi squeaks as she arrives at our table. "I can't have a conversation in a bar without you interfering? You can't mind your own business for a few minutes?"

"I'm sorry," I say immediately. "I won't do it again."

"Too late now!" she yells. "I know I'm funny to you. My dad has made sure of that. Rich kid with a shitty job and no money. Couch surfing and feeling like I'm underfoot all the time. So if you could kindly avoid ruining my fun for *one* evening, I'd appreciate it."

"Sit with us," Bayer says. "Drake, get the girl a chair."

"No, thank you! I can't, anyway. Someone will take a picture and write that I'm boinking the whole team." She turns on her heel and goes back to her barstool.

Now I've really fucked up, so I follow her to apologize. "Hey," I say, chasing her. "I'm sorry."

Heidi ignores me. "Pete, I'd like a glass of champagne, please."

The older man puts both hands on the bar and shakes his head. "We've been over this. How about a virgin margarita?"

She tosses something on the bar. It's a driver's license.

Pete picks it up and squints. Then he checks his watch. "Miss Heidi Jo Pepper of Tennessee! Let me be the first to say happy birthday. And your first legal glass of champagne is on me."

"*Wait.* It's your *birthday?*" My voice rises and breaks, like an adolescent's.

"It is now," she says as Pete pops the cork out of a bottle of Krug.

"Pour two," I tell him. "And one for yourself."

"I usually say no." Pete chuckles, lining up three champagne glasses on the counter. "But this is a great bottle."

"Didn't I tell you to get lost?" Heidi asks, turning her regal chin away from me.

"Nobody drinks alone on her twenty-first birthday." Heidi deserves better.

"Guys" I call. "We're making a toast." I snap my fingers in the air. "Silas, come here."

Pete pushes a full glass toward Heidi and then pours a bunch of smaller portions for the rest of our crew. I pass them out, and Heidi watches with a mixture of embarrassment and curiosity.

"Ready, boys?" I lift my glass. "As Charles Dickens once said…" There are a few good-natured groans, which I ignore. "He said, 'Fan the sinking flames of hilarity with friendship, and pass the rosy wine.' We all know that Heidi gets high marks for friendship as well as hilarity…"

A shy smile creeps across her face, and she shakes her head.

"I predict that Heidi's next year will be full of new challenges, new victories, and a few glasses of bubbly, rosy wine." I raise my glass higher. "Here's to Heidi."

"Hear, hear!" O'Doul echoes, raising his own glass. "To Hot Pepper."

"To Hot Pepper!" the whole bar shouts.

"Thank you," she says, her face pink. I watch her take a very ladylike sip.

One by one, my teammates wish her a happy birthday, and she looks pleased by their attentions. I try not to notice how infectious her laugh is when Silas tells her a joke. Or the way her tits bounce.

Giving myself a mental slap, I look away. I really don't know what to do with my attraction to Heidi. It's not good for either of us. If I could just shut it off, I would.

Instead, I sit on the barstool beside her to welcome her twenty-second year on the planet. We drink our champagne slowly, and I apologize again for chasing that dude away from her. "That was a dick move."

"And hypocritical," she adds. "But thank you. We should go home. We both have open practice tomorrow."

"Oh yeah? You working with Georgia on publicity?" Open practice is when the public is allowed to come and watch. It's kind of a circus.

"Not exactly," she says, sliding off her barstool. "Maintenance."

"What does that entail?"

"I don't even know."

I hand Pete my credit card, and we have to wait a couple of minutes while he closes out my tab. "Sure hope next week is easier than this one." That's the thing about Heidi—I don't feel like I have to be this perfect guy for her. She already knows I'm a moody, superstitious asshole. And she still puts up with me sometimes.

"You definitely had a rough week," she agrees. "But it's going to be okay, even if the strawberry jam isn't really getting the job done right now."

"Don't mess with my sandwich," I warn, just in case she's got some big ideas for how to fix me. Everyone else seems to.

"I would never." Heidi gives me frown. "How'd that get to be your pregame ritual, though? I guess it's more sanitary than always wearing the same pair of ancient socks, like some guys."

"The sandwich? A high school friend made it for me before my last game at home." It was my high school girlfriend, actually. But I never talk about her. "We won that game five to nothing against our rivals. And the next day I got a call from the Harkness coach, inviting me to play for him."

She whistles. "Nice timing."

"Yeah. I've been eating that sandwich ever since."

"Well then, let's see..." She tucks her bag onto her shoulder as Pete hands me the slip to sign. "I'm not very superstitious myself. But sometimes you need a little mysticism in your life. Maybe you could jumpstart the magic. What if you call up the old friend and ask him to FedEx you another sandwich?"

I can't, because she's dead. "That's not gonna work. I'll just have to bring back the magic some other way. Here you go, Pete." I hand back the check and wish him goodnight.

"Better luck on the road, kid," Pete says. "I'll be watching."

"Thanks. I'll try not to let you down."

[15]

HEIDI

JASON OFFERS to get us a cab, but I want to walk back to the Million Dollar Dorm. It was raining earlier, and now the nighttime sidewalks look freshly washed, and the air is misty. As we walk down Front Street, I hear the low honk of a boat on the river.

The champagne has made me feel pleasantly buzzy. And—if I'm being honest—the eloquent toast Jason made in honor of my birthday didn't hurt, either. I'm still annoyed with him that he's friend-zoned me. And that he treats me as if I'm his kid sister he has to protect from Stranger Danger.

My crush on him knows no bounds. But sometimes I feel sure it goes both ways. He drools like a Doberman when I walk around his apartment in my sleep shorts and the see-through tank that I keep laundering so I can wear it every night.

And when he'd said those nice things about me tonight, I'm pretty sure he meant them.

"Feliz cumpleaños, as my father would say." Jason touches my hand lightly. "Happy birthday."

"Thanks. Do you speak Spanish?"

"Barely," he says with a wince. "I did when I was little. But we lived in Canada and then Minnesota. The other kids in preschool didn't speak Español. So I started always answering Papa in English. Kinda regret it now. What do you want for your birthday?" he asks suddenly.

We pass a couple who are holding hands and laughing, and I feel a twinge of jealousy. "Nothing you can wrap in a box. And we've been over this. You know exactly what I want from you." To make my point, I reach over and give him a little pat on the bottom.

"Stop that," he growls.

"Oh, please," I complain. "The way you look at me is illegal in seven states. You'll look, but you won't touch?"

"That's right," he says primly.

"Why?"

"I'm a gentleman."

I stop walking. "You are *not* a gentleman. Gentlemen don't ogle."

"Everybody ogles. I'm just honest enough not to be subtle about it."

"Honesty, huh? That's what you're going with?"

He grins.

When I step into his personal space, that grin falls right off. "What else are you honest enough to admit?" I ask him. I'm wearing heels, which means we're eye to eye. Okay—not quite. We're eye to mouth. But it's a nice mouth. "If I weren't Tobias Pepper's daughter, and if there were no stupid picture of us that everyone's already forgotten, what would we be doing right now?"

"Nothing," he says.

"You're a liar."

He tilts his head back and laughs. "Sometimes. Come on."

He hooks his arm in mine and steers me down the sidewalk again. "Look—you don't want my grumpy ass."

"You're wrong."

"In the first place, there aren't any roundtrip tickets on the Castro train. No refills. No second helpings. No—"

"I get it! Jesus." Our arms are still linked, and I wish the walk home were even longer. Arguing with Jason is more fun than it ought to be. "It's awfully sexist of you to assume that I want to trap you into a relationship. Women are capable of wanting a hookup, too."

"Sure they are," he says. "But the women I hook up with aren't spending the next night on my sofa bed. That is not enough of a post-bang distance. Even the most cynical girl would want another ride. It's just the nature of the beast."

"Oh my *God!*" My shout of laughter echoes against the empty sidewalk. "The ego on you! No wonder you need such a big apartment. Your head wouldn't fit inside a smaller place."

Jason just shrugs and gives me another maddening smile.

"You know, it could be a front," I insist. "Maybe you won't take me to bed because it would be a letdown."

He snorts. "I see what you're trying to do here. But it won't work."

"I understand that you have a reputation to uphold. You can't have the intern walking around with the knowledge that you can't really deliver the goods. You'd have to kill me to keep me silent. And where could you hide the body?"

"You are—" He unhooks his arm from mine, but then reaches around behind me and hugs me against his side as we walk. "—such a pain in the rear."

"But I'm *your* pain in the rear," I tease. "And I'm sending your nephew a birthday present. I don't know what you'd even do without me."

"Eat Doritos," he grumbles. "And walk around in my underwear again."

"Feel free to do that anyway." I tuck my head under his chin and he sighs.

"You didn't say what you're doing for your birthday. Silas and I could take you out for dinner."

"And then a threesome?" I ask just to rib him.

He snorts, and drops his arm. *Hello friend-zone. I'm back!* We're walking side by side again, and the apartment building is in view.

"Actually, I have birthday dinner plans," I admit. "A nice boy has offered to take me out after work."

"A nice boy?" Jason asks.

"My ex-boyfriend, if you must know."

"The one who's terrible in bed?" he asks.

"No comment. But I'm never drinking tequila again."

Jason snickers as we step onto the red carpet that covers the entryway on Water Street. The late-night doorman opens the door.

We head for the elevator together. He doesn't have to hold me up, and I don't say anything embarrassing this time.

Inside the apartment, it's quiet and dark. I go right over to the sofa bed and begin the work of setting it up for the night.

"Need help?" Jason asks. He is a gentleman, damn it. But only when I don't want him to be.

"No, sir," I grumble.

"Happy birthday," he whispers. "You deserve a great year. I meant everything I said tonight when I made that toast."

"I know you did. That's why you're so irritating."

He chuckles as he disappears into his room.

Saturday morning I turn in a written report to Rebecca, detailing my experiences on every job so far. The apartment is totally quiet, since Jason and Silas are at the practice facility watching tape.

My phone beeps with continuous birthday wishes from my friends and family. I'll admit that it's nice to be remembered on my birthday. Although my father's message says, *Happy birthday, baby girl!* Baby girl, really? *Your mother sent you a gift. Why don't you swing by tomorrow and pick it up? I know you have a dinner date tonight.*

How does he know that? Eric must have called the condo, thinking he'd find me there.

Note that my father's message does *not* say: *Swing by and sign off on your inheritance.* Today is the day when I'm eligible for the big disbursement, if Daddy approves it. The money that Grandpa set aside for me is just going to sit there until my father decides I'm adult enough to handle it.

It's not like I deserve that money. I didn't earn it myself. But the fact that he's keeping it out of my hands just for spite? Infuriating.

My reply to him is terse. *Thank you, Daddy.* I don't want to speak to that man, so I'm not calling him back. And I will not beg him to do the right thing.

Mama gets a phone call, though. My parents live apart for much of the year. When Daddy got the commissioner's job, he bought a condo in New York and stays here most of the time. My mother doesn't seem to mind, so long as she has the country club to keep her company.

"Hi, honey," my mother greets me. "I hope you're having a lovely spa treatment on your birthday."

"Oh, I am," I assure her. And it's almost true. In the other room, I already have the hot water running into Jason's kickass tub. I'm going to take the world's longest bubble bath.

"Did you open my present?"

"Not yet! But I will. Can't wait." Mama loves wildly impractical gifts. The old Heidi wouldn't have minded, but the new Heidi would just as soon have some birthday cash.

"You take care of yourself," she tells me. "Get a deep-cleansing facial. Keep that New York smog out of your pores."

"Absolutely." Mama is easier to handle if you just agree with her all the time.

We chat for a few minutes, but I don't tell her that I'm not staying in Daddy's condo, and she doesn't seem to know. My father probably assumes that my departure is like a temper tantrum—if he ignores me, it will blow over.

"Love you lots," we tell each other before signing off. Then I run into Jason's luxury bathroom, shed my clothes, and slip into the steaming water. His tub is the kind that's separate from the glassed-in shower stall and sized for two people.

I'm couch surfing at the equivalent of a luxury hotel. This bath is my birthday gift to myself. I should probably feel guiltier for staying here. But they're heading out on another road trip tomorrow, and they won't give me another thought.

After a good soak, I straighten my hair the way Eric likes it. That takes forever, because my hair is a lot like me—it wants to take a walk on the wild side. But since Eric is going to treat his *ex*-girlfriend—the one who dumped him and moved away—to a dinner she can't afford, I'll show up with hair that's straight and tame.

I carefully pack my favorite little black dress and heels in my bag and then put on jeans and a regulation Bruisers sweat-shirt and jacket. Working in a different department every week means I have more costume changes than a showgirl in Vegas.

Today I'm part of the ice-maintenance team. But since this is a practice day and not a game, I'm *half* of the ice-maintenance crew. And when I show up at the rink, it's clear to me that the guy in charge of the practice-facility ice is pretty happy to have a minion for the day.

"Here's the ice drill," he says, smiling at me from underneath a walrus-style mustache. "You know how to use it?"

"Of course," I say, because a girl has her pride. I can already tell that he's going to make me do all the work while he sits around eating some of the donuts they've brought in for the fans. But I won't play stupid just because he's lazy.

"Cleats are over there," he says, pointing lazily at a table full of supplies.

I pull on a pair of ice claws over my boots—they're metal spikes that will keep me from slipping on the rink. Cleats are for losers, but I'd rather wear them than face plant in front of the team and the crowd.

My hair is perfect, too. Can't mess with that.

Walrus Mustache doesn't even get up to see how I'm doing as I walk out onto the ice with the drill. He's probably on donut number three as I kneel down in the goal crease and drill into the fresh sheet of ice where the net's anchors will rest.

"Hot Pepper!" Silas exclaims from the patch of ice where he's stretching his hamstrings. "What are you doing?"

"What does it look like I'm doing? Getting my nails done, obvs."

A bunch of the men roar, like I've said something funny. Whatever. When I have four perfectly placed holes, I set the drill aside and fetch the net from the edge of the rink.

The gathering crowd is watching me as carefully as if I were performing surgery in front of them. Honestly I don't even understand why people are spending a perfectly good Saturday afternoon watching our boys run drills. I've been dragged to hockey practices since before I could walk.

Maybe it's the free donuts.

I slide the net into position, which is a little cumbersome. Silas skates up to help me, and I let him because he's a goalie and he's probably set up nets his whole life. "Ice crew, huh?" he asks, dropping the pin into the hole I've made.

"Yeah. Could be worse, I guess."

"True," he says. "Better than cleaning more toilets."

Knowing my dad, I'm not sure that's off the table. "Have a good practice," I tell him.

"Thanks, Hot Pepper."

The other goalie—Beacon—helps me with the other side. And then practice begins. I think about having a donut and then think better of the idea. And then I wait. And wait.

Holy cow, practices are long.

"Kinda rough out there," Walrus Mustache says at one point. "Better get a shovel." He takes another sip of his coffee and just waits.

So I get a rink shovel—that four-foot mini plow they use to clean up the surface—and patiently tidy up the edges between drills. Or I try to. Jason Castro is leaning over the wall chatting with Bayer, who's on the bench. "Is it worse today?" he asks.

"Pretty bad," Bayer says with a grimace. "Trainer's gonna send me for another MRI."

"Shit," Jason says under his breath.

"Excuse me," I say, clearing my throat. "Can you be a good, concerned friend from a slightly different location?" I have a job to do here.

Jason does a double-take. "What are you doing, Heidi?"

"Obviously, I'm just here to admire the view," I say through a clenched jaw. Seriously—why do the players keep asking me that?

A beat goes by, and then Jason moves out of my way. "Sorry."

"Thank you."

"Your hair looks different," he says as I pass by.

"It's supposed to."

I should have eaten a donut, because practice lasts a long time, and Walrus Mustache keeps me busy doing his job.

At some point I scan the crowd and pick out a handsome

man in a suit, sitting alone in the top row of the bleachers. It's Eric. He's waiting for me, and Eric isn't a big fan of waiting.

"Are we almost done here?" I ask Walrus.

"Nearly," he says. "After you do the resurfacing, you can go." He tosses something toward me.

Startled, I catch it with only a tiny fumble. It's a single key. And the key fob reads ZAMBONI.

No. Really?

"Really?" I demand. "I haven't driven a Zamboni since high school." And that time it was just joyriding on a dare. My father grounded me afterward.

"Like riding a bike," he says. "Let's have a refresher."

He puts the machine into position. Then, during the last minutes of practice, he goes over the controls. "These here are your hydraulic levers for dropping the conditioner and raising the dump tank. You got your blade adjustment, which determines how much ice you're takin' off. Press down here for the snow brake—better hit that puppy once or twice during each pass..."

Good. Lord. I'm nodding like a bobblehead as he tells me all the things I have to do. Then the coach blows the whistle three times, and I know it's show time.

"Gotta move the nets first," says Walrus.

Right.

I trudge back out on the ice and remove the first net. But the second one is a problem, because there's a group of hockey players standing around it. O'Doul is basically using the thing as his pulpit as he sermonizes to Jason. "I think maybe it's a breathing thing," he says. "Like, you're not tightening your diaphragm when you release the puck."

"No! It's his shoulder position," Trevi argues. "He needs to shift his stance to accommodate the change of angle."

"I think O'Doul is onto something with the breathing," Beringer chimes in. "You gotta breathe through your eyelids."

And now I've had enough. "Don't *listen* to this drivel," I say to Jason. "That eyelids thing is a joke from *Bull Durham*."

"But it worked!" Beringer squawks.

"The only thing working right now is me," I snap, reaching down to remove the first net pin. When I stand up again, I brandish it at Jason. "He's the most over-coached forward in the league this week. Y'all just stand around yapping, which won't help. It's all muscle memory, for Pete's sake! This man needs you to snap five thousand passes his way, so his body can figure it out. He doesn't need your advice."

It's suddenly very quiet in the rink. I forgot that there were fans here to watch today. Whoops.

"Anyway," I say with my voice lowered. "I straightened my hair and my date is waiting, so if you could kindly move your padded bottoms off the rink, I can resurface."

"Muscle memory," O'Doul says slowly.

"I could send you some passes," Trevi offers. "We could all take turns."

They're all thinking deep thoughts about this, so I have to physically move O'Doul off the net to dislodge it from the rink. "Y'all wait over there," I say, pointing at the first row of bleachers. "Please and thank you. Now, I have a Zamboni to drive, so excuse me."

I'm halfway back across the rink when I realize my mistake.

"Hot Pepper is gonna drive the Zamboni?" Bayer asks. "I gotta see this. Anyone want to make a pool on the time?"

"I'm in!" Jason replies.

Well, shoot. If I hadn't mentioned the darned resurfacing, I might have done this without spectators.

But now it's a *thing*. The Zamboni pool is a rink game where people bet on how long it will take to clear the ice, and the closest guesser wins.

"Twenty-two minutes," Beringer says, starting the bidding.

Everybody hoots, because twenty-two is a really long resurfacing time. "Who's got a pen and paper?" someone else calls out.

"I'll take the bets," offers Jimbo, the young guy who works in operations. "Got some paper right here. One for you, one for you… Here's a pen, Castro."

"Better make this a good run," Walrus says as I climb up on the machine. "Seems you got an audience. Don't crash it, for fuck's sake."

A frisson of nerves runs up my spine as I put my hands on the wheel.

"Place your bets, boys! Who's timing this?"

Across the length of the ice, I see Jason holding a pen. He tilts his head to the side, as if considering his bet. Then he scribbles something onto the paper and hands it to Jimbo.

I ease the big machine onto the ice and get my bearings. While I may never have done this job before, I've *watched* a million resurfacings. They always do the edges first. But that's a bad strategy for me. I'll save the walls for last, when I've already figured out the turning radius.

These are my thoughts as I swing the machine into the first turn. I take it a little too far and have to overcorrect. There are hoots from the bleachers as I come out of the fishtail, and a fine sweat breaks out on my neck. I remember to pump the snow brake and check the surface behind me.

It's smooth as glass. And if Walrus can do this, how hard could it be?

Okay. I got this. Leaning forward in my seat, I set about discovering how much speed I can pick up on the straightaways and still have plenty of time to take it easy on the turns. I'll finish the job faster than the earliest bet in the pool. That'll show 'em.

Turn after turn, I lay down a fresh sheet of ice. The hoots grow louder as I near the ending. The last loop takes all my concentration, since I have to get close to the boards without mangling them. I'm vaguely aware of shouting and whistles as I make my final pass by the players.

When I finally pull the Zamboni through the open doors at the rink's far end, my arms ache from clutching the wheel more tightly than necessary.

"Official time is fourteen-thirty-seven!" someone shouts from the peanut gallery.

Whoever bet twenty-two minutes can bite me.

In the ladies' room, I do a quick change into my dress and heels. I nearly dislocate my shoulder trying to get the zipper fastened, but somehow I manage. Then I shove my work clothes into a bag and leave them in a corner of the maintenance room until tomorrow.

When I finally walk into the public end of the rink, I'm properly dressed for dinner. Eric is smiling at me from a seat in the bleachers. As he stands to come down and meet me, Jimbo appears and pats me on the shoulder. "Nice work with the Zamboni!" he crows. "You showed them."

"Did you bet?" I ask him.

His face turns sheepish. "Yeah. Didn't win, though. I bet twenty minutes."

"Who won?" I ask.

"Drake." Jimbo rolls his eyes. "Rookie luck. He picked sixteen minutes."

"Oh." The disappointment I feel is swift and brutal. It should have been Jason who won. He should have been the one who knew I could drive that thing when everyone else thought I'd fail.

Where do I get these ideas? And why do I even care? My gaze flickers toward Jason, who's already out on the freshly resurfaced ice with two other players. A woman shouldn't try to impress a guy who doesn't care.

He's *never* going to care. He said so already.

"Heidi! You look amazing."

And here's Eric, looking suave in a navy suit and perfectly boring striped tie. A lifetime of good manners allows me to smile and greet him without revealing that I feel unaccountably heartsick.

My ex wishes me a happy birthday and gives me a chaste kiss on the forehead. And that's fine. It's not like I want my ex to push me against the wall and force his tongue into my mouth.

Then again, if he'd ever pushed me against the wall and forced his tongue into my mouth, we might not have broken up in the first place.

Eric takes my arm with the same care that a nice boy takes with his grandma in church, and we take our first steps toward the door.

"Hot Pepper."

My body practically jerks to a stop at the sound of Jason's voice. "Yes?"

Jason leans on his stick and looks Eric and me up and down. His expression is grumpy. Maybe he's annoyed that I waded in earlier to tell his teammates to stop yawping at him. "Nice work on the Zamboni," he says finally. "And, uh, happy birthday."

"Thanks."

There's one more awkward beat before he turns around and skates back to his pals. They're doing a shooting drill, sending passes to Jason. So maybe he took my advice, after all?

Not my problem. My goal for tonight is not to think about Jason. Not even once.

Not all goals succeed.

"Table for two," Eric tells the host at the Peter Luger Steakhouse. "The reservation is under Tobias Pepper."

"Right this way, sir."

Following the host, I hiss over my shoulder, "It's under my dad's name?"

"Sure," Eric says easily. "I asked him for a little help. It's not easy getting a Saturday-night reservation at Peter Luger."

My temper flares—privately, of course. The thing is, when Eric asked where I wanted to go out for my birthday, I'd said, "Somewhere sleek and weird. Asian fusion, maybe? Brooklyn is full of new restaurants. Or I could come into Manhattan."

But here we are at a restaurant that's been a favorite of stodgy men since 1887. My father has brought me here a dozen times, at least. The steak is phenomenal, but the ambiance isn't. It's done up in a style I'd call Old Boy Network, with dark paneling and geezer-style chandeliers.

Our steaks will arrive on a platter with a plastic cow shoved into the meat to let us know how it's cooked. A red cow for rare or a blue for medium. So elegant.

I'm obviously a horrible person for thinking these thoughts. A nice girl would donate her birthday gifts to a worthy cause. Or at least say no to a dinner that makes her a little uncomfortable.

Then again, I'm not a nice girl. Why does everyone insist on thinking I am?

We're seated, and Eric gives me the better seat against the wall. He's a gentleman in so many ways. I sneak looks at his boyish face over the edge of my menu. He's objectively handsome. And he *is* a hockey player—totally my type. But I don't feel any zing.

Every zing and flutter I feel these days comes from one particular struggling right-winger on Brooklyn's greatest sports team.

"I'm told we're supposed to get the tomato and onion salad to start," Eric says, lifting cool eyes to mine.

"Great idea!" I hold his gaze and smile, willing my hormones to flash and pop.

Nothing.

"You look amazing tonight," Eric says.

"You're not so bad yourself," I say and then inwardly cringe. He's a good man. He'll make some girl very happy. Am I selfish to want more than Eric can make me feel?

This is way too much thinking to do on my birthday.

We order the salad and the steak for two, and side dishes as well. "What a feast," I say, trying to be a gracious date as the wine is poured and the appetizers served.

"It's really good to see you." He chuckles. "The Zamboni, though? I thought you had an office job."

"I did. But Daddy is in a snit. He's trying to force me to go back to school."

"He's worried about you," Eric says. "You moved out, and he hasn't seen you. I'm supposed to report back on your condition."

"Oh, Jesus." Eric's eyes widen at the curse. "I'm just fine, as you can see for yourself. And the jobs I'm doing at the rink aren't so bad."

Eric grins. "You're like their mascot. You actually know some of the team?"

Not biblically. "A little. Sure." Eric obviously hasn't seen that awful blog photo of Jason picking me up off the sidewalk. Small mercies.

"Why do they call you Hot Pepper?"

"It's just a nickname. I mean—it's catchier than Bell Pepper."

Eric chuckles.

But—wait. "Actually, that has a nice ring to it. Sorry, one second." It's horribly rude to use your phone at the dinner table, but I pull mine out and tap *Belle Pepper's Delivery Service* into my notes. Then I put it away again. "I need a name for my side hustle."

"You're hilarious," Eric says with a smile.

"That's the general consensus." I wonder what it would even feel like to be taken seriously. But enough about me. A good Southern girl knows how to keep the conversation balanced. "How was the interview at Goldman Sachs?"

"Brilliant," Eric crows. "I think I'm getting in. They'll let me know in two weeks when they finalize the incoming trainee class."

"Wow." I wonder what that kind of confidence feels like.

And Eric in New York? I don't know what to do with that idea.

Our steak—when it arrives—is delicious. I enjoy every bite and feel less bad about the world. The tasty Cabernet Sauvignon Eric ordered doesn't hurt, either. "Your dad said that 2013 was a good year for California wines, and I'd have to say I agree," he tells me.

I'm in a good enough mood to let another mention of Daddy go by without comment. And it's not too hard to fall back into a rhythm with Eric. So long as I ask about his hockey teammates, we don't run out of conversation.

"You must miss your sorority sisters," Eric says at one point.

"I don't. Not really." College just wasn't as fun as I'd hoped it would be. I was always trying to figure out how I fit in with the intellectual crusaders at Bryn Mawr. Even their parties were nerdy. The theme of the spring formal was "Kafkaesque."

What's a girl supposed to do with that?

"Why is the job better than school, though? I mean—driving the Zamboni looked fun, but..." Eric's question peters out, because he really doesn't understand me.

"It's *real* work. I love the Bruisers organization. I want them to succeed. They're underdogs. Last spring everybody was betting against them." The way my daddy does with me.

He smiles at me like I'm a cute little kitten.

"And the Zamboni *was* fun. I'll be better at it the next time. The steering is like a 70s Cadillac. Too much oversteer. It's a smooth ride, though."

He refills my wineglass as the dishes are cleared. "The players were timing you. Did you see who won?"

"Yep. Drake, the rookie. That's just beginner's luck, right? The rest of them picked times that were too long."

"Not all of them." Eric chuckles. "Somebody went over."

"Over?"

"Yeah—they were playing it like on the *Price Is Right*—closest to the time without going over. Somebody had fourteen minutes and didn't win the pool."

My heart skips a beat. "Did you see who?"

"One of the forwards. Not Trevi." He shrugs. "I think it was that Spanish guy. Castro?"

"He's not Spanish," I say without thinking. "His dad is half Brazilian and half Cuban American." Okay, that's too much information. Aren't I the perfect little fan girl?

"Okay?" Eric just blinks at me. "Mighta been him."

"I'm just going to powder my nose before dessert," I say brightly. "Back in a jif!"

Eric stands up when I do, because he's been taught how to treat a woman right.

As long as she has her clothes on.

[16]

JASON

TREVI, O'Doul, and I stay after practice. The two of them skate up and down the rink, sending me about a thousand passes, which I return as fast as possible. When we run out of pucks, we collect them all and start the whole thing over again.

"You know," O'Doul starts. "I think you—"

I hold up a hand. "Let's not talk about my failings for one whole afternoon. I just want to work out and feel my way through it."

Maybe Hot Pepper was only blowing off steam when she said that everyone should shut up and wait for muscle memory to work its magic on me. Or maybe she's some kind of fucking oracle, because if one more person tries to fix me, I won't be responsible for my actions.

"Okay." O'Doul suddenly shuts his trap and gets ready for another pass. And then another dozen. When I wear him out, Trevi steps in to play.

By the time we're done, I'm exhausted and starving. "You guys are the best. Let's shower and get some food. My treat."

But the two of them go off to spend the evening with their womenfolk, so I end up treating Silas to takeout instead.

We're sitting in the living room eating spicy chicken and watching our rivals lose to Tampa. Just like old times. Except I have this niggling feeling I can't shake. Like something's missing.

Or some*one*. Heidi isn't here. She's out on her date. I got a look at that guy who showed up in a suit to take her for dinner. Mr. Straight and Narrow, with his shiny penny loafers and his boring tie.

He's bad in bed, I remind myself. Although it's unclear why I care in the first place.

I shove some more noodles in my mouth and try not to wonder if she's going home with him tonight. Lord knows it's none of my business.

My phone vibrates with a text. From *her*. It's like I conjured her up with my inappropriate speculation.

I just have one question, she writes.

Eight inches, I reply, just to be a tool.

OMG, stop. She adds an eye-roll emoji.

Aren't you out on a date right now? I ask. ***I'll bet charm school frowns on texting another man when you're on a date.***

Charm school can bite me, Heidi replies, and I let out a bark of laughter. ***Just answer my question. What time did you write down for the Zamboni pool***?

Why? Does it matter?

It does to me.

Where are you right now? Are you coming home?

I can't believe I went there.

I'm in the ladies' room at Peter Luger, and I have to get back to my date. What did you bet?

14 minutes. If you coulda just been 27 seconds faster, I wouldn't have lost my 20 bucks to the rookie.

"Who are you texting?" Silas asks from the other end of the

couch. He takes a leg off the coffee table and swings it over to give my thigh a nudge, because only goalies are that flexible. "You're smiling like a goober."

Sorry about the money! I'll make it up to you.

I put the phone down to save myself from asking how she'd like to make it up to me. And because Silas is giving me a smug look. "It's Hot Pepper, right? You always look like a goober when you're thinking about her."

I rest my head back on the sofa's back and close my eyes. "Don't do that."

"Do what? State the obvious? Can you fall for a girl when she's driving a Zamboni? No, wait—I think you fell for her when she was beating me and Bayer at darts."

"News flash. I'm not falling for anybody." I used to think of Silas as an easygoing roommate. I don't anymore.

"You say that, but—" My phone rings in my hand. The phone number of the caller is blocked. Nonetheless I answer it so fast that Silas laughs. What if Heidi needs rescuing from her date? "Hello?"

"Jason." The voice on the other end is slurred by both alcohol and tears. *Fuck*. It's not Heidi, thank God. But it's a call that I dread nonetheless. "Honey. How are you?" the older woman asks.

"I'm well, Jolene. And you?" I hold in my sigh, because I know what's coming.

Her sob is loud and broken. "It's that time of year again. When I feel so blue! It's gonna be bad this time. I just know it."

Fuck.

It *is* that time of year again. I always struggle in the fall, too. Although Jolene is the kind of person who leans into tragedy. The first moment I met her I knew she was trouble. Jolene—my high school girlfriend's mother—is a hundred and two pounds of narcissism with a raging addiction to alcohol on the side.

"Me too, Jolene," I say. I've learned that agreeing with her is the quickest path to freedom.

"It's so hard. So hard to watch the leaves fall again and to know my baby girl won't ever see them again. She loved the fall. We used to go back-to-school shopping together."

I grit my teeth. There's some truth in what she says—Lissa loved every season. She was full of life and adventure. But Jolene had only been interested in her daughter when it suited her. And most everything Lissa bought she earned for herself.

"The high school looks just the same," Jolene says between sniffles. "*Just* the same! Kids with their backpacks..."

Silas is motioning to me from the other end of the couch. He's lifting his hand in imitation of drinking a beer.

I nod, and then reconsider. *Tequila,* I mouth. He gives me a salute and marches into the kitchen. Jolene goes on and on in my ear. "My sweet girl. So nice to everyone."

Tuning her out, I kick my feet onto the coffee table and settle in to remember Lissa the way she really was—an absolute hellion of the highest order. In a good way. When my parents were giving me grief about playing junior hockey instead of going to prep school, it was Lissa who'd said—middle fingers raised—"*Fuck that noise. You do you.*"

She was so strong. A lioness at sixteen. I fell hard.

Five years later, it's still so easy to picture her face. I only keep the one photo in my gym bag. But I can see her so clearly in my mind that I don't need more. She had a wide, laughing smile and bright, mischievous eyes. My wild girl. My Lissa. I loved her with the pure, bright fire of youth. I thought we'd have a hundred years together.

We got two.

"The Juliet to your Romeo!" Jolene wails. "Gone. A real-life tragedy."

It was. And it's one that I re-live through phone calls like this a couple of times a year. She always calls in October or

November. The accident happened over Thanksgiving weekend. Freezing rain. A slippery Minnesota road. I'd been four states away at a hockey tournament that I'd signed onto at the last minute.

"You can't leave me alone with the family on Thanksgiving!" Lissa had shrieked when I told her. "They're the worst on holidays."

It was all true. I shouldn't have left her there to fend for herself. Even so, Lissa didn't need to solve the problem by escaping into the car of a friend who was too high to drive...

Silas puts a bottle of Jose Cuervo onto the coffee table, along with two shot glasses. This happens right around the same time when Jolene steers the conversation to the other purpose for her call.

"My goddamn landlord," she weeps. "A man with no heart at all. I'm a little short this month, and he's threatening me. A lonely old lady. Can you believe the nerve? I'm between jobs right now. He *knows* this."

"How much do you need?" I ask immediately. There's no point in beating around the bush.

"You are such a good boy to offer," she sniffs. And I swear I can hear the distinctive sound of a match lighting her latest cigarette. I'm going to write her a check and she's going to blow it on cigarettes. "I'll lose this apartment if I don't come up with fourteen hundred real quick. Not that I have any groceries in the kitchen."

"Let me have your address," I say, grabbing a magazine off the coffee table and flipping it over.

I look around for a pen. Silas tosses me one with those quick goalie reflexes. *Thanks*, I mouth. When he's not busting my chops, Silas is the best roommate ever.

"Could you send it Western Union?" she asks with a sniffle. "I'm kinda in a bind."

"Why not," I say, eyeing the tequila bottle.

"I want to pick it up at the Walgreens on East Main Street. It's store number 111."

"Okay, sure. I'll do it tomorrow afternoon. I'm traveling in the morning. Better go, Jolene. Good hearing from you," I lie.

"Goodnight, honey. Be well. I'll pray for your safe travel."

We hang up and I toss the phone onto the coffee table and put my head in my hands.

"She's back, huh?" Silas asks, uncapping the tequila. "How much does she want this time?"

"Whatever," I grunt. Hell, if Jolene knew the terms of my new contract, she would have asked me for ten times as much. Luckily, she doesn't follow hockey.

Besides, taking care of Jolene is something I do for Lissa. The only thing I can do for Lissa. It has fuck-all to do with Jolene.

"I think you should tell her to fuck off," Silas says. "But if you won't, let's drink tequila instead." Silas hands me a bottle of water first, because it's important to stay hydrated the night before a game. Then he lines up the shot glasses and pours.

We dunk the first shot in silence.

"Can I ask you something?" he asks eventually.

"Maybe?"

"What would it take to make you serious about a girl again?"

"A frontal lobotomy," I say immediately.

Silas rolls his eyes. "I was being serious."

"Me too," I snort. "Dude, there is really no point. I'm used to being single now. I like it."

"Forever, though?" He leans back and looks at the ceiling.

I glance at my roommate and try to guess what's in his head. Silas is one of the most unreadable people I've ever met. "What's got you asking, anyway?"

He shrugs. "Hockey and dating don't really go together so well. But someday…" He doesn't finish the sentence.

"They don't," I agree. "But so what? You and I can get all the, uh, companionship we need without the commitment. So why do you even let it bother you?"

"One-night stands aren't really my style." He's not lying. Silas hooks up like maybe twice a year. "But I feel like I've been single so long that I don't even know how it's done."

"Every night in the locker room there's somebody who's all pissy over a fight he had with his wife," I point out. "Not sure you're missing out."

"And we may never find out." He sits up and pours us another couple of shots. "Want to kill some zombies?" he asks after he hands mine over.

"Absolutely." I down my second shot and get up to fetch the Xbox controllers. We hunker down and play a few rounds of our new favorite *Call of Duty*. It's getting late, and Heidi still isn't home to kick us off the couch.

Eventually Silas gives up and declares he's heading to bed. "You're going to get some sleep, right?" he asks me.

"Yeah. Soon."

"How about I put away the tequila?"

"How about you leave it here instead?"

"Suit yourself. You're waiting up for Heidi, aren't you?"

"No." But where the hell is she? "I don't think she's coming home at all."

Silas winces, which only means I've done a poor job of concealing that it bothers me. He walks behind the couch and then stops one more time. "Just don't finish the bottle, okay?"

"Right, Mom."

He actually tousles my hair like I'm five and then finally departs, leaving my brooding ass alone.

I help myself to another shot of tequila, just to keep my buzz going. Then I grab Heidi's pillow off the tidy stack of belongings she keeps in the corner. And when I lay my head down on the case, it smells like her. I take a deep breath of her citrus scent and wonder where she is right now.

It's selfish, but I want her here on the other end of the couch, giving me sass and telling me what to do. Silas was right earlier tonight when he said that I have it bad for Little Miss Perky. It's true.

But just because you want something doesn't make it yours. I have a poor record for taking care of beautiful girls who trust me. It's better for everyone if I stick to hookups and bachelorhood.

And she obviously went home with her college boy. So I don't even have to move my drunk ass off this couch.

I must have fallen asleep. Because the next thing I know I'm trying to roll over and my leg is dangling off the couch and my arm is trapped between the cushion and the back of the sofa.

Ow.

I stumble into my bathroom to take a piss and brush my teeth, blinding myself with the bathroom light.

My muscles are tight from practice, and the bed beckons. I drop my clothes a piece at a time as I make my way to the bed. Lifting the covers, I collapse onto the cool sheets.

Except they're not that cool. And as I roll toward the bed's center, I collide with something smooth and warm.

Someone gasps, and it isn't me. "J-Jason?"

"Mmm?" My hand finds soft skin. Bare skin. My fingers splay across the bliss of her silken stomach before I fully understand. "Heidi? You're naked *in my bed?*"

"You were asleep on the couch!" she sputters as I quickly withdraw my hand. "And all my nightgowns are in my bag under the coffee table. In the dark. I didn't want to disturb you."

"Oh, I'm disturbed." I sit up fast and fumble for the lamp. When I switch it on, I'm immediately sorry I did. The sight of sleep-tousled Heidi in my bed is devastating. The sheet is askew so that her breasts are partially revealed. I can only see one rosy nipple, but my mouth waters anyway.

"You're staring at me," she whispers.

"So fix it," I grunt. "Move that sheet."

Heidi's fingers find the edge of the sheet. She looks me dead in the eye. "Yes, *sir*." And then the vixen pulls it down instead of up.

Now all I can see are two full breasts, a sleek tummy that I'd like to measure with my tongue, and a tiny pair of black lace panties. "Jesus Christ."

Heidi puts a hand on her stomach. She stretches her fingers until her pinky finds the edge of the panties, and she lets that little finger slip beneath the elastic.

I finally find the willpower to look away. "What are you doing?"

"Who's asking? You're more naked than I am," she points out.

When I look down, my cock is tenting the sheet that's covering my lap. "I mean, what are you doing in my bed?"

"I told you." She sits up, and I'm powerless again. I turn my head just as her tits bounce from the motion. "My bed was occupied by a snoring right wing."

"Because I thought you went home with *him*." Okay, that comes out a little too forcefully.

Her eyes widen with surprise. "And that bothered you?"

I shrug, because it's already clear to both the naked people in this room that it did. And if that makes me an asshole, I guess that ship has sailed. "You thought about going home with him, right? You're wearing *those*." I point at the incriminating lingerie.

"Maybe I did think about it," she admits. "These are my lucky panties. And he asked me back to his hotel room."

"And you said no? Why?"

"Because he wants me to love him," she whispers. "And I don't, so it wouldn't be fair. If I slept with him, it would only be for birthday sex."

When her rosy lips form those last two words, my disobedient cock gives a throb. I force myself to look at the alarm clock. "It's two in the morning. Your birthday is over."

"Right," she snaps. "Like I said, I didn't come back here to beg you to jump my turnstile. Been there, done that."

"So you're here to torture me instead?" I'm so aggravated right now. Not one thing in my life makes any damned sense.

"No. That's just my consolation prize."

"I'm no *prize*," I grumble. "What you don't understand is that I'm saving us both a lot of hassle."

She rolls her eyes, tosses the sheet aside, and scrambles to her knees. "Now, you *listen up*." I can't, because her fearlessness turns me on like nobody's business. "If you're so smart and I'm so stupid, maybe you could answer a couple of questions for me."

"What's that?"

"Why was it so easy for me to turn him down? And yet, when you look at me like that—like you can't decide if you should kiss me or kill me—it makes me really wet?"

I let out a loud, unhappy groan. "Why did you have to *say* that?"

"Because you pretend you don't care! But you do. Here you are asking about my choice in lingerie, which clearly flips your light switch—" She waves a hand at my aching dick. "—but I'm supposed to be content with being the only woman in Brooklyn who's off limits."

Fuck me. The woman is listing all my flaws and inconsistencies, and every one of them is true.

"Why not me?" Her eyes flash as she continues her sermon. "If half of what they write about you is true, you've stamped the passports of—"

Check, please. It's fucking inevitable that I put my trembling hands on her soft body and push her down on the bed. The moment my palms meet warm skin, she stops ranting. *Finally.* But I'm not one to take chances, so I fit my mouth over hers just to shut her up. With my tongue.

The moment my mouth melds with hers, Heidi moans. She grabs me by the hair and pulls me closer.

Fuck me, but I love it. Leaning into her soft curves, I taste her more deeply. Her tongue tangles with mine, and she moans again.

That sound you just heard was the door slamming shut on my self-control. If Heidi wants to make bad choices, I'm done being the one to stop her. Women never listen to me, anyway. Not when it counts.

But she's paying attention right now as I roughly claim her mouth, my whiskers abrading her soft skin.

"Is this what you want?" I mumble against her tongue.

In answer, she arches her back, asking for more contact.

I deepen the kiss, plundering her mouth, kiss after kiss. "You didn't answer," I point out, because I'm still in a mood. "You want my mouth? How about my hands?" I run a palm down her curvy body.

She only moans.

"I can't hear you. You want more?"

"*Yes,*" she bites out. "And if you're just teasing me right now I'll—"

She doesn't finish that sentence because I push my hand inside her little tiny panties. Her legs part on a gasp. Holy fuck. My fingers find so much slickness and heat that I groan with impatience. "You're bare," I croak as my fingertips slide against soft perfection. And the truth hits home. "You shaved for him."

"He likes that," she gasps, lifting her hips to meet me.

"Why? Does he put his mouth on you?" The image of another man's face between her legs makes me feel a little more insane than I already feel. I stroke her sweetly.

Her forehead wrinkles as she shakes her head and shifts her hips.

"No? Then he's a *fool*." I give the panties a tug, but they don't give way. Maybe that only works in porn. "Lose the panties, I want a taste."

Big blue eyes measure me as she kicks them off.

"Good girl," I say. Heidi's pink lips part in surprise. And it dawns on me that being a good girl might be a habit that dies hard. This gives me even more ideas. "Take the sheet off me."

She blinks, and then her gaze drops to my waist where the sheet is still covering my cock, save the dot of wetness where I'm leaking against the fabric.

"I'm waiting."

"Hold your horses," she whispers crossly. But then she takes the edge of the sheet and yanks it down, exposing my erection. She licks her lips and reaches out a hand to touch me.

And I catch it midair. "Not yet," I say, having no idea why. All I know is that I have to keep the upper hand. "First things first. There are condoms in that drawer." I point to the nightstand on her side of the bed. "Take out as many as you think we'll need. If you don't want to go there, I guess that would be none. It's your call."

Our eyes lock, and I wait, wondering if she'll make the smart choice and shut me down. I want her so badly. But I'm sure I'll regret it later.

I exhale as she turns toward the drawer. Because the bed is huge, she has to crawl forward on her hands and knees to reach it.

I die quietly at the view while she reaches into the drawer.

My blood swims with desire as I picture myself bending her over the edge of the bed and—

Heidi turns around, holding a strip of no fewer than ten condoms. She tosses them to me with narrowed eyes.

A bark of laughter pierces through my lust. "Who's a funny girl?"

"You're so fond of giving me that speech about how there are only one-way tickets on the Castro train. Better make it count."

"Yes, ma'am."

What have I gotten myself into?

[17]

HEIDI

THE WAY he's looking at me right now? *Smoldering.*

My wish list has always been lengthy. I've wanted ponies and gold medals and trips to Paris. But I don't remember ever wanting anything as badly as I want Jason Castro right now. Nobody has ever made my pulse feel thready and my hands sweat.

This time I won't blow it. This time I'm not drunk, although I feel a little woozy anyway as I lean back against the headboard. I can hardly believe all the sass that's fallen from my mouth tonight, or my little acts of bravery. And I need to keep up the fearless-girl routine, so he won't see how shaky I feel right now.

But oh, the view! I've seen Jason shirtless before. I've admired those strong pecs and those lickable abs. But the way he's propped so casually against the pillows, buck naked, his penis hard and ready... *Gulp.*

Keep it together, Pepper.

"Come here." He crooks a finger.

Feeling a little shy, I put one foot on the floor, so I can walk around the bed.

"No," he says sharply. "Crawl to me."

Oh my. In for a penny, though, in for a pound. I get onto my hands and knees. Goosebumps rise on my skin, because I can feel how closely he's watching me. And—why not—I arch my back a little. "Like this?" I ask sweetly. Moving forward a little, my boobs jiggle. "Am I doing it right?" I exaggerate my Nashville accent a little, so that it's more Scarlett O'Hara than Reese Witherspoon.

"Fuck," Jason whispers as I approach. "I'd say you're doing fine. Climb into my lap."

My heart shimmies as I slide a leg over his thighs and climb on. I have to spread my knees, and that feels extra dirty, because his concentration is laser-focused. And even as I settle my bare pussy onto his lap, he doesn't reach for me.

He just stares. His gaze burns me up as it makes a slow scan of my face, my tits, and then my lower extremities.

"What?" I whisper. "You're going to give me a complex."

He grins. "I'm just admiring the view."

"But that's—" I gasp as he lifts his knees suddenly, causing me to pitch forward. My hands land on his shoulders and I find myself mere inches from his face. We're nose to nose. And the view into those big brown eyes has never been better.

"Impolite?" he guesses. "Hot Pepper, there is nothing polite about the way I feel right now.

"I was going to say *unnerving*," I whisper.

"Don't lose your nerve now," he whispers back. "It's just getting good."

It is, indeed. And it gets even better as he removes one of my hands from his shoulder and curls it around his thick erection. He's so heavy in my hand, and so *hot*. Like he's burning up for me. I love it. I swipe my thumb across the rosy head of him.

He bites his lower lip and makes a grunt of approval. "Give me that mouth. Right now."

It's easy to obey a command like that. I lean forward and find his lips with my softer ones.

Jason kisses the way he plays hockey. The minute our mouths align, he's all attack and control. It's *sublime.* I feel breathless as he reaches behind my head and gathers my hair in his hand. He gives it a tug and breaks our kiss.

With a gasp, I tip my head back. And his mouth finds my nipple not a second later. Before I can get my bearings, he gives it a good, hard, suck.

If I only get one night with him, I'd like to remember every second. But my poor brain is swimming in sensation as his tongue finds new ways to light me up. First my breasts and then my neck. I wrap my arms around his head and sift my fingers through his hair. It's silkier than I would have guessed.

Jason lifts his hips, lifting me, too. He lengthens his body on the bed, lying down flat and leaving me sitting on his hips, panting.

He reaches up and runs a hand down my body, his fingertips finishing their journey right on my mound. I hold my breath, and he holds them there, teasing me. I shiver, my nipples like little pebbles. "Come here, you hot thing."

"W-where?" I lean forward a couple of degrees, feeling my body flood with desire.

"Scoot," he says. "Here." And then—impatient with me—he grasps me by the hips and drags me up his body.

I land on his ribcage, then quickly dig my knees into the bed and grab the headboard for support.

"Almost," he says with a knowing smile. "A little further." His fingers splay on my bare ass, and he gives me a slow, dirty squeeze. "Come on now. Let me taste you."

I look down at him, stunned, but also very turned on. Still, I hesitate.

"While I'm young?" he prods. "Besides, who begged me for —" He actually makes air quotes on my bumcheeks. "—filthy, dirty sex?"

"You can't use a drunk girl's words against her!" I squeak. I will never touch tequila again as long as I live.

Jason lifts his head off the pillow, strains forward, then tugs me once again. His eager mouth lands on my lower belly, those hot lips searing my skin and his whiskers refusing to allow his kiss to be a gentle thing. "Give it to me," he murmurs, his voice strained. "I want it so bad."

The scrape of desperation in his voice is what finally breaks down my inhibitions. I inch forward on my knees until his hungry mouth finds my pussy. The sound I make when his lips first brush my clit is a high, keening thing.

His answering moan vibrates through my belly as he gentles his tongue against my body and tastes me in slow, reverent strokes.

Ten seconds in, I'm already a convert. I grip the headboard and hover above him with eager glee. He has a firm grip on my hips, tugging me closer whenever I retreat.

"So sweet," he rasps against my skin between kisses. His naughty tongue is urging me towards climax. Every stroke is a revelation.

My eyes slam shut, and all my muscles lock up tight, preparing for a wave of glory. But it doesn't come. Instead, I find that I've been lifted just out of reach.

"Not yet, baby," he rasps.

"That's just mean." I open my eyes and look down at his heavy-lidded eyes and wild hair. I've made a mess of him. A wonderful mess.

He slaps me on the ass—an actual slap—and then grabs the strip of condoms. "Break one of these off."

I take them with shaky fingers and tear the strip.

"Open it."

I try, but he doesn't like my progress because he drops me onto his body and opens it himself.

The next five seconds are very eventful. Without moving me out of the way, somehow Jason reaches down, rolls on that condom, and then lines me up just right. And I gasp as he jacks his hips up and fills me in one smooth stroke.

My mouth is open on a silent *oh* as I stretch to accommodate him. My head falls to his shoulder and I squeeze my eyes shut as my body hugs him everywhere.

Athletes. Wow.

"Jesus Christ," he groans, his hands on my hips. He rolls us to the side, and everything stops for a second except for my pounding heart. His big brown eyes blink at me once. "You were right."

"I was?" I can't figure out what he means, because I'm too dazzled by this perfect moment. My skin sings everywhere we're touching, which is lots of places.

"You said we'd be really good together."

"Oh." It's true. His strong arm loops under my knee and lifts it high on his hip, spreading me wider. I shiver at the boldness of it. "Well, duh," I say against his lips.

Then he thrusts his hips. *Hard.* And I don't say anything intelligible for quite a while.

[18]

JASON

YOU DON'T MAKE it in professional sports without a lot of willpower. Every big-league player knows how to control his body and how to deny himself.

Every one of them but me, apparently.

Kiss after scorching kiss, thrust after crazy thrust, I'm driving us where we both need to go. I feel wild. And whatever willpower I used to possess floats away on Heidi's desperate moans. I roll again, laying her flat on the bed, spreading her body beneath me.

Lord. I'm fucking an angel. It's not just that she's young and pretty and so tight I may lose my mind. It's the way she watches me with those big, impressionable eyes—like she doesn't want to miss a thing. Like I know all the secrets.

If only.

I'm breaking all my rules right now. Every one of them. But *man* does she make me feel worthy. Her fingers stroke my hair with reverence. Her mouth is sweet and welcoming. And I'm the brute who's helping himself to all these riches.

It's so good to be bad.

I bear down on her until Heidi's kisses get sloppy and her breathing comes quicker. "You're close," I rasp in her ear.

"Yes," she pants. "Yes. *Harder.*"

Jesus. "Not yet, you hot thing." I force myself to slow down, torturing both of us.

She groans and grips my biceps in two hands, straining upward to get more from me. Her pink lips form a perfect "O" as she reaches for her climax. It's so sexy that I might come just from the look on her face.

That's when I pull out.

Heidi looks up at me with unhappy eyes. "Why?" she demands.

"Grab the headboard," I order.

She rolls over slowly, like she's forgotten how her limbs work. She kneels in front of the headboard and takes it in two hands.

"Good girl," I whisper, coming up behind her. In the window's reflection, I see her big eyes watching me. Her chest rises and falls with her rapid breathing. I take her hips in my hands and fill her again.

The tight clench of her body is everything, and I let out another groan. I thought maybe I could last longer if I couldn't see her face. The problem is that I can. The lamp is on. If there's anyone in the office building across the street—not likely on a Saturday night—he's going to get an eyeful.

But I love watching that angelic face as she bites her lip and then tips her head back to rest it on my shoulder. I rock forward in slow, deep strokes. Her silky hair tickles my chest, and its clean scent wafts around me.

It's too much of everything good. I'm yearning for release. I wrap my arms around her, cupping soft breasts in my hands. "Are you ready?" I whisper. "You're going to get it so good."

"Please," she whimpers, and the sound makes my balls

impossibly tight. I take one of her hands off the headboard, guide it down between her legs, and press it against the place of our joining.

Then, digging deep, I pick up the pace, pinning her body to mine, thrusting in measured strokes. I flatten her palm against her pussy and brace it there. "Take it," I pant. "Let me feel you get there."

Heidi makes a desperate noise. My whole body is tight and straining. I actually clench my jaw to hold myself back.

"Oh!" she sobs. And then everything gets impossibly wet and tight and perfect. She tenses around me, and I can't wait any more. I relax onto my haunches, tugging her body onto mine, pinning her onto my cock as I shudder through my climax.

She turns her head to find my mouth with a deep, sloppy kiss. And I'm ready. I dive right in, but wrapping my arms around her destabilizes me, and we tip to the side. I tuck her face against mine as we go over, landing on the bed, luckily, and not rolling onto the floor.

"Oh my God," she gasps, and then falls silent. My arm is still wrapped around her body, so I can feel her pounding heart. "Wow."

"Yeah," I say, all my eloquence burned away by the hottest, most desperate sexual experience I've had with anyone since... *Yeah*. I steer my brain away from that thought.

And it isn't too difficult, because Heidi flops her exhausted body around and kisses me senseless.

Eventually we fall asleep, wrapped up around each other in the center of my bed. For a few hours my slumber is completely dreamless.

"Castro? Are you awake because...*whoa*."

It takes a second for Silas's voice to penetrate my consciousness. I pick up my head and say just one word. "*Out.*"

"Fine," my roommate says. "But there are these things called doors…" He pulls mine shut behind himself.

"Uh-oh," says Heidi from face-down in my pillow.

I glance at her, and while her bare back and my bare ass make it perfectly obvious that we're both very naked, none of her important parts are exposed.

Too sleepy to care about Silas—or about my newly complicated friendship with Heidi—I fall back onto the pillow again. I have to get up and head for the airport, but the bed is warm and when I stroke my palm down Heidi's bare bottom, I don't want to go anywhere at all.

"Airport," Heidi mumbles.

My hand suddenly stills as I try to take that in. "You're traveling with the team this time?"

She lifts her pillow-creased face and blinks at me. "No. I'm not. I meant that *you* need to go to the airport. So get that look of panic off your face."

Oh. I take a deep breath. She isn't wrong. I did panic there for a second. I'm still a little stunned by what we did and how much we both needed it. I'm confused by how much I like her.

That's new for me. My heart is made of stone. Or so I thought.

I'm not the only one who's confused. Heidi sits up, clutching the sheet to her breasts, as if I haven't already seen them or played with those nipples between my lips. "I get the first shower," she demands.

I open my mouth to argue, but nothing comes out. Heidi removes the sheet from the bed, leaving me naked, and wears it into my bathroom.

The door clicks shut, locking me out.

Well. This is already a little awkward. I guess I'll go use

Silas's bathroom. He's going to laugh his ass off, and I won't even blame him.

A half hour later, my bag is packed. I stroll into the kitchen hoping for a cup of coffee. And I find Heidi and Silas eating breakfast together, pretending like nothing happened.

Okay. I guess that works for me. "Any coffee left?"

"I poured it into my mug," Heidi says, spreading butter on a piece of toast. "Just snap your fingers on the team jet and they'll bring you as much as you want."

"But that's airline coffee," I complain.

Silas shrugs. "I'm guessing you need to catch up on your sleep, anyway."

"I don't have the first idea what you're talking about," I say.

Heidi bites her lip, and I don't know if that was the right thing to say or the wrong one. It's a shame that I am on my way out of town, because she and I probably need to talk. Just because I don't do repeats, doesn't mean I won't look her in the eye like a grownup.

She's ignoring me right now, though, handing a fresh piece of toast to Silas and offering to cut him a slice of melon.

"Can I have one?" I ask.

"Sure," she says stiffly.

Silas looks at me over the rim of his coffee mug, and his expression says, *What the hell did you do?*

I shrug.

"Check your email, both of you," Heidi says. "You'll find a link to a form where you can submit your errands and groceries to my new automated database. The deadline is Wednesday at noon. Requests submitted after that will be subject to a rush fee."

"Wow, fancy."

"It's going to help me with the volume." She hands me a plate with a slice of melon on it. And yet she manages not to make eye contact.

"What's your team job this week?" Silas asks.

"Ice crew at the practice facility. There's a tournament for the Adaptive Hockey League."

"Oh, cool," I say, just to make conversation. The adaptive league is pretty neat, though. The Bruisers lend out our ice when we're out of town so that disabled athletes can train.

"It'll keep me off the streets," Heidi says to the bottom of her coffee mug.

An awkward silence follows. I fill it with memories of last night. Heidi clutching me and kissing me like the world is ending. She's standing at the counter with her back to me. But it's like I've developed x-ray vision. I can picture her naked way too easily now.

Hopefully that will fade? I doubt it.

"I just have one thing to say, and then I'll never mention this again," Silas says.

Both Heidi and I turn to him with matching wary expressions.

"Castro, when it's my birthday night next month, you really don't have to go all out like that."

Heidi groans, and I throw a balled-up napkin at him.

"No really." He laughs. "Just get me a nice bottle of scotch."

"I think I hear your jet leaving," Heidi grumbles.

Still laughing, Silas gets out of his chair. He puts his plate and mug into the dishwasher, then stops in front of Heidi. "Be well. And thank you in advance for the errands."

"My pleasure."

He leans forward and pulls her into a quick hug, which she returns.

I have a sudden and very unreasonable urge to yank him off her.

"Cheerio!" Silas says. "Coming, Castro? I'll hold the elevator."

"Yeah, totally." I wait for him to leave the room, then I take a step closer to Heidi. "You good?"

"Absolutely," she says, turning the faucet on.

I shut it off again.

"What did you do that for?" She turns her chin and gives me a grumpy look.

"Hey." I catch her chin in my hand. "I just want to say—" What do I want to say? "—you're amazing."

Her blue eyes dip. "Thanks. You're not so bad yourself. Now go on. There might be traffic."

"Right." I lean forward and give her a peck on the lips. She tastes minty, and I'd rather have another kiss than walk away.

But her blue eyes bore into mine, and she's wondering what the hell I'm doing.

That makes two of us. So I give her cheekbone a single stroke with my thumb, and then leave the kitchen. I grab my phone and my suitcase and head for the door.

"Wait!" Heidi comes trotting out of the kitchen with a little paper bag. "I almost forgot to give this to you."

"What's that?"

"Your sandwich. Now go! Beat Chicago." She presses the bag into my hand and makes a shooing motion.

"Dude, you coming?" Silas calls from the elevator bank.

I'm not, because I'm staring at the bag in my hand. "Peanut butter and..."

"Strawberry jam," she says. "I didn't mess it up, jeez. Go on."

"Thanks." I snap out of it and head for the elevators.

[19]

JASON

FOURTEEN HOURS later I'm sitting on the visitors' bench gulping water as the third period winds down. We're up two to one. The Chicago crowd is starting to thin in the cheap seats.

Our opponents' fans are giving up. It's a beautiful sight.

Even more beautiful was the assist I got during the second period. A quick pass to Drake, who shot a flying saucer into the upstairs corner of the net.

No lie—I celebrated even harder than him. "Baby, I'm back!" I'd said to Silas who'd held the bench door open for me when I'd returned. "Don't know why it's working tonight, but it is." *Finally.* I feel lighter and faster than I have since switching to right wing.

Silas had given me a smirk. "Maybe it was the unexpected night of—"

"Shut it," I'd growled.

But it's clear that my teammates are relieved. They need me back in the saddle, because we're down a veteran player. We had to leave Bayer behind in New York so he could have another knee surgery. I'm on a line tonight with the rookie Drake and with Bryce Campeau, a recent trade from Montreal.

Trevi and his boys look good out there, though. They're running Chicago up and down the ice, looking for another scoring opportunity against our opponent's defense.

In ten minutes we're notching this game into the winner's column. Or I'll die trying.

When coach puts his thumb on my shoulder blade to let me know I'm up next, I vault over the wall without hesitation. I don't even hesitate in finding my new position on the right wall. Somehow it's stopped feeling wrong. Not only that, but passing from a dominant arm that's closer to center ice is finally starting to make sense.

Campeau sends me the puck, and I flick it to Drake without having to cross my body first. And then—as the Chicago defenseman moves to get into Drake's way—a beautiful opening presents itself. Drake sees it, too, and in the next microsecond he returns the puck to me.

In less time than it takes to say "mine, suckers!" I snatch it off the ice and send it sailing toward the goalie's five-hole. Right between his legs.

Boom! The lamp lights for me.

Thank you, Jesus. I pump my stick in the air and give a yell as the stadium DJ blasts "Crazy Train," an upbeat riff meant to keep Chicago's fans from making a mutual suicide pact.

My relief is complete. We set up for the next faceoff, and even though I've been skating all night and every inch of my body is drenched in sweat, I feel light.

Finally. I've proved it. I can still bring the magic. I only need to do it seventy-five more times this season. For the first time in a month, that seems possible.

After the game, the locker room is a happy place. We blast our win song and argue about how we're going to celebrate.

"Ribs," Drake demands.

"Chicago-style pizza," Trevi argues.

"Nah, it's overrated," I complain as I towel off from the shower. "I'm with Drake. Let's eat barbecue."

"Gotta let the night's scorers decide," Beacon says, pulling a shirt on. "Give these boys what they need. Plus, the ribs joint is closer to the hotel, so…"

"Ladies," says a snarky female voice. "Congratulations."

I look over my shoulder and spot Miranda Wager—my least favorite reporter. Funny how I don't hate the sight of her quite so much after a win. "Be right with you," I say, because my ass is bare, and I don't want to be that rude athlete who waves his dick in her face like it's a dare.

"Take your time," she says. "I was just hoping you'd comment on your comeback."

I pull on a pair of underwear and then my trousers. Only then do I turn around and dignify the question. "My comeback?"

"It's been weeks since you had any points."

I consider my response carefully. *A particular awesome, sexy woman made my sandwich this morning…* I smile, just picturing Heidi. But I still need to answer the question. "Obviously I just needed some ice time to figure out how to play right wing. You know the ten-thousand-hour rule? Mastering new skills is a lengthy process."

"I'm aware," Miranda says. "But ten thousand hours? That would take four hundred and seventeen days, if you didn't sleep."

My irritation flares at this handy demonstration of mental math. But I remind myself of what Heidi said—how everyone is hard on Miranda. And even though I don't trust this reporter, I dial down my attitude. "I don't know how many hours it's been.

But just think how unstoppable I'm gonna be after my ten-thousandth hour?"

She actually rolls her eyes as she scribbles on her notebook. "Thank you for that humble quote."

"It's entirely my pleasure." I give her a big, friendly smile. We stare each other down for a second.

She blinks first. "There's a young woman in the hallway looking for you," she says. "Have a nice night." Then, thankfully, she turns away to sink her reporter's talons into Beacon.

Good riddance.

I finish dressing quickly. A young woman waiting for me? I don't know who that could be. As I tuck in my shirt, my traitorous subconscious leaps right to the place it shouldn't. *What if somehow it's Heidi in the hallway? Yay!*

Thanks, brain. Or—let's be honest—my brain isn't the only body part that's kept Heidi in mind all day. I can't stop hearing her voice in my head. Specifically, her voice moaning, *yes, yes, harder.*

Oh, the irony. I'd told Heidi we couldn't sleep together because she'd only want more. And I'm the one who's still hot and bothered, playing last night on replay. She's gotten under my skin. The sex was spectacular.

But also? I *like* her. The idea of her waiting for me outside is strangely appealing. A horrible idea, but appealing nonetheless.

Either way, I owe her a phone call. In the first place, we're friends. And friends don't bang friends without a check-in afterwards. And I need to thank her for the sandwich. When the puck went into the net twenty minutes ago, my teammates all screamed my name. It had been a while since I'd heard them do that.

I tie my shoes, grab my bag, and then head for the door to see who's outside. Maybe there's nobody there, and Miranda Wager was just fucking with me.

Or maybe it's somebody I hooked up with some other time

in Chicago? That would be awkward. The reason I only have sex with randoms is that it avoids entanglement. That's worked just fine for me for years.

Yanking the locker room door open, I look right and left. "Jason!" somebody screeches. And I smile immediately, because I'd know that screech anywhere. I've been hearing it for most of my life.

"Silli!" I yell, grabbing my little sister into a hug and lifting her off her feet. "You didn't tell me you were coming."

"I didn't know! Put me down, and I'll explain."

When I set Silvia onto her feet, she punches me in the arm. "Ow! What's that for?"

"Making me look bad. Our nephew *loves* that bear you sent for his birthday. I bought him books."

"Serves you right. Come out for dinner—we're all getting ribs. I'll buy."

"In that case, I'm in," Silvia says. "I spent sixty bucks on a ticket in the nosebleed section, and all because I can't plan my life."

"You know I woulda got you a seat…"

"I know," she says, looping her arm in mine. "But I asked for the night off and I thought they turned me down, but I didn't read the schedule closely enough." Silvia works as a nurse in a Wisconsin hospital. She's also getting a graduate degree in public health, because we're a family of overachievers. "This afternoon when I realized I had the night off, I just got in my car and drove."

"Where's your car?"

"Parked at your hotel."

I laugh. "So that's how it is, huh? Your plan is to get drunk and crash in my hotel room?"

"There a problem with that?" she asks.

"No. It's great to see you," I say, because it is. The shittiest thing about professional sports is that it keeps me on the road so many days a year. Dinners with my family are scarce.

"You looked fantastic tonight," she says. "I've been worried."

I groan. "Thanks for the vote of confidence." If you can't count on your family to point out your failures, who can you count on?

"Look, I don't care if you ever score another goal. But I know *you* care. And you're a very grumpy bear when things aren't going well."

"Things are fine," I grumble.

"I noticed. We all worry about you more in the fall, anyway."

"That's ridiculous," I insist.

She gives me the side-eye, implying that it's not. "Mom and Dad are planning a surprise visit to Brooklyn, too. To check up on you."

"They're visiting me? When?"

She shrugs. "I didn't listen to the details. But you've been warned."

My family is great, but I don't like them to worry about me. Although it's true that autumn is not my favorite time of year. Ever since Lissa died on a clear November day, I've never been a fan of the season.

And then it hits me like a six-foot-six defenseman. "Oh, shit." I forgot all about the call from Jolene last night. "I'm such an asshole."

"Tell me something I don't know."

Ignoring her, I pull out my phone. I'm sure it's possible to send the money via a website or an app. Except I can't remember that number Jolene gave me identifying the right drugstore. It's still on my coffee table, scrawled on a magazine…

Oh. And now I know how I'm going to solve the problem.

"Silli, I need a minute." I push open the stadium door, finding the team bus ready with its door open.

"Hi Silvia," Jimbo says with a smile. "You guys need a car?" Jimbo asks me. Sisters aren't allowed on the team bus.

"We sure do. I'm heading to that ribs joint where we went last year. You in?"

He checks me off on his tablet with a stylus. "Sure. I'll be late, though." The transport guys aren't done for the night yet.

"Come whenever. I'll buy you dinner."

"Thanks, man. I'll grab you a car. Prolly take three minutes."

"Awesome. I'll be right over there." I cross the asphalt to the stadium wall and then look up Heidi's phone number. As it's ringing, my sister sidles up beside me.

"I need a minute."

"Yeah, but I like to eavesdrop."

"You're a pain in the—"

That's when Heidi's phone picks up. "Belle Pepper's Delivery Service. How may I direct your call?"

"Can I, uh, speak to Heidi?" I ask.

"It's me, genius!" She laughs. "Just playing with you. What do you need?"

"In the first place, I just wanted to say hi." My sister is staring at me, and it's throwing me off my game. "How are you doing? I should have, uh, called you earlier but…"

"You were busy beating Chicago! Nice goal, by the way. I was so excited."

"Well, thanks?" She sounds completely upbeat. And that's terrific, right? I want her to feel cheerful. But her tone is so *casual*.

But didn't we have earth-shattering sex less than twenty-four hours ago? Did she not notice how amazing it was?

"Just do that eighty more times, okay?" Heidi babbles. She's still talking about the game, and I'm distracted by the way her voice vibrates through my soul. I can picture her tilting her head to the side and smiling. "Maybe Denver won't stand a chance."

"Right. Okay. You're worse than Coach." I lift my eyes and find my sister hanging on every word. I shoo her away with a wave of my hand, and she moves maybe six inches.

"Is there something you need?" Heidi chirps. "Because my bubble bath is waiting."

Bubble bath. An image of Heidi lying naked in my bathtub assaults me, and I close my eyes.

"Hello?" she prompts.

"Um..." My concentration is shot. "A favor. I was hoping you could help me with something I forgot. I wouldn't ask but someone's depending on me..."

"Sure! Name it! While I'm still young, though."

My sister chuckles, and I step to the side to try to get away from her prying ears. "On the coffee table there's a magazine, and I wrote something on the back of it—the store number for a drugstore in St. Paul."

"Minnesota? Um, okay. A phone number?"

"No, it's the store's code number. I need to use Western Union to wire money to somebody who will pick it up at that store. Could you do this tomorrow? Find a Western Union and send sixteen hundred dollars cash?"

"Sixteen hundred?" my sister gasps.

"Sixteen hundred?" Heidi echoes in my ear. "Sure. Can you send me an email with all the details? And where am I getting this cash? If I had that kind of money, I wouldn't still be couch surfing in your apartment."

I smile in spite of myself. "I keep a spare credit card in my bottom desk drawer, and the pin number is on a piece of paper that's wrapped around it. I'll put that in the email, too. I was supposed to do this today..."

"Don't worry. Consider it done. Just go beat Denver."

"Thank you," I say, "thanks a ton, I really—"

The line goes dead.

"Who was *that?*" my sister hoots. "I haven't seen that look on your face in a really long time. Ooh! Our car is here. You can tell me all about it on the way."

Silvia hooks her arm in mine and drags me toward the car. All of this happens before I can process the fact that Heidi just hung up on me.

[20]

HEIDI

Ladies and gentlemen! The academy award for indifference after a life-changing night of meaningless sex goes to…HEIDI JO PEPPER.

After disconnecting the call, I set my phone down on the coffee table and then flop face-first onto the sofa cushions. I take a deep breath and exhale.

Okay. Phew. I've been dreading my first interaction with Jason. And it was every bit as difficult as I expected. He was right that sex would make things weird. Or at least very tingly. From now until eternity, every time we chat about errands I'll be undressing him in my mind.

I have got to move out of this apartment. My game face isn't sturdy enough to face him in the flesh. And what lovely flesh it is. Is it possible to leave smile marks on a couch? Just to be safe, I roll over and grin at the ceiling.

By now I've had eighteen hours to process the experience, but I still can't stop thinking about it. *Hot loving with Jason Castro.* It was so, so good. And not just because he knows his way around the female body. He was so *invested*. The smoldering look in his eye when he pushed me down on the bed? It will live in my memory forever.

And the helpless groans? The whispered curses? *Wow*. Now I know how the other half lives. And it's even better than I'd thought.

Except now it's over. My lips are still swollen from roughened kisses, but for how much longer? Lifting my fingertips to my mouth, I gently explore the abraded skin. But, heck. Touching my lips reminds me of his kisses. And if I relax into the sofa I can picture his hard body pressing me down again, pinning me to the bed with his pumping hips—

Whoops. I could get seriously carried away with this train of thought.

I sit up to try to clear my head. Two things are immediately clear. One: the happy glow is going to last a long time. Two: it's going to leave behind a craving for more.

He was right, darn it. Once isn't going to be enough.

The silence of the living room mocks me. I have three days to figure myself out. Jason won't want me here anymore. He was very clear about his one-and-done policy. And who needs a permanent house guest who gives you a worshipful gaze every time you cross the room?

Nobody, that's who.

I need an affordable apartment, and I need it now.

Time to get to work.

Unfortunately, the New York City housing market does not suddenly get cheaper just because I've made my life difficult. I still can't afford to use a real estate broker to find an apartment. I'm not even close to having enough money saved.

My mother always says that word of mouth is the best kind of marketing. So I write emails to all the young women I went to private school with in Nashville. ***Hello from New York! If you know anyone here in the city looking for a roommate, please let me know***. Etc.

But then I run out of ideas.

With no real estate miracles on the horizon, I turn my focus to earning money. By Tuesday morning I'm hard at work filling orders for Belle Pepper's Delivery Services. I have requests from every player who lives in the neighborhood, except one.

The shopping I did last time was so popular that I'll be buying as many groceries this week. I might need two taxis just to transport it all. I don't have an order for Bayer, though. So I shoot him a text, reminding him of the deadline.

My phone rings about a minute later, and it's him. "I'm not on the trip, Hot Pepper. I'm having knee surgery today instead."

"Oh no! That's terrible!" Not only is surgery a drag, but it's bad news for Brooklyn. The team needs him. "Is there anything I can do?"

"Well." He chuckles. "Can I book a couple of hours of your time for something a little unusual?"

"It depends? I don't wash windows."

He laughs. "No, this is more like a babysitting job. I need someone to check me out of the hospital after my outpatient surgery this morning. I know it's not on your menu of services..."

"Goodness! Just tell me how I can help."

"Well, I'm waiting for them to call me in, and the surgery itself should only take an hour. So if you're here by ten or eleven o'clock, that should work out. I'll be free to go as soon as the anesthetic wears off. But they require me to have someone sign me out, and all my friends are on the road."

I can't imagine going into surgery all alone. "I'll be there. Don't you worry."

"Thanks, Heidi Jo. I really appreciate it. I'm emailing you the details right now. Charge me overtime or whatever."

I would never do that, of course. Instead, I get to the hospital early, just in case he's ready. But when I arrive, he's still in the recovery room being fussed over by nurses.

Everyone looks pale and horrible right after surgery. I know this. But it plucks my heartstrings to see this powerful man—a seventeen-year veteran of the NHL—laid out like this, his knee bandaged up, an IV in his arm. "Oh my," I say softly, slipping into the chair beside him. I take his hand and give it a squeeze.

He opens his eyes and squints at me. "I'm okay, angel," he slurs. "They have really good drugs here."

"I'm sure they do," I agree. "Just wish you didn't need them."

"Me too," he grunts. "It's gonna be a while until they let me out of here."

"I know that," I explain, releasing his hand. "Just didn't want you to wake up alone."

His hand lands on top of my head. "You're a good girl, Heidi Jo."

"Everyone says so," I grumble.

"It's a good thing to be," he slurs. "You won't end up all alone like me."

Oh my. Anesthesia is its own kind of truth serum, and he's still under the influence. "How's your pain?"

"Fine. I'm a tough old stone, Heidi. Probably out for the season, though."

"*What?* That's terrible!"

He doesn't answer. He just pats me clumsily on the head.

While he dozes, I pull out my laptop and get to work trying to figure out how to solve Jason's Western Union problem. I have his credit card in my pocket, as well as an email and the scribbled destination, torn from the magazine. I can do the whole transaction online, although it doesn't work the way he thought. There's nowhere to input the pickup location.

"Bayer?" I ask.

"Hmmm?"

"Do you know how Western Union works?"

"Is that a hockey team?"

I'm taking that as a no. So I do some more research and figure it out myself. Then I email Jason.

To: Jason Castro

From: Heidi Jo Pepper

Sir—Western Union doesn't work exactly the way that you implied. You don't need to give them a pickup destination. Instead, you need to tell Mrs. Jolene Skinner to bring her ID to any Western Union location and give them tracking number KP7742-11.

Paying with a credit card cost you $26. Sorry. They asked me if I wanted to charge the recipient for the fee and I said no. I figure I'll just spend $26 less on your grocery list. Those blueberry waffles you asked for have too much sugar anyway.

Beat Denver.

Your humble servant, HJP

The nurses come back to Bayer's bedside and lift the bed to a sitting position. He gives me a wobbly grin and a thumbs-up.

"Once you're taking liquids, and you're able to urinate, we can send you home," the head nurse says.

"Roger that." His eyelids drift closed.

I get an email from Jason not five minutes later.

From: Jason Castro

To: Heidi Jo Pepper

Thank you so much for handling the wire transfer! I really appreciate it—and it's fine that I paid the $26. I felt like a dick for forgetting to handle it myself. But I got really distracted Saturday night. It's basically your fault, now that I think about it.

That's a joke, okay? And it had better be a joke that you're saving money on waffles. What is the point of shopping for me if you're leaving out my favorite things?

—JC

From: Heidi Jo Pepper

To: Jason Castro

I'm great! I'm super busy getting everything the players asked for, and looking at apartments in Queens and the Bronx.

The waffles will appear and so will your dry cleaning. They couldn't get the pizza stain out of your red tie, but honestly the world is better off without that old thing. You're replacing it with something nicer from Barneys.

You also need some new shirts. Just saying. The blue striped one is particularly ragged. What's your shirt budget, is $2000 too much?

—H

From: Jason Castro

To: Heidi Jo Pepper

$2000? You can't be serious. And don't toss the striped

shirt! We beat Dallas twice when I was wearing that. Seriously, don't toss it. Don't toss anything. I don't know which tie you mean because they all have pizza stains. The one with kittens on it is lucky against Tampa.

Leave the clothes alone, okay?

—J

I let out a cackle.

"What's so funny?" Bayer asks in a perkier voice.

"Jason Castro is the most gullible man in sports. It's a miracle his opponents don't deke him on every single play."

Bayer tips his head to the side and studies me. "I think he's a cynical kid. Reminds me of myself. Except where you're concerned, maybe."

I squint at him. "I don't know what you mean." Those meds are still impairing his brain. And now my phone is ringing, and I have to dive into my bag to shut it up before the nurses eject me. And it's *him!*

"Hello?" I whisper into the receiver. "Jason?"

"Heidi? Why are you whispering?"

Oh my. A now familiar tingle rolls over me as Jason's deep voice reaches me from afar. "I'm in a very posh store," I whisper. "On Fifth Avenue. Did you know there were silk ties with actual gold threads in them? They're *beautiful.* I think you should buy one. Five grand isn't too much, right?"

"For a *tie?*" There's horror in his voice. "My clothes are *fine,* Heidi. I just need the dry cleaning. Don't throw anything away. I know some of my things are looking worn, but you won't know which ones are lucky."

"You, sir," I whisper, "are hilarious. And it's a little too much fun to tease you. I'm not going to throw away a single thing. I was kidding about that."

He exhales into the phone. "Okay, thank you. And also thanks for taking care of that other thing even though I gave you shitty instructions."

"It's my pleasure, Jason Castro." And, whoops! That comes out sounding flirty and dangerous. I need to dial it down.

He lets out a sound that might be a groan. "I better go. You take care of yourself."

"Oh, I will. Are you sure you don't want a purple silk tie with little golden stripes…"

"No," he says briskly. "O'Doul is waving me down."

"Bye, killer."

"Bye, Hot Pepper."

Bayer is grinning at me and sipping water through a straw. "What was that?"

"What was what?"

"What's the deal with you and Castro?" Bayer asks immediately.

"Nothing." My voice cracks on the word, because I'm a terrible liar. "Why?"

He rolls his eyes, and I'm pleased to see a little color returning to his face. "He can never stop staring at you, for starters. And why did he sound like a stammering teenager on the phone just now?"

I give him a stern look. "Don't eavesdrop on my calls, or I won't spring you from this hospital."

He laughs again.

Pro athletes are not to be underestimated. Who else can be charming and infuriating ten minutes post-op?

After another hour, Bayer passes all the nurses' tests, including a very slow trip to the men's room on crutches. "Don't watch me walk away," he says as they ease him off the bed.

"Why not…*oh*." I get a glimpse of his bare ass through the open halves of the hospital gown.

"Your girlfriend can wait outside now," the nurse says. "You'll be out of here in thirty minutes tops."

Bayer cackles as he shuffles towards the john. "Be honest. Do you think she's too young for me?" He gives me a wink over his shoulder.

"No comment," the nurse says.

Eventually, we're set free. I get a taxi for Bayer, his new crutches, his pain medication, and ten pages of instructions. Bayer grits his teeth every time the car goes over a little bump in the asphalt. But he looks a lot happier as we ride the elevator inside the Million Dollar Dorm.

Luckily, Bayer lives on the third floor—the same one as Jason and Silas. That'll make it easy for me to keep an eye on him tonight. But when we walk into his apartment, I see that it's configured completely differently. Bayer has a duplex—there's a set of spiral stairs up to his loft bedroom.

"Wow, this is super cool," I gush, turning around in the open space. "But you can't climb those stairs tonight." And tomorrow doesn't look good, either.

He crutches into the center of the living area. "I have the sofa."

"Does it fold out?"

"Sure does."

Still. My own knee throbs in sympathy at the idea of six-three Bayer on a sofa bed. "Tonight I'll help you set it up. But first let's find you some lunch. Could you eat?"

"Always," he says.

I get him situated in a chair with a footstool propping up his knee. Then I order lunch from the ramen place near the waterfront.

We eat noodles together in companionable silence. "You don't have to babysit me, kid," he says as he takes a sip of the ice water I brought him. "This isn't my first knee surgery."

"I know that. And I promise you I'm leaving for a few hours

to do some work for my boys. But I'm right down the hall. I'll be over later to change the bandages."

His eyes widen. "Really? I hate that part."

"Of course. That's on page two of the instructions." I get the paperwork out of my bag and set it on the coffee table. "Hey—I should check to see if the money Jason sent was picked up." I pull out my laptop. "It's for some lady in Minnesota. His family, maybe?"

Bayer shakes his head. "That kid is such a fucking martyr."

"How's that?"

"Well..." Bayer frowns, as if he's not sure if he should say. "If he's sending money to Minnesota, it's for the dead girlfriend's mother. She treats him like an ATM."

"His *dead*..." I can't bring myself to say it.

Bayer's eyes widen. "You don't know that story?" He shakes his head. "It's not mine to tell. But it explains a lot about that boy. He's only twenty-five, but he thinks it's totally fine to be alone." Bayer waves a hand around his apartment. "This is where he'll be. Paying someone to bring him home from the hospital after his last knee surgery."

"Hey! You're not paying me."

"Sure I am."

"No way, dude." He gives me that smile that so many people do—the one that implies I've said something cute. Usually it drives me crazy, but somehow I don't mind when it comes from him. "I was never billing you for this. We're friends, right?"

He tips his head to the side and considers me. "Yeah, we are. You're a great friend, Heidi Jo Pepper. I just hope that dumbass Castro gets his head out of his ass and tells you how he really feels."

I have no response, because I can't imagine that Jason has anything to say to me on the subject. "I need to run now. You need anything, you text me."

"I'll do that."

"Don't take any risks with that knee, okay? I'll be back in a few hours."

"Got it." He salutes me. "Go forth and conquer the shops of Brooklyn."

So I do. An hour later I'm standing in a tailoring shop in Brooklyn Heights, picking up a dress for Ariana, the team massage therapist. "You're a lifesaver, Heidi!" she'd said when I confirmed her request.

Hey, maybe I'm not curing cancer, but at least I make busy people happy.

As I wait for the tailor to charge my credit card, I get a text message from my sister Jana. ***The blogs love Jason Castro. And he sure is nice to look at!***

My heart ricochets. There can't be another picture of Jason and me, can there?

I click on the link, and it takes me to a blog called Puckrakers. The first thing that loads is the headline, "Hockey's Latin Lover Strikes Again."

I roll my eyes. That's so trite, and racist, too. But when the photo snaps into focus on the screen, I gasp for a completely different reason. My sister was right—it's a very attractive photo of Jason. Except that he's arm-in-arm with a gorgeous brunette. He's smiling at her, while she eyes the camera with laughing eyes.

I want to punch her in the throat. No—scratch that. I want to punch Jason in the throat. Or maybe the nuts. Because according to the caption, this photo was taken on Sunday night, after the Chicago game.

A mere twenty-four hours after I handed him the remote control to my entertainment center.

"Um, miss?" The tailor's assistant is staring at me, possibly because I've begun growling like an angry honey badger.

"Yes?" I snap.

The poor thing slides my credit-card slip across the counter with a wary expression. I sign it hastily, thank her, and leave the store.

Breathe, I coach myself as I step outside. The October air is cool and fresh, and I can see lower Manhattan in the distance across the river. Nothing has changed. It doesn't matter.

This was inevitable, really. He warned me. I slept with him, anyway. I made that choice, and now I'll have to live with it.

I don't, however, have to like it.

[21]

JASON

TO MAKE it in professional sports, you have to drink your own Kool-Aid. You have to invent your winning narrative and never question it. That puck isn't going into the net if I don't believe it will. The game can't be won unless I believe it's possible.

In Denver, I believe.

And I'm *en fuego*. Now that I'm back to believing that the puck can find my stick and then the net, it does. *Twice*. I feel unstoppable in the third period. I run the opponent so ragged that Campeau gets his first goal of the season.

Tonight is Silas's victory, too. Coach is putting him in goal more often and resting Beacon, our star goalie. To make it to the playoffs again, we'll need depth everywhere.

And it all feels possible.

"Everything is right with the world," I say to my roommate as we touch beer glasses in the hotel bar.

"It was a good night for Apartment 302," Silas agrees. "I'm so tired, though. Can't wait to go home tomorrow. The apartment will be clean, because Esme is back from Puerto Rico. And the groceries will be stocked, because Heidi is a goddess."

"Mmm," I say, picturing Heidi's face for the millionth time. It's been three days now and I still can't stop thinking about her. The idea of her flitting around our apartment is surprisingly appealing.

I know I gave her a whole speech about one-and-done. But now that seems hasty. It doesn't help that I'm full of post-game adrenaline. I'd like to exorcise this buzzy feeling in my veins by getting her very naked and demonstrating my appreciation.

I pull out my phone and text her. ***Thanks again for helping with my Western Union thing. The recipient got the cash and is happy. Also I forgot to tell you that my nephew loved the bear.***

She doesn't respond right away. A couple of women approach Silas and me, asking for autographs.

"Great game," says the smiliest one. "Well done tonight."

"Thanks," I say, signing her cocktail napkin. "It was fun."

I don't invite her to sit down, though. Any other night I might have, but I'm waiting for a text from Heidi and nobody else will do.

It takes a while until I can check my phone for Heidi's response. When I finally read it, I'm instantly disappointed. She wrote: ***Glad to hear it.***

"Four words?" I yelp, staring at the screen.

"What's the matter?" Silas says, waving down the bartender for a check.

"Nothing." I shove the phone in my pocket. "Let's call it a night. I'm so tired I can't feel my legs."

I can't believe Heidi didn't comment on our victory. Didn't she tell me to beat Denver? And didn't I just make Denver cry?

What is going on in that girl's head? Maybe I'll go upstairs and call her.

"You know it's after one in the morning in Brooklyn," Silas says as he slides off the barstool. I swear he reads my thoughts.

"Oh. Shit. And get out of my brain."

He grins. "You are so goddamn entertaining. I should sell tickets."

"Fuck you," I say, and he laughs so hard I want to smack him.

We land Thursday at one p.m., and there's a meeting with the offensive coordinator at three. So I only have time for lunch and for dropping my luggage off in my sparkling apartment.

Heidi isn't there. But I leave her a note on the coffee table. ***We're home! I'd love to catch up with you. Text me if you want to catch up later.***

Hours pass, and I get no response. None.

I don't make it home again until evening, because the guys drag me out for a fried-chicken dinner. I text Heidi to see if she wants to meet us at the restaurant.

Again—no response.

After the check is paid, the boys want to head over to the whiskey bar. "I'm beat," I tell them, peeling off from the group.

"Night, weakling," O'Doul says with a laugh.

I don't even give him the finger. I just walk home by myself. When I open the apartment door, the living room is dark, and I only hear silence. My disappointment is swift and fierce.

But then I spot a glow of light coming from the open door to my bathroom. Hope springs up inside my chest so fast I can't even believe it.

Now there's something to contemplate later.

Kicking off my shoes, I walk on silent feet toward the bathroom. And then I'm rewarded—Heidi is there, humming to herself while she picks up about fifty different beauty products she's scattered around my bathroom. One by one she's dropping them into a quilted overnight bag.

My happy buzz dies instantly. "Going somewhere?" I ask.

She lets out a shriek, whirls around, and lunges at me with a hairbrush.

"Ow!" I yelp as the brush connects with my chest. "What the hell?"

"Jason!" she squeaks. "You scared the bejesus out of me. Don't sneak up on a girl!"

"I do live here," I point out, possibly unreasonably. "What are you doing?"

She glances into her bag. "Packing up. Who wants to know?"

"I do." And now I'm getting the feeling I've fucked things up in some fresh new way. "What's the matter?"

"Not a thing," she says briskly. "And luckily I don't have a heart condition. That's the second time today that you scared me senseless."

"I haven't seen you today!"

Her eyes narrow. "No kidding. But your lovely housekeeper Esme has now seen me naked, seeing as you didn't mention you had a housekeeper. We startled each other this morning right after my shower. The poor woman dropped a bucket of water. It took us a half hour to clean it up."

"Uh-oh," I say slowly.

"I'll say." She zips up her bag and sets it on the floor.

"But back up. Why are you packing? Where are you going?"

"I don't have all the details worked out yet."

"Where will you sleep tonight?"

"In your teammate Bayer's bed."

"Say *what?*" A hot pang of jealousy shoots through my chest.

"Before I go..." Heidi sets down her bag and grabs a folded paper out of her pocket. "Here's your itemized grocery receipt, as well as your change."

I open the receipt and scan it. "Forty-three dollars. Thank

you." The amount of change is a puzzle, though. "Didn't I leave you two hundred bucks? There's only seven dollars here."

She points at the last line on the page. *Assorted gratuities, $150.* "You tipped the concierge for helping me bring twenty-seven grocery bags into the building—a dollar a bag. You tipped Esme for her trouble. You tipped your drycleaner delivery person, the FedEx guy, and someone who delivered a shipment of hockey tape to the rink earlier. He looked like he was having a bad day."

"Wow. I'm so generous," I say drily. "Did all my teammates display the same largesse?"

"Nope," she says, dusting off her hands. "Just you. And the very last expenditure was for a new pair of lucky panties. For me." She lifts her perfect chin and levels me with an angry gaze. "You're not the only one who's allowed a superstition or two. And my lucky panties have obviously lost their magic."

Every time her rosebud lips say the word *panties*, a zap of electricity shoots through me. "Am I familiar with this pair? The black lace? Did you retire them? I don't think a pair of panties can get any luckier than those got on Saturday night. They should be framed and hung on the wall, probably."

"Not exactly." She licks her lips. "I threw them right in the trash. This new pair could be an improvement. They can steer me toward a guy who stays off the blogs for at least twenty-four hours after testing my suspension."

"What?" I blink. "The blogs?"

With the world's most impatient eye-roll, Heidi pulls out her phone and shoves it in my face.

I immediately recoil. "Oh, gross! That headline!" *The Latin Lover Strikes Again*. Yikes.

"Yes, it's horribly racist," Heidi snaps. "But what about the photo?"

"Forget the Latin shit," I argue. "They can't use *'lover.'* That's my sister for Christ's sake. *Ew*."

"Your..." Heidi snatches the phone back from me. "*Sister?* But you showed me her picture! And that girl looks nothing like you."

"I have *two* sisters," I grumble. "Tell me this—do you look exactly like your sister?"

Heidi's eyes widen. Slowly she shakes her head.

"Then you ought to understand that Jackie and I favor my dad. He's half-Brazilian and half-Cuban American. But—newsflash—my mom is a white lady from Canada. Not that the author of this blog post was interested in that detail."

Heidi gasps. "Oh *no!*" She covers her face with her hands. "I'm a horrible person. I made a shallow assumption based on imperfect observations of implied ethnicity! No wonder I didn't fit in at Bryn Mawr."

Didn't I say this girl is hilarious? I grab her hands from her face. "No, Hot Stuff. The real stupidity here is believing a gossip blog. Like you don't know any better than that? Please."

She gazes up at me. "I'm sorry. I mean—I'm not supposed to care. You can hook up with whoever you want. I'm not supposed to get jealous. You warned me."

"Aw. You were jealous? Is that why I tipped half of New York City?"

She drops her chin.

"You're right," I whisper. "You're not a good girl at all. I think you need to make it up to me." I cup a hand under her drooping chin, and find her sad blue eyes. "I can't stop thinking about you. Come over here and kiss me."

Confusion crosses her features. "Jason, you gave me very clear rules. 'There are only one-way tickets on the Castro train.'"

She does a startlingly good impression of me. And she's right. This is entirely out of character for me. For the first time in years, once isn't going to be nearly enough. I'm starting to clue in, although it took long enough.

"Okay, listen," I try. "The Castro train left the station without me. I threw away my own rulebook way back when I kissed you in the carwash. Or maybe it was all the way last spring, when you sassed me for eating the last blueberry muffin." Silas was right. We've been circling each other for months.

"What are you saying?" she whispers.

"I'm saying that you and I should be a thing."

It's quiet for a moment while we both take that in. I can't tell which of us is more surprised. I mean it, though. She's more to me than a one-night stand.

"But that's confusing," she says eventually.

"Tell me about it." I never had any trouble with my one-night rule before now. "But you're all I can think about. So let's just see where it goes. We could start right now. Come here and kiss me hello."

She doesn't move.

"Look." I chuckle. "I'm sorry to confuse you. And I know my track record sucks. But I think you like me, too. So kiss me, or tell me I'm wrong."

Heidi tips her head to the side and considers me. But she doesn't move.

I snap my fingers, just to be a dick. "I'm waiting." There's a part of me that's still fighting to keep my distance. But that part is quickly overruled as Heidi stands up straighter and looks me dead in the eye. She wants this, but she's afraid to trust it, too.

Although it's torture, I stay where I am and wait. But when she moves forward, I can no longer control my expression. I give her a hungry, desperate look as she steps into my personal space.

"Good girl," I whisper, as my hands pull her body against mine, the way I've dreamed of doing these past few days. My soul exhales as I take her into my arms.

But I don't kiss her yet. It has to be her choice.

Slowly, she takes my face in both her hands, rises up on her tiptoes, and brushes her lips over mine.

I make a low, needy noise. But she sets herself back down on her heels and releases me. "That's all I get?"

"What do you want?"

"You," I grunt. "Naked. Often."

"I'm still thinking," she says at close range, as her fresh, citrus scent overwhelms me. "You were a one-night stand. I don't know how to wrap my head around this."

"Why don't you wrap some other things around me while you think about it? Just try me out."

"Like a free sample?" She squints at me.

"Yeah." I take her smooth hand and place it right over my erection. "Sample that, if you need convincing."

Her lips part in surprise. And since a good hockey player always finds his opening, I lean forward and slide my tongue between those sweet lips. The sound she makes is half gasp, half groan. I kiss her deeply, wrapping my arms around her waist, and finally, *finally* pulling her body against mine.

Oh, hell yes. She relaxes against me, her mouth melting under mine. And everything is right with the world.

[22]

HEIDI

I USED to think I was a smart girl. Not so much right now.

Every time Jason kisses me, I get a little stupider. And, let's face it, this is probably just a whim of his that he'll reconsider by morning. Good thing, too. If I saw him naked every day, I'd probably lose all my executive function. I'd walk into doors and leave my phone in the refrigerator.

But right this second, lucid thought is overrated. The slide of his tongue against mine turns all my thoughts to a staticky hiss. My hands find the hard planes of his back and then the warmth of his neck. I give in and cling to him while his wide hand coasts down my ass and lifts my skirt.

Oh. Oh, wow. That bossy maneuver makes my pulse quicken. I wore a short skirt today just in case I ran into him. I wanted to look very hot and unavailable. But now I'm feeling hot and *very* available as his palm skims over my panties.

"Is this the new pair?" he whispers against my lips.

"No." In truth, there is no new pair of panties. That was just bluster. But I'm not ready to admit it. "I was saving those for a special occasion."

His fingers breech the edge of the fabric. "I'll show you a special occasion."

"P-please," I hear myself beg. I know better than to lose my heart to Jason. But here I am, anyway. His touch makes my heart race. I crave him. So even if this ends badly, I don't want to stop.

There's no subtlety in his touch. That naughty hand slips down my ass, parts my legs and cups my pussy. As his fingers meet sensitive flesh, my breath hitches in the middle of our kiss.

Jason smiles against my mouth. "Somebody missed me," he whispers as his fingertips find slickness and heat.

"Shut up," I say, reaching for the buttons of his shirt. "Don't ruin it with your giant ego."

"My giant ego missed you, too, though," he says, and I melt a little more. "And now I'm going to show you how much."

Our clothes come off piece by piece right there in the bathroom. We're naked and lip-locked as we sway together under the bright bathroom lighting. "Come right this way," he whispers, nudging me toward the bathtub. "I've been thinking about you naked in here for days."

He grips the faucet and starts the flow of warm water into the bath. "Hop in there. I'm going to shut the bedroom door."

"Good call," I say in a shaky voice.

With a hockey player's speed, he skates out of the bathroom. I step into the tub and sit down. The shallow water is nice and hot and causes my skin to form goosebumps and my nipples to harden. And then self-consciousness sets in. My sex life up until I met Jason has been missionary position on a bed. I feel exposed right now.

Jason reappears in the doorway, a condom in his hand. He dims the lights and his eyes darken when he spots me in the tub.

"Now that's what I wanted to come home to," he says in a voice like gravel.

Well, okay then. I'd better up the ante. I unhook the little hand shower from its wall mount and turn it on. Then I turn the spray onto my bare breasts.

I'm rewarded by a guttural sound of longing from deep in his throat. About two seconds later he's in the tub with me, taking up all the extra space and pulling me into his lap. "Let me do that," he says, grabbing the sprayer from my hands.

"Careful," I say as he aims warm water at my tummy. "You're going to splash the floor."

"Who fucking cares?" He drops the hand shower into the tub and finds my mouth with his.

Oh my. That bossy tongue is back and ordering mine around. I get more of his deep, scorching kisses. Now that his hard body is naked and under mine, I feel desperate. I turn my body until I'm straddling him. As we kiss, I rub myself against him in a deliciously undignified manner.

Jason breaks our kiss, breathing hard. *Oh, yay,* I think. *He's going to get the condom.* Only he doesn't. He just waits there, his naked body hot and hard, and he's smiling at me as the steam rises around us.

"What?" I whisper.

He reaches up and turns the water off—the tub is already halfway filled. "Nothing. I'm just taking my time tonight."

"But I don't need you to," I argue. "Don't be polite."

"I'm not," he insists. "But I've discovered something about you."

"What's that?" I pant.

"You only let me boss you around when we're both naked. When you're dressed up in your cute-as-fuck little outfits, I can't tell you anything."

That sounds about right, so I don't argue.

"And I like to be in charge," he adds. "So I think you're going to have to spend a lot of time without your clothes."

"Oh." I shiver happily at the thought.

He actually laughs. "Yeah, I know. The hardship. Now I have a few questions. And you're going to answer them."

"Right now?" I whine.

"Yeah, baby. You have to talk to me or you don't get the good stuff."

"Then make it snappy."

He kisses me once on the nose. "Riddle me this—if you were upset with me this week, why didn't you tell me?"

"Because…" Why didn't I? It's hard to think when you have the hottest hockey player in North America naked between your thighs. Oh, right. "It wasn't relevant. You told me not to expect anything more from you, so I didn't."

His smile disappears as he runs a finger along my cheekbone. "I told you not to expect more sex, because I didn't anticipate this. But I'm not a shitty friend, Heidi. I wouldn't spend the night with you and then pick up a random less than twenty-four hours later."

"You do have a reputation," I point out.

"Right." He shrugs. "If the blogs say it, then it must be true."

Whoops. "I'm sorry."

He leans in to give me a quick kiss. "Don't let them turn your head again, okay?"

"Okay," I agree.

"Even if you and I are a thing, they won't stop making up shit about me."

"Right."

"I'm the only one who gets to turn your head."

"Mmm." I stare up at his flexing forearm as he reaches for the condom.

"I didn't hear that," he says, pausing with the packet in his hand. "Did you agree with me?"

"Yes," I whisper. "Yes, *sir*."

"Oh, man." He drops his head back for a second and lets out a hot breath. "I like the sound of that. Here." He hands me the condom.

I unwrap it with clumsy fingers. I've never done this part before. I squint at the condom in the dim light, trying to see which way it's rolled. But, heck. This shouldn't be my job.

Glancing up at him, I catch Jason watching me with greedy eyes. He's enjoying this. It's dawning on me that he's always keeping me on my toes, seeing what I'll do next.

So I slide backwards down his thighs, lean down, and lick the fat crown of his cock.

"Oh, fuck," he gasps. "Did I say you could do that?"

"You said I could have a sample," I point out. And then I open my mouth as wide as I can and take him inside.

All his muscles go rigid. I hollow my cheeks and suck, and he makes a broken noise. His fist closes around my hair as I go to town, licking and mouthing him eagerly.

Now *this* is power. He thinks he has my number? I also have his.

His curses echo against the bathroom walls as I work him over. I'm no expert at this, but my enthusiasm shines through. I've never heard the Lord's name taken in vain quite as frantically as Jason does tonight.

Eventually he pushes me off, then leans back against the tub with a sigh. "No more of that or I'll disgrace myself." He grabs the forgotten condom out of my hand and rolls it down his length with haste.

I sit back, arms crossed in front of my damp body, wondering what happens next. My face feels flushed, and the ends of my hair are damp and wild.

"Don't get shy now," he says, beckoning to me. "Let me look at you." When I drop my arms, his gaze makes a slow sweep of my body, lingering on my breasts, my tummy. And then my lady parts.

A lifetime of good-girl habits isn't easily shed. That dirty gaze gives me the urge to close my legs. But I resist it. My fingers tingle with the need to cover myself, but I let him admire me. After all, this is exactly what I asked for. I want him to see me as a woman.

So instead of hiding, I rest my hands on the sides of the tub and actually spread my legs a little farther.

"Fuck," he says in a broken voice. And then he moves, gripping my hips and sliding my body closer to his. We're of one mind as I brace myself over him. Quickly, he lines up beneath me and then lowers me down onto his cock, filling me with one long stroke.

"Yes!" I gasp as my body stretches to accommodate him. I grip his shoulders and grind against him. I can't help myself.

He groans happily. "You…" He takes a deep breath and begins to move his hips beneath me. *Finally.* "…are exactly what I need."

I couldn't agree more, but I don't want any more conversation. So I grab his face and kiss him. Hard.

Afterward, we wrap towels haphazardly around ourselves and stagger to his bed, where we lay together in a steamy heap. "I have a theory," he pants.

"Murmph," I say, because my lips have forgotten how to say anything other than "oh god oh god" and "YES! YES! YES!"

I really hope Silas isn't home yet. We weren't exactly quiet.

"You told me that men always treat you too carefully. Because they're intimidated by your daddy."

"It's true." I sigh, trying to slow down my breathing.

"Nah," Jason says with a chuckle. "I think they're intimidated by you."

"What?" I gasp. "That makes no sense. I'm not intimidating."

He rolls over to look at me with those big brown eyes. They're full of warmth. "See, your fearlessness is a real turn-on for me," he says, reaching out to wrap a lock of my damp hair around his finger. "But some men can't handle that. It makes them wonder if they're enough."

"But you can? Your exceptional ego can handle it?"

He grins. "Most of the time."

"I don't know if I buy it," I confess. Still, it's one of the nicest things anyone has ever said to me.

Jason's smile doesn't dim. I've never met anyone like him. My other boyfriends always wanted me to agree with them. Jason seems just as happy when I argue. Now he reaches out and pulls me onto his chest. He smooths my hair back with one hand and lets out a contented sigh.

I never expected him to be cuddly, damn it. It's nice. I like it a little too much.

"My ego didn't like one thing, though," he says. "What's this bullshit you were spinning earlier about spending the night in Bayer's bed?"

"Ah." I'd meant for him to get the wrong idea, and I guess it worked. "It's true that I was going to sleep there. But Bayer wouldn't have been in the bed. He can't climb up the loft stairs, so he's sleeping on his sofa. I should text him and see if he needs anything."

I sit up to look around for my phone.

"Not yet. Don't go." Jason pulls me right back down again. It's gentle, but still bossy.

"You just manhandled me," I complain from a comfortable spot on his pec. My fingers find his happy trail, and I trace it softly.

"We're still naked, so I'm still in charge," he says, stroking a hand down my shoulder. "Now tell me about the rest of your week."

"Oh, it was just the usual. Working at the rink. Looking for cheap apartments and grocery shopping for hockey players. Oh! Listen—I had an idea for Silas's birthday next month."

"Time to hire the strippers!" His perfect abs bounce with a chuckle.

"No!" I argue. "My idea is so much better."

"I'm only kidding. When it's someone's birthday, we usually go out for a ridiculously pricey dinner and make a rookie pay. But what's your idea?"

"Well, my plan is still pricey. I saw that Delilah Spark is playing Madison Square Garden the night before his birthday. And the team should be flying back from Seattle that morning."

Jason cackles. "You think we should buy him a ticket to her show?"

"No, we should buy a bunch of tickets. Let's get a block of them—maybe even VIP access. It would be a hoot."

"Holy shit! If Silas met Delilah Spark he'd wet himself."

"It would be a really cool gift. It's not often when you can give a grown man something that would make him so happy."

"That is true." Jason puts his lips against my cheekbone and gives me a slow kiss. "You made me happier tonight than I've been in a long time."

My heart gives a stunned little flutter. "I don't know what to say about that."

"Just say you're happy, too."

"I am happy," I say slowly. "But what happened to Mr. One Time Only? I don't know what to think."

"You don't trust me," he says.

"Would you?"

"Well, I'm pretty great. You just need more convincing.

Now, how do we get these concert tickets? Won't it be sold out?"

"There's a price for everything."

"Ah. And I'm sure I'll be paying it. Do I actually have to go to this concert? Her music is not my taste."

"Someone has to go. And why not you?"

"Let's make a deal," he says.

"What kind of deal?"

"I'll go to the Delilah Spark concert and sit in the front row. I'll give her a standing ovation after every song. But only if you'll be my date."

"But..." Did he even do the math? "It's a month away."

"I heard you the first time. You and I are going to be a thing."

"A thing? What's that?"

"It's whatever we want it to be. It's our thing."

"And our thing lasts a month?"

"At least." He shrugs maddeningly. "A month from now I'll still want you in my bed. Isn't this nice?"

It is, damn it. But I don't know if I can have an ill-defined relationship with Jason Castro. "I didn't agree to date you yet."

"You will." He says this like it's not infuriating. "Hey—did you get those cookies I asked for on my shopping list?"

"No," I say immediately, and I'm not even a little sorry.

"Why, because they're not healthy?"

"No, because I was mad at you."

He laughs. "You weren't mad at me a few minutes ago when you were having your second orgasm."

"Don't rub it in," I warn him. "Unless you're, um, rubbing it in." I feel a happy spasm just thinking about it. Even though he's confusing, I'm ridiculously attracted to him. I don't think I can walk away from him. Not just yet.

"So you're saying I deserve those cookies?"

"I suppose," I grumble. "The best I can do is ice cream. I hid a quart in the back of your freezer. I bought it for myself."

"Heidi," he whispers. "Will you share your ice cream with me? Fantastic sex makes me hungry. And then will you share my bed, so I can hold you all night long?"

"Okay," I say, caving in immediately. And I have a feeling this might become a trend. "But I also need to check on Bayer."

"We'll get Silas to do it," Jason says. "I don't want to share you tonight. I'll text him right now."

He gets out of bed, and I admire his shapely backside as he jumps into a pair of sweatpants.

I don't want to share you tonight. Such a bossy sentence!

It makes me tingle, damn it.

We're sitting at the kitchen table eating Chunky Monkey out of the container when Silas eventually comes home. He takes one look at us and smirks. "I see how it is."

"Don't judge," I say with a sigh. Jason and I are dressed in hockey T-shirts yanked from his drawer and we both have sex hair.

"Wouldn't dream of it." He drops his jacket over a chair. "So this is how it's going to be?"

"We're having a thing," Jason says, digging his spoon into the ice cream.

"A thing?" Silas asks. "Is that, like, a relationship? I thought you were over those."

"So did I." Jason shrugs. "Did you get my text?"

"Sure did. Just came from Bayer's place. I brought him a glass of water and tucked him in, so you're off the hook."

"Thank you." I feel guilty, though. "How is he?"

"Fine, but…" Silas shakes his head. "He keeps saying the R word."

I'm stumped. "Relapse? Revenge?"

"Retirement," Silas and Jason say at the same time. And I swear both of them shudder. "That's horrible, man," Jason says.

"Yeah." Silas clears his throat, and the mood is as somber as if someone died. "Early pre-game skate tomorrow."

"I'll set an alarm," Jason promises.

Silas gives us a wave and heads off to bed.

"You have to work tomorrow?" Jason asks.

"Sure do. At the stadium, too."

"What's your new job this week?"

"Oh, you'll see," I promise. "You won't be able to miss me."

[23]

JASON

THE NEXT MORNING, I feel...reflective. I guess that's the right word. It's not that I regret asking Heidi to trust me. Our "thing," as I insisted on calling it, is something I want.

But as I shower after the morning skate, I wonder if my rusty heart still knows what to do. Let's face it—the last time I started dating anyone I was sixteen years old. I didn't have to shave every day, and I thought a trip through the drive-thru at McDonalds was a fun night out on the town.

Heidi deserves only the best. I just wonder if that's really me.

On the way home, I stop at the florist's. Flowers never go out of style, right? "What should I bring home for my new girlfriend?" I ask the tattooed woman behind the counter.

"Honey," she growls. "This is New York City. I have seventy-six different flowers in that cooler, from all over the world. Columbia. California. Ecuador. The Netherlands. Even Thailand. You gotta give me some guidance." She opens a binder on the countertop that's filled with photos of arrangements. She flips to a tab labeled *Clueless Boyfriends & Husbands.* "Here. This is your section."

"Wow. You got us all figured out?"

"You've got *no* idea. Prices range from forty bucks to three hundred and fifty. And if you need to narrow down the occasion, I can guide you."

"Guide me, then." I point at an overflowing bouquet of pink flowers. "That's nice, right?"

"Yeah, but those orchids say *I'm sorry I forgot our six-month anniversary.*"

"Oh." When did flowers get so complicated? "What does this one say?" I point to another bouquet in red.

"That's for when you canceled a dinner date because you had to work late."

"Well, I'm looking for the bouquet that says we had a fun time together. That's all. I want her to know I'm thinking happy thoughts about her."

"Ah. You're not up to page three yet. You're still on page one." She turns back a page.

"How many pages are there?"

"Thirteen."

"What's on page thirteen?"

Her glance is filled with disdain. "You don't want to know. Listen up, Mr. Page One—we have some nice Peruvian lilies that just arrived. They look smashing with yellow roses."

"Sold," I say, slapping my credit card down on the counter.

"Okay. I'm on it." She moves over to the cooler and opens the door. "How big a bouquet are we talking about, here?"

"Impressive," I say. "But not obscene."

She turns to me slowly. "Can I give you a word of advice?"

"Okay?" I'm not sure I have a choice, anyway.

"I'll make you up a medium-sized bouquet, and she's going to love it. But save the impressive bouquet for another time."

"Why? Not enough roses in there?"

She shakes her head. "It's easy to celebrate new relationships. You haven't fucked it up yet. But someday you're gonna come through my door again and say, 'I need some flowers because I'm an imperfect human and started a fight about nothing.'"

"Yeah, okay," I agree just to move things along.

"You don't believe me," she sniffs, pulling some pretty orange lilies out of the cooler and laying them gently onto a work surface. "But the rough times always come."

"Yeah, thanks." As if I need help remembering that.

Fifteen minutes later I walk into my apartment building carrying a very pretty bouquet. "For me?" Miguel asks. "You shouldn't have."

"Who's a smartass?" I ask him, and he laughs.

"Nice choice for Heidi," he says.

"How do you know they're for her?" I ask as he presses the elevator button for me.

"Cause I got eyes. Have a good game tonight."

"Thanks, man," I say as the elevator door closes on his smirk.

I open my apartment door, hoping Heidi is already home. Striding into the living room, I find that she is. Unfortunately, half my hockey team is there, too, taking up all the sofa seats and sprawling on the floor.

To a man they all swivel their heads to watch me enter the room carrying a bouquet of flowers.

Heidi is seated at the front of the room, her computer on her lap. She looks up quickly, her eyes widening as she takes in the flowers and my startled expression.

As I watch, her cheeks pink up, and her mouth parts. And—boom—every hesitation I had this morning is gone. There's just her intelligent eyes and that pencil behind her ear. She's busy taking over the world, and I'm the lucky guy who gets to be here to watch.

"Hi," I say into the silence.

"Hi." Her blush deepens. "You're late."

"For...?" I'm a little confused right now.

"The meeting!" Bayer says, his bad leg propped on my coffee table. "Somebody doesn't read his texts."

"Whoops," I say cheerfully. Then I cross the room, set the vase of flowers on the coffee table and lean in for a kiss. Our lips meet in a quiet *snick*, but there's nothing quiet about the way I feel. I'm filled with a rush of optimism and gratitude as I help myself to a quick taste of her perfect lips before forcing myself to stand up again. "Carry on, then. Anybody want a water?"

When I turn around, I'm met with a row of astonished faces. Nobody raises his hand.

Whatever. I head into the kitchen to help myself. Someone joins me a couple seconds later. It's Leo Trevi.

"Hey," he says.

"Hey, yourself. What's this meeting about?"

"Silas's birthday surprise. Georgia is going to be pumped when I tell her we're going to a Delilah Spark concert."

"Heidi found the tickets already?"

"She's called, like, six ticket brokers, asking them to compete on price."

I laugh because my girl is hilarious.

"So?" Trevi says. "You and Heidi? I didn't see that coming."

"Apparently you and I are the only ones." I reach into the fridge for an apple that I didn't have to shop for.

"That's big, man. Her dad is going to lose his shit, though. Didn't he threaten you at the fundraiser?"

I just shrug. "He hated the idea of his little girl in a trashy blog post. But that won't happen again. Besides, he's not the coach. He's not the team owner or the GM. What's he actually gonna do to me?"

Leo grins. "I don't know, but maybe we need a secret panic

phrase. If you think your life is in danger, text the secret phrase to my phone."

"What phrase should we use?" I ask, humoring him.

"Butt pimple," Leo suggests. Then he laughs.

"Somehow I don't see myself needing a rescue. But thanks, man." I fill up a glass and hand it to Leo. Then I get one for myself.

"Checks are fine," Heidi says as we reenter the living room. "Or you can use the Belle Pepper Pay Portal."

"Awesome," O'Doul says, rising. "I'm in, but I gotta get back to my place now. It's nap time."

"Class dismissed," Heidi says. "Watch for my invoice."

"Yes, ma'am," Leo says. "Hey—when do we get to tell Silas? I need a video of his face when he hears."

"Not yet!" Heidi says. "I want the whole plan nailed down before he hears about it."

"Can I just pay and not go to the concert?" Bayer asks, planting his crutches on the floor and rising carefully.

"No way, man," I argue. "If I'm going, you're going."

"It's like a suicide pact for our ears," Bayer complains.

"Nah, I like Delilah Spark's music," Leo says. "So does Georgia."

"*Whipped*," someone mumbles.

My teammates file out of my place with the usual amount of bickering and smack talk. And when the door finally shuts on them, I have Heidi all to myself. At least I think I do. "Where's Silas, anyway?"

"Getting a massage," she says, snapping her computer shut. "He's in goal tonight."

"Awesome." The moment she stands up, I cross the room and pull her into my arms. "That means we're home alone."

Her arms wrap around me, and it feels fantastic. I've gone years without regular affection, and I'd forgotten how this feels. "It's nap time," Heidi says, laying her head against my shoulder.

"Then let's nap. Naked," I suggest.

She gives me a squeeze. Then she lets go and steps back. "No can do. You need your rest."

"We'll rest," I argue. "Between rounds."

Heidi shakes her head. "There will be no sharpening of your pencil before this game. Talk to me after you beat Tampa."

"Wait, really?" I step closer to her and kiss her smooth forehead. "So if we lose, I'm cut off? What if it isn't my fault?"

She takes my face in her hands and smiles. "How about this—if you score, then you *score*. I hate Tampa. Always have. They're the smuggest expansion team."

I tip my head back and laugh. "Okay, sure. But if I *obliterate* Tampa, what do I win?"

"You'll just have to find out." She yawns.

"Hey." I can't seem to keep my hands to myself, so I hug her again. "You need an actual nap."

"Don't you? We didn't sleep much last night."

It's true. "If I keep my hands to myself, would you lie down with me?"

"Can you be good?" She tips her face toward mine.

We're nose to nose. Heidi feels just right in my arms. "I think so," I confess. "It won't be easy. Let's try."

She takes me by the hand and leads me to the bedroom. Heidi takes off her jeans, but replaces them with a pair of my Bruisers shorts. We lie down together in the bed, and I'm aware of the unique silence as she settles into my arms.

This is new. It's been a while since I held someone without removing all her clothes. I still like it, though. I like it a lot.

And then it's almost like Heidi reads my mind. "How come you never told me that your high school girlfriend died?"

Oh, fuck. "It's not the kind of thing you just bring up. It was a car accident. I wasn't there." That last thing is my confession, but Heidi probably won't catch on to that. But it's true. I wasn't there when she needed me. And now she's gone.

"That's so sad," she says. "How old was she?"

"Eighteen. We'd known each other forever. You know how I have all of Romeo & Juliet memorized?"

"Yeah. You're kind of famous for that."

"She was Juliet. I was Romeo. Ninth-grade play."

"Oh God!"

"See? I don't talk about it because there's no making sense of that."

Heidi doesn't try to. She just tucks her body a little more tightly to mine and holds my hand.

While I drift off to sleep, she's breathing slowly beside me. I feel more peaceful than I have in a long time.

[24]

HEIDI

I WAKE up two hours later beside a sleeping Jason. His hand is heavy on my hip. Remaining very still, I spy on him for a moment. His inky eyelashes fan out toward handsome cheekbones. His strong chest rises and falls with each breath.

When I told him I couldn't wrap my head around us as a couple, I wasn't kidding. He could have anyone. Not only is he an amazing athlete, he's handsome. He's witty. And *kind,* too.

The mark of a good man isn't the way he speaks to me when he's trying to impress. It's in the way he speaks to all the little people in his life—the doorman, the taxi driver, the bartender.

Jason Castro is a rare combination of gentle and fierce. He's exactly my type. If he wants to actually date me, that's a dream come true. Yet I worry.

He never used to date. Why now? And why me?

Here's the weird thing—I used to think of myself as a catch. I was a queen bee in high school. I'm smart and funny, too. And it's not bragging to say that the Pepper family gene pool was kind to me and that I take good care of myself.

But my self-esteem is on pretty shaky ground these days. I didn't fit in at Bryn Mawr, and it threw me for a loop. I let a couple of confusing years get me down.

My lack of self-confidence is a new problem for me, and I know I'm not supposed to let it get me down. If this beautiful (though slightly bossy) man thinks we should be together, then I'm going to give it a spin. On my terms, of course.

But first, I have a night of work to get through. I slip out of bed, letting my man get his rest, and head for the shower.

An hour later Jason stumbles into the kitchen, his hair crazy and his eyes half-mast. "Hey," he grunts. "Naps always—" He yawns.

"—turn you into a zombie?" I finish. "Sit." When he plunks himself into a chair, I set a mug of coffee in front of him.

He cups the mug as if it were a treasure, then raises his sleepy brown eyes to me. "I knew I picked the right girl."

"Is that all it takes?" Moving to stand behind him, I run a hand through his messy hair. Then I put my hands on his shoulders and squeeze.

Jason lets out a happy moan.

I work his shoulder muscles for a few seconds. "Now drink that coffee. We need you sharp for Tampa."

He lifts a hand to catch mine. "Heidi, can I ask you a weird favor?"

"Sure. Shoot."

"Would you make my sandwich again?"

"Oh." I take two steps toward the counter and pick up the paper bag I've set there. "It's already done."

His eyes widen when I set it on the table. "You're amazing."

"Thank you. Beat Tampa, and then I'll allow you to show your complete appreciation." I don't point out that it took me three minutes to make that sandwich. If he thinks a little PBJ makes me Supergirl, so be it.

"I have a good feeling about this game," he says, gulping the coffee. "You're going to be there, right?"

"Unfortunately, I am." My job tonight is a pain in the backside. But the smile he gives me might even be worth it.

Jason reports to the arena at four, while I have to show up at five. I'm working on the ice-maintenance crew again, but the job looks a whole lot different on game night. And not in a good way.

"This won't fit me," I tell Mr. Randy Cavanaugh, the head of the ice crew. My friend the walrus isn't in charge on game night, and I already miss him.

Randy is a surlier boss. He wears a goatee and a permanent scowl. And he just handed me a ridiculous uniform.

"This is extra-small," I explain. "I'm a small or a medium, depending on the fit."

"Shoulda got here at the beginning of the season," he says. "Put it on. You got seven minutes until doors."

"But..."

"No buts." He sneers. "This is bullshit anyway. Tryouts were three months ago. You're not even *trained*. Can't believe I gotta have you on my crew just 'cause some boss thinks you're a hot piece."

My mouth flies open, but no words come out. His crudeness has stunned me into silence. But even if it hadn't, I don't ever tell my short-term bosses who I am, or why I'm suddenly assigned to them for the week. Nothing good will come of letting this asshole know that my daddy is in charge of hockey, or that I'm taking notes on everything I see.

So I force my mouth closed, turn around, and retreat into

the tiny dressing room, where five other women are all trying to touch up their makeup in an undersized mirror. "Is he always such a charmer?" I ask the room full of strangers.

"Sometimes he's worse," says one of them. "You're the new girl? Did he fire Amber?"

"I sure hope not," I say, tugging my jeans off. "I'm just a temp. I might not last the night if this bra top won't fit me."

"They stretch," another woman promises. "I'm Lydia, hon. Yell if you need help."

"Thanks," I gasp, pulling up the tiny skirt they gave me. It has a built-in panty brief. So as long as the seams don't split apart, I won't be flashing Brooklyn. But Lord, I can't even breathe when I pull it up.

"Wow, you poor thing," Lydia says, eyeing me in the mirror. "You can probably order the next size up online. There's an option for rush shipping, but it costs forty dollars."

"Great," I grumble, stretching the bra top to try to pull it down over my head. "Did y'all have to buy your own uniforms, too? He said he was taking it out of my pay."

"Of course," another girl chirps. "This is practically a charity gig when you count up the unpaid time and the uniform. Nobody tells you this shit when you try out. They're all—*think of the exposure you'll get!*"

They're right about the exposure. Ten minutes later my whole body is repeatedly exposed to the chilly nighttime air as the arena doors open and shut in front of me. I've just learned that being a Bruisers Ice Girl is a literal description. My cleavage is quickly turning to ice.

The Ice Girls' main job is to skate across the rink during the game, removing accumulated snow. But we won't get to lace up our skates for another ninety minutes. First we have to stand here mostly naked and greet the guests as they arrive.

I brace myself as the doors open again, admitting a group of red-faced men and another blast of arctic air.

"Smile," grunts Cavanaugh from somewhere behind me.

I want to choke him. But I paste on my charm-school grin instead. "Welcome to the Brooklyn Arena! Drinks are half price until warmups are over."

"Thanks, honey," says a beefy guy with a Yankees cap pulled down low on his forehead. "You could join me for a cocktail. And maybe a *sausage*." He winks, and his friends crack up.

"Have a great game!" I say through a clenched jaw.

Randy Cavanaugh is watching me, so I resist the urge to tug at my so-called clothing. It's forty-two degrees outside, and I'm basically dressed in a bikini. My boobs are practically spilling out of the V-neck bra top.

Who designs a bra top with a plunging V-neck? A man, that's who. Rebecca is going to get a long email about this. With shouty caps and photo illustrations. And if I could somehow hide a recording device in my tiny clothes, I'd give her an earful of this man's tone every time he speaks to me…

"Smile, damn it," he snarls behind me.

I hate men who tell women to smile. Would Coach ever order his players to smile? No he would not.

And I hate my father. He thinks he's teaching me a lesson. I think he's giving me pneumonia instead. Ice Girls don't have health insurance, either.

The doors open again, and I grit my teeth.

[25]

JASON

TONIGHT I NEED to bring the magic again. If I score, that makes three games in a row. It's the poor man's hat trick.

Also, if I score, I *score* with the hottest, feistiest woman to cross my path in a long time. I won't lie. As the first period heats up, it's helping my motivation.

We miss Bayer, the poor bastard. Drake and Campeau and I are trying to find our rhythm. But I'm skating with two new guys and we don't have enough history together to make this easy.

My first several shifts are hard fought, but we don't manage to create any scoring chances. The defenseman who's guarding me tonight does an excellent job of getting in my way. I'm going to have to punish him for it before the night is through.

Then Tampa scores at the goddamn seven-minute mark. I'm not on the ice when it happens, but it still burns me.

There I am sitting on the bench, chugging water and thinking about my strategy when I spot some familiar blond curls whiz by me at top speed.

Holy shit. Heidi is skating with the Ice Girls tonight.

I don't usually spare a glance at the Ice Girls. I'm too busy thinking about the game. Not this time, though. My gaze is locked on Heidi as she accelerates toward the far corner.

Can she handle this? The Ice Girls skate fast and in formation. They need to clean the whole rink in two minutes flat. What if Heidi stumbles and goes flying? They're not even wearing helmets!

As I watch and worry, Heidi steers her shovel in a stylish arc around the boards, her bare legs executing a series of perfect crossovers.

Huh. I guess she can skate. Maybe you'd have to if you grew up in the Pepper household. She never mentioned skating before. But she moves like a natural.

I'm not the only one who's paying attention, either. Some asshole lets out a deafening cat whistle. He's a few rows up, behind the plexi, but his voice is so loud I can hear every word. "Nice rack on the new girl. Praying for a wardrobe malfunction, here. Show us your tits!"

I'm on my feet immediately, turning to scan the crowd.

"Take it easy," Trevi says under his breath.

But I am not easy. And then I spot the guy as he calls out, "Hey, honey! Resurface this!" He grabs his crotch while his buddies laugh.

My fist makes an equally deafening crash against the plexi. "Hey, asshole! Is that how you speak to women?"

Every fan in earshot turns to stare, including the asswipe I'm yelling at. And then he opens his ugly mouth again. "Just do your job, brutha," he chirps. "How much do they pay you to lose to Tampa?"

I ought to climb over the plexi and flatten him.

"Sit the fuck down," Coach snarls. "Christ. You know better."

He's right, but I still want to slug the guy. Nevertheless, I turn my back and sit.

"He's not worth it," Beringer mutters to me.

As if I don't know that. At the ref's whistle, our starters skate out for the faceoff. The game wears on. I dig deep on every shift, but I'm struggling.

And that asswipe fan's voice has some kind of direct line into my ears. Every time he chirps a rude comment, I can hear it. "Get the lead out, fucktard!" he yells when Leo Trevi doesn't quite get to a puck in time.

It's the typical bullshit we learn to tune out. But tonight I'm gritting my teeth.

And then the Ice Girls come on again.

This time I'm paying rapt attention as Heidi glides out like a goddess, her chin high, her movements sharp. Her attitude is all business.

"Smile, new girl!" yells some dipshit wearing a goatee and a Bruisers Ice Crew jacket.

Heidi bares her teeth.

"Why so grumpy?" yells the asshole behind me. "I'll give you something to smile about, baby."

My growl sounds like a rabid beast's. That's when Coach puts his thumb on my shoulder blade.

I leap over the wall as the Ice Girls retreat and head out for the faceoff, my blood pounding in my ears. Campeau wins the puck and flicks it to me.

Feeling angry and unruly, I snatch the puck and drag it behind my body, attempting to deke the D-man. And it works. For a split second his gaze lags on the wrong side. And then I fire the puck like a missile through the smallest gap between players that I've ever hit in my life.

And, fuck me, but it works! The lamp lights, and for a half second I'm just stunned. But there it is—a one on the scoreboard where there had been a donut before. I scored.

A slow smile breaks across my face, and I turn to try to find Heidi on the sidelines. She's nowhere to be seen, but Drake and Campeau charge me for a celly while the DJ blasts the Beastie Boys.

First goal of the night, ladies! It belongs to me.

When I finally go back to the bench, the asswipe yells to me, "Not bad for a skinny shit!"

"Kiss my skinny ass!" I holler in the general vicinity of his seat.

Then I turn around and tune him out for the rest of the game.

We win 3-2 during a sloppy overtime period. But it still counts. I'm dog-tired when it's done, but I'm still smiling.

The glow lasts until I come out of the showers to find my least favorite reporter waiting for me.

"How does it feel to be back?" Miranda Wager asks.

"It feels like I never left," I fire back. Then I turn my back and drop my towel.

"I walked right into that one, didn't I?" she asks my naked ass.

"Pretty much."

"Fine. You want to give me a better quote?"

"Not really. That flying saucer of a goal speaks for itself, don't you think?"

"Okay, modest one. Do you have any comment about the racist fan who heckled you tonight?"

"Racist? Did I miss something?"

"He called you 'brutha.'"

Rolling my eyes, I pull up my boxers. Then I turn around and shrug. "Is that a thing? I'm sorry, but I didn't have any opinion about him at all, other than he was irritatingly loud and

I was in a grumpy mood. It faded the second I got the sweetest goal of my life. Then I forgot all about him."

She eyes me sullenly. I'm sure her job is more fun when the athletes take her bait. But she can peddle it elsewhere tonight. "Good game," she says eventually. "Have fun with your parents."

"My parents?" What bullshit is she spinning now?

"They're in the hallway. You look exactly like your dad." She walks away to bust someone else's balls.

Good Lord, but that woman is nosy. Before I make it out of the locker room, two more journalists corral me. But all these dudes want to talk about is team readiness, my awesome goal, and our next game against Philadelphia. They don't try to psychoanalyze me.

When I finally sling my duffel bag over my shoulder and walk out, the first people I see are my mom and dad. "Hey!" I shout. "Look who it is!"

"Sweetheart!" Mom shrieks. I get a bracing hug. "Great goal! Like threading a needle!"

"Thank you for noticing." My parents might not love hockey, but they do pay attention.

"Good work, kid," my dad says. "Sorry we didn't call."

"Eh, Silvia warned me that you were planning a surprise attack."

"We got cheap airfare. Two hundred bucks!" Mom gushes. She loves a bargain. And since I always send my comp seats for home games to my parents, they don't really have to plan ahead.

"No hotel, though," my dad says with an apologetic smile. "Hope that's okay."

"No problem," I say immediately. That's why I bought the pull-out couch in the first place. "Where's your luggage?"

"Right here," he says, showing me a backpack. "We travel light."

"Great. Okay." I'm wrapping my head around this change of plans. Heidi is going to have to wrap hers around it, too. And that's going to cause a stir. "Let's get out of here. But first I have to find someone."

I pull out my phone and text Heidi. ***Still here? Where can I find you?***

She doesn't respond right away. "Hungry?" I ask my parents.

Mom shakes her head. "We ate dinner before the game." Of course they did. Mom would rather lose a limb than pay twelve bucks for an overpriced stadium cheeseburger.

"Wouldn't turn down a beer, though," my father says, proving that in spite of our differences, I'm probably not adopted.

"Okay. We could go to the tavern or have a beer at home. Let me see what Heidi wants to do."

My mother's eyes grow as wide as saucers. "Who is *Heidi?* Jason Lucas Castro—do you have a *girlfriend?*" Her voice gets a little higher with every word.

And that's when I notice that Miranda Wager has left the locker room and is leaning against the wall, watching us.

"No," I say immediately. "A friend." I'll be damned if I give a reporter any fodder to write about my personal life.

Mom frowns and Dad chuckles.

"Let's go," I say, heading toward the players' exit.

My phone chimes with a text as soon as we get outside. ***I'm by the front doors,*** she says. ***I have five more minutes on the clock and have to grab my things.***

"Mind if we walk around the stadium?" I ask.

My parents follow me gamely around the big structure. "I thought we'd go out for brunch tomorrow morning," my mother says.

"Sure," I say, mentally crossing off the leisurely morning I'd planned in bed with Heidi. But my parents only get two or three nights with me during the season. I always spend a week in Minnesota with them during the summer. Sometimes we rent a cottage in Ontario, near the place where I grew up.

I love my family, even if they aren't good at planning their visits. Although I suspect that's intentional. Castros are nosy. Every one of us.

When we round the front of the building, I spot Heidi outside. That ought to be good news, except she's still wearing her skimpy Ice Girls uniform and I can see her shivering from fifty paces away.

"Hey!" I say, breaking into a trot. "What are you doing out here wearing that?"

"It's the r-r-rules," she says, her teeth chattering together. "We have to work the d-doors."

I don't even think, I just pull her against my chest. "Jesus. Do they know it's forty degrees out here?"

"The g-girls are allowed to stand inside when it dips below freezing."

"That's some serious bullshit," I grumble, tugging my trench coat off and wrapping it around her. "Take my coat. Your lips are *blue*. Jesus." I pull her hands into mine, and they're like two popsicles.

"N-no need," she says with a shiver. "Mine will do. I can punch out now and change."

"Jason?" My mother comes huffing towards us. "Do we get to meet your friend?"

Heidi peers around my shoulder. "Wait. Are those your—"

"—parents," I confirm. "They surprised me tonight." *And I'm sorry in advance for all the unwanted attention you're about to receive.*

Heidi steps back and smiles politely, prepared to greet them properly. But then she looks down at her getup—the tiny, tight sports bra and nonexistent skirt. Her smile fades. "Oh Lord," she says under her breath.

"Mom, Dad," I say brightly. Because Heidi has nothing to fear from my parents. "This is Heidi. She needs to change out of her work clothes before you can chat her up. But say hello before she freezes solid."

"It's l-lovely to m-meet you," my girl says in her perfect charm-school voice. She pulls my coat more tightly around her. "If you'll just excuse me for a m-moment…"

"Oh, *sweetie!*" my mother squeals, lunging for her, and hugging Heidi so tightly I'm a little worried for her spine. "It's amazing to meet you! Jason is a terrible son, obviously, because he failed to tell us he was dating such a delightful, beautiful girl."

"Well, um," Heidi says, her charm-school training failing her as she meets my gaze with nervous eyes. "It's, uh, new."

I smile apologetically. No girl should have to meet the parents until a relationship is at least forty-eight hours old. That ought to be a rule.

"This is Matheus, Jason's father. He's just as excited to meet you, but I probably won't let him get a word in edgewise."

"Not an exaggeration," my father mumbles, shaking Heidi's cold hand.

"It's lovely to meet you both," Heidi says again. "Let me just change out of this. I'm not usually dressed like a member of the Hooters tennis team."

I bark out a laugh, and wrap an arm around poor Heidi. "You are a great sport, do you know that?" I'm as attracted to her attitude as I am to her rocking body.

My mother watches us, her face in an expression of rapture. "I can't believe this. It's been *years* since I've seen him like this." Jesus, I knew she'd make a big deal out of me being with someone again. "Matheus! Isn't this *amazing?*"

"Well—"

"We have to celebrate!" my mother declares.

"Can you let the poor girl put on clothes?" I beg, cuddling

Heidi a little closer. Then I release her. "Go on. Make a run for it."

"Yes!" Mom agrees. "Sorry, honey. Go warm up. Or you'll catch your death!" My mother takes a breath. Then she realizes what she just said.

Then she bursts into tears.

[26]

HEIDI

JASON SHOOS me toward the doors and hugs his sobbing mother. "Take a breath, Mom," he says. "You're scaring Heidi."

"But it's just so wonderful!" Mrs. Castro sobs.

Oh, jeez. I leave them behind and dart for the Ice Girls' dressing room. I can't believe I met Jason's mother in an ill-fitting Ice Girls uniform. *Thanks, Daddy. Thanks a whole lot.* Could this night get any worse?

It takes me twice as long to get dressed as it should, because my fingers are numb and slow. I have trouble zipping my jeans and buttoning my coat.

"Good job tonight," Lydia rasps. "Bring food and a thermos of coffee next time, okay?"

"Will do," I say between shivers. We don't get a dinner break, and I didn't know they'd try to freeze me to death. Live and learn. Lydia tried to share her food with me, but I wouldn't take it from her. *I'll be fine,* I kept saying.

Except I thought I could recover from this evening on

Jason's sofa, wrapped in every blanket he owns. But now I have to put on a cheerful face and greet the parents.

He's worth it, I remind myself. When he spotted me outside the front doors, the look on his face is something I won't forget for a long time. First joy, followed quickly by concern. He'd wrapped his long arms around me and held me close...

I hurry outside again now, because I want more of those hugs. "Here's your jacket, sorry for the wait!" I babble when I find all three Castros waiting at the curb.

"No trouble," Mr. Castro says. "We've got a taxi waiting. Hop in, young lady."

I end up in Jason's arms on the far side of the back seat, while his mother sighs happily on the other side. "Should we order in some food?" he asks me, then kisses my forehead. "You're still cold. Did you eat dinner?"

"No. It's a six-hour shift with no break. I'm starving."

"Soup!" Jason's mother shouts. "She needs soup."

"Is the ramen place still open?" I wonder aloud.

"Matheus! Call the ramen place!" Mrs. Castro demands of her husband in the front seat.

"What's it called?" he asks with a sigh.

"I got it, dad." Jason pokes at his Katt phone. "What's your order, Hot Pepper?"

"Oh! You have nicknames already?" his mother gushes.

He gives me a long-suffering look and smiles.

"I like the sh-shoyu."

"I'm on it," he says, pressing the phone to his ear. "Do you happen to know if we have beer in the fridge?"

"Yep," I say. "Two six-packs." I lean shamelessly into the warmth of his body.

"Wait—you bought the beer, but not my cookies?" he asks.

"There's Silas's needs to consider."

He laughs, and his mother clasps her hands together. "You're living together?" she breathes.

"It's temporary," I say quickly. Jason only chuckles.

My teeth don't stop chattering until I finish the giant bowl of steaming soup at Jason's kitchen table.

"I'm gonna have a word with the asshole that made you stand out there in the cold," Jason says, his hand holding mine under the table.

"Don't," I say quickly. "He'll retaliate. Rebecca will hear all about it from me eventually."

"That uniform, though," Jason growls. "Last year they had pants and sleeves, right? Am I crazy?"

"There was a uniform change," I say, pushing my empty bowl away. Jason's mother snatches it up and puts the spoon in the dishwasher. "I think it was the new guy's idea."

"A *bad* idea."

"It'll be okay," I insist. "Let me handle it."

Jason's mom pats me on the shoulder. "You're impressive. She's a fighter, Jason. Not a spoiled rich girl."

"Oh, I totally am," I insist. "And hope to be again very soon."

She laughs like I've said something cute, but of course I'm dead serious. And when I yawn again, she insists that I pack myself off to bed. "You need your rest after that long shift."

"True," I say. "Let me sort out the sofa bed for you, though." I'm the last one who used it, after all.

"No!" she says, scandalized. "I'll handle everything, honey. Off you go."

It's not polite to let Jason's parents sleep on the sofa bed while I bask with their son in his king-sized bed. And it's not polite to turn in before everyone else.

But—after grabbing all of my belongings from the living

room—I do both those things, anyway. I need my rest, and I need it now.

First I take a nice hot shower in Jason's luxurious bathroom. Then I blow dry my hair. And finally—finally—I'm truly warm again.

When I emerge from the bathroom wearing only a towel, I'm startled to find Jason sitting up in bed, his bare torso propped against the crisp white pillowcases. He gives me a sexy smile.

Certain parts of me are still conscious enough to tingle in response. But I walk right over to my suitcase and pull out a purple cotton nightgown and matching robe.

"Yes!" Jason says as I drop the towel. "Noooo," he counters a second later when I pull the nightgown over my head. "I liked you better naked."

"Shhh!" I scold him, hurrying over to my side of the bed. "Don't say 'naked' with your mother one room away." I slip into the bed and tuck myself in.

He shuts off the lamp and then slides down to meet me under the covers. "Do you know the best way to warm someone whose body temperature has slipped below the healthy range?" He pulls me closer. "Skin-on-skin contact."

"I'm perfectly fine," I insist.

"Let me just make sure," he whispers, and then kisses my neck. "Mmm. Okay right here." His lips take a sensuous journey across my collarbone. The loose neckline of my nightgown allows him to kiss his way across my chest. "Everything is looking good on this side, too." His whiskers give me goosebumps as his kisses venture toward my cleavage.

As he ministers kisses to all of my available skin, I relax into the warm bed, and the tingles multiply.

"This is gonna be a very thorough once-over," he whispers. "This is in my way." He tugs on the nightgown.

Against my better judgement, I lift my hips and let him

sweep it off my hips and over my head.

"That's a good girl." He chuckles quietly. "Aren't you warmer now?" He covers me with his muscular body, his erection cradled between my legs.

"Oh." I sigh under his hardness. "We shouldn't," I whisper. "Your mother probably has her ear against the door."

He snorts and buries his face in my neck. "She's nosy as heck, but only up to a point," he promises. "Besides, I still haven't verified that you're okay." He lifts his head and cradles my breasts in his hands. "Let me just see..."

When he begins dropping gentle kisses on my breasts, I know I'm not going to be able to help myself. My nipples tighten and my body cries out for more. "Those are very famous," I say quietly. "They were on network television tonight."

"Oh, I know." His tongue does a slow circle of my nipple, and I feel my body soften and then tighten.

"Does that...bother you?" I ask, distracted by my own arousal.

"No," he says, stroking a thumb through the slickness he's created on my breast. "You can show them to whoever you want. Just as long as I'm the guy who gets to do this." He drops his head and sucks my nipple into his mouth.

"Oh," I gasp. The pull of his tongue is exquisite.

He lifts a hand to my mouth and settles his palm over my lips, reminding me to be quiet. And then his brown eyes bore into mine as he sucks greedily on my breast.

Oh my. I push his hand off my mouth. "You're a very bad boy," I whisper.

"Why?" he mouths.

I crook my finger, and he slides up to put his ear right beside my mouth. "Because," I say so quietly that it's almost inaudible. "It's bad timing. And now I just want to be..." The rudeness of the word describes exactly how I feel. "*Fucked*."

Jason presses his face into the pillow and lets out the world's quietest groan. Then he rolls his face toward my ear. "Now you've done it," he whispers, his mustache tickling the shell of my ear. "I'm calling in my reward. Don't know if you were watching. But I *scored*. You know what that means, right?"

"I do." I wrap my arms around his head and whisper into his ear, "I never go back on my promises. Just do it quietly."

He lifts his chin to whisper back at me. "Politely?"

"No!" I mouth. "Never."

He grins. And then his mouth takes mine in a hot kiss. I weave my fingers through his hair and tug until he rolls on top of me again. And everything is right with the world.

We lie drowsing together afterward. "I apologize in advance for every nosy question my mother asks you tomorrow," he says.

I'm lying on his chest, allowing my fingers to explore the sleek skin on his ribcage. "Why is your mother so excited to meet me?"

"Because you're awesome?" he tries.

"Jason."

He sighs. "Moms like that stuff. And I just haven't dated. They all think it's because I'm too afraid to get close to anyone."

"Are they right?"

He snorts. "I'm here with you right now, aren't I? I'm not afraid of you. Unless you're driving my car or sorting through my lucky ties."

"I won't touch your ties. That was a joke."

"And the car?"

"I can't *wait* to drive it again. How does tomorrow sound?"

He laughs so loudly I have to cover his mouth with my hand.

[27]

JASON

IN THE MORNING, my parents take us out for brunch in Manhattan.

Heidi's right—my mother is over the moon about me having a girlfriend again. Every time we interact, Mom gets a moony look on her face, as if I've just announced our engagement instead of merely pulling out Heidi's restaurant chair for her.

In fairness, Heidi is spectacular company. Even though she looks a little weary today, she's charming and bubbly. "It's true that I dropped out of Bryn Mawr," she confesses. "I felt really lost for the three years I was there. I couldn't see a path toward finishing."

My mother—who has two masters degrees, a PhD, and would skin any of her children alive for dropping out of college—pats her hand. "One day you'll figure out exactly what you're meant to do. And everything will fall into place."

I swear, Heidi's next words could be, *"I'm a cult member and I have an addiction to methamphetamines,"* and my mom would smile and offer to help score her next hit. She's that far gone.

Meanwhile, my dad and I polish off twin plates of eggs Benedict with extra bacon. If my dad has an opinion about Heidi and me, I can't tell what it is. My dad is a man of few words. Thank the Lord.

"We'd better get to *el aeropuerto,*" Dad says after we stroll through a few shops in Lower Manhattan. "There could be traffic." Also, shopping is not his favorite activity.

"I'll get you a car," I say quickly. I love my parents, but I've had my fill of parental involvement. Plus, practice starts in two hours.

"It was lovely meeting you," my mother gushes three or four more times before I can tuck them into a taxi. "We always come to the Minnesota game when Jason plays! It's only fifteen miles from home. Any chance you'll be coming, too?"

"You never know," Heidi says lightly. "My work routine is a little unpredictable."

My mother hugs the poor girl again. "You take care. Jason, I'll call you when we make it home."

"Excellent," I say, wondering whether I'll be grilled. "Safe travels."

I close the car door. As the driver pulls away, I let out a gusty breath. "Wow. You are a trooper, Heidi Jo Pepper."

"She's awfully nice," she says, stepping closer to me. "But since my mom is incapable of demonstrating that level of enthusiasm, she took some getting used to."

I sling an arm around her shoulders as we walk up the street toward the subway station. "Ready to head home?"

Heidi shakes her head. "I have to trek up to Daddy's place and pick up my birthday gift. My mother keeps asking if I like it."

"Want company?" I hear myself ask.

"Sure?" she says. "Well, I don't know if my father is home. He works really weird hours. You might be walking into the lion's den."

"I told you I'm not afraid of him." I raise my hand, hailing a Yellow Cab.

"He might be a dick to you."

"Heidi, I'm paid to face down enforcers all night. This is just another day at the office for me."

She giggles as I open the car door for her. "78th and Park," she tells the driver.

Tobias Pepper's condo building is a sleek apartment tower, and the doorman's buttons are so shiny I almost have to squint.

"Hello, Miss Pepper!" says a beefy guy with one gold tooth. "I do not believe your father is at home."

"Oh well!" says Heidi happily. "I'll just have to catch up with him another time." She squeezes my hand as we step into the elevator together. "Oh snap," she says as the doors close. "I won't have to listen to a lecture."

She's practically whistling with joy as she opens the door with her key card a few minutes later. "This is Daddy's place," she says, holding it open for me. "I was really just a squatter here."

"Does your mother ever visit?" I ask.

"Barely. She doesn't like the city."

"Oh." Still, that doesn't make much sense. "But does she like your father?"

"She likes him in Tennessee. I think four months of the year is perfect for her."

That saddens me, but I don't say so.

"Now I just need to grab this gift..." She trots toward the rear of the apartment. "One second!"

I'm *this close* to jokingly calling out my offer to have a nooner in her dad's condo when I hear another key in the lock.

Uh-oh.

That's when the front door opens again, and her father walks in. Naturally, I'm the one he spots first. First his eyes widen, and then they narrow.

"Hello," I say with an awkward chuckle. "I didn't break in. I swear. Your daughter is back there." I gesture toward the bedrooms and try to look innocent. Which I'm not. Not really.

He says not a word to me. Just closes the door behind himself and waits for his daughter to appear.

"Daddy? Hey." Heidi emerges a second later. "I was just stopping by to pick up whatever mom sent me."

His jaw is rock-hard. No hello kiss for his baby girl? He points at me instead. "Why is *he* here?"

Ah, straight to the point, then.

"Jason and I were out to brunch together. With his parents." Heidi puts her hands on her hips and faces him down. "We're close. But I don't see why you'd care."

"I care because of your self-destructive behavior!"

"Oh, please!" she squeaks. "I work an obscene number of hours a day, thanks to you. Who has time for destructive behavior?"

"Go back to school," he says heavily.

"We already had that discussion," Heidi fires back. "And I'm not doing it."

"Where have you been staying?"

"It just occurred to you to ask now?"

"You don't exactly answer my calls," he points out. "Where are you living, Heidi? I told your mother I'd find out."

Heidi flinches. "That's a private matter."

Tobias Pepper rolls his eyes, and for a split second the family resemblance shines through. Heidi gives me that same face sometimes. It's way cuter on her, though. Then the man turns to me and asks, point blank, "Is she staying with you?"

"Yessir." I don't even hesitate. "For as long as she needs."

He makes an unhappy grunt. "Heidi Jo, your ten weeks just became twenty."

"*What?*" she shrieks. "You can't *do* that! I've done everything you asked! Every stupid job! Every humiliating moment! And I haven't complained."

Oh, Jesus. I would've waited in the lobby if I'd known I would cause this scene.

The old grump is already shaking his head. "You need to learn how the real world works. And you can't learn it by ingratiating yourself with a hockey team."

Heidi has gone white. Her hands are in fists. She looks like O'Doul just before a sudden second-period brawl. "I can't believe you," she whispers.

"You'll believe me by March," he says. "That's the point."

She closes her eyes for a moment. Then they fly open again. She stomps toward a console table against the wall. "This must be from my mother?" There's a gift box with a ribbon tied around it. Heidi checks the card and then tugs violently on the ribbon. "Ah," she says, opening the lid of the box. "It's good to know my parents are on the same page." Heidi lifts something from the box. A scarf? A wrap?

I don't speak women's fashion, but it's diaphanous and beaded.

"This is very useful!" she snaps. "I can wear it over my Ice Girls' uniform between resurfacings. Or sell it on eBay. Whether or not you know it, I am a very practical girl." She drops it back into the box and snatches it off the table. "Let's go, Jason." She stomps toward the door and opens it almost before I catch on.

Heidi makes it to the elevator before I'm even out the door. But I hesitate anyway, turning to glance at her father on my way out. He's standing quite still in his living room, looking like a grenade with the pin pulled.

"Look," I say, and he turns to look at me with angry eyes.

"Don't punish her for spending time with me. She doesn't deserve that."

If possible, his jaw gets even harder.

"She works really hard. I just want you to know that. She tackles the jobs you assigned to her, and she has a side hustle to earn more money." I shake my head, thinking of all the hours Heidi works. "And she's a good friend. She's looking after my teammate who just had knee surgery. And she planned a birthday surprise for my roommate. She's a good worker, and a good person. She's *impressive*. If I were you, I'd be proud, not angry."

He closes his eyes for a brief second, and then turns his back on me.

Having said my piece, I join Heidi at the elevator bank. Her eyes are red, and her shoulders are tight.

When I pull her into my arms, she doesn't resist.

[28]

HEIDI

"HE *DOUBLED* MY JAIL SENTENCE," I tell Jana. "I'm having a dying duck fit, here."

"Deep breaths, Heidi Jo," my sister says. "Stress wrinkles the face prematurely."

"I'll look like a hag by the weekend, then! Why is he doing this to me?"

"Maybe Daddy is having a midlife crisis," my sister muses. "He snapped at Mama over the weekend, too. Right in the middle of the country club dining room."

"Oh, Lordy. Did she lose her squash at him later?"

"No idea. I stayed clear of the two of them after brunch. He was giving Mama a hard time over her credit card bill."

"What a *grump*." Although Mama is known for bringing armloads of shopping bags home every week. And she never worked a day in her life.

Unlike me. "If you happened to watch the Brooklyn game on TV last night, you would have seen me skating with the Ice Girls again."

My sister giggles. "When's the next home game? I have to see this."

"Friday."

"I'm making a note. Is the uniform awful?"

"It's the worst. Not just because it's too revealing—it's *cold*. And the jerk in charge is always touching us—like he's at the grocery store trying to choose a good melon."

"Ew!" Jana shrieks. "I'm surprised you haven't kneed him in the walnuts already. Our Heidi Jo doesn't suffer fools. Tell Daddy. He'd hate that."

"I will *not* ask Daddy for help." There's a better way. "I'm going to write down everything the guy does and report back to the team owner." In fact, I'm walking into the Brooklyn Bruisers headquarters right now to meet with Rebecca. "He's going to get an earful from management."

"That's showing him," my sister says. "Now, you hang in there. If you need money, maybe I could give you a loan from my trust fund. The lawyer could help me with that."

"Wow. That's generous of you. If I get really desperate, I'll ask. I'm only halfway to banking the five thousand dollars I need for my own apartment." I pause in the lobby to finish our conversation.

"What?" she yelps. "Why so much?"

"Everybody wants first and last months' rent as a deposit. And then there's the brokers' fee. And I don't own a stick of furniture." Heck—if you add all that up, it's more than five grand.

"Come home," Jana suggests. "Find a job in Nashville."

"I can't! Because then Daddy wins." Also, my subconscious has a brand-new problem with that idea. *Jason is here in Brooklyn,* my heart whispers.

It's way too soon to plan my life around his. But my subconscious doesn't know it.

"You hang in there," Jana says. "Gotta jump! The spa

manager is giving me the stink eye for using my phone in here. And it's time for my full-body facial."

I let out a little sigh, just picturing it. What I wouldn't give for a day at the spa right now. "Enjoy!" I tell her. "Toodles!"

After we hang up, I hurry down the shiny hallway floorboards and into the executive suite. But instead of continuing into Rebecca's office, I skid to a stop right in front of the reception desk where Rebecca used to sit.

There's someone else sitting at it now. A stranger.

My pulse jumps and not in a good way. I'm staring down at a young woman with a shiny manicure, a crisply tailored suit, and perfect hair. There's something familiar about her. Oh wait—that's because she reminds me of *me*. Last year I was the glowing young intern who always showed up for work after a good night's sleep and with perfect grooming.

She's me, only without the exhaustion from a month of petty humiliations. And what the heck is she doing at this desk? "Can I help you?" I ask her.

The girl looks up at me, startled. "I'm pretty sure that's my line."

"Who are you?" I demand.

"Again, I'm the one who's supposed to ask those kinds of—"

"Heidi Jo!" Rebecca interrupts by calling to me from within the owner's office. "Come right in."

I give the newcomer a searing look and then march toward Becca's office. "Hi," I say stiffly. "Did you already hire someone for—" I jerk my thumb toward the outer office.

"She's a temp," Rebecca says kindly. "It's a rent-to-own situation."

"But I want a shot at that position." *That's my job!* I want to scream. "How much more experience could she have than me?" My voice gets high and squeaky when I'm upset.

"I understand," Rebecca says. "Nothing's been decided. But I can't leave that desk empty for months. And your father sent me an email demanding that you work through your internship jobs for an additional ten weeks."

"He's being irrational," I argue. "I'll calm him down and make him understand."

"Okay. Let me know how that goes." She gestures towards a chair. "You said you needed to talk about the Ice Girls' gig?"

"You bet." I plunk down and face her. "Randy Cavanaugh is —to use a technical term—a dick weasel."

Rebecca flinches. "I don't enjoy his company, either. And if his behavior is unprofessional, I'm going to need specifics. Start at the beginning."

So I do. I give Becca chapter and verse about the tiny uniform and the arctic breeze that turns my toes to popsicles as we greet the fans before the game. "'Welcome sir! Here is my cleavage for your viewing pleasure. Ignore the blue tint of my skin! Beer is half-priced until warmups begin. Now retrieve your eyes from my ass and have a pleasant day!'"

Becca claps a hand over her mouth and tries to suppress her giggle. "I'm sorry to laugh, but you are a cutup."

"I don't see how it's legal to freeze me."

"It's not." She shakes her head. "There was no reason to change the uniform. Last year they wore long black spandex tights and long-sleeved tops. They were still low cut and bare at the tummy." Becca rolls her eyes. "But they had to be warmer, more practical."

"If the team had matching warmup gear, it could still work," I point out. "But he has us dressed the same as his dance team, even when we're just standing around shivering."

"You're right. What else?"

I hesitate. "Where did the new guy come from, anyway? There's just something off about him generally. I know this is unhelpfully vague, but he took this girl named Amber aside last night, and afterward she was crying."

Becca's eyes widen. "Did you ask her why?"

I shake my head.

"Well." Becca looks thoughtful. "If Amber was late for work six nights in a row, he might have simply delivered a well-deserved warning. Or he could be a horrible man asking for sexual favors."

I can't even hide my shudder.

The boss taps the tips of her fingers together. "Listen, I have an idea. You are under absolutely no obligation to do this, though."

"What is it?"

"Let's keep you on the Ice Girls team for longer than this week. We'll work in your other jobs around it. I'd want you to pretend to be really invested in advancement—tell Cavanaugh that you want to try out for the dance team. Tell him you'll do whatever it takes."

"Goodness!" I gasp. I'm afraid to know what it takes.

"Let me be clear," Rebecca adds. "You are not to endanger yourself in any way, or to do anything that makes you truly uncomfortable. And meanwhile, you're going to collect evidence to support the fact that he's mistreating his employees. Buy a thermometer and record how cold it is where you're standing. If he touches the girls, take a photo."

I let out a bark of laughter. "Hiding my phone is going to be tricky. The skirt is about four inches long. No pockets."

"Heidi Jo, you are the most resourceful person I've met in ages. Feel free to go all James Bond on this man. Find a camera on the internet that looks like a pen. Save your receipts."

"Oh, wow." Suddenly, I see the possibilities. "This could be a whole lot of fun."

Rebecca gives me a devious smile. "This man was hired very suddenly last spring, after the woman who ran the program quit to move to Alaska with her girlfriend. Unfortunately, he has a multi-year contract. I need evidence if he's created a hostile work environment. At the very least, I want to address the uncomfortable working conditions."

"I understand."

"Meanwhile, you're going to have to fit in more of the work from your father's list of jobs. But you'll get overtime pay."

That's certainly good news.

"Oh—and what if I told your dad how amazingly helpful you are? I could let him know that your ability to work everywhere in the organization is working out so well that you and I are *both* giddy about it."

"But—" I don't want Daddy to think this was a great idea.

"Come on, don't you have siblings? Reverse psychology, baby. You know it's no fun to torture someone if they're enjoying it."

"Oh," I say slowly. "You're very devious, too, Rebecca."

"I know!" She gives me a gleeful smile. "Hang in there, Heidi Jo. Not only are you doing me a big favor—one that I won't forget—you're also doing those other women a big favor. After you've been around for a while, maybe they'll trust you enough to confide in you."

"Okay." Helping the other girls would be killer. And helping Rebecca isn't such a bad thing, either. "Say no more. I'm in."

Even if my boobs freeze off, it's for a good cause.

[29]

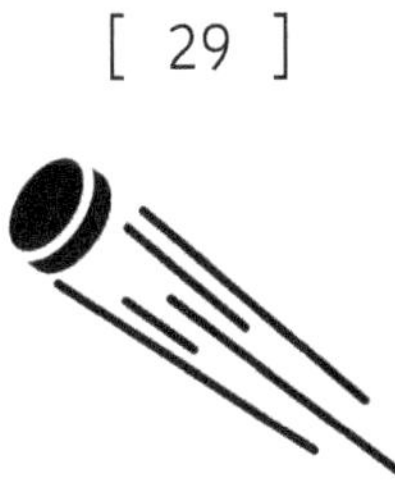

November

JASON

"HEIDI SHOULD KEEP LOOKING," Silas says as he zips up his suitcase for our road trip. He keeps his voice low as he adds, "That place is *not* the right apartment for her."

"I was afraid you'd say that."

Last night Silas accompanied Heidi to the Bronx to look at a rental. I'd wanted to see it myself, but Heidi said I was too judgmental. I've earned this reputation by pitching fits about the other three apartments I scoped out with her.

In my defense, every one of them was in a dark, dangerous spot and had poor security. "How bad was it?" I ask Silas.

He makes a disgusted face as he picks up the suitcase and carries it past me. I follow him into the living room where he sets it near the door. "A total dump. And in a shitty neighborhood."

"There are safety bars on the windows!" Heidi yells from

my bathroom—which is mostly her bathroom these days. "I took a photo to show you, Mr. Bossypants."

That's me in this scenario.

"It also has roaches," Silas points out.

Gross. "Is there a doorman?"

Silas says "no" at the same moment that Heidi yells the opposite. "Well." Silas chuckles. "There's a homeless man who holds the outer door in search of tips. But he's not exactly a union employee."

"He was very nice," Heidi insists. But then she sighs and changes the subject. "Guys, our car is four minutes away."

"We're ready," I call, walking toward my bathroom. "What takes you so long, anyway?"

But the moment I spy her in the mirror, I forget the question. Heidi stands there in a short wool skirt and black tights. But it's not only her curvy backside that's so captivating, it's the way she's leaning toward the mirror, stroking some kind of makeup product onto her eyelashes, and humming softly to herself.

It's her *essence*. She's populating my bathroom with beauty products and taking over my dresser drawer with lacy little pairs of panties, and I don't even mind the invasion. Because I love the way her arm curls around my waist at night and the sound of her raucous laughter when I tell a joke.

Every time I walk into a room where she is, I feel lucky. Life has been pretty kind to me for the last month.

Heidi, however, hasn't had it so easy. In the first place, Rebecca still has her working on the Ice Girls team, documenting Randy Cavanaugh's offenses. That means Heidi has skated in all eight home games this month.

And when the team is away, she does every other job her father invented for her. She's cleaned the locker rooms at the practice facility. She's stacked bandages for the training staff.

She's sold tickets in the box office. I get tired just thinking about it.

My life, on the other hand, has only gotten better. I come home from road trips to a fully stocked apartment and an affectionate girl in my bed. And it's funny how easily I've slipped into the role of being someone's boyfriend, even after all these years. It's like riding a bike. When I'm in town, I take her out for dinner and rub her feet. I do my part to shore her up, but I can tell she's feeling worn down.

This week, though, she's heading out on a road trip with the team. So that's new. "Are you about ready? I'll carry your bag downstairs."

"Almost. I have to finish my lashes."

"No you don't," I argue. We still bicker all the time, and sometimes our arguments get heated. The dumber the argument, the more stubborn I become. I swear Heidi almost punched me last night when we were arguing over which pizza toppings are the most all-American.

I can't even remember what position I took in this great debate. I think I made a speech about the importance of sausage, and she made a speech about the patriarchy. After we fought it to a bitter draw, though, the make-up sex was spectacular.

"You know, babe," I say, instigating yet another argument just because I can. "Eyelashes don't really matter. No guy ever turned to his buddies in the bar and said, 'Look at the lashes on that one.'"

She doesn't take the bait. She screws the cap onto whatever diabolical dye or paint or glue she was using and then turns to face me. And this is how I lose arguments, because she's so pretty I get a little distracted. "Jason, the lashes aren't supposed to be noticeable. But they're part of the whole *effect*." She makes jazz hands to emphasize this point.

And, fuck, I guess she's right. Because the whole *effect* is making me wish we had a few extra minutes, so I could pull up that soft-looking sweater and…

She snaps her fingers in my face. "Don't do that."

"Do what?"

"Don't make your horny face. It's time to go." She slips past me.

"I have a horny face?"

"Of course! All men do. Yours is sort of cross-eyed, and your tongue hangs out of the corner of your mouth." Her phone pings.

"No it doesn't! *Jesus*." I chase her toward the kitchen, hoping for a kiss.

She puts her coffee cup in the sink. "The car is downstairs. Saddle up!"

"Oh fuck." I sigh. "I need two more minutes. I forgot to make my peanut butter and…"

Heidi grabs a paper lunch bag off the counter and thrusts it into my hands. And from the weight and shape, I know it can only be another peanut butter and strawberry jam sandwich, cut diagonally just how I like it.

"*Ohh*." I let out a moan of happiness. And, fuck. My tongue *is* hanging out—but just a little. And only for a second. "You're the best girl in the whole fucking world." *And can I take off your sweater now?*

"Had to do it," she says. "Can't break the streak. San Jose looks tough this season."

"But I'm tougher, right?" I actually puff out my chest.

"Of course, baby. That's just a given." Her heeled boots click importantly on the wood floor as she hefts her suitcase off a chair.

"Hey now," I say, stopping her. "I said I'd carry that."

"I can lift my own bag," she says at close range, those big eyes going slightly soft now that we're nose to nose.

"Sure you can," I whisper. "But you're not going to carry it when I'm standing here with two functioning arms. Thanks again for the sandwich. I know you're doing it for the whole Brooklyn franchise. But I sure do appreciate it."

Her gaze softens again. "I know you do. And I'm not superstitious at all. Peanut butter and jam can't beat San Jose. I only make that sandwich because it makes you happy."

Well, now I have to kiss her. I duck my head and quickly skim my lips across hers. She stands up on her tiptoes and wraps her arms around me while I slowly claim her mouth.

"Mmm." Heidi sighs against my tongue as we kiss.

Didn't I say it's been a great month? I pull her body against mine and her warmth does nice things to my heart.

"Keep the make-out sesh brief," Silas says from the front hall. "Isn't it time to go?"

My girl pulls back with a smile on her face. "I'll let you carry my bag if only to save your tender male ego."

"Good call." I steal one more kiss. "It will be nice having you in my hotel room tonight."

Slowly, she shakes her head. "The support staff are staying at a Holiday Inn near the airport."

"What? No! I need you close to me."

"We'll see," she says. "I don't want to look like a prima donna."

"You're not," I insist. "And please don't rent a shithole apartment just to prove your independence. It doesn't need proving."

She lifts her blue eyes to mine. "Maybe it does. To *me*."

"Oh." I really don't see why that would be. But I'm a smart enough man not to say so. "Let's go to California. What job did you say you were working on this trip?"

"I didn't say." She strides into the hallway in front of me. And I swear there's an extra little butt wiggle there that's meant to torture me.

My girl is right. San Jose does look tough this season. The game is a gongshow. It's dirty. So many of our opponent's hands are grabbing various parts of my body, that it's more like a rave than a hockey game.

Midway through the second period we have a hard-fought 1-1 draw. I'm gulping Gatorade when Coach says, "Let's mix it up a little. I'm putting your line up for the faceoff next time."

"Sure thing."

But after the next whistle there's a media timeout, so we all get a chance to breathe. I ruminate on our opponent's defense squad and try to formulate a plan. Meanwhile, the team mascots take the ice. There's a furry blue fish and our own Brooklyn brown bear. They're having a faux-fight—the kind of thing I always ignore.

But for some weird reason, I feel a tingle at the back of my skull. And I glance up to see the bear do a graceful spin in front of the penalty box.

"Holy shit." Trevi whistles. "Our bear can skate."

My eyes widen as the Brooklyn bear executes a double axel, landing with its furry brown arms outstretched. There are hoots of laughter from the crowd. But not from the other mascot. The fish swerves, cutting off the bear's path, moving in and punching the bear right in the neck.

"That doesn't look very sportsmanlike," a teammate says.

But the San Jose fans like it. "Fight! Fight! Fight!" they cry.

Our bear squares himself to the fish, and raises a pair of furry fists. But anyone can see that it isn't a good matchup. The fish towers over the bear. And even though flippers aren't known as weapons in the wild, this fish winds up and clocks our bear right in the chin.

"Fuck 'im up!" yells some cretin in the stands.

Our bear seems to realize he can't win with brawn, so he goes for flair instead, executing a roundhouse kick that neatly avoids actually touching the fish, and then follows that up with a stylish spin maneuver.

"Holy shit!" Silas laughs from the other end of the bench. "Now we know what job they gave Heidi this week. Mystery solved."

Holy shit indeed. That tingle moves down my backbone as I realize he's right. Only Heidi could bring such flare to the bear suit. And she said she used to compete at skating when she was little.

The fish is unimpressed, though. He keeps trying to jab at her, while Heidi is literally skating circles around him. He flaps those long flippers, spoiling for a fight.

Then Heidi skates toward him, as if she means to engage. But—psych! She's too quick. The fish punches and misses. The crowd howls.

You'd think that a guy in a whole-body fish suit couldn't look angry. But you'd be wrong.

"*The bear won't fight!*" yells some asshole in the crowd.

"*The bear is a pussy!*" screams another.

"Take it like a *man*, bear!" As if that makes any sense at all.

I grow increasingly uneasy, because Heidi doesn't seem to sense the anger in the room. Or maybe she does, and she's just running down the clock. Then again, no sensible person would do what she does next—skating up fast and then pulling a hockey stop so sudden that she sprays the fish with ice shavings. It's the ultimate burn in hockey.

And then? Heidi opens her furry arms as if to say, *I'm right here. What's the problem?*

The shark lunges. The crowd roars. As my heart climbs my throat, both mascots go down in a heap of blue and brown fur.

"*Fight fight fight!*"

"Oh, shit," Trevi whispers as the mascots begin to grapple.

Heidi has the fish by its snout. She gives him a shove and then tries to roll away. A wave of nausea rolls through me as the fish whips his skates around in an arc.

A sharpened skate can *kill* you. I'm on my feet now.

"Hey," Trevi says, pulling me back down. "Heidi's smart. She won't get herself in trouble."

For a few beats of my heart, I actually believe him. Heidi pops to her feet and skates away from the shark. But then she looks over her shoulder at him. She puts her big fuzzy hands on her big fuzzy hips and shakes her giant padded ass. *You can't catch me.*

He tries, though. A mad fish is a fast fish. He's practically on her little bob of a tail already. Heidi weaves and dodges down the ice. Her footwork is amazing, but the fish has a longer stride. When he closes in on her, the asshole uses one of his skates to sweep her legs out from under her.

All my blood stops circulating as he reaches down and picks her up in his flipper arms. I'm on my feet again.

Heidi flails while the crowd roars.

"Sit down!" Trevi hisses to me. "You set foot on that ice and they'll penalize the team and also fine you."

I can't even breathe as the fish staggers forward and hurls Heidi into the hockey net. I'm already over the wall and skating toward them even as her head bounces off the surface of the ice.

"Goal!" yells some asshole fan.

The next three seconds are a blur. I reach the goal crease as the fish is celebrating and Heidi is trying to scramble to her feet. But she's caught in the net.

"What the fuck, man?" yells the fish as I push him out of the way.

I reach into the net and pull the Brooklyn brown bear into my arms. "Let me go!" Heidi shrieks. "I'm going to kick his ass!"

"You know you're beating up a *woman*?" I snarl at the fish.

The ref is blowing his whistle like crazy as I stand up, carrying my girl.

"What are you doing?" Heidi squeaks as I skate quickly toward the chute, where a very puzzled rink official pulls open the door so I can set her onto the rubber padding. "I could have won!"

It's dawning on me that twenty thousand people are watching as I glare at Heidi through the mesh eye holes of her costume. I put a hand on her fuzzy head. "Are you hurt?"

"No! I'm fine! You just got yourself in trouble for *nothing!*"

That's when the game announcer calls a two-minute bench minor against Brooklyn for delay of the game.

"See?" she yells, flailing her furry arms unhappily. "Now the fish gets a power play!"

I'm vaguely aware of an entire stadium laughing.

"You do your job, I'll do mine!" she yells, her furry arms outstretched.

The ref's whistle slices through the air, calling me to the penalty box.

Gritting my teeth, I go.

[30]

HEIDI

"I CAN'T BELIEVE you have a black eye!" Rebecca fusses.

"It's not black," I argue. "Just a little purple. And it's *tiny*."

Becca gives me a knowing look and hands me an ice pack. "Sit there on the desk." We're in a barren little office underneath the San Jose stadium. "Maybe we should have the doctor go through the concussion protocol."

"No way!" I yelp. "Did you see how thick the padding is on that bear suit? It's like wearing a beanbag chair on my head."

"Then how'd you get a black eye?

She's got me there. "The head rotated a little. I bruised my eyebrow on the face frame when I landed. It's nothing."

"I guess there's not much swelling." Rebecca leans over me, clucking like a mother hen. "But I feel terrible. This assignment was supposed to be *fun*. It was your reward for suffering through all those other horrible jobs you've been doing."

"Whatever," I reassure my boss. "We shall not speak of this again."

Rebecca sighs. "Okay. It's in the vault."

I'm deeply embarrassed about the whole thing—about losing a fight to a stuffed fish and about letting him get me so riled up. I didn't even know I was capable of that kind of blood lust.

All the battle scenes in Outlander make more sense to me now, at least. Given the right set of conditions, I could run a sword through my enemy. Daddy wanted me to learn some things about myself? He didn't count on this.

Nothing can make me feel better, either. We lost the game 2-1. San Jose scored during Jason's penalty minutes. I'm still almost as mad at Jason as I am at myself.

Almost.

"I guess we can look on the bright side," Rebecca says. "The footage is hilarious."

"That is *not* the bright side," I grumble.

"When you shook your butt at the fish..." Rebecca's giggle shakes her whole body. "Priceless!"

I don't want to see the footage. I wish the linoleum floor would open up and swallow me. Instead, I tap the screen of my phone, checking the time. We're waiting for the post-game press conference to wind down. Can I make my escape yet?

At least I'm no longer wearing a smelly bear suit. I'm dressed in yoga pants and a Brooklyn hoodie that I stole from Jason. I'd rather be invisible. I just want to go back to the Holiday Inn and pull the sheets over my head, pretending this night never happened.

But the support-staff bus won't pull up until every player has cleared out of the locker room. I'll probably have to help the travel team load hockey gear onto the bus, if only to speed them up.

Georgia Trevi breezes into the room looking fresh and happy in spite of our loss tonight. "Heidi, there you are! The first blog posts are up and just look at this photo someone got!"

She's smiling, but I brace myself anyway. The last time

Georgia had a photo to show me, it was me as a stumbling drunk. Tonight it's bound to be me in the bear suit, tangled up in the hockey net.

They must be scratching my name off the charm-school graduates' list by now.

"Puck Buddy's is actually doing a *Caption This* contest! Check it out." She thrusts her Katt Phone into my hands.

There I am, standing tall at least. Small blessings. The fish isn't in the shot, either. This photo is Jason and me, face to face, his hand on the top of the bear-suit head. The deathly serious expression on his face is in direct contrast to the silly bear's smile on my costume.

My heart can't even sort out all the things I feel when I look at this picture. All I want is to be treated like an adult—by my father and by Jason. But it's always one step forward and then two steps back. Here he is scolding me like a child.

Although Becca and Georgia have no trouble seeing the humor in it. They're giggling away. A hockey player scolding a stuffed animal? Hilarious!

Privately, I'm grinding my teeth. It's yet one more instance of a man trying to rescue me again when I don't need rescuing.

And here comes the man himself, stalking into the room, trailed by Tommy, the other publicist. Jason is wearing a well-cut suit and a scowl.

I whip the ice pack off my eyebrow, but I'm a little too late.

That scowl deepens. "You're hurt? Jesus Christ." He strides over to cup my chin possessively. Then he squints at my tiny bruise. "He gave you a *shiner?*" Those dark brown eyes get dark and wild.

And, fine, his caveman expression gets me a little hot. I'm only human. But I wish he'd save this show of protectiveness for a private moment when we're both naked. Although I feel naked right now, because Becca and Georgia are watching with great interest.

"I'm fine." I push his hand off my face. "Don't fuss."

But he only relocates those hands to my shoulders. "I'm not a fan of you getting hurt."

"I'm not a fan of you telling me off in front of twenty thousand people! If you think I'm sneaking into your hotel room after that, think again!"

Becca and Georgia lean in, fascinated. *Whoops.* I swear they're paying more attention right now than they did to the actual game.

"You don't want to hear me get upset? Then don't pick fights with assholes!" Jason says.

"*He* started it!" I squeak. "But everything was under control!"

It's a lie. I lost that fight. Jason's expression says he knows the truth, too. I brace myself for more of his scolding. But instead he does something more brutal. He leans down and kisses me *right* on the lips.

And it's no quick peck—it's a bossy, hungry, *claiming* sort of kiss. My toes curl inside my ankle boots as his tongue seeks out mine. I get a hold of my senses and pull back, although now I can't remember the finer points of why I'm angry.

"Well, *well*." Becca chuckles. "Who knew Castro had a thing for bears?"

Georgia high-fives her, and they both crack up.

"Not funny," Jason growls. "How could you put Heidi in that position tonight?"

Becca sobers up quickly. "Usually the mascots meet beforehand to discuss their shenanigans. But the fish was unavailable. Turns out he was getting high in the men's room. I've already asked Hugh to write a letter to the team, demanding an apology for Heidi."

"Oh, let's not make a federal case out of it," I snap. "The worst thing about tonight's job is that the bear costume smells like B.O." I had to sneak into the visitors' locker room during the third period to shower.

"Am I getting in some kind of trouble with the league for leaving the bench?" Jason asks.

"I doubt it?" Becca shrugs. "Hugh and your agent will sort it out. The league could technically fine you. But since you left the bench to *stop* a fight, not to start one, it's unlikely they'll want to make an example of you."

"I won't apologize," Jason says. "That was an unsafe situation."

"We get it," Becca says with twinkling eyes. "Carry on, then." She walks out of the room, still smiling.

"Actually..." Georgia walks over to the office door and closes it. "I have something else I need to talk to you about, Jason. It doesn't have a thing to do with tonight's game. It's a private matter."

A beat goes by, and then I realize that was my cue. "I'll go," I say, sliding off the desk.

"No, stay," Jason grunts, catching me by the hand. "Ice that eye. Whatever Georgia has to say, you can hear it. I don't have any secrets."

My anger instantly cools. The press of his hand against mine is nice. And I can't deny that I get a thrill every time he says, *"Stay here with me."* Whether he says it with his words or with his hands or with his eyes, I fall a little further into his thrall.

I've never been so obsessed with anyone in my life. It's exciting, but it's also trouble. This *thing* that Jason and I have going on is even better than I'd hoped for. Little by little, I'm falling for him. I don't know if that's allowed, but I don't know that I can help it.

"So here's the issue," Georgia says, her voice oddly hushed. "Earlier today I got a weird call asking for a meeting with you, Jason. It's an unusual request. I told this young woman that I'd get back to her in a week or so. So let me share this with you now so you can think about it."

"Okay?" He looks confused, and I don't blame him.

Georgia sits down on a broken desk chair and puts her chin in her hands. "So there's a young woman in Minnesota. A senior at the university, playing her last college hockey season."

"That's nice?" Jason says. "How do I fit in?"

"Six years ago she wasn't able to play hockey. She was basically dying. A surgery she'd had went wrong and damaged her liver. But then she was gifted a liver transplant, by a young woman named…"

Out of the corner of my eye, Jason visibly braces himself. "Melissa Skinner."

Georgia nods.

"Wait," I whisper. "That's Lissa—your high school girlfriend who died?"

"Right," he grunts.

"Did you know she was an organ donor?" Georgia asks softly.

Jason is quiet for a moment. "I only have hazy memories of the week she died. But there was something about organ donation."

Georgia clears her throat. "I hadn't heard that story before. After I got this call today, I googled Melissa Skinner. There are some old news articles about you and Melissa and the accident. Your hockey team raised money for Melissa's funeral. I'm so sorry, Jason. I didn't know you lost your girlfriend when you were…"

"Eighteen," he bites out. "That was a long time ago. I don't think about it so much anymore." Although his tone makes him a liar.

"Well, I'm still sorry for your loss," Georgia says.

"What does the girl want?" he asks, probably hoping to get to the end of this conversation. "Money?"

"Not exactly. See, she's pretty happy to be alive and playing goalie for her college team. She was hoping to meet you when the team travels to Minnesota. Her name is Carrie, and she runs a campaign every year at her school so that other students know how important it is to check the organ-donation box on your driver's license."

"Oh," he says slowly. "That's a good cause."

"It is," Georgia agrees. "She's in touch with another organ recipient, too. Both women feel a lot of gratitude toward Melissa. They'd like to meet you."

"Me?" he asks. "Why? The other woman plays hockey, too? What are the odds?"

"No," Georgia says quickly. "Only Carrie plays. The other girl—they're just transplant buddies."

He frowns. "She got a transplant, too? Of…?"

Georgia looks really uncomfortable now. "Eyes." Her voice cracks on the word. "She was blind."

"Eyes," he repeats. "I see." And then, as I watch, Jason's face drains of color. His face turns white and then grey, and even his lips go pale. "Excuse me," he grunts. Then he walks away from me without a backward glance, flinging the door open so hard that it bangs against the wall.

He disappears, and for a long moment afterward, Georgia and I just stare at the doorway where we last saw him.

"Holy cow," Georgia says, recovering first. "I didn't mean to upset him. I had to bring this to him, though. Didn't I?" She turns to look at me with wide eyes.

"Sure," I say, although I'm not sure about anything at all.

"There's no road map for this," Georgia says.

"Right? I'll give him a few minutes and then track him down. I'll make sure he's okay."

"Would you?" she asks. "Text me, okay?"

"Of course."

Georgia leaves, still looking worried. I throw away my ice pack, gather up my things, and go in search of Jason.

But by the time I've checked the locker room and the equipment room, Jason is gone. He's already on the team bus, from what Jimbo can tell me.

I check my phone. No messages.

[31]

JASON

I'M LYING in bed in a luxurious room on an upper floor of the Fairmont Hotel. I've left the lights off and the drapes open, and the Silicon Valley sparkles out the window in the distance.

Only I'm not really here at all. I'm back in Quebec in a stadium with my juniors team. We just won our third tournament game in a row. I'm covered in sweat and grinning like a maniac. But then my coach pulls me aside. *Come here, Castro. Sit down, son. There's been an accident.*

A car accident, as it turned out. And Lissa was just *gone.* I remember sitting there on the bench in the stinky locker room, trying to process what he was telling me.

But it took me hours to understand and another day or so to cry. Because your girlfriend can't just up and *die* when there are so many complicated things between the two of you.

Except it turns out that she can.

Most people don't learn this lesson at eighteen. Some people never learn it at all. I still envy everyone who doesn't know what it's like to have a major chunk of your world ripped away on the Saturday after Thanksgiving. It's a kind of violence on your soul.

And violence always leaves a mark. I felt physically ill tonight when Georgia explained who wanted to meet me. Bile rose suddenly in my throat, and I fought it back all the way to the hotel.

Good night, good night! parting is such sweet sorrow, That I shall say good night till it be morrow. Lissa and I had starred in *Romeo and Juliet* at school in ninth grade. To this day I still have every line memorized. "A Shakespearean Tragedy" our local paper had titled the story of Lissa's accident.

That play will forever be snarled with November and loss in my mind.

Jesus fucking Christ. I can't meet somebody who has Melissa's *eyes*. I'll write a big fat check to whatever charity these girls are supporting. But I don't want to meet them.

I roll over and stare at the hotel room ceiling. I need to pull myself together. That's something I had to learn at eighteen, too. A man doesn't fall apart. There are too many people depending on me. Even at eighteen, I had the dysfunctional mother of the deceased blubbering in my arms at the funeral. And my own family watching me warily—my mother soaking her way through a supply of tissues.

You don't cry when anyone else is around. They need you to be okay. They're counting on it.

Across the room, my phone lights up with another text. My parents always reach out after a game to let me know they watched. And my teammates are probably wondering why I'm not down at the bar.

Then there's Heidi. This afternoon I slipped a hotel key into her pocket and told her to meet me here later if she could. But then I pulled a runner tonight after that weird little meeting with Georgia. Heidi is almost certainly wanting to know if I'm okay.

And I will be soon. I always am.

Sleep comes for me eventually. I drift through its shallowest waters before slipping under the surface entirely. I barely register the beep and click of my hotel room door opening. A few moments later, a soft body curves toward mine. My arm is lifted and then lowered again. My hand—relaxed in sleep—comes to rest on smooth skin.

I inhale, taking in citrus and warmth.

Heidi.

I'd begged her to come to my hotel and warm my bed. But I hadn't counted on needing a night of solitude to get my crazy head in line. So now I lay very still and slow my breathing, asking my body to sleep. It's the only way to get out of my head.

But Heidi's scent is too present, her skin too warm, her curves tucked against my greedy body. Unbidden, my thumb strokes the underside of her breast. And the sigh she makes is full of awareness and heat.

My blood stirs. Of course it does.

Right after Lissa died, I assumed I wouldn't think about sex ever again. But I was an eighteen-year-old guy. My libido barely took a vacation. I spent the year after I lost her horny and upset about it. Then I went off to college, where nobody knew me as the boyfriend of the dead girl. So I started hooking up on the regular. No relationships, of course. Just sex.

And that was the way it went for six years. Until now.

Heidi tries to roll over, reaching for me. But I can't let that happen. She'll see all the pain I'm in.

So I use my strength to stop her. I force her to remain on her side, facing the other way. So what if she lets out a shocked gasp at my rough treatment? She likes me in control. I kiss the back of her neck as a show of tenderness. She tastes sweet, and

I let my tongue linger. Meanwhile, I give each of her nipples a rude pinch.

She moans, and I close my eyes against that sound. It feels wrong to do this. I shouldn't fuck one girl while I'm all tangled up over another one. Worse—I shouldn't shut Heidi out. She cares about me. I know in my gut that she'd want to hear what's on my mind.

If I stopped right now—if I wasn't slipping my hand down between her legs—she'd be happy to listen. She'd hold me and say all the right things. There's probably a unit at charm school for what to say to the fucked up and grieving.

But I don't do the right thing. I lock my arms around her, dipping my fingertips into her pussy, sliding her wetness over her clit until she clenches her thighs around my hand. I suck on her neck and tease her until my hand is drenched, and my cock is so hard I can't stand it.

Heidi and I have the kind of sex that you don't have with strangers. It's raw and trusting and free. I've really let down my guard with her. I see that now.

And maybe that was a mistake. As I lift her leg and line up my cock, I feel unhinged. So much for keeping my emotions on lockdown. With a broken cry, I push inside her slick heat. No condom. We discussed this already, so it's not a violation of her trust. We're protected against pregnancy, and I just got tested.

But I'm not protected against losing my ever-loving mind. Tonight I'm all about the pain and the self-torture. She feels so good that I have to hold still for a moment, groaning into her hair, clenching my muscles around her small body. My eyes are hot, and my skin is on fire.

I don't deserve to experience such intense physical pleasure. My heart shreds itself into tiny pieces as I begin to move. I've got Heidi in an iron embrace. She struggles, clenching her sweet body around my cock, rocking her hips—or trying to.

But everything is on my terms. It has to be. Anything else

will break me tonight. So I slow my breathing and fuck her slowly. She moans every time I slide deeper inside. Her smooth hands are locked onto mine. They're begging me to touch her further.

I close my eyes and try to hold on to this exquisite moment. My mouth explores the side of Heidi's neck, as I try to drown all my senses in her body. My teeth find the cord of muscle between her neck and her shoulder. I bite down gently, and Heidi whimpers.

Then she gets impossibly wet, and my control begins to slip. I fuck her more urgently. I slip a hand over her pussy, and she sobs in gratitude, riding my hand, taking my cock in heated thrusts.

Usually I run my mouth during sex. Tonight words fail me. In the silence, I hear Heidi take a deep, shuddering breath. Then she gasps as she climaxes around my aching cock. I feel every ripple, every flutter as she comes. And I just lose it. I make a broken sound, and shoot inside her, biting my lip, groaning, and trying not to remember that the last person I filled up with my come had disappeared from this earth forever.

"Jesus," Heidi breathes into the sheets a moment later.

I still can't make myself talk. But I do roll her gently onto my chest and kiss her mouth. My hands wander lovingly through her hair, and my fingertips caress her back.

Right now I'm two people. One of them is closed off and silent, unable to get past the horror of years past. The other one is a tender lover, returning affection like a good boyfriend should.

"Are you okay?" she whispers, curling closer to me.

"Yeah," I lie. "Of course."

[32]

HEIDI

"HEIDI, SLOW DOWN," my sister says into my ear. "You're not making a whole lot of sense right now."

She's right. I've been rambling into the phone at her, because everything is wrong, and I don't know how to fix it.

"Let me get this straight—you said Jason is acting too much like a boyfriend. And then you said he isn't acting *enough* like a boyfriend. Do you see why I'm confused?"

"But it's true," I hiss. "He went completely caveman-protective of me, and I didn't like it."

"That wasn't a fair fight," my sister argues, and I bristle that she's taking his side.

"You watched?"

"It's on the Hockey Fights website," she says.

"Really? What's my rating?" I hear myself ask. I can't help it. I was born with a competitive streak.

"You have fifty-five percent!" she hoots. "That's better than O'Doul got in his fight."

Unbelievable. "Then it was a fair fight. Statistics don't lie."

"Sure they do!" my sister scoffs. "Everyone loves an underdog. Plus, that butt wiggle…" She giggles.

I groan. "Okay, forget the fish. The bigger problem is that Jason is *sad*." He hasn't been the same since Georgia told him about the transplant recipients. "I swear he hasn't looked me in the eye in four days." We're in Seattle, on the final leg of our road trip. And Jason is just not himself. He seems cold inside. "I've asked him what's wrong, and he says *nothing*."

My sister makes a sympathetic sound. "The male ego cannot be vulnerable. He's wrestling with something, but it's not in his nature to tell you."

I know she's right. But I hate it anyway. "What should I do?"

"Patience is your only choice. Oh, and sex. Maybe you can boink him into a better mood."

"Maybe," I whisper. I've had to stay with the travel crew these past two nights. Coach gave the boys a curfew after two losses in a row. "Tomorrow we go home to Brooklyn. Then there's the Delilah Spark concert tomorrow night."

"I'm so jealous!" Jana says. "Second-row seats with some hockey hotties at a concert? You poor thing."

The ticket cost a fortune, though. "First, I have to fight a salmon."

"What?"

"Seattle's mascot is the Sockeye Salmon. The West Coast really likes their fish."

My sister snorts. "Please tell me it won't turn out like the last one?"

"It's fine. I met the mascot already. Swear to God, I outweigh the guy. He's a fifty-year-old ex-circus clown. It's going to be fine. We're doing a mime routine where he's selling popcorn, and I don't have the money to pay for it."

"Just like your real life!" Jana says cheerfully.

"Yeah."

"Chin up, Heidi Jo. Give your man some space, and kick that salmon's hindquarters."

"Will do."

A few hours later, everything goes off without a hitch. Brooklyn beats Seattle 3-1. Jason gets a goal. And I spend two and a half minutes on the ice, dressed in a bear suit, pretending to steal popcorn from a salmon. It doesn't make a lick of sense, but I don't get another black eye so I'm counting it as a win.

I shower quickly and then help out in the equipment room, pitching in with Jimbo to pack the hockey sticks into their protective tube and gathering all the gear we can before the players are finished in the locker room.

"Tonight we tell Silas about the concert, right?" Jimbo asks as we stack empty Gatorade bottles into their carrying carton. "He's gonna die."

"Yes! It's going to be epic." Our flight is tomorrow morning. We take off at eight a.m. and land at four thirty. I have a reservation for twenty people at Brother Jimmy's Barbecue for six, and doors open at the concert at seven. "You're going, right?"

"Totes!" says Jimbo, grabbing a hockey stick that we missed on the first pass. "Bayer went home to his dad's place while his knee heals. So he gave me his ticket."

"Nice."

"They're done in the showers," Jimbo says, peering into the next room. "Let's get the towels. Do you think they'll wait to tell Silas until we make it back to the hotel?"

"They better!" I say. "I want to see his face."

It takes us another hour to clear the locker room of Brooklyn gear. When it's all packed away on the truck, Jimbo and I grab a taxi. As we head for the hotel, the first snow flurries I've seen this year dance through the fresh air.

"I'll take a video when you tell him," Jimbo says. "We can immortalize this moment."

"Deal," I say, grabbing my phone. "I'm texting Trevi to let him know we're on our way. He wants to be the one who breaks the news. He's going to sing a Delilah Spark song in the bar and then hand over the tickets."

"Cool. How come you don't have a Katt phone like the rest of us?" Jimbo asks.

"I covet the Katt phone, but I'm not an official employee of the team."

"You're not?" Jimbo yelps. "You've done every job there is for the team. You practically run this place."

"Dude, I will have the Katt phone or die trying."

He laughs as the taxi pulls up in front of the hotel. I pay the driver, file the receipt away in my wallet and climb out. Trevi has replied to my text: ***We're right inside at the bar. But come and see me first. There's something you need to know.***

Hmm. I don't like the sound of that. But now we've arrived, and as soon as Jimbo holds the door open for me I spot Trevi and Jason standing shoulder to shoulder, shot glasses in hand. I hurry over to them. "Hey guys! Great game!" I stand on my tiptoes and kiss Jason on the chin.

"Shouldn't you be wearing a jacket?" he asks. "It's fucking cold out there."

I step back, a little stunned. "That is not how a man greets his lady, but I'll let it pass, because I'm in a good mood." I turn to Trevi. "Is it time? Are you ready to sing?"

"Buddy." He puts a hand on my shoulder. "There's bad news about the concert."

"What?" I gasp. "It *cannot* be canceled! I planned it all out."

"It's going to snow," Jason says. "Six inches by midnight and twelve by morning."

"Our flight is already delayed until noon," Trevi adds.

"*Noon,*" I breathe. "Four hours. So we'll land at eight thirty.

But there's an opening act, right? She might not take the stage until eight or eight thirty anyway."

"It'll take us an hour to get there, even if we don't drop off our luggage," Trevi says, squeezing my shoulder. "I'm sorry, buddy. There's no way we're making it."

"But…" My mind spins as I try to rewrite the rules of physics. "It was *perfect*. Maybe the forecast is wrong. A snow storm is like a man. You never know how long it will go or how many inches you're getting."

Every hockey player in a ten-foot radius bursts out laughing.

Trevi hands me his Katt phone, and we both look down at the weather app. "They've upped it, actually," he says. "Fourteen inches now. This snowstorm is hung."

"But it's *November*," I wail.

Jason puts an arm around me and puts his chin on my head. It's a silent show of support, and I do appreciate it. I lean into his warmth and let out a frustrated sigh. "I hate everything in the world," I whisper. "It was going to be perfect."

"What's the problem?" Silas asks, sliding a beer onto the bar in front of me. "This is for you."

"Thank you." I feel like crying. "Silas—I made a plan for your birthday. A *big* plan. And now the snowstorm has ruined it."

His eyes widen, and the other players in the bar get quiet. "What kind of plan?"

Leo Trevi reaches into his jacket pocket and pulls out a little envelope—the kind that tickets are kept in. Wordlessly, he hands it to Silas.

Silas opens the envelope and pulls out a fat stack of tickets. His head actually jerks back when he sees what's written on them. And his expression flickers with something unexpected. Pain. I'm sure that's what I see, but only for a split second.

Then he actually lets out a strangled laugh. "Second row." He shakes his head. "You're shitting me."

"I tried," I say, wiping the tears off my cheeks. "We *all* tried."

Silas raises his chin and takes in the whole team in a glance. "You guys were really going to this concert with me?"

"Totally!" Trevi says. "I practiced singing 'Make You Mine' just for you."

"Jesus," Silas says, shaking his head. "Well, it looks like you're off the hook. Close call, guys."

Everyone laughs.

"Let's put these on StubHub," he says, holding up the envelope. "Or maybe Georgia can quickly find a charity who could use them."

"Hey, that's a good call," Leo agrees. "Want me to ask her?"

"Absolutely." Silas drops the envelope in front of Trevi, like it's a hot potato. "Now who needs another drink?"

"I do," Jason says. "Tequila, right? We don't have to get up early anymore. Heidi, want a shot? For old time's sake?"

I shudder. "Nope. Tequila and I aren't friends."

He smiles, but it doesn't reach his eyes. "I'll drink yours, then."

"Let's get sloppy," Silas says. "I'll buy the first round." His smile looks sketched on, too.

My men aren't doing so well tonight. And I'm all out of good ideas. So I order a glass of wine and try to pretend that I'm not worried for both of them. "Does this place have a dart board?"

"If it does, we'll find it," Silas says grimly.

"Good, because I feel like throwing things."

Again, the team laughs. But I'm a hundred percent serious.

[33]

JASON

I'M DRIBBLING a puck down center ice, swerving between orange cones. The practice rink is my favorite place in the world. I'm at home with the sounds of pucks echoing off the boards and the murmur of male voices between drills.

Heidi skates past me in her Ice Girls uniform. "Hey!" I call. "Where's my kiss?"

She doesn't turn her head. Her curly hair flies out behind her as she accelerates away from me. Her legs look a million miles long in that microscopic skirt. It gets so quiet now that I can hear her blades scraping against the ice.

"Don't make me come over there!" I call playfully. "That's no way to greet your man."

She plants the toe pick of her skate into the ice and jumps. She's spinning through the air so fast that all I can see is a blur. And when she lands, the scrape of her blade against the ice is unnaturally loud. She stumbles, and my stomach drops immediately.

But Heidi doesn't fall. She recovers herself and then picks up speed again. She's going to do another jump.

"Hey!" I shout. I suddenly don't want her to jump. "Heidi! Babe!" Now there's no one here but the two of us. And I'm shouting, but the sound of my voice doesn't carry. I can feel the sound waves die, so I yell even louder. "HEIDI STOP."

Head down, she's skating toward me now. Finally. She executes a perfect set of back crossovers and then spins around to face me.

When she looks up, her eyes are gone. There are only bloody sockets looking back at me.

I sit up in bed with a wet gasp, the horrifying image still burned in my vision. I'm covered in sweat, and I have to clap a hand over my mouth to prevent myself from making any more noise.

Jesus Christ. Another bad dream. They won't stop. And what the *fuck* was the point of that one? It was so nasty that I feel sick and disoriented.

It doesn't seem to matter that I'm home in Brooklyn, and Heidi is lying peacefully in the bed beside me. I'm full of adrenaline. My heart pounds while I try to control my breathing.

Taking stock, I notice that it's daylight already. The clock says 8:05. That's a relief. I don't even want to go back to sleep—not if I'm going to dream morbid horror-movie dreams.

Heidi rolls over. Her eyes flutter open, and to my relief they're just as blue and perfect as they should be. "Are you okay?"

"Yeah," I say immediately.

"Bad dream?" she squints at me.

"The worst."

"What was it?"

Later I'll look back on this moment and see it for what it is—another chance to prevent myself from ruining everything.

But I don't do the smart thing. "Lost the puck to Dallas a minute before the buzzer."

Heidi's gaze holds mine. She pushes herself up on one hand, and the covers fall away, revealing a tiny little satin nightie. She's staring at me with a rare intensity.

Now I'm self-conscious, so I gather her hair up in one hand, feeling its silkiness against my palm. "What?" I demand.

Those blue eyes narrow. "You freak out like that, and you want me to think you're dreaming about the Dallas defense?"

College degree or not, Heidi is as smart as they come. And yet I do the asshole thing anyway. "Yes," I insist.

Our gazes lock. Heidi is trying to decide whether or not to call me on my bullshit. Four nights in a row I've had these dreams. In one version, I'm in the car that hit Lissa's. When I get out of the vehicle to see what happened, her body is lying on the side of the road.

I'm a fucking wreck, and I don't know how to stop being one.

Heidi makes up her mind. Instead of chewing me out, she gets up on her knees and positions herself behind me. She puts her smooth hands on the back of my neck and begins to rub her thumb against the stiffness she finds there.

Grateful, I drop my foolish head. She can't see my look of relief. I don't want to talk about it, and I doubt she really wants me to. Heidi is attracted to the Jason Castro who has his shit together. She doesn't need to know that I feel like a big bag of crazy. That my mind is full of violent images and terrible possibilities.

Heidi's hands dig into the knots at my shoulders. Nonetheless, I feel a huge gulf opening up between us. I've gone back to being a frozen man, and I don't know what to do. "That feels amazing," I say, so as not to be an ungrateful bastard.

In answer, she lowers her mouth to my neck and gives me a lingering kiss.

Goosebumps break out on my body as she kisses me again. Her soft lips trace a line along the back of my neck. Her hands wander to my bare chest, where her fingertips trace my nipples, and then coast down the center of my abs.

My libido responds to her, as it always does. I feel my cock begin to grow heavy as she drops open-mouthed kisses onto my shoulder. Her tongue tastes my skin, and her hands coast down my body. I'm a lucky man. The luckiest.

Except for one thing. There's still acid in the pit of my stomach. The fight-or-flight response I had to that dream is still lingering just beneath the surface of my skin. When I blink, my eyes are hot.

My body is all heat and confusion, lust and remorse. Tension tightens my chest, as if chains of steel were there instead of her arms.

I'm so caught, and I don't know what to do. If I turn around and push Heidi down on the bed, I could lose myself in sex. I could unleash myself on her. I could take her like a beast.

Part of me craves that release. I want to fuck her long and hard, and I also want to burst into tears. It's even odds which of those things might happen. Or maybe both.

I feel *insane* right now. And that's no way to make love to your girl.

Catching Heidi's hand, I stop its journey into my boxer shorts. Because I'll protect Heidi against anything. Even myself. "Come here," I mumble. I give her a little tug, and she takes the hint, moving around to my side.

From there I pull her into my lap and wrap my arms around her. I tuck my chin onto her shoulder and bury my nose in her hair. My hug is as tight as a Titanic survivor's grip on the life raft.

And Heidi rolls with it. She ruffles my hair with one hand. She tucks her cheek against my chest and sighs. Best of all, she doesn't ask for an explanation. She just holds me.

This is what I was always afraid of. My frigid heart is back. And I'm not the only one who will suffer.

"Coffee and bagels," I mumble eventually, after my pulse finally slows. "Want to go out and grab breakfast?"

A beat goes by before she answers. "Sure."

My heart drops again. I can hear her disappointment, and her confusion. This is why I haven't dated anyone for five years. This awkwardness right here is the reason. Heidi wants sex, and so do I. But she also wants real intimacy.

Today I just don't have it in me.

Heidi makes me want to be the kind of guy who isn't too damaged for easygoing weekend morning sex. But I'm not that guy today, and there aren't any words to explain. Because I don't really understand it myself. What kind of idiot turns down sex just because he had a bad dream?

Things improve for me at One Girl Cookies. Coffee is a miracle drug, for starters. I buy us two giant cappuccinos and one of everything they make—quiche, muffins, croissants. We cut every offering in half and share.

I'm soothed by the scent of baked goods and the coffee shop noises. It's harder to feel crazy over the clink of coffee cups and the sound of the milk frother. Heidi makes all the conversation. She tells me her daring plan to finish up her time with the Ice Girls.

"I'm going to audition for the dance team. And I'm going to record all the rules he has for the dancers—that he'll fire me if I gain ten pounds, and that I'm not allowed to fraternize with the players."

I choke on my coffee. "You little rule-breaker!"

She smiles. "I know! Like it's any of his business who I'm

with. I can't wait to see his face when Rebecca terminates his contract. He's going to be so mad."

That's a sobering thought. "Honey, I don't think you should approach the man after Rebecca lets him go. If he's angry, I don't want you near him."

Heidi makes an angry noise. "Think about what you just said. You can't forbid me to talk to him, just like he can't forbid me to talk to you! Do you hear yourself?"

Whoops. I really should have phrased that differently. "Good point," I say quickly. "But I respectfully suggest that you don't put yourself in an angry man's path when you're alone, at least."

Heidi eyes me over the rim of her coffee mug. "The only time you ever make me mad is when you don't treat me like an adult."

Ah. Well, it's good to know that I'm off the hook for every other nutty thing I've done this week. "I'm sorry, sweetheart. If you weren't an adult I wouldn't like you half so much as I do."

This wins me a tiny smile. Her phone bleats. Heidi picks it up and squints at the screen. "It's my sister. I should probably talk to her."

"Actually, I have an errand down the block. Meet you back at home?"

"Sure," she says brightly. "I'm going to grab a muffin for Silas before I call my sister back. I'm worried about him."

"He's okay," I say instinctively. Sometimes a guy just needs to make a few poor life choices to exorcise the demons in his head. The other night in Seattle when we got snowed in? Silas and I both got plastered. And to the surprise of pretty much everyone in the bar, Silas picked up a hockey fangirl and took her upstairs.

Silas never bangs the fans. But that doesn't mean he shouldn't indulge if he feels the urge.

"Still," she says, stacking our empty plates. "I'm going to bring him a pastry."

I take the plates out of her hands. "You're the best girl in the world. I got these. Go buy muffins and call your sister."

She gives me a grateful smile that I don't really deserve and picks up her bag. "See you in fifteen."

When I leave the coffee shop, I head straight for the florist on the corner. The same surly woman is behind the counter again. "You're back," she says. "Does that mean it's going well?"

"Uh," I say stupidly. But the question catches me off guard. "It was the best of times, it was the worst of times."

She cackles, but I'm not joking. Heidi is fantastic. I care for her a hell of a lot more than I ever planned to. But I don't know how to navigate my own drama. And I sure as hell don't want to drag her down with me.

"Page four, I think." She flips open her book. "This one here is for fighting over nothing." She taps a multicolored arrangement. "Does that fit?"

"Not exactly. What kind of flower says—I'm sorry I'm trapped inside my own dumb head?"

"Hmm." She squints at me. "I'm going to do up some poppies and draping ivy. It will look smashing."

"Thank you." I slap my credit card down on the counter.

"But it won't do the trick," she adds.

"What? You're the master of floral expressions. It says so right on that wall!" I point.

"I am," she agrees. "But you look like a smart man. Or at least not the stupidest one I've ever met. So you probably already know that spilling your guts is the only fix for what ails ya."

Suddenly I don't even want the fucking flowers. I just want to punch something. Because if I open my mouth to spill my guts, nothing but darkness will come out. How does that help?

Wisely, she picks up my credit card and walks toward the cooler, while I stand here feeling empty. "It's all up to you," she says, plucking out a gorgeous pot of red poppies and turning toward her workspace. "The next time you're in my shop, you could be a page one again. Or a page thirteen."

I hate that she's right.

Five minutes later I sign the slip in silence. The flowers are stunning, as she'd promised. "Thanks," I grunt, picking them up.

"You're welcome," she says cheerfully. "Come back any time."

I wonder if I will.

[34]

HEIDI

IN THE CORNER of the dressing room, I hurry to lace up my skates before everyone else. With shaking hands, I pop the microphone Rebecca gave me into my phone and set it to record.

This is it. I'm going to record Randy Cavanaugh's sins and fix his fate for good.

It's only a practice, not a game. But all the other girls are still fixing their makeup. I tuck my phone into a Brooklyn sweatshirt I borrowed from Jason—it's roomy, so the phone doesn't show in the pocket—and I hurry out of the cramped dressing room and down the hall.

Randy Cavanaugh is right outside the stadium door, smoking a cigarette. I'm feeling very James Bond as I step outside to talk to him. "There you are," I say in a breathless voice. "It's time we talk about my dance-team audition."

He blows smoke out of his greasy nose, and I try to smile through my horror.

"You're a fine skater, Heidi. Haven't had to fire you yet. But

I got a million girls who can dance. Auditions aren't until spring."

"Just give me a chance," I beg.

"You want special treatment, huh? You have the look of the kind of girl who thinks the world should fall at her feet."

"Maybe I am that kind of girl," I agree, trying to keep the conversation going. "If I don't expect a lot, then how am I going to get it?"

He actually rolls his eyes before taking another puff on his cancer stick. Apparently he's unimpressed by girls who show initiative. But I already know this about Cavanaugh. He likes girls he can push around. The ones who never make a wish list. He wants the girls who don't even know they *should* make one and keep dreaming big.

After this I'm going to go home and add a dozen things to mine. Just for therapy.

"Maybe you'd be a great addition to the dance team," he says finally. "Imma leave it up to you to convince me."

Here we go! "And how am I going to do that?" I give him my most innocent face.

"I'll leave it up to your imagination. Here's my private number." He pulls a card out of his jeans pocket. "You want to meet up and talk about it, you can come over tonight."

"What are we going to talk about?" I try. "You should see me dance, maybe."

He throws the cigarette on the ground, cementing my fine impression of him. "Yeah, okay. Wear something sexy."

"Like what?" I just need him to say one really crude thing. "Look, I study to get an A. Tell me what it takes."

He sizes me up, as if trying to decide how much he's willing to say. I have goosebumps everywhere, and I hope I don't look as creeped out as I feel.

"Look. I dunno if you're cut out for the dance team. My

favorite auditions are the ones with no clothes at all. You call me if you think you might want to try out."

"Okay," I say quickly. Now I'm fighting a smile. I may be a terrible actress, but I have just won this war.

"Now get inside," he says. "Let's clean some motherfucking ice." He steps past me, opens the rear door and disappears inside.

After practice, I find a voicemail on my phone from Rebecca. "There's something I need to tell you," she says.

That sounds a little ominous. On the other hand I have something to tell her, too! I race from the stadium to the Bruisers headquarters to share my Randy Cavanaugh data. I've got seven different temperature readings to document the unsafe work conditions. And I've got Randy on tape asking for sex. I've taken photographs of girls standing on the freezing sidewalk without their jackets, and I have a list of skeevy things Randy has said to us in the dressing room.

I documented all of it. And I can't wait to find the owner and share it all.

Unfortunately, there's a press conference that's just finishing up, so the building is full of strangers. I'd forgotten that today was the day Bayer officially announced his retirement. Rebecca may be tied up, but I have to check.

I skid to a stop in front of Rebecca's old desk in the outer office where the temp still sits. Same girl. Although a few details have changed. Disgust rises up inside me as I notice the framed photograph of a cat on her desk and the Brooklyn teddy bear on the ledge behind her.

The temp is making this space her own! She's moving in on my territory. "Hi," I say, although it comes out sounding surly. "Is Becca in there?" I jerk my thumb toward the office door.

"No luck," the girl says with a jolly smile.

I feel the irrational urge to slap her. What is with me lately? First the fish, and now this.

"Let me just see if I can track her down, Heidi Jo."

She even knows my name, and that just upsets me more. It should be me sitting at that desk memorizing everyone's name! I'm good at it, too!

Then I die a little inside. Because the temp picks up her phone to summon Rebecca. *And it's a Katt phone.* Only permanent members of the organization get those. The temp is no longer a temp.

I am filled with grief and rage.

Spinning on my heel, I march away, leaving the temp behind.

"Heidi Jo!" the young woman calls.

I ignore her. I must find Becca. It's already too late, but I'm going to plead my case. Mama always said not to deliver a sermon in the heat of passion, but I'm going to do it anyway.

Or I'm going to try. But Rebecca is not in the press room at the end of the hall. So I poke my head into every office down the row. She's not in the travel department. She's not in marketing.

The last place I look is publicity. I stick my head around Georgia's partially open door, and there's a woman standing there by Georgia's desk. It's not Becca, but…

I do a double-take. It's Miranda Wager, the journalist. Her phone is lit up in her hand. And she's alone.

"What are you doing in here?" I blurt out.

"Looking for Georgia," she says immediately. "I have a question about the charity event next week."

The hair stands up on the back of my neck, because I know she's lying. For one thing, there is no charity event next week. The team is traveling to Minnesota and Ottawa. And Miranda wouldn't be standing so close to the desk if she weren't snooping. "You," I say in a heavy voice, "were reading the papers on her desk!"

The journalist's lip curls. "Don't be ridiculous! I walked in here about one second before you. I haven't read a thing! I was looking for a sticky note to leave her a message."

The explanation slows me down for a second. It almost makes sense, but my spidey senses are still pinging like crazy. I glance toward the hallway, hoping Georgia appears. No luck.

Miranda's eyes narrow, and she steps away from the desk, slipping her phone into her pocket. "Whatever you're thinking about me, just go ahead and think it. I've nothing to hide. *I'm* not the one having a top-secret relationship with Jason Castro."

"What?" I yelp. But then I cringe. Because Jason and I are absolutely having a thing. Even if our thing is confusing the heck out of me right now. But that's no reason to stoop to Miranda Wager's level. I won't lie. "It's not top secret," I admit. "We're having a thing."

"A thing? Is that what the kids are calling it these days?" Her eyes brighten. "So Daddy knows? How *is* your father holding up, anyway?"

"Yes, he knows." And here I thought Miranda Wager was a *real* journalist. "Like I said—I don't have anything to hide. I don't need to sneak around like a thief." *Like you are.* The unspoken words just sort of hang there in the air between us.

Miranda's eyes narrow with anger as she realizes she hasn't fooled me. I've never had a cat fight before, but today could be the day. I've already fought a six-foot fish, so this should be a piece of cake.

"If you've nothing to hide," Miranda hisses, "maybe you'd like to make a statement?"

"About what? Jason and I? That's not news. Nobody cares."

"No?" She gives me an evil grin. "How do you feel about dating the league's only Hispanic player?"

I blink. "He is?" That can't possibly be true. And what a ridiculous question! "I..." How to shut her down? "It's a non-issue! He's just Jason. We don't sit around and discuss his father's heritage. Why would you even ask that?"

"No?" She steps around me, wearing a smug little smile. "What color is his dick?"

I literally gasp with outrage. Jason was right about Miranda. She's a horrible human being, and a ridiculous one. "It's rainbow-colored!" I shriek. "And it sings to me in Spanish! Are you kidding me right now?"

She laughs. "I was, actually. Later, Hockey Barbie."

Miranda slips out the half-open door, leaving me with nothing but outrage and the sound of her heels clicking down the hallway.

I just got played. She got me off the topic! She changed it from snooping in Georgia's office to... Jason's penis.

My mind whirls. What was she looking for in here, anyway?

Feeling shaky with outrage, I step closer to the desk, putting myself where I found her three minutes ago. I glance around as quickly as I can, but Georgia's office is a bit of a disaster. There are shelves over her desk lined with every kind of hockey memorabilia. There's even a photo of my father and some other retried players at the Brooklyn ribbon-cutting ceremony three years ago.

The photos trigger something in my subconscious. Miranda was gripping her phone when I came in, and the screen was lit. Then she tucked it out of sight. Maybe she took a photo, too? Of what?

When I glance down at Georgia's desk, I get a shock. Right there on the blotter is a print-out of an old newspaper clipping. *Tragedy strikes senior class. Hockey team raises money for victim's funeral.* Jason stares up at me from the accompanying photograph. He has his arm around a beautiful, smiling girl. *Melissa*

Skinner would have turned nineteen years old next month, reads the sad caption.

Jason's smile, though. That's what really grabs me. It's so open and happy. It's the smile of a boy who hasn't a care in the world. I want him to smile like that again. So badly. The back of my throat burns, and my eyes get hot.

Beside the clipping is a legal pad where Georgia has scribbled: *Minneapolis Center for Organ Donation, 2pm CST arrival for 2:30 photos*. There's a photographer listed and some phone numbers.

The meeting! Jason didn't tell me it had already been scheduled. My heart drops. I asked him if it had, and he changed the subject.

I take a deep breath and try to calm down. Jason didn't want me to know about this meeting. But now Miranda Wager has the details. She stood right here and took a photo of Georgia's desk. I'd bet my trust fund on it.

Now she's going to write a story about this painful part of Jason's life. That's just cruel. I won't let her do it. And there isn't much time to stop her.

I fly out of Georgia's office and run down the hall toward the stairs.

[35]

JASON

"WHAT'LL WE HAVE FOR LUNCH?" Silas asks as half a dozen of us file through the lobby.

"Anything but pizza," I suggest.

"I was kind of thinking about pizza," Silas confesses.

"You're *always* thinking about pizza."

"How about Chinese?" Trevi counters, opening the street door. "Georgia wants to come with us, and she is always up for Chinese."

"Sounds good," I say quickly, before Silas can argue.

"Is Heidi coming, too?" Trevi asks. "Where's she going so fast?"

I'm about to ask what he means, but I spot her as I step out the door. Heidi is flying down the sidewalk, and I don't know why. As I glance up the street, I see another woman, hand in the air, trying to hail a taxi.

The next few seconds seem to happen in slow motion. I see a Yellow Cab pull an illegal left turn off York to try to get the fare. He swings around fast. And I see Heidi suddenly leap off the curb, toward the woman, as if to catch her.

There's a deafening squeal of brakes as the cab tries to stop in time. Bile rises up in my throat as Heidi lurches, trying to change her body's direction. But momentum causes her to tip toward the street.

She goes down. My mouth is wide open in a silent shout, because nothing comes out.

HEIDI

"What the fuck was that?" Miranda screeches. "Are you fucking insane?"

Everything is noise—the taxi brakes, the cab driver who's standing beside the taxi, cursing at me in a language I don't understand. There are players shouting at me from the curb, I think.

Breathless and freaked out, I pick myself up off the asphalt. There are little bits of grime imbedded in my skin. "Don't write the story," I wheeze. "Give me your phone."

"You are one crazy little bitch," Miranda says. "You don't get to tell me what to write, even if you do have a death wish."

"He doesn't deserve that invasion of his privacy!" I straighten my shaky spine and look her square in the eye.

Miranda steps back, opens the cab door, and positions it between herself and me, proving that I must look as deranged as I feel. "You can't protect him, Heidi. He's got a fiduciary responsibility to the entire league. Financial prudence is a job requirement. Now get out of the street, you idiot." She gets into the cab and slams the door.

Not one word Miranda just said makes any sense at all. I'm

trying to play them back in my head when two strong arms lift me bodily off the street and then deposit me on the sidewalk.

"What the fuck was that?" asks a voice that's too angry to be Jason's. Except it is. When I turn around he's standing there, fists clenched, eyes flashing. He looks like a bomb that's about to go off.

"I…" I swallow hard. "She was snooping in your business. Taking pictures, I think. I wanted to see her phone."

"So you jump in front of a *moving car?*" he shouts. I've never seen him this angry. I've never seen *anyone* as angry as he is right now. "What the actual fuck?"

"I'm sorry," I say immediately. Because that's what you say to someone who looks like he's about to lift the parked Audi beside him and hurl it across the road.

"You're *sorry,*" he snarls. "You'd be even sorrier if that cab's brake pads were any worse off than they were."

"Calm down!" I squeak. I'm already shaking. I don't need my boyfriend yelling at me in front of the team.

Leo Trevi speaks from somewhere behind me. "Take a breath, Jason. It's okay now."

It's not, though. Nothing is okay. There's a vein bulging in Jason's neck. "I didn't mean to scare you," I try. "I know you have some bad memories…" My brain is finally catching up with the situation, but there is a giant lump in my throat as I try to make myself clear. "I know you said yes to that meeting. But you didn't tell me about it."

"So fucking what?" he snaps. "Don't change the subject."

"I'm not," I insist. "You're freaked out. I'm sorry. But you're taking it out on me."

"Bullshit!"

"No, you are." This isn't a great conversation to have on the sidewalk, but he isn't giving me a choice. "We're a thing, with no definitions, right? I didn't mind before. Except now I do. Because a *thing* is apparently not the kind of relationship where you tell me when you're upset. A *thing* means I'm only allowed to guess and try to wait you out and not feel bad."

"You are *way* off topic." His eyes are full of thunder.

"I'm not," I insist. "And just now I was trying to stop Miranda from writing about you. Because someone has to. You're welcome. I care about you, even if you're a mess and you won't admit it."

"That's bullshit."

"Is it? Were you ever going to tell me about that meeting? Did you think I wouldn't care?"

He shrugs. That's all I get. A shrug. That's the gesture of a man who doesn't care. So it's time I read the handwriting on the wall. He's still a sad Romeo who's in love with his Juliet. And no amount of wishing is going to untie that knot.

"Well," I choke out. "I guess we just found the limits of our 'thing.'"

"I guess we did," he agrees.

The words are a cruel blade slicing through me. But I'm standing in the cold, with half the Bruisers looking on in sympathy. "I see," I say stiffly. "Good to know. I think you need some space, then. Correct me if I'm wrong."

"Sounds okay to me," he grinds out.

"Castro, you idiot," Silas whispers from a few feet away.

My eyes get hot and my throat is scratchy. I'm not a crier, though. I take a deep breath through my nose and lift my chin. I turn my back to Jason and to the four or five teammates standing there gawking at me.

Georgia is jogging toward me and the group. "Are we going to lunch? Did something happen?"

Why yes it did. My heart got shredded right here on Hudson Street at the corner of York.

Nobody says anything for a beat. And then Georgia's husband Leo speaks up. "We're, uh, gonna need to drag Jason off and calm him down. Maybe you and Heidi should have lunch without us."

Georgia blinks. "Um, okay?"

"I need to talk to you, anyway," I say, finding my voice. "There was an incident in your office."

Her eyes widen. "Let's go. I know just the place." She hooks her arm in mine and gently leads me down the sidewalk.

Georgia is a very smart woman. A genius, probably. "You should apply for Mensa," I say, leaning back in the massage chair while someone else rubs lotion into my bare feet. If anything can calm me down, it's a pedicure.

She smiles from the chair beside me. "Happy to help out. Becca and I get lunchtime pedicures whenever we need a break from the office. None of the men ever come in here, obviously. It's the only place we ever felt we could talk freely."

"I don't know if I want to talk freely," I grumble. "I don't have anything nice to say."

"Ladies!" I look up to see Rebecca hurrying towards us. "What did I miss?" She tosses her jacket onto the last pedicure chair.

"Heidi chased down a journalist who was snooping in my office. And then there was a close call with a taxi making a U-turn," Georgia says. "Poor Jason has car-accident PTSD and lost his shit. The boys dragged him off to calm him down. Hopefully not with liquor because it's game night."

Rebecca blinks. "How close a call?"

"Not *that* close," I say. "It probably looked bad, though. And I'm sympathetic to everything that's going on inside his head. But he won't *talk* to me." Instead, he cut me loose in front of his friends.

That hurt so much.

"Men," Georgia says, shaking her head. "Leo is not a sharer, either. The bro code pretty much says that you shouldn't express your feelings."

"They're not all bad," Becca chimes in. "Nate is pretty good at sharing."

"Really?" Georgia says, shaking a nail polish bottle. "It took that man five *years* to tell you he loves you."

"Fine," she says, and I smile. "But he's good at it now."

"So they're educable," Georgia agrees. "But you have to be strict with them."

I try that idea on, and I'm not sure it has merit. Jason either loves me and he needs space to grieve, or he doesn't love me at all. Either way, I can't make him share himself, even if he needs to. This morning he bought me some beautiful flowers. I would rather have had two minutes of real talk instead.

"Jason has been through a lot," Becca says. "He can still recite every word of *Romeo and Juliet*. One drunken night he told me that he rereads it every year so that he won't forget. It's his last connection to her."

Ouch. I care too much about a man who's still grieving. It's nobody's fault, but it still hurts.

"This is the first time he's dated anyone," Georgia says carefully. "He's come a long way."

"I know," I admit. "But maybe he's come as far as he can."

They're nice enough not to agree with me out loud. Instead, Becca reaches past me and grabs the bottle of nail polish out of Georgia's hand. "Pink *again?*"

Georgia grabs it back. "I like pink. If you want to experiment on somebody, torture Heidi."

"Nobody torture Heidi," I complain. "Like this day isn't long enough. I have to skate with the Ice Girls tonight, too."

"No you don't," Rebecca says. "You've done enough time. I thought you said you were done?"

"I am. And I have one last recording for you. But I still have to show up tonight and skate with the girls. If I don't show, there won't be enough people. And Randy will be extra horrible and yell more often."

"You're a good person, Heidi Jo," Becca says.

I'm not feeling like one right now. "I could also use the paycheck." I need a place of my own, even if it's terrible. Which reminds me that I have a burning question. "Rebecca?"

"Yes?" She adjusts her massage chair and leans back into its robotic embrace.

"Why does the temp have a Katt phone and photos on her desk? She looks awfully cozy in my chair."

Rebecca's eyes fly open. "I hired her permanently."

"Oh," I say softly as all my hope drains away.

"That's what I wanted to talk to you about. It's not the only job in the organization, Heidi Jo. There are other possibilities..."

"I understand," I say. Because I really do. Becca is running a business, and that's hard. I know because I'm running one myself. But it's occurring to me that I might soon leave the Bruisers with nothing—no job. No boyfriend. I put my whole heart into everything I do.

Sometimes the universe just doesn't care, though. You can make a wish list as long as you like. And come away with nothing.

I want to bawl, I really do. But not in front of Rebecca.

She reaches over and squeezes my hand. "I know you're hurting. Have a little patience. Just a little, okay?"

"I am not a naturally patient person," I admit.

"None of us are!" Rebecca admits cheerfully. "But sometimes patience is all we've got."

Now there's a lesson I never wanted to learn. Thanks, Dad.

[36]

JASON

"DID SHE RETURN YOUR TEXT?" Leo Trevi asks me. He has to shout, because the stadium is echoing with music.

"No!" I yell back. We're suited up and standing on the blue line, facing the other team. The lights are down, and spotlights crisscross the surface of the ice.

"Did you leave her a voice message?" Silas asks from my other side.

"Did you do a really good grovel?" someone else wants to know.

The game is supposed to start in less than a minute, so at least I know when my friends' scolding will end. "Why are we still standing here, anyway?" The starting lineups have just been announced. Now is the moment when the lights should come up for the national anthem.

But they don't. It's the weirdest thing.

"Hey—look," Leo says. "Somebody had a warmup cocktail." He lifts his chin toward the red carpet that's been rolled out onto the ice. I follow its path to the end, where there's an aging pop star in a leopard-patterned jacket holding a microphone.

The hockey franchise asks someone new to sing the anthem at each game. Various has-been singers show up for this honor. It's never Rihanna or Bono. That's not in the budget.

And this guy isn't doing so well. He's supported on one arm by that prick who runs the Ice Girls crew, and on the other arm by Jimbo. But it's not enough. As I watch, he doubles over and collapses onto a heap on the red carpet.

"Now what?" Silas asks. "We could be standing here all night, right? It's in the league rules that the national anthem must be sung."

Maybe he's right, because there's a frantic commotion on the sidelines. The pop star is scooped up and carried off by Jimbo and another guy from logistics. And now the officials are involved, their black-and-white uniforms converging in a huddle to discuss what to do.

"We could do this singalong style," Trevi suggests. "Who has a karaoke app on his phone?"

"My muscles are gonna tighten up from standing too long," Silas complains.

But now the referee is holding up the microphone, and they're escorting someone down the chute toward the red carpet.

"Please rise for the national anthem," the announcer says again as the lights finally come up.

I blink. And then I blink again. Because it's Heidi who is stepping out onto the red carpet. She's wearing a Brooklyn jacket over her tiny Ice Girls' skirt, and she's frowning as she whispers with the official. He says something I can't hear and then points at the microphone.

Heidi's reply—if I'm not mistaken—is: "Do I have to do everything around here?" She takes the microphone and walks further onto the carpet.

In spite of everything that happened today, I smile. With Heidi, it's impossible not to. Singing the anthem to twenty thousand people would terrify most people. But not Heidi. She lifts the microphone, as well as her perfect chin.

"Oh say can you seeeeee..." rings out a clear voice. Chills run through my body immediately, and a glance around the stadium fills me with uncharacteristic awe. "By the dawn's early light..." sings the incredible girl on the carpet. Twenty thousand people lean forward, hands on their hearts. Heidi sings the anthem in tune. It's not Rihanna, but it's competent.

And it's so fucking *brave*.

I can feel Leo watching me, wondering what my problem is. There's no denying it. Heidi is incredibly special. She's probably the coolest person I've ever met. And if I'm honest with myself, I love her.

But when I close my eyes tonight, I'm going to see her go down in front of that taxi again. That fear will never leave me alone. Every day is a day when your coach can pull you aside and say, "Come here, son. Sit down. There's been an accident."

I know it. And I can't unknow it. I'm like a burned-out lightbulb in the middle of the row. I can't be lit up anymore when I've already seen the darkness.

Heidi doesn't deserve that. She needs someone who can love her without reservation. She wouldn't even want a guy who's as dark inside as I am right now.

She nails the high note and then finishes the song to applause and also to catcalls. And she doesn't glance my way as she exits the red carpet.

When I walk into my bedroom four hours later, I know immediately—all of Heidi's things are gone. The place looks utterly sterile. I open a dresser drawer, even though I already know her lingerie has disappeared. I wander into the bathroom, and it looks completely lifeless without fifty-seven different beauty products on the counter.

It's all gone. Everything is right back to the way it was last summer. Empty and quiet.

Except those goddamn flowers. When I walk into the living room they're still centered on the coffee table looking way too bright and cheerful.

Just in case I wasn't convincingly crazy yet, I seal the deal by lifting a foot and kicking the arrangement—and its glass vase—right off the coffee table, where it shatters on the wood floor.

A Delilah Spark tune abruptly cuts off in Silas's room. His door opens a second later. I hear him pace toward me and then stop, just taking in the scene. "So we're not being robbed?"

Slowly, I shake my head. Getting robbed would be less awful than I feel right now.

"Do we have a broom?" He disappears into the hall closet and emerges a moment later to hand me a broom and a dustpan.

I start sweeping up the mess.

Silas appears a second time with a roll of paper towels, a garbage bag, and two beers. Then he watches me clean up the mess, one wet stem at a time. I'm wiping up water and tiny bits of broken glass by the time he says, "Want to talk about it?"

I turn and give him an evil look over my shoulder. "What good would that do?"

He takes a swig of beer and studies me. "See, there are some problems that talking about won't help. Sometimes you're in love with the wrong girl, and there's nothing you can do about it." He takes another drink. "Your thing is different, though. You could have everything, man. You really could."

I pick up another bit of glass and throw it in the bag. Silas is wrong. Nobody can have everything. They only think they can. And I'm like the guy who already knows the awful truth.

So I don't spoil it for him. I just clean up my shit and then drink my beer.

"She's staying at Bayer's, still," Silas says as we wait in the charter terminal at LaGuardia a couple days later.

"Awesome. Thank you for checking." I'm incredibly relieved to hear it. We're leaving town again, and I was awake in the night wondering if Heidi had finally rented some shithole in a bad neighborhood. I texted her at four a.m. to ask if she was okay, just because I had a bad feeling.

There was no reply. She's avoiding me. Smart girl. I made a few overtures to apologize to her. I left her a voicemail saying how sorry I was that I flipped out at her. And how sorry I was that she'd left.

I didn't beg her to come back, though. We both know I'm not in a good place. That means I owe her one more giant apology. I'm sorry that I asked her to be with me when I clearly wasn't ready. That's something I want to say in person.

And here I am at the damned airport.

"So you don't have to worry about her this week, okay?" Silas adds. "And—bonus—you can turn in a shopping list, and she'll deliver before we touch down on Wednesday." Silas rubs his chin. "I expect we'll get billed for her time, though. No more free stocking of the peanut butter, dude."

"Shit!" I say suddenly.

My roommate's eyes widen. "Dare I ask what the problem is? You didn't forget your sandwich, did you?"

I did. Rising from my chair, I squint at the terminal coffee shop. They have bagels, but no regular bread. "What are the odds that they have strawberry jam?"

"Not good," Silas says. "You can find a deli near the rink

and order a sandwich on your phone. Or ask the new girl to help you."

I glance over at Rebecca's new assistant, who's poking at her Katt phone and bopping to a song in her earbuds. I don't even want to try to explain to her what I need. Nobody ever understands on the first try.

Everything is shittastic. It just is.

Doctor Mulvey is the team psychiatrist. We all have to meet with him once every six weeks or so. It's routine. Or, rather, it's supposed to be. After I threw my tantrum on the sidewalk, my appointment got mysteriously moved up.

We're 30,000 feet over the Midwest, heading to our game in Arizona. And Dr. Mulvey and I are together in the little office at the back of the jet, drinking shitty coffee.

"Look on the bright side," he says with a smile. "You won't have to take time out of your week for this now."

I give him a weak smile. I like Dr. Mulvey. Everyone does. It's just that none of us look forward to these appointments. Talking about yourself is the worst. And it's not like I can lie. Doc has all our files, so he knows my whole life story.

"Tell me about this meeting you're having on Tuesday."

Ugh. "You probably know as much as I do about it," I say. "There's a girl who got a transplant liver, and another one who got…" I was doing pretty well delivering this message until the last part. "Eyes," I say as my throat closes up. And for a second, I feel nauseated again. But I take another gulp of shitty coffee and swallow hard.

Dr. Mulvey misses nothing. "So you're really looking forward to this meeting, then?"

I actually laugh, but it sounds a little manic.

"Lots of people struggle with the idea of organ donation.

There's an uncanniness to it. I could read you some excerpts from Freud."

"That's okay," I say quickly. "I just have to get through it."

"True," he agrees. "Although it might help you to know that 'eye transplant' is a misnomer."

I blink. "It is?"

"Yep." He nods. "The cornea is currently the only part of the eye that can be transplanted. It's a very small bit of the inner eye. Not the part you see when you look at someone's face."

"Oh," I say slowly. Well, fuck. "It would have been pretty helpful if someone explained that to me before."

He watches me with a kind of quiet patience they must teach at shrink school. "I can only imagine how gruesome your dreams have been lately."

"*Jesus*. Get out of my head."

"Okay," he agrees. "That's the same thing I'd ask of you, though. What would have happened if you told someone how troubled you felt? Maybe a friend—or your soon to be ex-girlfriend—could have talked you through it."

My stomach drops, because I can actually picture Heidi sitting on the sofa with me, googling eye transplants and explaining about corneas. Not that I gave her the chance.

"You can get through this meeting," Dr. Mulvey promises. "And while I don't expect you'll enjoy it, you might actually feel better afterwards."

"You mean… Like maybe there was a purpose to her death? I don't think my mind works that way. 'Everything happens for a reason' sounds like bullshit to me."

The doctor smiles again. "Preach. But there's a middle place between believing that your girlfriend's death was fated and feeling torn up about it all the time."

"I'm not," I say automatically. "Not all the time," I add, because Dr. Mulvey has a finely tuned bullshit sensor.

"Really? Yet you're not ready to be with another girl who loves you?"

Christ. The man doesn't hold back. "It didn't quite get that far with Heidi."

"Didn't it?" He leans back in his chair. "How convenient. If she's not The One, then you don't have to do the difficult work of forgiving yourself."

"You are in a *mood*. Jesus."

He grins evilly. "I like you, Jason. You've been sitting across from me for a year, telling me how great everything is. The whole team likes you, too, because you're upbeat a lot of the time. You're a fun guy. Always quick with a joke."

"I am," I agree, hoping that counts for something.

He shakes his head. "Because you're so fatalistic. The man who's met death can often laugh at a joke. You live in the moment, because you expect to be in pain again at any second."

"*Harsh.*" But, shit, that sounds more accurate than I wish it did.

"It's not," he insists. "There are worse coping mechanisms."

"Then are we done here?" He seems to have me all figured out already.

"Not a chance. Tell me why you broke up with your girlfriend on Hudson Street after she almost fell in front of a taxi."

"Because…" I try not to sound defensive, but the guy is starting to piss me off. "It wasn't serious with her."

"No? She doesn't love you?"

"I didn't *ask*."

"Because you don't love her? Or you don't think you could?"

Of course I could. If I were somebody else. "I wasn't feeling like a very good boyfriend, and I didn't see the point of dragging it out."

"Why did you think you weren't a good boyfriend? Did you cheat?"

"No way! And don't be dense on purpose." My anger is as bright as the sun. "I was in a funk, and nobody likes that."

"So you took that decision out of her hands."

"Yep! I guess I am a shitty boyfriend. See?"

I wouldn't think shrinks are supposed to roll their eyes at their patients. But Dr. Mulvey does it anyway. "Nice try, son. Your coping mechanism is to keep everything light and easy."

"Exactly," I agree.

"It's a smart strategy."

"Yeah."

"It's smart as long as you don't mind being lonely. How's that working for you this week?"

"Not bad," I lie.

He smiles. "Heidi was staying with you. Where is she now?"

"In Bayer's apartment. He went home to his dad's."

"So you're keeping tabs on her, making sure she's okay. Do lots of guys who break up from unserious relationships do that?"

"I dunno," I say. "They should, maybe."

He nods. "You're right. You're a good man, Jason Castro. Ask anyone. But I only wish you were a little nicer to yourself. It's really sad that you lost someone. But you could stop blaming yourself."

"Why would I do that?"

"Oh, I don't know? Maybe because you were a thousand miles away when she got into a car with a drunk driver who killed her?"

"If I had come home that weekend when I was supposed to, she wouldn't have been in that car."

He shakes his head. "She could have called a friend. She could have called a taxi. She made a terrible, regrettable choice. She paid the price. And you're still paying interest on it."

I don't say anything, because I've heard this sermon before.

"Lucky for you," the doctor adds, "you'll probably live

another sixty or seventy years. You've got time. I hope, though, that the right girl comes along when you're finally ready to set down this burden—and not beforehand. Timing is everything. Hockey players know that even better than me."

"Yessir," I agree, glancing at my watch. Maybe he'll move on to torturing someone else now.

"Is there anything I can do for you?" he asks.

I shake my head quickly. "Not unless you know where I can find a peanut butter and strawberry jam sandwich between touchdown and warmups."

The shrink looks thoughtful. "Tell you what. I'll go find you one myself."

"Really?" Now that's full service.

"Sure. If you can explain why it matters."

"Oh." I chuckle. But then I open my mouth and nothing comes out. How can I explain something so obvious? "Do you give all the guys a hard time about their superstitions? I hear Leo has a lucky jock strap."

"Nah. I'm used to athletes and their superstitions. But yours is the only one I know that's a talisman from beyond the great divide."

Oh Christ. "It's...a reminder to live up to my full potential. My career has been on an upward trajectory since I started eating that sandwich before games."

"Here's the thing," the shrink says, sitting back in his chair. "Nobody's career goes only in one direction. Ask your friend Bayer about that. And then ask yourself why you think you don't deserve a living, breathing girlfriend, but you can't live without a sandwich from a dead girl."

"Um..." Does he really expect an answer? "Okay. Will do."

"Good."

A beat of silence passes. "So... Are you really going to find it for me?"

Mulvey puts his head in his hands. "Sure, kid. I'll get it somewhere after I check in to the hotel."

"Sweet! Thanks."

He waves me out of the tiny office, and I go gratefully back to my seat.

[37]

HEIDI

"I'M SO angry at Jason, because I didn't go looking for a relationship!" Yet now I feel awful anyway. "He started it!" I whine to my sister from the middle of the rug in Bayer's apartment.

"You sound like a seven-year-old," she says.

"You shut up," I reply, proving her point.

"Look—it's not very Heidi Jo to take this lying down," she points out. "You always run straight at the things you want and then grab them by the neck."

"I *did*," I wail. "It failed."

"Bullcrap," my sister fires back. "Either the two of you have something special, or you don't. That man is scared. You told me yourself. Why are you letting him off the hook so easily?"

"Because you can't make somebody love you. He has to want it."

"But what if he does? He told off *Daddy*. Nobody does that. And he defended you from a fish. He moved you into his *home*."

"That last thing is open to interpretation." I moved myself

in. And that's the whole problem—I don't really trust my view of events. I was too busy getting swept off my feet to notice that he's still in love with someone else.

"You're not a quitter," my sister points out. "No matter what Daddy says. Hey—speaking of Daddy—has he called you this week?"

"No. We aren't speaking much right now. That's another failed relationship of mine."

She's quiet a second. "I don't think it's you. Something is up with him. Mom is flying to New York this weekend, too. I got a bad feeling about it."

I sit up from the rug, nerves racing through my belly. "You think there's something wrong with Daddy?" My mind is full of horrible ideas now. Cancer? Heart trouble? Our mother hates New York and doesn't often come up.

"Maybe I'm just being dramatic," Jana says. "But I'll call Mom and ask her if everything is okay."

"You'll tell me if you hear anything, right?"

"Of course. Now I have to run. Things to do. People to meet."

"Me too," I say, because I'm waiting for the hockey game to start. Maybe I'm breaking up with my hockey player, but I'll never break up with hockey.

I turn on Bayer's giant TV and find the game broadcast. While I wait for the faceoff, I use my phone for my other hobby—searching Miranda Wager's byline for new articles. If she writes something invasive about Jason, I may not be responsible for my actions.

I still care about him, even if he doesn't return the favor. And his stressful meeting with the transplant recipients is the day after tomorrow.

The camera cuts away from the sportscasters and makes a sweep of the bench. I lean forward eagerly. There's O'Doul talking to Trevi. And the new kid, Drake. Then I see Jason, and my heart seizes. Maybe I'm just projecting, but he looks sad behind his face mask. Those dark eyes have known more unhappiness than I guessed before I got to know him.

I wonder how he's doing tonight—whether he's steeped in sad memories. And I can't help but wonder who made his sandwich. Did they use creamy peanut butter? Was the jam done right, or did it leak out of the sides?

Jason is a big boy, I remind myself. He can make his own freaking sandwich. But I liked doing that small thing for him. Not because he needed the help, but because he appreciated it so much.

There's a knock on the door, and I startle. Everyone I know is in Arizona at the game.

When I peer through Bayer's peephole, I see Georgia Trevi. "Hi!" I say, swinging the door open. "I thought you'd be in Phoenix."

"Tommy has this trip covered," she says. "Although I'm heading out to Minnesota tomorrow night to take Jason to his meeting."

"Oh," I say, waving her in. "The game is about to start."

"I know!" She glances at the TV to make sure we're not missing any action. "But I was just packing for my trip, and I wanted to tell you something."

"What?"

"I'm flying commercial tomorrow. American has an eight p.m. flight to Minneapolis-St. Paul."

"Oh?" I'm not sure why this is relevant. "Did you need me to do something?"

"Nope!" she says cheerfully. "Just thought you should know."

My mind whirls. "You think I should go to Minneapolis? Why?"

Georgia sighs. "I'm marching Jason into a meeting he's dreading. And I don't think I'm the one he wants there."

"I'm not, either," I point out.

"Are you sure?"

No? Yes? "I'm not sure of anything."

"Hear me out for a second. I was once like Jason—traumatized by my past."

"You *were?*" That's hard to picture. Georgia and Leo are like poster children for a happy couple.

"Yes. And I was too stuck inside my troubles to trust myself. I'm not proud of it. But Leo had to be the bigger person and have patience with me. Even when I pushed him away."

"But..." I struggle with myself for a moment. "What if I show up and he really doesn't want me there? I already feel like the third wheel."

"It's not a foolproof plan," she admits with a wince. "But he's unhappy, and you're unhappy. That's where Leo and I were, too. Just saying."

"I see."

She pats me on the shoulder. "I'm going to go yell at the TV with my mother-in-law. Come join us if you want. I'll pour you a glass of wine."

"Thanks," I say. "Um, maybe I will. Later." The minute she walks out that door I'm going to google flights to Minnesota. Damn her.

She smiles like she knows what I'm thinking. "Until then. Have a good game."

Georgia leaves just as the players on Bayer's screen line up for the faceoff.

I sit down on the couch and pick up my phone. There are, in fact, several flights to Minnesota tomorrow. But the one that Georgia is taking costs $1255 for a last-minute ticket.

There's no way I can afford that. Problem solved.

I lie down on the couch and watch the game. Jason is on second shift. He skates with grace and power, staring down the defenseman, stealing the puck and passing it with finesse. He doesn't look like a man who needs me.

But then I get a look at him on the bench. He's wearing his closed-off game face. Every player has one—a face that threatens to tear down anything in his path.

We all have that face, actually. But it's an act. I wear mine when I'm feeling particularly friendless.

I ponder that for a moment. And then I pick up my phone again and search flights for the following morning. Maybe I'm looking at this the wrong way. Jason might not be ready to love me. But he could really use a friend in Minneapolis.

Maybe Georgia has a point. Loving someone means supporting him without expecting anything in return. It's making him a sandwich, or standing beside him when he's facing the worst part of his past.

I can be that friend. Even if it hurts.

To make a grand gesture, you need a few things: courage, airfare, and cooperation from the universe.

That last thing proves to be a problem.

My cheap flight has a layover in Detroit. That costs me an hour and a half. And then my connecting flight to Minnesota is forty minutes late.

But I can still make it, I tell myself as I run toward the taxi line outside the airport. It takes me ten minutes to make my way to the front of the line. When I finally throw myself into the back of a cab and blurt out the address, I only have twenty-seven minutes until the meeting will start.

Cue the traffic. It's pretty bad once we get off the highway. I see signs for the hospital and think I'm in luck. So I sit back and fix my face as the taxi inches through various intersections. I manage not to stab myself in the eye with the mascara wand as the driver steps heavily on the brakes. "Accident," he says. "Sorry, miss, they're gonna make me turn here."

I look out the window and spot a policeman setting up a detour, and my heart sinks. A glance at the time tells me that the meeting starts in four minutes. And I can see the hospital from here!

Damn it! How can I be a great and selfless friend when I'm stuck in the back of a cab?

I could walk the rest of the way. That's how.

This idea energizes me. "I'll get out here," I say, passing cash to the front seat.

"You're kidding me," he grumbles, and I pass over another twenty. I'm getting there if it kills me.

It doesn't kill me. I'm just very winded by the time I roll my carry-on through the hospital doors and present myself at the information desk. "Organ. Transplant. Center," I wheeze at the man behind the desk.

His eyes widen. "Are you okay, miss?"

"Fine! I'm late for a meeting..."

"Go through those double doors. Take the second elevator to the B wing. Then follow the signs toward surgical."

"Got it!" I take off again.

But, Lordy, I didn't know a hospital could be so big! It's another ten minutes before I see the transplant unit. There's a *Meeting Room* sign over one door, so I sprint over to it. I skid to a stop outside, breathing hard, peering through the glass pane, looking for Jason.

And there he is, looking gracious in a gray suit and blue shirt. He stands tall beside... Well, everyone. His mother and father are there. And both his sisters. Georgia, too. She's holding a bag of Bruisers gear. And there's a gray-haired woman I don't recognize. They're standing in a semicircle with two young women, one of them in a hockey team jacket, the other one in a dress.

As I watch, the hockey-playing girl steps forward. She looks up at Jason with pure joy, and then gives him a big hug. The look on Jason's face is impossible to describe. It's full of pain, but also love. He squeezes his eyes shut and bites his lip.

And now my eyes are fountains. I brush away my tears and take a series of steadying breaths. When I look more closely at the meeting room, it doesn't make things easier. The walls are covered with photographs of smiling people, in sets of two. Donor and recipient. Loss and life. Loser and winner.

The other girl steps forward now. Jason meets her gaze and makes himself smile. Then he pulls her into a hug.

Now I'm a *mess*. The tears come again, and even though I can't seem to stop them, it feels gratuitous. I'm blissfully uninvolved in everything that's happening here. I've never lost anyone so violently, nor have I ever bargained with God for the chance to live a healthy life.

My wish list is mostly luxury cosmetics. Never once did I have to put kidney on there.

I turn away, chastened. There's a box of tissues on the reception desk, and I take one.

"Can I help you?" the woman behind the desk asks.

"N-no," I stammer. "No, thank you." I retreat down the hallway again. Jason didn't need me after all. But at least now I understand what it means to truly be spoiled.

Daddy had it all wrong. It's not the jobs you work or the brand of your shoes.

Spoiled is not having to look into the darkness.

[38]

JASON

CARRIE IS ADORABLE. The fact that she plays college hockey makes this a little easier somehow, like we have one thing in common that's not tragedy. And Georgia is standing ready to give her a jersey and some other Bruisers' swag.

"You know I'm a Brooklyn fan now," she says. "It's really amazing to meet you."

And meeting Anita—the other recipient—isn't so horrible, either. It helps that she looks nothing like Lissa did. "I have 20/20 vision," she whispers after hugging me and Lissa's mother. "I'm sorry for your loss. I can't even imagine it. But I wanted you to know that Lissa changed my life. I'm pregnant." She puts a hand over her tummy. "When my baby is born, I'll be able to see her. Just like any mom."

That's it. I'm done. Fat tears roll down my face. I'm the last to break; my family is quietly crying, and Jolene Skinner is wailing like a wounded animal.

"My baby girl," she howls. "If she had to go, I'm glad she could do this for you."

I blow my nose and pull myself together. Somehow Jolene's theatrics make it easier for me to keep it together. Somebody has to. I feel wrung out. That's what nobody ever tells you about grief—it's exhausting, and you're never really done with it.

Georgia must sense that I've had enough. "Ladies, I have some gifts from our team, and I have tickets for tomorrow night's game for everyone here. But we need to get Jason back to the hotel for a team meal."

"I want to help you with your participation drive," I tell Carrie. "Send Georgia the information, and we'll see what we can do."

"That would be amazing," she says, wiping her eyes.

We take a couple of photos together, then Georgia does a great job of wrapping things up. Carrie and Anita leave first, and Georgia puts a blubbering Jolene into a taxi. I walk my family to their cars in the parking garage.

"See you tomorrow night, honey," my mother says, squeezing me tightly. "You were a rock in there. I don't know how you do it."

Praise doesn't help. My recent behavior hasn't made me feel like anyone's rock.

"Where's Heidi, by the way?" my dad asks.

"Ah, about that," I say with a sigh. "I don't know if that's going to work out."

"Oh no," my mother says. "Why?"

"It's all me," I admit. "I have been difficult, and she got fed up."

"You, difficult?" My sister Jackie snorts.

Mom's eyes grow sorrowful. "Maybe it's not too late? I really liked her."

"You never know," I say. I feel so much relief at having survived the meeting that anything seems possible. "See you tomorrow!"

"Go Brooklyn!" my dad says as he starts the car.

After they pull out and drive away, I walk back over the pedestrian walkway toward the hospital. Georgia has texted me. ***Making a quick call. Be with you in five minutes. Find the taxi stand? It's out in front somewhere.***

Will do, I reply.

I head to hospital's main entrance. Outside, there's a bus shelter that might also serve as a taxi stand, so I wander towards the busy spot.

My subconscious snags on a young woman who's facing away from me. And I immediately get this indescribable lift inside—like there's suddenly more space in my chest. I take a second glance, and notice that her honeyed curls look a lot like Heidi's.

That's ridiculous, of course. There's no reason why Heidi should be sitting on a bench waiting for the bus in Minneapolis. But just the *suggestion* of Heidi makes me so happy. That's something I'm going to have to think about later.

Then she turns her head, and I'm astonished to see that it is actually Heidi Jo Pepper sitting on that bench in the brisk November wind. She dabs her eyes with a tissue.

She's here. It's really her. And she's *upset*.

I'm running to her before I even realize it. When I reach the bench, I pluck her into my arms and wrap both arms tightly around her. She gasps but then quickly settles against my chest.

And somehow everything clicks into place.

HEIDI

"What are you doing here?" Jason asks.

The question lacks finesse, but his hug is *perfection*. My poor little heart starts tap dancing to the tune of hope. A girl can be meticulous at prioritizing her wish list, but sometimes her heart scribbles out all the attainable things and scrawls JUST THIS FOREVER at the top of it.

And how do I even explain why I'm here?

"I had this idea that you needed a friend today, even if we can't be together. But then I got here late and you had your family around you and didn't need me." I'm starting to babble, but I can't stop. "But I also see now that I'm way out of my depth. And it's okay because I get it now. I finally understand. I brought your sandwich, though, so you might want to eat it anyway."

His lips are coasting over my cheekbone, causing goose-bumps to break out all over my body. "You brought me a sandwich."

"I thought you might need it." And right then, I have a flash of insight. "Jason, did Lissa make the first sandwich for you?"

"She did. I should have told you that. I should have told you a lot of things. We need to talk," he says.

"Okay." I hate those words. But he's still hugging me tightly. So at least I have that.

"I'm sorry I've been awful."

"It's all right. We can be friends. I meant that."

"No, see, we can't."

My heart drops. "We can't? Is it because we already had filthy, dirty, sex?"

"No." He chuckles in my ear. "We can't be just friends because you're much more to me than that. Even if I've been too big of a punk to admit it. I'm still struggling, Heidi. November is always a rough month for me. But if you can give me another chance, I swear I'll do a better job."

"Of what, though?" I lean back and look him in the eye. "If you're still in love with someone else, I'm not going to try to compete with that."

"No." He shakes his head. "See…" He sits down on the

bench and takes my hand. I let him tug me down to sit beside him. "It's like this—the part of me that's still eighteen will always love an eighteen-year-old girl I once knew. And—this is the greater problem for me—I'll always feel bad about not being there for her. But I'm not a teenager anymore."

"You still carry her picture around in your gym bag," I point out.

He winces. "Yeah, I think it's time I put that in a drawer."

"Not for my sake, though."

"No," he agrees quickly. "For mine. You proved to me that it's time to move on. And I *want* to. With you. Because I *love* you."

I take a deep breath and try to take that in. "You didn't plan on loving me."

"Nope!" he says cheerfully. "'I love you against reason, against promise, against peace, against hope, against happiness, against all discouragement that could be.'"

Do not cry, I order myself. But who could resist a man who says things like that? "Is that Shakespeare?"

"Dickens," he says. "The man was good at telling it to you straight. And he knew that the scary stuff was just the other side of the happiness coin." He kisses my eyebrow. "I believe him now."

"Well..." My tummy flutters. "I didn't plan on loving you, either. But I do. You're basically irresistible, except when you're telling me what to do."

He smiles at me, and his brown eyes look as warm and beautiful as ever. "Sometimes you don't mind that."

"True," I admit. "It depends on whether we're wearing clothes. But when we're fully dressed, I need you to see me as an adult. Not a flighty child."

"I do," he says, kissing my ear. "I swear. Except when I think you're in danger. But I'm working on that, okay? I promise. You can call me on it, too. And I'll listen. We can start by calling this thing by what it is—a relationship."

"Wow," I say. "All right." I nuzzle his warm cheek. "Does this mean we can keep having dirty, filthy sex?"

"You bet." He kisses me then. And—jeez—his kisses are even better than his hugs. I'm leaning in for more when someone clears her throat.

I startle and find Georgia standing over us.

Whoops.

"I called us a car," she says cheerfully. "So maybe you two want to take it down a notch until after tonight's game?"

Jason chuckles while I turn red.

"Actually," I say, as I stand up. "I have to find a hotel room. My flight home is tomorrow at eight in the morning."

"You can bunk with me," he says. "Georgia won't rat us out to Coach, right?"

The publicist shrugs. "Leo and I aren't saints, either. So I guess it would be hypocritical to turn you in. Let's go, kids. I think that's our car."

Jason takes my hand as we stand up, and he holds it all the way to the hotel.

[39]

HEIDI

THAT NIGHT I watch Brooklyn beat Minnesota. And then I sneak into Jason's hotel room so the two of us can stay up half the night making out and talking.

"Will you please come home with me tomorrow?" he asks. "It's not the same without you there."

"I need to pay some rent," I insist. "It's not fair to Silas if I don't."

"Fine. We'll work something out," he says, kissing my neck. Then he rolls on top of me, and I forget all about paying rent.

Now I know how it feels to get everything I want.

No—wait. My wish list is still full of small and large dreams, some of them sparkly and expensive and some merely impractical. Wanting things is what keeps me alive and optimistic.

But now I know how it feels to get everything I actually *need*. I have a job (of sorts) with the possibility of a better one. And I have the love of a man who makes my heart go pitter-patter. Beyond his smoking-hot exterior, there's a whole lot of good stuff in there. He's loyal and passionate. And he quotes literature really well.

I'm so gone for him. As we stand at the luggage carousel the next day, waiting for our bags, I can't keep my eyes off him. I'm like a cartoon character with hearts in its eyes.

Jason's phone rings, and he answers it. "Hello?" As I watch, he frowns. Then he glances right at me. He covers the phone with his hand. "This is the weirdest call. This woman claims she's calling from Belle Pepper's Delivery Service."

"Oh, she is!" I explain. "That's my call center in India. I had to do some outsourcing so I could take this trip."

"I got the same call a couple minutes ago," Silas says, pulling his suitcase off the carousel.

Jason's eyes soften. "Have I ever told you how formidable you are?"

"Not lately," I say in a teasing voice. "Tell me now."

"Jesus," Silas complains. "I'm going to need my own cab home, aren't I? Can you two keep it PG-rated for another half hour?"

"No," Jason says, just at the same moment that I say, "Yes."

"But I have to go to Manhattan," I confess. "I took all my stuff to my dad's condo. I didn't know where else to go."

Jason plucks my bag off the conveyor belt and then puts a hand over his eyes. "I'm sorry. It's my fault that you packed up and left."

"It's okay," I assure him, stepping in to hug him. "You can make it up to me tonight."

"Check, please," Silas says, rolling his suitcase away from us.

Jason kisses me on the nose. "Tell you what. Let's take a car into Manhattan and get your stuff."

"Really? You have time for that?"

"For you? Absolutely." His lips brush mine, and I can't help kissing him again.

Someone makes a gagging noise, and we don't even stop.

Somehow we keep it PG in the taxi. When we reach East 78th Street, the cab can't even get close to the building, because there are news vans in front of Dad's high rise.

"Just another day in Manhattan," Jason says. "I wonder which movie star just made the papers? Let's get out here."

He pulls our luggage from the trunk, and off we go down the crowded sidewalk.

"Staying overnight?" the doorman asks as we roll two suitcases into my father's building.

"No, can I park these with you?" I ask him.

"Of *course*, Miss Pepper! Anything for your family. Give my regards to your parents." He wrings his hands, which is a little strange.

"Parents?" Jason asks in the elevator. "Like, plural?"

"Well..." It's just dawning on me that Mom might be visiting. Didn't Jana mention that? "It's possible that you're about to meet my mother. She never comes to New York, though, so I could be wrong."

When I let myself into the condo a minute later, though, they're both right there in the living room. "Hi guys," I say cheerfully. "What's this all about?"

"Oh! Heidi," my mother chirps. "I'm leaving your father."

"What?" I gasp.

"She won't," he says in a voice full of misery. "She's just in shock."

"About what?" I'm frozen in the entryway, afraid to walk inside. As if staying out of the room can help me avoid whatever is wrong.

Jason gives me a gentle nudge. He closes the door behind me and then squeezes my hand. *I've got you,* it says.

Unwilling to let go, I tow him into the living room with me.

"Evening," he says. "Mrs. Pepper, I'm Jason."

"Nice to meet you, too." She gives him a feral head-to-toe examination, then turns to me. "Well done, Heidi. Is he good at managing his assets? Or will he bet your entire net worth on his ex-roommate's pharmaceutical company and lose everything?"

I replay this outrageous sentence in my head and try to decipher it. "What's happened?"

"Sit down," my father says, indicating the sofa. When Jason and I sit down beside one another, my father gives Jason a polite nod of greeting. "Heidi, I have difficult news."

"A cancelled dinner reservation is difficult news!" my mother shrieks. "This is Armageddon!"

My father closes his eyes in a show of distress and then opens them again. "I'm sorry to tell you that when I sign over your trust fund next week, it won't be much good to you."

All my blood stops circulating. "What? Why?"

"Because I invested it in Kafi's company. And the FDA just shut them down for fraudulent practices."

"Oh, shit," Jason breathes beside me. "The Kafnar Corporation? I read about that. They were falsifying their lab data."

My mother begins to cry silently.

"Omigod," I say like a braindead girl. The foundations of my secure little world are crumbling. I thought the money would be waiting for me. And it isn't. "You knew!" I gasp. Everything makes so much more sense now. "It's not that you didn't want to give the money to me! It was gone!"

My father hangs his head. "Until last week I still hoped that it would turn out okay. I trusted Kafi and his team."

My anger recedes just a little. Kafi and my father played hockey together in college and then in Philadelphia, although Kafi retired when he was only twenty-seven to work at his father's drug company. Of course my father trusted Kafi. You're supposed to trust your best friend of thirty-five years.

"And I was upset that you'd left school. You're going to have to work for a living like most people."

I weigh this idea, too. And while I've hoped my trust fund could help get me the start I want, I realize that working isn't a scary thing. I *like* working. That's why I'd left school in the first place. Bryn Mawr felt so impractical. "If only you'd let me go to NYU for business," I say in a whisper.

"That would have been..." He closes his eyes again. "A fine idea." He sighs. "I'm so sorry, honey. I didn't listen way back then. But you were only eighteen, and I wanted you safe in the hills of Pennsylvania."

Jason and I exchange a glance. He smiles. "Everyone wants you safe. But none of us knows how to get it right."

I take a deep breath and straighten my spine. Then I smile back at Jason. It's an exercise in will. "Okay. This isn't the end of the world," I say slowly. "I enjoyed being a spoiled little rich girl. But it isn't everything."

Jason's expression turns serious. "You impress me every day," he says. "I hope you know that."

I swallow hard, because it means a lot to hear that.

"And you're pretty fun as poor chick, too. Besides, I just happen to know an apartment in Brooklyn that can't wait to welcome you back." He puts an arm around me.

"Thank you," I choke out, leaning against him. What a year this has been!

My father clears his throat. "I'm truly sorry, sweetheart. I never thought it could turn out like this."

I still don't really know what's happening. "Are you losing everything?"

"My liquid assets are probably gone." He flinches. "I thought Kafi's developmental drug was a safe bet. But I still have my job. For now. I may have to sell the Nashville home and downsize."

Mom's sobbing increases in volume.

"And the country club membership will have to go," he says over her tears. "Everything frivolous."

I eye my mother, wondering what she does any given day that isn't frivolous. "Mama, calm down. Your mascara is starting to smear."

She straightens up immediately and reaches for a tissue. "My poor girl," she says, turning her teary face toward me. "This is devastating."

It isn't, though. Devastating is losing everything in an earthquake or a fire. Devastating is losing the person you love. My mom will come through with most of her designer clothes in a downsized condo somewhere swank.

"Hang in there, Mama. That's just the shock talking."

She leaps up, crosses to me, and grabs me into a tight hug. "You're a good girl, Heidi Jo! Such a good girl."

I glance beyond her perfumed arms to Jason, who lifts an eyebrow at me. His expression says, *Sometimes you're a very bad girl and I know all about it.*

My smile pops into place. I'm so grateful to have him here with me. And I can't wait to show him my gratitude.

"Mama," I say gently. "Is there anything I can do for you right now?"

"No," she sniffs. "I'm going home to Nashville to mourn."

I bite back my opinions and pat her arm. "Well, call me when you're feeling calmer. I have to head to Brooklyn and beg Rebecca for a full-time job." I stare down my father. "Can I assume that you won't stop her from hiring me?"

He waves a hand in a gesture of assent. Poor Daddy is worn out. I feel a pang of sympathy for his stubborn self.

I kiss my parents goodbye and then let Jason steer me back into the elevator. "You're going to be okay," he says.

"Oh, I know it."

"Sorry about the money. It doesn't make you a spoiled brat to be mad about it."

"Doesn't it?" I sigh. "That's going right to the top of my wish list."

"What is?"

"Becoming spoiled again. That sums things up pretty well."

He laughs. "I'll spoil you later, Hot Pepper. I can't wait."

[40]

JASON

In the elevator, I pull out my phone, because we need an Uber back to Brooklyn. But I'm distracted by the fact that I have twenty-five new texts.

I read the one on top first. It's from Silas. ***Oh shit! Is Heidi okay?***

Hmm. It's possible that the media has this story. The next text—from Trevi—has a link attached. ***This sounds bad,*** he writes. The headline reads: "Hockey Commissioner's Personal Finances Engulfed by Kafnar Scandal."

And the byline is Miranda Wager's.

"Oh shit," I whisper as the elevator doors open. Out the windows I spot the news vans on the street. And now I know why they're out there.

Heidi spots them, too, and stops in the center of the lobby. "Do you think they're here for..." I can hear her mind clicking along. My girl is smart.

"I'm afraid so," I say, tucking my arm around her. "Does this place have a backdoor?" If they decide that Heidi is part of the story, she could end up with her face in the news stories alongside her dad.

The flustered doorman brings our suitcases out. "You could exit through the parking garage," he says. "Can I call you a car?"

"Yes, please," I say immediately.

"Right away, sir." He rings for the elevator again, and Heidi and I get onto it, this time heading toward the basement.

My girl's lips are in a thin, worried line as we exit into the cool underground space and walk toward the exit. "I'm worried about my mom," she says. "The woman has never worked a day in her life."

"Maybe she won't have to," I point out.

We emerge onto East 77th, and the first person we see is Miranda Wager herself.

"Shit."

Heidi gasps as Miranda takes a picture of her.

"Cut that out!" I bark. "She's not the story."

"No kidding," Miranda says. "She never really was. And neither were you, so she can stop lunging at me in the street." Miranda rolls her eyes.

"You are not a nice person!" Heidi squeaks.

"Who is?" Miranda snaps. "That picture of your dad and Kafnar Jr. in Georgia's office, though. Now that's news."

"It isn't!" Heidi shrieks. "Write about Kafi if you want a scandal."

"You don't think it matters if the league commissioner trusts the wrong dealmakers? He's responsible for the financial well-being of the entire sport."

Well, ouch. I steer a red-faced Heidi away from her. "Nice to see you, Miranda. Always a pleasure."

Heidi wiggles under my arm, trying to get away from me. So I stop on the sidewalk and face her. "Look. I promised not to protect you when you don't need protecting. And I guess this counts. But do you really want to have it out with a journalist on the sidewalk? She probably records every interaction."

"Arrrrrgh!" Heidi shrieks. "I want to wipe that smirk off her face."

"I know," I say in my calmest voice. "And I'd love to watch. But it's still a bad idea."

Heidi's eyes are wild. I want to throw her over my shoulder and carry her away from here. My fingers actually itch to do it.

But I don't. I take a slow breath and just wait.

Heidi's shoulders slump. "Let's go home and throw darts at her picture instead."

"Yes! I call first shot. Ten bucks a point." I lift my hand for a high five.

She slaps it. "Still want to choke her."

"I know, baby. And I still want to stop you. But look at me being all adult about it."

A smile flickers across her face. "Thank you for what you did in there." She tips her head toward the building.

"I didn't do a thing."

"You did," she insists. "You were there for me. No advice. No drama. Just...sturdy."

"I can do that," I say, and I realize it's true. Maybe I'm not a horrible boyfriend, after all.

"And I appreciate it. Drama is really not the Pepper family style. I'm kind of shaken up about it."

Our car pulls up at the curb. "Let's go home, okay?" I open the backdoor for her. "No more drama today. No parents. No apartment hunting, for God's sake. Let me take care of you, with movies in bed and takeout food. I'll have a team meeting later, but mostly I get the day off."

"That sounds *great*." She hops into the car. "Let me just call Becca." She pulls out her phone. "Oh, crap. It's dead."

"Use mine." I hand her my Katt phone as I get in and close the door. "Becca's cell number is in there."

"Sweet." As the car pulls away, she dials. Because we're in a small space, I can hear a tinny version of Becca's voice say, "Hello? Jason?"

"This is Heidi," my girl says. "I needed to tell you—"

"Are you okay? I just saw it on the news. Your poor dad."

Heidi flinches. "Yeah, it's bad for him. And I need a real job now. He won't stand in my way. I'm open to any department. But I have to ask if maybe your new assistant isn't working out..."

Becca says something I can't understand, and Heidi's grip on my hand tightens. "I understand," she says stiffly.

"*However,*" Becca's voice says before becoming unintelligible again.

Heidi sits up straighter. "Really? YES! YES! I mean—I'd consider that. Sure. If the terms were right."

I bite back a chuckle, because my girl is already negotiating.

"Of course I can come in tomorrow. Nine o'clock is fine. Uh-huh. Full time. I'll be needing benefits. Right. Oh—and this job comes with a Katt phone, right?" She hangs up a minute later, smiling like the sun itself.

"Well?"

"Rebecca has plans for *two* office managers! She thinks I would be perfect for assisting Hugh. There's travel. But it's the real deal. A full-time position!"

"Baby, that's *amazing.*" Not that I'm surprised. Heidi is like a category-four hurricane when she wants something. Who wouldn't want that kind of gale force on his side?

She turns her head and smiles at me. "Are you sure you don't mind me sticking around your place? We'd be seeing an awful lot of each other."

"But that's how I like it." Just to prove the point, I reach over and slide her closer to me on the seat. "See?"

"That is nice."

"I love you, Heidi," I tell her. "Thank you for putting up with my grumpy ass."

"I love your grumpy ass. And I'm going to get this job," she says as the car accelerates on the FDR.

"Yes, you are," I say, wrapping an arm around her.

"They'll forget to interview anyone else."

"They won't even bother," I agree.

"You're just yessing me," she complains. "You're really thinking about sex now."

"No way!" I argue. Although that's a nice idea. "Maybe you should wear your lucky panties to the interview. The new pair."

She snuggles closer to me. "I have a confession."

"What's that?" She smells like flowers. And I can't wait to get home.

"The new pair isn't real."

"No? Are they like the clothes in that fairy tale? The Emperor's New Underwear?"

"Pretty much," she says, putting a hand on my chest.

"That's very affordable," I whisper. "And you can model them when we get home."

"If you're lucky, I will," she says with a wicked smile.

And because I'm very, very lucky, she does.

The
End